Christmas is for Children

Christmas is for Children

ROSIE CLARKE

An Aria Book

First published in the UK in 2019 by Aria, and imprint of
Head of Zeus Ltd

9 7 5 3 1 2 4 6 8

A catalogue record for this book is available from
the British Library.

ISBN (PB): 9781788549936
ISBN (E): 9781786693013

Typeset by Silicon Chips

Printed and bound in Great Britain by
CPI Group (UK) Ltd, Croydon CR0 4YY

Head of Zeus Ltd
First Floor East
5–8 Hardwick Street
London EC1R 4RG

WWW.HEADOFZEUS.COM

Christmas is
for Children

'You – get in line!' the gaffer's voice was harsh, angry. He shoved the man who had dared to step forward back into the line of thin-faced men with anxious eyes. It was a chilly November morning in 1932 and only one ship was being unloaded on the docks, the majority of the cranes motionless, like black spiders outlined against the grey sky. Dust and debris scurried across the empty crates and abandoned tarpaulins littering the dock, as men stood or lounged, watching the horizon hungrily for any sign of a new cargo ship. Since the stock market crash in America in 1929, trade had slowed, work was scarce and agricultural prices had dropped by sixty per cent: a combination of disasters that had left whole countries reeling and men standing in line for work. 'When I want volunteers, I'll ask for them…'

'He's been standin' here for three days and you haven't given him one job,' Robbie Graham spoke up for the older man, who looked drained and ill, despair weighing him down. 'What's Josh done to deserve bein' ignored?'

'Shut yer gob, Graham, or you'll find yerself at the end of the line wiv 'im.'

Robbie glared at the gaffer, his fists balling at his sides. Robbie Graham was a tall, well-built man with dark almost black hair, eyes that were blue rather than grey and a strong jawline. If he chose, he could knock that cocky devil from here to kingdom come and one of these days... But any sign of violence and he would be out for good. It was humiliating being forced to wait all day like this, more often than not nothing would come into the dock, and if it did, the work would go to the gaffer's favourites. Men like old Josh there would get nothing and Robbie was lucky if he was given the filthy crates and lorries to wash down; unloading and stacking was reserved for the favourites and there was no chance of Robbie being offered his real work of carpentry.

'That's it, no more work today,' the gaffer announced after he'd pulled three men from the line. 'Come back tomorrow early and maybe yer'll be lucky.' His grin was evil as he heard the groans, because he knew the power he had over these men. Work was scarce, not only here on the East India Docks, but all over the country. Men had marched to the capital earlier that year demanding bread, but all they got were blows and curses as a peaceful march turned into a riot.

Robbie turned away with a sinking heart. He had a shilling in his pocket and two motherless kids at school, and his pride had prevented him from signing on to the dole to receive the pittance of perhaps seventeen shillings a week if he was lucky. The national government had reduced the rate because of a crisis with the gold standard and to receive the money, each household had to pass a means test, which was hated by everyone. The dole was only payable for twenty-six weeks in a year and Robbie had believed he could earn more; most weeks he had. However, since his wife had died and the Depression had begun to really bite, he'd hardly been able to afford to put food on the table, let alone clothe his children properly. His misfortune had started when he'd had an accidental fall from the roof of a house he'd been helping to build and been flat on his back in bed for weeks on end, and then, just when he thought he was getting back on his feet, the recession had started and he'd been let go from his firm.

Robbie's wife, Madge, had fallen ill a few weeks after he'd been sacked. He'd thought it was just a nasty chill, but then it had turned to pneumonia and suddenly she was gone, leaving him with two children under ten years to care for. Robbie's marriage had not been particularly happy at the end, but he'd grieved for her, remembering the good times when they'd first met when he was on leave from the army. Latterly, her scolding tongue had driven a wedge between them and then it had been too late. She'd wanted to be in Yarmouth near her folks so he'd had her cremated and buried her ashes near her mother; it was all he could do for her and cost every last penny he had.

Once, they'd been happy, racing across the sands at Yarmouth, he a young soldier on leave, and she a carefree girl on a rare holiday from her work as a parlour maid. Because there was a war raging, they'd married quickly, believing the magic of love would last, but it hadn't and, standing over her grave, Robbie blamed himself. Madge had known there was someone else – someone he could not forget – and it had soured her.

With every penny he had gone, he'd joined the men waiting in line on the docks. At first he'd got his fair share of what work was going, but for some weeks now, he'd only been offered what the skilled men didn't want...

'You shouldn't 'ave stood up fer me, lad,' Josh said, catching up with Robbie's long stride. 'The gaffer's got it in fer me and now he'll take it out on you.'

'It ain't fair,' Robbie replied. 'You deserve a chance same as the rest – but I get the worse jobs and he don't even give you the job of slopping out the bone lorry.'

'I'm used to it,' Josh admitted, resigned. 'I'll look for work elsewhere tomorrow. What's the point in standin' in line, when yer know you ain't gonna be picked?'

Robbie shook his head. Times were hard now. In

1931, the government had been forced to devalue the pound and they'd reduced the rate of pay for all government employees, including the postal workers and the servicemen. This had caused protests and strikes and even a small mutiny by the Royal Navy, but when it left many of the ratings – ordinary sailors with no rank – with no more than twenty-five shillings a week, some protests were to be expected. In the north, shipyards and factories had closed their yards. Because of the massive unemployment now most people no longer bothered to protest; everyone was in the same boat and you took what you could get.

'Suppose not,' Robbie said. 'I went down the exchange on Monday, but there was a queue as long as two football pitches and someone said they'd got nothing to offer.'

'I'll do anythin' – I ain't proud…' Josh looked desperate.

Robbie fingered the shilling in his pocket. 'I'll buy yer half a pint, mate,' he offered as they approached the pub.

'Nah, I can't buy yer one back. I'm skint…'

'Half a pint ter wish yer luck,' Robbie insisted.

He smothered his guilt as he took the protesting Josh into the pub; he was a mate and needed a bit of help. There was some bread for toast and a bit of dripping in the pantry. The kids wouldn't starve and tomorrow he'd go looking elsewhere for a job. He was a skilled carpenter and he might find some work if he had the courage to look...

'Are yer comin' down the rec?' a lanky boy called to Ben Graham as they left the junior boys' school that afternoon. Ben was a miniature version of his father, tall for his almost ten years and full of energy. It was a late November evening and the mist was coming down, making it feel cold and damp.

'Nah, I've got to fetch me sister,' Ben replied and watched the boy run off to join a crowd of five others intending to play football on an open piece of ground near the docks. He would have liked to join in their game, but Ruthie would be waiting for him to fetch her. If he wasn't there on time, she would cry and sniffle all the way home.

'They ain't worfth the bother them lot...' another boy sidled up to Ben as he turned towards the girls' school, which was just around the corner. 'I'll walk wiv yer...'

'All right, if yer want,' Ben agreed. Mick was thinner and shorter than Ben; half-Irish, he sounded more like a Londoner. He and his father had moved here some six months or so earlier and Mick had enrolled at the school, but he'd spent more time away than in class. Mick's father was Irish and the only time Ben had seen him had been when he fetched Mick back from school once; he'd been drunk, lurching about and swearing. The headmaster had gone after him, but Mick's father had raised a fist to him and he'd paled and backed away.

'You ain't been to school for a while?'

'Nah, me dad was sick and I 'ad ter look after 'im,' Mick said. 'I fought he might croak it, but he never. He's back on the booze again now.'

'My dad likes a drink, but he grins all the time and gets daft if he has one too many – yours swears and gets violent.'

'Dad ain't bad when he's got work.' Mick grimaced 'He's a labourer and there ain't much goin' fer 'im at the moment. He says the bloody government ought ter make jobs fer men like 'im – roads and stuff – but they ain't got no sense...'

Ben frowned, because he could just recall a time when things had been better. His dad had been working full-time on the building sites and his mum had set the table for tea with a spotless cloth and glass jam dishes with a silver spoon, but things were different now.

'We was learnin' about the recession in class this mornin' and the teacher says it all started in America...' Ben looked at the other boy. 'You should come ter school, Mick. My teacher said us kids need a better education so that we're not all in the same boat when we get older. He said the workin' man relies too much on heavy labourin' and not enough on his brains... He reckons that's why the Labour party got defeated in the election last year.'

'School is a waste of time,' Mick replied because Ben was just repeating what his teacher had told him and it went straight over his head. ''Sides, they told me I had ter wash and get me clothes washed and all – and there ain't nowhere to wash 'em where we live.'

Ben was aware of the ruined tenement buildings not far from the East India Docks, where his friend and his father lived in squalor. They had been merchant seamen's houses once, but for many years they'd been subdivided into rooms and allowed to fall into disrepair as too many families squeezed into the row of semi-detached houses. Years ago, the authorities had evicted the tenants, condemned the buildings and boarded up the windows and doors. Left to fall to ruin, the tramps and homeless had started to squat there and no one bothered to turn them out.

They passed a small factory that had finally closed its doors in the summer after trying to limp along on half-time for months. The blackened chimney stack had no smoke issuing from it and posters advertising cinema films were plastered all over the walls and boarded up windows. There was a film showing called *Tell England* and another with Laurel and Hardy – and at the Odeon up west there was a film on with Norma Shearer starring.

'I ain't never bin to the flicks,' Mick said, looking at the posters with a kind of hunger. 'Have you?'

'Mum took us once to a Charlie Chaplin film for my birthday,' Ben said. 'I remember it was funny but it was a long time ago… and I liked the cartoons best…'

Ben and Mick were approaching Ruthie's school now. She was only six and Ben was nine, ten next January. She looked to her big brother to look after her, because Dad was hardly ever home until late and Mum was dead… Ben frowned as he saw Ruthie was standing by herself and looking miserable. Her ribbon had come off and her fine fair hair had tangled in the wind, and her blue eyes were drenched with tears. Some of the other girls were pointing at her and laughing.

'What's the matter?' he asked when she ran to him in distress.

'Me dress split under the arms again 'cos it's too small. The teacher said I had ter get it mended or stay home. She caned me 'ands and stood me in the corner and the kids all laughed at me…'

'Bloody teachers; they cane yer fer anythin'. I think they enjoy it,' Mick growled. 'You take no notice of 'em, Ruthie. They're all rotten…'

'I like goin' ter school. We're makin' cards fer our friends in class,' Ruthie muttered and sniffed. 'I'm 'ungry…'

'So am I,' Ben said. Mick nodded his head. They all knew what it was like to have that familiar ache in the pit of their tummy. 'I've got three pennies – we could buy some chips with that and share 'em…'

'I've got tuppence,' Mick offered. 'They'll give us some crispies for that and we can put salt and vinegar on 'em...'

The three of them traipsed into the fish and chip shop on the corner and Ben pushed their five slightly sticky pennies over the counter.

'Can we have chips and some crispies please, Mr Fred?'

Fred Giles nodded, picked up a sheet of newspaper and scooped two large portions of chips into it, adding a full scoop of bits of batter off the fish. All the kids and some of the adults asked for them, but Fred gave them to the ones he liked most – and Ben cleaned his windows for him every Saturday morning. He did it better than most window cleaners and he was always polite. So Fred sprinkled salt and vinegar over the chips and gave Ben the package, and then he took a buttered roll and popped it on top.

'See you on Saturday mornin', Ben?'

'Yeah, thanks, Mr Fred...'

Ruthie and Mick followed Ben out. He broke the roll into three pieces, but Ruthie was only interested in the chips, so he gave Mick two shares of the roll and they all dipped into the chips and crispies. Ben felt sorry for his friend, because he knew there was a warm bed waiting for him at the end of the day and his dad would have food for him when he got home. Ben and Ruthie had a free school dinner, because Mum had applied for it when Dad was sick – but Mick often went without food all day. His father wasn't registered in London as unemployed so he didn't qualify; what work he did was cash in his pocket and no one was any the wiser, because he spent his money at the pub as soon as he got it.

When they reached the end of the road leading up from the docks, Ben saw his father approaching their cottage from the opposite direction. The houses where they lived were once all seamen's homes, hundreds of years old and most were in bad repair. They could smell the river from the back garden and in the summer, it stank.

Ben looked at Mick and, knowing he had only the dark and cold waiting, because his dad wouldn't be there, asked if he wanted to come in for a while.

'Dad will make a cup of tea,' he said. 'He won't mind if you stop for a warm by the fire, Mick. I ain't sayin' there'll be much ter eat – but you can have a hot drink...'

'Yer dad is all right,' Mick said and kicked at a stone in the road as he tagged on behind them.

'Ben, Ruthie...' Ben's father called to them. 'Hello, Mick – do yer want a cup of rosy lee?'

'Yes, please, Mr Graham...' Mick grinned and followed the others inside to the large kitchen.

It was warm from the range, which was kept going

on cheap coke all the time when Ben's father had money in his pocket. At one end of the room stood a big oak dresser with lots of china, mostly blue and white willow pattern, displayed on it; a pine table was in the middle of the room and a sink with curtains underneath and a wooden drainer to both sides was under the window. The curtains at the window matched the ones under the sink, and the covers on the armchair and the old sofa also matched. Ben's mother made them before she died. Neither of the boys ever spoke of their mothers, because it hurt.

'It's just toast and drippin' this evenin,' Robbie said as he put the kettle on the range. 'But you can have cocoa if you'd like rather than tea…'

They all asked for the cocoa and the chocolatey smell was delicious, as was the taste. Mick and Ben ate a piece of toast and dripping, but Ruthie shook her head and complained it made her feel sick. She found a jar of jam in the cupboard which had just a scraping left of the sweet strawberry conserve and she scooped it out to put on her toast.

Mick perched on the lumpy old sofa; it was heaven compared to what awaited him at the dark and damp derelict house that should have been pulled down long ago. His bed was a pile of old sacks and he had one blanket he pulled over him at night. He hated living there and didn't want to go back – and it wasn't just that his dad might be in a foul temper; there were others using the derelict buildings as somewhere to sleep and he was afraid of one of them in particular.

'It's cold out tonight,' Robbie said and eyed Mick's thin jumper. It had holes at the elbow and didn't look as if it would keep him warm. 'I've got an old jacket – it will be a bit large for yer, lad – but yer welcome to it...'

Robbie took the jacket down from behind the door and offered it. Mick hesitated and then took it. He put it on and rolled the cuffs back. The jacket hung on him, but he wrapped it round him and Robbie gave him a bit of string to tie it in the middle.

'That will keep yer a bit warmer, lad...'

Mick thanked him, bade farewell to Ben and went out.

Ruthie wrinkled her nose when the door had closed behind him.

'He smells...' she objected. 'He's all right – but he smells...'

'I dare say he could do with a wash,' her father told her and frowned, 'but he's not a bad lad, Ruthie. We might not have much, but we share what we can – right?'

'Yes, Dad,' Ruthie said and then pulled a face. 'My dress split again today...'

'I'll mend it when you're in bed,' Robbie promised. 'As soon as I get a proper job I'll buy you a new one, love...'

Ruthie went to kiss his cheek, her mouth sticky with

the last of the strawberry jam. 'I love you… but I wish Mummy was still here.'

'Yes, love, we all do,' Robbie said. Madge would have made her daughter a new dress for school, even if she'd had to cut down one of her own. 'Go to bed now – and Ben will be up soon…'

He looked at his son after she'd gone up to bed. 'I'm goin' to try for work somewhere else in the mornin', Ben. Maybe I'll have more luck than I've had lately on the docks…'

'I had threepence for doin' a job,' Ben told him, 'but we spent it on chips – I'll find some more jobs ter help yer, Dad…'

'You keep yer pennies, son,' Robbie said, feeling guilty over the few pennies he'd spent on beer for himself and Josh, but he'd wanted to cheer his friend. 'I'll sell somethin' to tide us over if I don't get a job tomorrow…'

Ben nodded and headed for the stairs.

Robbie sat on by the fire for a few moments. His eyes moved round the room. Truly, there wasn't much left that was worth more than a bob or two down at Uncle's, as everyone called the pawnbroker. *Uncle* would take anythin', even your Sunday suit if you had one, but Robbie didn't want to part with the few bits he had left. That nice blue and white teapot was his first gift to Madge when they moved here. The marble mantle clock might fetch a pound, but he'd never know the time without it... He could only think about his wife's clothes, smart handbags and personal items. He hadn't touched anything from her wardrobe yet, but unless he could find work that paid more than a couple of bob he might have to open it and pawn Madge's best coat.

2

'Yer don't know what it's like stuck up here in this bed,' Ernest Hawkins said to his daughter Flo. 'I get fed up on me own – and if I could get to the commode by meself I wouldn't ring for yer...'

'I know it's hard for you, Dad,' Flo said and brushed a lock of soft fair hair from her forehead. For work, she wore her hair pulled into a neat pleat at the back of her head because it was tidy that way and she could tuck it under the little white cap she wore when cooking her cakes and home-made sweets to sell in her shop. Her blue eyes were saddened as she looked at her father. 'I'm sorry you had to ring three times, but we were busy in the shop.'

'I know that bloody shop is more important than me...' he grumbled and glared at her. 'It's yer own fault if I've wet meself. I couldn't hold it no longer...'

Flo sighed but she didn't answer her father back. He'd been very ill and for some weeks the doctors had thought he might die after his last stroke, but of late he'd seemed more aware – and his temper hadn't improved.

'I'll change the sheets while you're on the commode...'

'Fat lot of good sitting me on that now,' he mumbled but accepted her help in rising.

Once he was up, he seemed quite steady and she was able to settle him in a suitable position while she changed the sheet.

'There, that's nice and dry for you, Dad,' she said. 'If you're ready, I'll get you back to bed – and then I'll go back to work.'

'I'd rather sit in a chair for a while,' her father replied and she took him to the comfortable armchair her neighbour had carried upstairs for her only recently. 'And you can tell the girl to bring me a cup of tea and a bit of cake as soon as she's ready...'

'Her name is Honour, as you well know,' Flo replied, thinking of the beautiful girl with dark-honey hair that fell in soft waves to her shoulders and eyes more green than blue. Good-humoured, hard-working and loving she deserved far more than she got from him. 'She's your kin not your slave...' In fact, she looked very much like Flo and people often remarked on how alike they were, for Flo was still slim and attractive, always smiling and good-natured despite all the work.

'Yes, I know what she is,' he retorted and his eyes

snapped at her. 'I might have had a stroke but I didn't lose me wits – just the use of me damned legs...'

'They are a bit better, though,' Flo said encouragingly. 'Kick your feet as much as you can, Dad – like the doctor showed you. He said if you exercise them you'll get the use of your legs back sooner.'

'All right for him to talk,' her father muttered. 'Stop fussing, girl – and next time answer the bell when I ring...'

He was spoiling for a fight and Flo wasn't in the mood to oblige him. It was a Friday and the weekend trade was brisk. Some days Flo wondered if it was worthwhile opening her little cake shop. Often, she'd sell just a few rock buns, perhaps a sponge cake and a couple of penny lollipops from the jars on the shelf at the back of the counter. Their main trade at the start of the week was the little soft bread rolls Honour baked and filled with cheese, tomatoes or corned beef.

Flo's mother had never sold filled rolls, which were mostly bought by single men or girls on their way to work. Mrs Hawkins always made enough from her cakes and buns to clothe herself and her family and save for the future, but the recession that had plagued the country for the last few years had turned into what people now called the Depression. Everyone's trade was affected and there were desperate men begging on the streets. Some had a cap by their side with notices written on cardboard begging for help to feed a wife and family.

Children were going to school hungry and it was only the free meal they received there that saved them from starving. All over London – and probably the rest of the country from what Flo read in the papers – enterprising bodies had set up soup kitchens and in the middle of each day a line of men would form for the cup of soup, hunk of bread and mug of tea they were given by well-meaning volunteers. Bread and potatoes were the staple food in most households, because they filled up the spaces left by inadequate meals.

The streets of London's East End looked almost as dismal as they had during the Great War. Small shops and businesses had closed; their windows were either smashed or boarded up and posters had been stuck on them. Unions urged men to strike to help their unemployed brothers, and government posters begged the people to behave like responsible citizens. Some popular shops like Flo's just off the market and a short distance from Poplar High Street just about kept going, but she managed it only because she and Honour worked all hours. Flo paid Honour a few shillings a week for her work and she was forced to give her father the share he'd always demanded of their takings, but she took very little for herself, saving every penny in case it was needed.

Honour was in the kitchen when Flo walked in, setting the kettle on the range. 'I've left the hall door open so I'll hear if the bell goes,' she said. 'What was wrong this time, Flo?'

'He needed the commode and I wasn't in time so there's another sheet to wash.'

'You should send them to the laundry,' Honour suggested. 'Sometimes I think he does it on purpose.'

'No, I don't think so. He gets angry when he makes a mess.' Flo smiled at the girl she loved. To the world she was Flo's younger sister, born seventeen years apart, but the love she felt was of a mother for her daughter. It was her secret. One Honour did not share – though Flo was almost certain her father did, even though he'd been working up north in the shipyards for months before the birth. Flo had been forced to bottle-feed her child and believed that her mother had successfully kept their secret from her father, but sometimes now he hinted and she wondered – could he know that Honour was Flo's bastard, born in shame and hidden from the world?

All these years she'd been forced to keep her silence, because her mother had threatened what her father would do to them both if he knew.

'If he ever learned of your shame he would disown you, Flo. He would not have a wicked girl like you under his roof...'

Flo's tears had been shed in private. Was Honour's

birth the reason her father seemed determined to humiliate and punish her?

The shop bell rang as Honour was pouring hot water into a pot and Flo went to answer it. Her customer was a well-dressed man. He smiled and tipped his hat to her.

'Good afternoon, Mr Rolf.'

'Good afternoon, Miss Flo – I was wondering, is that sponge filled with buttercream and your special strawberry jam?'

'Yes, it is, sir,' Flo answered. He was a businessman for he carried a little briefcase. 'It was made fresh this mornin'.'

'Then I shall buy it. My daughter likes strawberry jam in her sponge cake. I seem to recall that last year you made some extra treats for Christmas…?'

'Yes, sir, that is right. We make sugar mice for the children, coconut ice, fudge, chocolate truffles and some marzipan fancies. I don't start makin' them until the end of the first week of December – though I am takin' orders for my rich fruit cakes now. I make them in November, store them in tins, and ice them last thing, so they are lovely and soft…'

'Yes, I bought one last year. Please order a large iced cake for me – and I will purchase some of your other delights when I come in to fetch the fruit cake.'

'Certainly, Mr Rolf…' Flo smiled and made a note on her pad, because he was a good customer. She made most of her profit at Christmas, because her trade did not rely on local customers. People came from all over to buy her chocolate truffles, fruit cakes and sugar mice. Some of them had been coming for years, when Flo's mother ran the shop, but many more had begun to visit at Christmas since she and Honour started to make their home-made sweets.

After he had gone, Flo knew she may as well shut the shop. There were only a few rock cakes left and they could eat those for their supper. She smiled because that was the fourth order for an iced cake she'd taken that day. It seemed that despite the terrible Depression, everyone who could meant to make the most of Christmas.

Robbie jangled the few coins in his pocket. He'd been in the right place at the right time and earned enough to buy sufficient basic foodstuffs to feed the children for a few days. A traffic accident had happened just as he arrived outside a factory making nuts and bolts. A truck turning into the factory had been run into by a brewer's cart and the truck had turned on its side as the heavy horses reared and stampeded, causing chaos and fear; the shrill screams of the injured horses mingled with the cries of the truck driver as it went over and spilled its load of scrap metal in the road.

Robbie's first reaction had been to catch the horses'

reins and help the driver calm them. After that he'd found himself clearing up the spill of metal and shovelling it into wheelbarrows and taking it into the factory. He'd helped the injured truck driver to tell his tale and, with some other men from the factory, he'd righted the truck and got it into the factory yard.

The manager came out and thanked him, giving him five bob for helping out. The work had taken up most of his afternoon so he couldn't continue his search for more permanent work that day, but at least he had some money in his pocket. He decided to go home and call in at the grocer's on his way, to pick up some butter, jam, cheese, a quarter of loose tea, which was expensive since the government put a tax of four pence on it in April, and a tin of cocoa. He might manage a slice of ham as well if he was lucky...

The small corner shop was next door to the fish and chip shop. Fred Giles was just starting to get ready for the evening service and the smell of the hot fat was tantalising, but Robbie stuck to his plans. The five shillings he'd earned had to buy basic food for a week and couldn't be squandered on fish and chips, however tempting the smell. He needed a bob for the gas meter or it would probably run out before they had finished their meal and they'd have to light the candles.

Walking into the grocer's, he saw a young woman standing there with her basket on the counter. She was dressed in a blue coat with a velvet collar and a matching cloche hat over her fair hair. Her shoes were patent leather with a sensible heel and he noticed she had shapely ankles.

'I'm going to need twelve pounds of sugar, the same of ground almonds, two large tins of cocoa and twelve pounds of mixed dried fruit, spices, three pounds of butter and the same of marge, ten large bags of plain flour and the same of...' she paused to give the grocer time to make notes and turned her head, glancing at Robbie for the first time and seemed to start and then carried on reading from her list. 'And we need a tin of plums and a packet of Bird's custard powder please, that's for Dad's tea not the shop...' She gave a nervous laugh.

Robbie's heart stood still as the years rolled back and he saw his first love – a reminder of the stupid idiot he'd been at seventeen... 'Hello, Miss Hawkins,' he said. It wasn't the first time he'd seen Flo since he'd returned to the East End, but it was the first time they'd come face to face.

'Robbie... Mr Graham...' she murmured and her face had gone very pale for she recognised him. 'How are you?'

'Very well,' Robbie lied. His chest was in the grip of a huge vice and all his breath had been squeezed from him. 'You sound as if you expect to be busy?'

'It will be Christmas next month,' Flo said and she was smiling easily now, as if she had taken their meeting in her stride. I have to order my supplies in time or Mr Johnson might run out... and I always trade here.'

'Local trade for local people,' Robbie agreed. 'You run that cake shop just off the High Street, don't you?' He'd passed but never allowed himself to enter.

'Yes, we do – Honour and me...' Flo looked away from his bright gaze as she lied, 'she – she's my younger sister.'

'We live a few streets from you, where the old seamen's cottages are.' Robbie swallowed hard. 'My wife used to make cakes for the kids, but they don't get much like that these days...'

Robbie was floundering and knew it. Flo just took his breath away. It was years since he'd caught more than a glimpse of her in her shop and she looked older – but she was still just as lovely as she had been at sixteen when they'd first met...but surely, she would have forgotten their friendship for it had been too brief.

'I'll leave the order with you and come back tomorrow,' Flo told the grocer. 'Goodbye, Mr Graham. It was nice to see you...'

Robbie heard the doorbell ring as she left but didn't allow himself to watch her.

'She's my best customer,' Mr Johnson asserted. 'She could buy a lot of this wholesale if she liked – her mother did, but Miss Flo buys from us. She says by the time she adds the delivery charge on it costs just as much, but I think she just likes to help out her local traders.'

'Know her well, do you?' Robbie asked. 'Never married then?'

'If you ask me she never had a chance – that mother of hers was a tartar, proper despot; harsh words is all Flo ever got. Mrs Hawkins never bought from me unless she ran out and then she never stopped moanin' about me prices…' He put Robbie's goods on the counter. 'Her father used ter buy his fags 'ere – he were all right once, but he turned a bit sour as he got older. I reckon it were his missus as turned him that way – a naggin' woman would send any man to the bad…'

Robbie smiled, agreed and paid the three shillings and eleven pence three farthings he owed. He picked up his shopping and left. It had been a shock meeting Flo like that after all these years, though he'd known she ran the shop that had been her mother's.

If he hadn't been such a fool… Regret and memories swirled in his head but he pulled himself up sharp. No good brooding over something that couldn't be changed. He had to think about where he was going to try his luck the next day. He'd been turned down at every shop, factory and pub he'd tried. No one was hiring. He'd even tried a builder's yard, asked for work as a skilled carpenter. Robbie had been lucky he'd been on the scene when the accident happened, but that wouldn't happen again, and if he couldn't find work he would have to go and stand in line on the docks again...

Mick stood shivering outside the derelict buildings. No light flickered between the cracks in the boards that covered the windows and he knew his father hadn't got back yet. He didn't want to go in alone, because there were rats and he hated the way they ran over his feet when he lay under his blanket at night – but it wasn't the rats he was most terrified of. It was him... the man who stood by the entrance they all used to get into the old tenements. He was big and had long hair, a bushy beard, wild blue eyes, a row of rotten teeth and foul breath – and he was always grabbing hold of Mick and hitting him.

He didn't want to go past him and so he stood out in the icy evening, waiting for his father to turn down the small dark lane that led off from Dock Road. Hardly any street lights worked in this area and no one bothered to contact the council to get them repaired; it suited the folk who came and went here – tramps, thieves, hard men who wanted a place to stay for a few days.

Mick's feet and hands were frozen. He tucked his hands under his arms and stamped his feet. Inside, he could start a little fire in the old can his father boiled their kettle on – but to get there he had to get past that filthy brute and he would rather freeze.

'What yer doin' out 'ere, yer daft lump?' the sound of his father's voice made Mick smile and he dodged the cuff round the ear Taffy aimed at him and breathed a sigh of relief. He knew his father had come home sober for once and that made him happy.

3

It was the beginning of December now and the cake shop had pretty coloured lights in its windows when the two children approached hand in hand. They pressed their noses up against the glass, looking longingly at the delicate glass stands with their offerings of delicious cakes. There were all kinds of mouth-watering treats: sponge cakes dusted with icing sugar and filled with buttercream, soft buns covered in sticky pink icing, almond tarts, madeleines and rock cakes, crisp meringues filled with buttery cream, as well as the beautiful iced Christmas cake right in the centre. Also, piled up in little glass dishes, were chunks of coconut ice, chocolate truffles, fudge and, the best of all, right at the front of the window, two sugar mice: a pink one and a white one.

'Look, Ben,' Ruthie cried. 'Sugar mouses… pink for me and white for you…'

'It's sugar mice, Ruthie,' Ben said, looking at the sweet treat as longingly as his sister. 'Perhaps Dad will get us one each for Christmas…'

Ruthie looked up at him, her eyes large and dark blue like her late mother's but filled with knowledge that a child of her age should not have. A single tear slid down her cheek, because she knew they wouldn't get a stocking this year. Their dad was out of work again; last night he hadn't even had a shilling for the gas and he'd lit a candle to see them to bed. She knew he lined up down the docks every morning hoping to be given a job, because Ben had told her that was why he was so miserable.

Everything was horrible in Ruthie's world. Ma had died nearly nine months ago and since then things had got steadily worse. The house was often cold and empty, no food in the pantry. No one looked after her any more; her clothes split and got dirty, and her pale hair tangled; she needed someone to brush and comb it and put it into plaits, because it was so fine that otherwise it went all over the place in the wind.

Mum had done her best while she was able. She'd cooked and scrubbed and looked after her kids, but over the last two years her cough had got worse and worse. The doctor said it was bronchitis and wanted to send her away to a place at the sea where she might get better, but they didn't have any money and there was a long waiting list for such places if you were poor. Mum had finally died in March, and that had left them alone with their father. He did his best but it wasn't the same without Mum.

Dad got up early to give them breakfast before he went down to the docks to stand in line, but the work was scarce and more often than not he came home without even a shilling in pay – and when he did, he often stopped at the pub at the end of Fettle Street to have a drink. His mates who had worked that day shared a few pence when he was broke and so when he had work he repaid them by buying drinks he could not afford. Sometimes, when he was very down he didn't stop at one drink, and when he came home, he was laughing but couldn't stand up properly – and those days there was never any money for the gas meter and very little to eat.

Ben told his sister it didn't matter. Their dad wasn't a bad man; he wasn't a violent man who knocked his kids about and deliberately neglected them. Robbie did as much as he could for his kids, but recently he'd been passed over for all the better jobs. Ben had heard him telling Fred at the fish shop that the gaffer didn't like him because he'd stood up for one of the older men.

'You should go to Mr Penniworth,' Fred had told him. 'I'm sure he doesn't know how unfairly the gaffer treats the men.' Mr Penniworth was the overall manager for the East India Docks, but the men hardly ever saw him on the dock and no one went to his office unless invited.

'I couldn't do that, Fred,' Robbie had sighed. 'I'd be marked as a troublemaker and then I wouldn't get work anywhere in London.'

'Well, it's a rotten shame, that's all I can say. You're a decent man, Robbie Graham, and you deserve a bit of luck.'

Dad had laughed and thanked him for his kind words, paying a shilling for two fishcakes and sixpence worth of chips. Fred had filled the bag right to the brim and Ben, his sister and their father had eaten well that night, but that was days ago now and it had just been bread and dripping since.

It didn't matter to Ben that he had shoes that were down at the heel, holes in his socks and didn't get a threepenny piece for sweets on a Saturday like some of his friends. He knew that times were hard and money was tight. Ben wasn't the only boy in school with trousers bought off the second-hand stall and cut down to fit. Nor did he mind that he and Ruthie had to come home to an empty house after school. He could get their tea, a bit of bread and jam or some chips if Dad gave them three pennies. What made Ben unhappy was the way his father's shoulders hunched when he came home at night with a few coppers in his pocket after working hard all day.

The old cottage belonged to Ben's father, because it had been left to them by his grandfather, who had been a seaman all his life, and it was the reason they'd all come to live here, leaving the rooms they'd rented near his mother's home in Yarmouth. It wasn't really much of a place, but it was somewhere warm to sleep, because the range in the kitchen heated that room and the rooms above it. The only time they ever used the parlour was when Ben's mother died and her coffin stood there for three days before the funeral.

'Look,' Ruthie pulled at Ben's sleeve as the door of the sweet shop opened and the nice lady came out. 'It's Miss Flo...'

'Hello, you two,' Flo Hawkins greeted the children with a smile. 'It's cold this evening. You should hurry home, because I think it might snow.'

'I like your sugar mouses,' Ruthie said and gave them a last lingering look before Ben took her hand firmly. 'When I see them, I think it will soon be Christmas.'

'Yes, it will,' Flo agreed. She held out a brown paper bag to them. 'It's almost time to close – and these won't keep until the morning. I thought you might like them.'

'Oo, thank you,' Ruthie squealed in excitement and took the bag quickly before Flo could change her mind. 'It's ever so kind of you, Miss Flo.'

'It's perfectly all right,' she said. 'Perhaps your father will buy you a sugar mouse for Christmas.'

Ruthie shook her head sadly. 'Dad can't find a proper job,' she said and pulled at Ben's hand. 'Miss Flo gave us buns with icing on top. I love your buns, Miss Flo.'

'You're very kind, miss,' Ben thanked her a little stiffly, because it wasn't the first time the cake shop lady had given them a cake she claimed wouldn't last until the morning, but every time it was fresh and delicious. 'I'll clean yer windows for yer if yer like, miss.'

'Thank you, Ben, but my sister does them every morning herself,' Flo said. 'One day I'll find a job for you, but you don't have to work to pay me for a cake I can't sell…'

With that she went back into the shop and closed the door.

Ben took his sister firmly by the hand. 'Don't eat yer cake until we get home, Ruthie. It's rude to eat in the street.'

'I'm 'ungry,' Ruthie grumbled and her tummy rumbled to prove it, but she kept the bag shut, holding on tightly so that she wouldn't lose it.

'Dad wouldn't like us taking charity,' Ben said. His eyes were stinging with the tears he was fighting. Miss Flo's kindness always made him want to fling his arms round her and hug her, but his pride held him back.

'It isn't chari— whatsit…' Ruthie said and pulled on his hand. 'Miss Flo is just a nice lady and she told us the cakes wouldn't last until the mornin'…'

Ben didn't bother to answer her. He was nearly ten but Ruthie was only six. She could be stubborn and if she didn't want to understand that it was wrong to keep staring in the window until Miss Flo brought her a cake, she wouldn't listen.

'Shall we visit Mrs Millie and Mr Bert?' Ruthie asked him. 'It's Friday night and Dad warned us he might be late…'

Ben nodded. It would be cold in the cottage, because they couldn't afford to keep the range going all the time now. Dad soon got a little fire going with wood logs when he got home, but Ben couldn't quite manage it on his own.

'All right,' he said. 'We'll visit and see how they are – and then we'll go home.'

The terraced house in Silver Street where the elderly couple, Mr and Mrs Bert Waters, lived was just round the corner from their home. Ben knocked at the door and it was cautiously opened just a crack by Millie. As soon as she saw them, a big smile appeared on her wizened face and she opened her door wider.

'You never know who is about these days,' she said. 'I've had three men round askin' ter clean me winders this week – and I 'ad ter send 'em all away. I give them a sandwich 'cos I was sorry fer 'em like, but I can't afford ter pay 'em.'

'I'll clean yer winders, Mrs Millie,' Ben offered. 'I don't want sixpence. I'll do 'em fer nuthin'.'

'Bless you, lad. I know you would,' Millie said. 'Come and sit by the fire and I'll give you a cup of tea and a piece of my carrot cake…'

'Miss Flo gave us a bun with icing,' Ruthie told her and took one out to show the elderly lady.

'Well now, there's a thing,' Millie exclaimed, her wrinkled face creasing so much that her watery grey eyes almost disappeared. 'Wasn't that kind of her, Ruthie? Well, you keep that for when you get home. Your dad might like a piece of something like that.'

'Ruthie can eat hers,' Ben said. 'I'll share mine with Dad when he gets home. I like your cake, Mrs Millie – if you can spare it?'

'Of course I can, lad,' Millie said. 'My Bert has gone out the back to chop some wood and fetch a bucket of coal...'

'I'll help him fetch them in,' Ben offered, jumped to his feet and went out of the back door, leaving his sister by the fire. He'd brought in coal and wood many times and enjoyed helping Bert Waters with little jobs in his back yard. Bert's eldest son, Terry, had once been a car mechanic and Bert had lots of interesting bits and pieces in his shed that Terry had collected. He'd finished chopping the wood and had filled the log box. He was shovelling coal into a pail when Ben reached him. 'Can I help you, Bert?'

'You can carry the wood in for me if you will. I've got enough wood and coal to last us for a day or so...' He looked up at the sky. 'I think it will snow before long...'

'Yes, that's what Miss Flo thinks,' Ben replied and

grinned as he picked up the heavy box of logs. 'I'll come round on Sunday and help you stock up with wood and coal again so you don't have to go out if the snow comes.'

'You're a good lad, Ben,' Bert told him. 'I'll bet your dad is proud of you...'

Sighing, because Dad was always working or looking for work and had no idea what his son got up to, Ben followed his elderly friend back into the large warm kitchen. The walls had a dark green distemper to them, but they had been washed to remove the mould so many times that it had gone streaky and was black in some places. The furniture was scarred pine and old, the sofa sagging, its springs sticking through the material in one place, but the sturdy wooden rocking chairs by the fire were comfortable with bright cushions on the seats and backs. Little ornaments and fairings were crammed on the mantle and on the pine dresser, mixed with odd plates and cups, mostly blue and white, and there was a pair of imposing brass candlesticks complete with candles in case they ran out of shillings for the gas.

'Shall I get your shoppin' in the mornin', Mrs Millie?' Ben asked and the old woman smiled.

'Yes, lad,' she said. 'You and Ruthie can go down to the market fer me in the mornin'. Come round first thing and I'll give yer me list and the money.'

'I'll be here,' Ben promised. He took the slice of cake he was offered and sat on the peg rug in front of the fire munching it and sipping from the mug of hot tea sweetened with condensed milk.

A warm fire, good friends and something to eat: for the moment Ben was in heaven...

4

'G ivin' the profits away again?' Honour Hawkins
teased as Flo came back into the shop clapping
her hands on her arms to instil some warmth into them.
'If you give cakes to all the kids who press their noses
to that window, you'll end up broke.'

'Nonsense,' Flo said. 'I don't give all the children
cakes – but those two…' She shook her head, because
she didn't know why those two pulled at her heartstrings
so much, because it shouldn't mean anything to her that
they were Robbie's and yet she knew it did. 'I just can't
resist those eyes somehow.'

Honour's eyes met hers in understanding. There were
nearly eighteen years between them, because Honour
had been born when Flo was just seventeen. Yet they
were close, loving each other as sisters, which Honour
believed they were, working together and sharing the
burden of looking after their father. Ernest Hawkins
had been a sour-tempered man for as long as either
of them could recall. Honour thought he'd treated his

wife Faith abominably while she lived, acting as though he owned the property and the business despite them having been left to Faith by her grandfather. Faith, and after her death, Flo and then Honour as well, had run the shop for years. Ernest had been a ship's carpenter until he had a stroke five years earlier, since which his temper had got worse and worse. A year previously he'd had a second stroke and this one had taken the use from his legs. Now, Honour thought resentfully, he lay upstairs in his bed and tried to dictate their lives, making them run after him time and again. They took it in turns to answer the little bell he kept by the bed.

Honour liked making fancy things, like the sugar mice, iced buns with little sprinkles on and the beautiful iced cakes they took orders for at Christmas and sometimes for birthdays. They shared the baking and took it in turns to serve in the shop. In the evenings they scrubbed their little kitchen, cleaned the shop and prepared as much as they could for the next day. Flo got up first to begin baking for the day and Honour made breakfast for all of them, carrying her father's up to him. He always demanded that Flo help him to the commode and if Honour tried he would throw things at her. So Flo had to leave the baking to her sister and go up to help him. It was always Flo who had to see to his needs for he would not allow Honour to touch him.

'I think he hates me,' Honour told Flo now as they began to tidy away empty cake stands ready to close the shop. 'I tried to make his pillows more comfortable when I took him a cup of tea and a piece of your jam sponge and he pinched my arm.'

'He does that to me all the time; it's just that he's so frustrated.' Flo excused their father even though she knew he did not deserve it.

'Father can be very cruel, Flo. Mum said he hit her a few times but always where it didn't show. He is a bully and the stroke made him worse. I think his mind is affected...'

'I'm not sure; I think he's just angry...'

'He was always cruel,' Honour began, halting as the shop opened and a soldier entered. He was wearing his uniform as a sergeant and looked handsome with straight dark hair cut short, grey eyes and a generous smiling mouth. 'Good evenin', sir – how can I help you?'

Honour smiled because Roy was her beau. He'd started coming in several times a week almost a year ago now, making sure that she was free to serve him. Then he'd asked her out. At first she'd just laughed and shaken her head, but then she asked Flo if it was all right and her sister told her she saw no harm in it. Since then he'd taken her to the flicks, for a drink and to a social at the church hall a few times.

'I don't need to tell you to behave and be careful,' Flo had warned. 'Don't be later than ten o'clock – and don't tell Father yet. Let him think you've been out with one of your girl-friends.' Honour's best friend Kitty lived next door; they'd been school friends and were often in and out of each other's homes, though not as much since her father's stroke, but Roy was Honour's first boyfriend and Honour had been excited but nervous the first time he'd taken her for a walk and a coffee. Now when she saw him, some months after their first outing, her heart beat faster in anticipation of being asked somewhere nice.

Flo took a cake stand through to the kitchen. She knew the young man by now and thought him respectable. He'd introduced himself as Sergeant Roy Sharp and he was quite obviously paying court to Honour. As yet, he hadn't asked her to marry him, but it was possibly just a matter of time. Flo didn't grudge Honour her happiness, but she dreaded losing her and hoped she would not marry for a long time.

Flo lingered as long as she could before returning to the shop. Honour had just filled a box with sweet treats and the soldier was paying her. He smiled at Flo and looked pleased with himself as he left. As soon as Flo had turned the 'closed' notice in the door and pulled the blind, Honour grabbed her round the waist and hugged her.

'He asked me to go to the pictures with him tomorrow. It's Charlie Chaplin and you know I love his films – I can, can't I?' Honour looked at her pleadingly.

'You mustn't let Dad know where you're goin',' Flo warned. 'I'll tell him you've gone to the church hall with Kitty. He doesn't mind either of us going there at nights – but if he knew you'd gone out with a soldier he would half kill you…'

'He might have once,' Honour agreed, 'but he can't get out of that bed without help…'

'Don't be too sure of that,' Flo warned. 'I caught him puttin' his legs to the floor the other day. He made out he fell as he tried to stand, but I wouldn't mind bettin' he can do more than he lets on. He wants us runnin' after him all the time.'

'The crafty old devil,' Honour cried but laughed, because she wasn't spiteful. 'I don't mind helpin' him if he lets me – but he makes so much work for you.'

'Well, I send his sheets out to be washed now and I told him so,' Flo said with a tight smile. 'He knows that it costs money to make a mess so perhaps he'll be a bit more considerate in future.'

'Dad has never considered any of us, not even Mum.' Honour frowned. 'You don't mind if I go out with Sergeant Sharp, do you?'

Flo hesitated before speaking. Honour didn't remember their father before the bitterness turned him into a bad-tempered old man, but she could just remember a different person who had smiled more and given his daughter a treat on a Saturday morning.

'No, of course I don't,' Flo told her and gave her a hug. 'You're young and you should have some fun. I want you to be happy – and one day I hope you will fall in love and get married.'

'You should get married too,' Honour teased. 'I know someone who likes you a lot...'

'And who would that be?' Flo asked, even though she knew Honour meant John Hansen.

'Are you going to the mission tonight?' Honour asked. 'I'll see to Father. I don't mind...'

Flo liked it when Honour was in a happy mood and didn't mind her teasing. Neither of them had much fun in their lives and Flo had given up expecting more than she had. She'd once made a mistake and this was her punishment. She had to stay here to make a life for herself and her darling Honour and nothing would make her give up the bequest her mother had left to her and Honour, even though her father had hidden the deeds to the property and refused to give them up even to the lawyer. He claimed he did not know where they were, but Flo knew that he'd hidden them the night his wife died. Yet she could do nothing to prove it and he threatened to turn them out with nothing unless she behaved and gave him his share of the profits.

Flo put up with his unkind words, his pinching and the way he made a mess just so that she had to clear it up – but as yet he hadn't tried to stop her going to the mission once a week. That was because if she hadn't gone, John Hansen would have come round and lectured her father about the evils of selfishness.

John was a Church of England vicar and spent his Sundays preaching to his congregation and the rest of his week caring for the poor of the area at his Christian mission. Here those who were destitute could always find a hot meal of soup, bread and tea. Sometimes, there were hot baked potatoes filled with cheese or a knob of butter as well as the soup, and on very rare occasions, like Christmas Day, there would be a meal of some kind.

Friday nights was tombola night at the mission and everyone who could afford to spend a shilling or two went along to play. Small prizes were given and the money earned over and above the cost of the prizes was saved towards the meal for the elderly and destitute on Christmas Day. Flo helped on Friday nights by serving tea and making sandwiches for the players and those who came in just to watch and warm themselves by the fire – and she always managed to take a few spare cakes with her, which were a special treat for those lucky enough to get a share.

'Yes, I am going this evening,' Flo told her sister. 'I'm taking the rest of the rock cakes and the sponge we cut today. I'll make fresh in the morning…'

'I'm goin' to make some more sugar mice this evening while you're out,' Honour said. 'I think I might make some iced biscuits as well. If I wrap them in cellophane they keep fresh for several days and people like to give them as gifts.'

'It's a bit too soon for Christmas gifts yet,' Flo suggested, but she knew Honour enjoyed making fancy things and she made them look beautiful, tied up with pretty ribbon. In the last days before Christmas people queued to buy her treats – although not quite as many as they had before so many folk were out of work. Yet most families saved a few pennies every week for Christmas and some people paid two pennies a week into a club at Flo's shop to buy festive cakes and sweets for their children.

Flo locked the shop and both girls went into the kitchen. They washed the used dishes from the shop, made a supper of pilchards on toast for themselves and then Flo took freshly made toast and melted cheese up to her father. She always cut the crusts off for him and arranged the little fingers of toast so that they were easy for him to eat.

Honour said that he was sour and bad-tempered, but she'd seen only the loving side of their mother. Flo still remembered when she'd been young and her father had been much kinder to both her and her mother. She was not certain why he had changed. Her mother had a cutting edge to her tongue and Flo had heard the echoes of bitter rows but never knew the reason for them; they had begun long before she fell for a child and it was after one terrible one that had come to blows that her father had gone north to the shipyards and not returned for over a year. Flo had suffered at the hands of both parents and yet she had nursed her dying mother and would do the same for her father, no matter how cruel he was. Only if he hurt Honour would she strike back at him.

He put down his newspaper and Flo saw he'd been reading an article about scientists in Cambridge smashing the atom. She wondered what possible benefit that could be to anyone. If they had money to waste, they should use it to discover something useful – something that would help people.

Flo plumped up her father's pillows. 'Right, you'll be all fine for a while now, Dad. I'll see you when I get back…'

'Where do you think you're goin'?' he demanded as she turned to leave.

'It's Friday. I go to the mission on Friday.'

'You should stay here in case I need your help.'

'Honour will help you, Father.'

'I'll not have that little trollop touchin' me…'

'Father, please do not speak of Honour in that manner. She isn't a trollop… and I won't have you say it.' She looked at him warily, holding her anger.

'She'll turn out just like her mother…' His bony fingers dug into Flo's arm. 'I'm not stupid, girl, even if you and your mother thought I was – that little bitch is none of mine…'

'Let go of me, Father.' Flo looked him in the eyes. 'If you persist in saying these things we might decide not to answer your bell…'

'Selfish little bitch!' her father shouted and flung his arm out. 'Go to the wretched mission then and leave me 'ere alone in me bed unable to move…'

'I think you could manage very well if you chose,' Flo said and gave him a hard look. 'This property belongs to me, Father, as you well know, because Mum left it to me in her will; her father's will said it should be passed on to her first child – and you've always had your share of the profits. If you're not satisfied you're welcome to leave, find yourself some lodgings…'

'You wicked girl! You'll go to hell for this,' her father threatened. 'If John Hansen knew how you talk to me, he wouldn't think the sun shines out of yer arse! If he knew what I knew, he'd want none of you, girl.'

'That sort of language is beneath you, Father, and I shall not listen to it,' Flo said, walking from the room without looking back. He yelled obscenities after her but she did not turn or give any sign that she had noticed. This language had started after his second stroke and was not like him, not like the man he'd once been. Her eyes stung with tears because her father had driven all chance of real happiness from her life long ago. She knew that she would never marry and sometimes that made her heart ache, though she accepted it was too late to recover lost dreams. Yet if he truly knew their secret – the secret Flo and her mother had kept from the whole world – he could make life very hard for her and for Honour.

Flo suspected that he had guessed Honour was hers, but he could not know the name of her child's father. Flo had told no one, even though her mother had threatened her with the whip. She'd kept that to herself and it would remain her secret until the time came to tell Honour.

No, her father could not know her secret. Flo had hidden it from the world, and even the man she'd loved so much that she'd foolishly given both her heart and her virginity to him had no idea that Honour was her daughter. Flo had not even told Honour and would not while her own father lived...

5

John Hansen looked up as the woman entered the mission hall: set up by the parish church, it was for the benefit of the local community and intended to give the residents somewhere to go for an evening of company that was not a public house, and once a week they had a social evening for the men, women and children of the area. However, of late, its main purpose had been to feed those near to starving, giving everyone who asked a meal of bread, soup and a mug of hot tea. It was a mission to the poor of London, but John did not think of himself as a missionary; he was just a simple man helping the people he cared for, just as he did when he spoke to them from the pulpit on a Sunday – though it had to be said that he saw fewer men on a Sunday than he did in his mission.

His gaze returned to the woman who had just entered. She would not be considered young now but her face had a sweetness and soft beauty that tore at his heart whenever he saw her. His feelings threatened to make

set her apart and made people look at her, though he knew that beneath the sweetness and thoughtfulness, there was strength. The strength that made her able to stand up to her father's cruelty. 'Has Mr Hawkins been playing up again?'

'I think lying helpless in bed makes him worse,' Flo admitted. 'It can't be pleasant, hardly ever seeing anyone, never going out and needing someone to help him all the time.'

'Perhaps if he'd been kinder to his neighbours he might have more visitors,' John said, because he knew that he was the only person outside the family to visit Ernest Hawkins. 'It is a sad thing to drive everyone away.'

'Yes, it is,' Flo agreed with him. 'I had best get to the kitchen. I brought some small cakes and some corned beef and my own pickle to make sandwiches.'

'We've used up all the ham donated,' John admitted. 'They will be glad of whatever you've brought.'

Flo nodded and he watched as she walked off to the kitchens to start filling plates with sandwiches and cakes. The fruit cake she'd sent earlier had almost gone and there were still more folk squeezing into the hall in the hope of food and a cup of tea or cocoa.

John's eyes moved over the men, women and a sprinkling of children in the hall. Some of them came to play the games he set up on a Friday night, hoping to win five or ten shillings as the top prize, but a packet of biscuits or sweets was another welcome gift, because no one in this hall had more than a few pence in his or her pocket. Everyone who had a job thought themselves lucky and knew that it could be snatched away from them at any time. Firms who were old and respected were going to the wall every week.

Lingering, John listened to the banter of the men and boys. Most of them were talking about their football team, West Ham, who were in division two, and wondering how many goals Vic Watson would score that weekend in the league. He was their top scorer and was helping the team to win their FA cup matches too; those who could read studied the football results in the evening paper of a Saturday night, for not everyone had a wireless at home and the pubs that had were crowded when the results came through. A good win for the home team lifted spirits even when things were bad.

John looked around for Robbie Graham. He'd met the man standing outside the pub earlier that day looking miserable and asked if he would bring his children to the mission that evening, but he'd shaken his head and his eyes had flashed with anger.

'I don't ask for charity, John Hansen,' he'd grunted. 'And don't be thinking I've spent every penny in the pub, because I stood all bloody day and they didn't give me more than an hour's work washing down a trailer stinking with maggots and bones and I'll not spend that money even though my throat is parched for a beer.'

John had nodded, not answering the accusation in Robbie's eyes, because he understood his anger; he'd seen it in the eyes of many men standing on street corners recently. 'You're a carpenter by trade, aren't you?'

'Aye, and a damned good one,' Robbie had grunted, still angry. 'But they won't give me my proper work. All I get is filthy, stinkin' jobs that pay pennies. How am I supposed to clothe and feed my kids like that?'

'I might be able to find you a few hours work at the mission,' John had said. 'We need some structural repairs and I could manage to pay you some shillings – but it would only be for a few days...'

'Proper work?' Robbie had demanded. 'I don't want you making a job for me out of charity...'

'Oh, the work is needed all right,' John had told him with a grin. 'If I hired a firm, it would cost a fortune – but perhaps you could help me out and do some of the repairs. If you tell me what I need, I can buy the wood...'

Robbie had nodded. 'I'll take a look and if there's a job to be done... I'd be glad to do it...'

'Come to the tombola this evening and bring the children. We have a bit of tea for the elderly folk and everyone has a good time.'

'Mebbe,' Robbie had said and touched the tip of his tongue to his lips as the door of the public house swung open and they caught the odour of stale beer. 'I'd rather come round during the day...'

John had nodded and walked on. He knew that you couldn't push a man into doing something that went against the grain and it wasn't worth trying. If Robbie made a good job of the work at the mission, there was a chance that the Church authorities would take him on. Goodness knows, there was enough restoration work in the churches of London to last a man his working lifetime. Getting the Church Commissioners to spend their money was another matter, though John happened to know that several buildings in the district were approaching the stage where either work was done to stop them becoming dangerous or they would need to close. However, there was no point in raising a man's hopes only to dash them. If Robbie did the jobs necessary at the mission, John would do his best to find him more, but he couldn't promise anything. Besides, Robbie had to make the first move.

Robbie stood outside the mission. It was cold and the lights in the windows were inviting him, tempting him to go inside, but he'd seen someone go in and knew he couldn't – not if *she* was there. He couldn't let her see how low he'd sunk. He'd loved her once or thought he did...

Robbie had walked past her little shop often enough, pausing to look at the tempting treats in the window and wish he could take some of them home for his children. Ben had given him half a sticky bun when he got in from work that night and he'd eaten it, asking where it had come from as he chewed the delicious cake, even though he knew already.

'Miss Flo gave us both one,' Ben had told him. 'I offered to clean her windows, Dad. She promised she would find me a job one day – so it's not charity. 'Sides, Ruthie wanted hers, so I couldn't say no.'

'Make sure you go round there and sweep the path for her, if nothing else,' Robbie had growled. He didn't like his kids taking charity from anyone – but it was worse coming from her. Yet how could he forbid it when he was seldom able to give them anything more than a bit of bread and scrape or a few chips if he'd been paid for a couple of hours unloading?

He cursed as he thought of the days when he'd left the army with a trade as a carpenter and there had been lots of work on the docks, as well as on the building sites and he could turn his hand to anything that used wood. He loved the smell and the feel of it and took a pride in his work. It had broken his heart when he'd had to stand in line at the docks.

'Are yer comin' in, Robbie,' a voice asked and he turned to see one of the men he sometimes stood in line with. Jack Goodrum had had better luck than him recently and he'd taken up a couple of quid at the end of the day. He didn't need charity.

'I don't go in for charity…'

'Nor me, mate.' Jack Goodrum grinned. 'No. I'm lookin' fer a game o' cards with some mates of mine. Yer can sit in if yer like...'

'I ain't got any money ter spare fer cards...'

'Nor ain't we,' Jack said. 'We play fer matchsticks – and then the one who loses the most buys the other a half on the way 'ome...'

Robbie hesitated. He had a couple of bob in his pocket, enough to buy a couple of half-pints if he lost. It was years since he'd played with other men – not since he was in the army. He'd joined up when his parents died and the war had been on... But the memories didn't make for good thoughts.

So why not play cards for a change? The kids were next door with a neighbour. They would be all right for an hour or so and it was a long time since he'd done anything but work and go home to sit in an empty kitchen when the kids were in bed.

'All right then, but I've only got two bob in me pocket so don't expect me to buy more than a half...'

Jack grinned and Robbie followed him into the mission. It was packed, mostly with older folk, but a few men and women of his own age and one or two kids. Robbie regretted not bringing his, as John Hansen had invited him to do, because it would have been a bit of fun for them.

He followed his friend and sat down at a table with three other men – that was four half-pints, five if he had one himself. He might have enough left over for a bag of chips on Saturday for the kids...

Sitting at the table, he was asked what he wanted to play and given a box of matches to use as his stake. Glancing round the room, Robbie saw her. She was carrying two plates of food to a table, where people were helping themselves to sandwiches and cakes. For a moment Robbie thought she'd seen him and it seemed that their eyes met until she turned away.

Sighing, Robbie concentrated on his cards. He would much prefer that he was the one being bought a drink rather than having to spend what little he'd earned on beer instead of his kids...

Flo saw him sitting at a table with four other men. Robbie was playing cards for matchsticks. John wouldn't allow them to play for money in the mission of course, but Flo suspected that the men went to the pub afterwards and who knew what changed hands then?

She looked round for Robbie's children, but he hadn't brought them with him and that made her frown, because if he was coming out for an evening of pleasure the least he could do was to bring his children for a treat. It would have cost him nothing and they might have won games and prizes, and enjoyed a nice corned beef and pickle sandwich. It made her wonder if he was a little selfish and she deliberately avoided looking at him.

Flo listened to the numbers being called for the tombola. She always bought a card and gave it to one of the elderly women to play, because she wanted to contribute to the funds for the mission. She bought raffle tickets too and sometimes she won a little prize, but if she did she always gave it back to John afterwards. He put it into the draw for the next week.

'I don't want to win anything,' she'd told him the first time she won a packet of Bourbon biscuits. 'I only buy a ticket to help out.'

Flo didn't have much money for herself. By the time she replaced her flour, sugar and other ingredients, paid Honour a small wage, given her father the money he demanded, bought their food, and settled the other bills the shop incurred, it left only a few shillings for her own use.

She occasionally made herself a new dress or skirt, but because she wore a smart striped apron in the shop most of the time Flo didn't bother about new clothes for herself much. She liked Honour to have nice things and when she could save a few pounds she gave them to the girl and told her to buy a new dress or some shoes. Honour took the money but often used a little of it to buy something for Flo, because she was a generous girl. She'd bought the lovely twinset Flo was wearing now for her birthday and it was Flo's nicest thing and that was why she wore it at the mission.

Watching some children playing pass the parcel, Flo smiled as they tore off each layer of newspaper wrapping the small treat inside. They were as excited as they would be on Christmas morning. Thinking of Christmas, Flo smiled as she recalled something she'd seen at the market that she wanted to buy for her sister. It was a silver bracelet made of twisted wires and had a little heart charm hanging from it. Flo had seen it and known that Honour would love it, but she hadn't had enough money in her purse. She would go back on Tuesday morning, which was her day for shopping in the market, and buy it – but she would hide it away, together with the pretty hankies and an imitation silk scarf she had already bought as presents for Honour.

Flo did a bowl of washing up and left one of the other helpers to dry as she carried the last plate of food out to the table. She caught sight of Robbie rising from the table with the other men and frowned, because he looked so miserable. It seemed obvious to her that he'd lost the game of chance he'd been playing and she doubted – with the state of things in the East End – he could afford even the few pence he'd probably pledged. For a moment he looked directly at her and Flo felt so sorry for him that she forgot her earlier annoyance with him and smiled. A dark colour spread up his neck and he turned to leave until John Hansen tapped him on the arm and spoke to him. Robbie nodded agreement and then dashed off, as if he someone had poured hot water over him.

'Have you finished now?' John asked, coming up to her. 'I've called time so we'll be closing as soon as I can get them all to leave.'

Flo laughed up at him. 'You make it too comfortable, Mr Hansen. No one wants to leave and go out in the dark…'

'Apart from Jack Goodrum and his friends,' John agreed and frowned. 'I got Robbie to come this evening, but I didn't think he would fall in with them… they think I don't know they bet with matchsticks and then the loser buys the drinks later, but I'm not blind.'

'I think Mr Graham lost…' Flo bit her lip, because John looked at her oddly.

'I dare say the idea of a free drink was appealing. It's a good thing I offered him a few hours work. It won't amount to much, I fear, but you never know what may happen…'

'Now what are you plotting?' Flo turned as Nurse Mary walked up to them. She worked at the infirmary but gave what time she could to the mission, treating men and women who couldn't afford to pay for treatment and would neglect themselves rather than get into debt for a doctor's bill. 'Ah, Nurse Mary. Mr Hansen is up to something…'

'I see you've finished for the night,' Nurse Mary said. She smiled at Flo, but her smile didn't reach her eyes. 'I just wanted to tell you, John, that I shall be here in the morning for my clinic as usual…'

'Thank you, Nurse Mary,' John said. 'Mr Potter has a nasty cough – and I think Nellie Jones's hip is playing her up again. I'm sure you will have your usual crowd waiting when you arrive.' She smiled at him and looked content.

'I'm leaving now,' Flo told him. 'I enjoyed helping, Mr Hansen. Goodnight, Nurse Mary.'

Flo went into the office and picked up her coat, wrapping her scarf around her neck. She had sensed the nurse's silent hostility and wasn't sure why the older woman did not like her. They were both interested in the same thing – helping John Hansen to keep his mission running. It was hard to find the funds because money was tight everywhere. Customers often asked for credit, and though most paid as soon as they could, it meant that everyone had to cut their profit margins to keep going.

Flo knew that she and Honour were lucky, because although a lot of people could not afford much in the way of luxuries, a cake or a few squares of coconut ice were little treats that helped them to face their hard lives. With Christmas on the horizon, more people would use what they had managed to save to buy sweet treats for themselves and their children – but afterwards, when they all tightened their belts, Flo would expect a sharp drop in profits. It was as well that she still had a little of the money her mother had secretly given her just before she died.

'The money is hidden from your father,' Faith Hawkins had told her daughter. 'Use it wisely, Flo, because you will find it hard to replace once it has gone. Your father has always grabbed a share of what the shop makes, though he has no right to a penny. I only gave in because he would make both your life and Honour's a misery if I denied him – and I know I've been harsh with you, but you hurt me when you brought shame on us.'

Flo had not touched a penny of the little nest egg her mother had saved. She never went near it, because she did not want her father to discover it and snatch it away from her; it was for Honour when she needed it.

Going out into the cold night air, Flo heard a loud bang and saw the Austin 7 car backfiring at the other end of the lane. Not many motorised cars were seen in these streets, other than the occasional baker's van and the bus. The brewery and a lot of other small tradesmen still used horses to pull carts or waggons and only the visiting businessmen or the gang members ever had a car.

Flo knew that criminal gangs still held sway in some of the worst streets of the area, though she'd never actually met anyone or seen anyone she knew to be a gang member. She'd heard whispers there was an illegal bookie somewhere about, but she'd never tried to discover where it was situated; it would be behind a normal house door, for all the world just another home, and somewhere in the back room bets would be taken and laid.

Shivering, she hurried through the streets, suddenly wanting to be home. It was easy to tell those families that carried on illegal forms of gambling and other vices; they were the ones with money and cars. She wondered if some of them came to buy sweets at her shop. If they did she didn't know, but the thought was enough to make her glance uneasily over her shoulder. However, the street was empty.

6

'I can't wait until Roy comes this evening,' Honour said on Saturday morning as they were tidying the shop. She'd spent the previous night with her hair wound up in rags and it looked bouncy and fresh, drawn back off her face with clips.

'What will you wear?' Flo asked and smiled as Honour told her exactly what she'd chosen. The excitement of being courted was in her eyes and Flo could see just a trace of colour on her lips; she'd been experimenting ready for her trip to the cinema.

Singing to herself, Honour went back to the kitchen to fetch some freshly baked cakes and Flo got on with her cleaning. She didn't think she'd ever seen Honour so happy and wondered if her friendship with the young soldier was more serious than she'd imagined. At first she'd thought it was just the fun of being taken out, because he was her first boyfriend, but now after they'd been dating for some months, she thought she'd noticed a change.

Flo frowned, because if Honour had fallen in love with Roy it would mean Flo would have to speak to her father. She wouldn't allow him to forbid Honour to see her young man, but he would be angry – as much because they hadn't told him, as anything else. Perhaps she ought to have made him aware from the first, but Flo didn't see why Honour should suffer the way she had. If he had his way, Honour would never be allowed out of the house! Yes, Flo had once made a mistake, but Honour was more sensible. They'd spoken briefly about behaving modestly when out with a young man, but Flo had been too embarrassed to say more – she would have to if Honour was thinking of marriage.

When her beloved daughter returned with the cakes, her eyes sparkling and a spring in her step, Flo felt tears on her lashes, which she hastily blinked away. Honour was beautiful and Flo ought to have known she would find a man to love one day. Of course she was too young to wed; at eighteen she could not marry for another three years unless Flo gave her permission. Ernest Hawkins might try to stop her but Flo was her mother, even though the world believed otherwise and hers was the last say. She knew that when the time came she would not stand in Honour's way...

*

Ben looked at Bert Waters' eyes when the old man let him in that Sunday morning. They looked red and puffy and he thought his friend had been crying.

'Is there anythin' I can do, sir?' he asked. 'If you're not too good I can fetch in the coal, chop the wood if yer like?'

'No, lad, I've chopped the wood, but you can bring some coal in for me...' Bert sighed. 'It's my Millie. She started coughin' terrible in the night and this mornin' she looks proper bad. I think she needs the doctor, but she says she doesn't want him to come.'

'Mum used to say that when she was ill,' Ben said wisely. His tenth birthday was not until the following January, but his mother's death had forced him to grow up swiftly. 'You 'ave ter get 'im anyway.'

'Yes, I think so,' Bert nodded. 'She worries about the money, you see. We've got a little bit tucked away but not much – but I think she needs the doctor and I'm goin' to ask if you will run and get 'im fer me?'

'Yeah, 'course I will.' Ben grinned at him. 'She'll have a go at yer, Mr Waters, but you'll not mind that...'

'Why don't yer call me Granda?' Bert asked with a smile. 'You ain't got a grandfather and I ain't got no grandchildren. My boys both got killed in the Great War – the bloody Germans killed 'em both on the Somme...'

'Yeah, I know,' Ben said, because he'd heard the story before, from Bert and others. Ben was always running errands for neighbours and they told him things, about the terrible war that had taken the flower of Britain's young men. 'I reckon that was rotten luck fer yer, Granda.' He grinned at him as he used the name for the first time. 'I like that – I reckon Ruthie will too. We ain't got nobody but Dad and each other.'

'Well yer 'ave now,' Bert said. 'Cut along and get that doctor then, lad. Yer know where Dr Miller lives, don't yer?'

'Yeah, I know. He came to Mum,' Ben said. 'I were with her and he weren't much good, though he done his best – but she still died and left us...'

'Yes, I know, lad. I was sorry about that – yer mum was a nice lady...'

'Yeah...' Ben caught back the tears that might shame him. Boys of his age didn't cry, even if their mum was dead. 'I reckon I'll go and fetch the doctor. He'll probably charge yer double fer comin' out on a Sunday.'

Bert nodded grimly, but Ben knew there was no other choice. Millie needed the doctor now and if he didn't come she might die...

Flo was wiping out the shop window when she saw Ben running by. He was plainly in a hurry and she wondered who was ill, because the look on the boy's face told her it was urgent. She remembered Robbie going off with the regular card players. He'd looked desperate – but he wouldn't do anything foolish would he?

Flo's father had started banging on the floor upstairs with his stick. She ignored him as she finished her work. He hated her working on Sundays, and said both she and Honour needed to sit and read the Bible. Flo hadn't had a chance to ask Honour if she had an enjoyable time with her friend at the pictures. Her sister had got up early and was busy making sugar mice, rum truffles and some biscuits with coffee icing on the top. She was going to make little boxes of mixed treats and wrap them in cellophane. One box would go in the window and she would have another two inside the shop on the glass counter. If people liked them and ordered them, she would make lots more ready for Christmas week, which was still some way off yet.

Flo had already made two dozen rich fruit cakes, which were stored in tins in the large pantry. She would ice them Christmas week so that they were fresh and the icing was soft. The cakes themselves had been made a month ago because they got better if you tipped a little brandy into them once a week and let them mature ready for Christmas.

Flo was looking forward to trying one of Honour's biscuits with a cup of tea and having a good chat about the previous evening, but she was waiting until Honour was ready to tell her. She didn't want to pry into Honour's secrets, because she knew how that felt – her father had done that to her for years.

Hearing her father's stick bang on the floor again, Flo drew the little net curtains behind her window and was about to leave the shop and go upstairs when she saw Ben returning. She went to the shop door and opened it, calling out to him, 'What is wrong?'

'I went fer the doctor,' Ben said. 'Millie Waters was taken real bad in the night. The doctor weren't there. His missus said he was out but he'd come when he could…'

Flo nodded, because it was often the same. There was a great deal of sickness in the lanes and ancient courts of London's East End, and often the doctors here were overworked.

'Is there anythin' I can do to help?'

'Nah, I doubt it. Granda is lookin' after her, but he says her cough is somethin' awful…'

'I know someone who might come,' Flo said. 'You go back to Mr Waters and I'll telephone the infirmary and ask for Nurse Mary. I think she might be finishing her work soon and she might call on her way home…'

'Right, ta,' Ben said and nodded. 'I'll tell Granda that…'

'Tell him that I'll pop round later too…'

As Ben set off at a run again, Flo returned to the shop and then popped up to see her father. Having settled him, she went through to the kitchen, where Honour had just finished tying up an open box of biscuits and chocolate truffles in cellophane and a pink ribbon.

'Is that for the window?' Flo asked. 'They look delicious and that is a lovely combination – coffee icing on the biscuits and rum truffles.'

'I put a little Jamaican rum into the mixture as well as the essence,' Honour said as she pushed a little plate forward. On it were two biscuits and two rum truffles. 'These are for us to try...'

'I've been looking forward to these.' Flo picked up the freshly made truffle and bit into it, her eyes rolling as the flavour washed over her tongue and filled her mouth with its exquisite softness and taste. 'Oh, they are lovely, Honour. You've got the balance just right. I think these are the best you've ever made, love.'

Honour picked hers up and bit into it. She moaned with delight as she swallowed. 'That is so lovely,' she crooned. 'I think we shall get asked for a lot of these... Roy is coming in tomorrow to buy a box of treats for his mother. She is an invalid and lives in a nursing home... His father died when he was a boy and they lived with his mother's brother. Roy couldn't look after his mother, because he is in the army so when she became paralysed they put her in this home. Roy says it isn't too bad... not like some, which are awful, but it's expensive and he couldn't afford it if his uncle didn't help. Roy visits as often as he can and takes her presents. He says I can go with him one day...'

'He seems a pleasant young man,' Flo said.

'He wants me to go for a walk this afternoon… can I?'

'As long as you're back for tea,' Flo agreed. 'I must go to the phone box and ring the infirmary and ask Nurse Mary to visit Millie Waters – and I've promised to visit her later, and I can't leave Dad alone here…'

'I don't see why he can't look after himself,' Honour said. 'I caught him using the commode himself early this morning. He grumbled at me and claimed he'd been callin' for us, but that was a lie. I wasn't asleep and I would have heard him.'

'I've thought he can get out of bed alone if he wants,' Flo agreed. 'He won't admit it, because it suits him to have us runnin' after him – but he lies easily. Even so, I couldn't leave him all alone…'

Honour looked at her in silence for a moment, then, 'What would happen if I wasn't here all the time? How would you cope on your own?'

Flo felt an icy tingle at her nape, because she didn't want to think about the day Honour left home. 'That won't happen just yet – unless you don't want to work here with me?'

'It isn't that, Flo. I'll always be here for you and I can probably work some of the time – but I… might want to get married and then you'd be on your own with him.'

'Honour! You can't be serious? You hardly know that soldier…'

'He has been comin' in the shop askin' me out for ages now – but he says he thinks the world of me, Flo. He says he knows it's too soon, but he wants me to marry him one day…'

Flo stared at her, heart pumping. This was what she'd dreaded! 'Be certain he's serious – and be sure how you feel, love.'

'I know he makes me want to smile and walk barefoot in the park in the dew,' Honour said and her eyes lit up. 'I dreamed about a cottage in the country and us living there with two little children…' She blushed and laughed. 'You must think I'm daft, but I get so fed up with our life here, Flo. I hate looking after Father and I know he hates me. I don't want to desert you – but I can't waste my life the way you have…' A shocked look came to her eyes. 'I'm sorry, Flo. I didn't mean that the way it sounded…'

Flo felt the hurt strike deep, but she couldn't blame Honour. Of course it must look to her as though the woman she thought of as her elder sister had wasted her life.

'I know you didn't mean to hurt me,' she said, her throat restricted. She wanted to cry but held back the tears. 'You're right, of course, but I had you to care for – and besides, there was no one I wanted…'

And that was a terrible lie, because she had someone, loved him so much that her sixteen-year-old-heart had behaved like a giddy spring lamb. She'd sneaked out to meet him that summer night when her parents were sleeping and they'd gone to walk by the river. Flo remembered that she'd taken off her shoes and stockings and walked barefoot, not in the morning dew but in the evening-damp grass.

'I love you so very much,' he'd whispered, though he was barely a year older. 'I want us to run away and be together forever…'

So many sweet words as they lay together on his jacket and kissed, touching, exploring each other's bodies. Flo hadn't really understood what was happening when they loved and she didn't think he knew much more; it was a funny, fumbling, sweet attempt to make love. Strange then, that the consequences should have been so overwhelming, to her life – and her mother's. Flo's mother had protected her young daughter when she realised she was in trouble, though she called her a fool and many worse things. Flo knew her mother had suffered at the hands of her husband, because he'd never believed that Honour was his and when he returned from months away in the north, he'd accused her of being unfaithful and lashed out in the only way he knew, with his fists…

'Oh, don't cry,' Honour begged as the tear slid down Flo's cheek. 'I love you so much. You've been everything to me; sister, mother, friend – please, don't cry…'

'You didn't make me cry,' Flo said and reached for her hand. 'It was an old memory, because there was once someone who made me feel the way Roy makes you feel, my dearest. It was a long time ago and it was over before it started...' Though it could never truly be over because of what had happened that summer night.

Honour stared in surprise. 'Why – did our father make you give him up?'

'Dad never knew,' Flo told her. 'My... my friend just went away and I never saw him again...' But that was a lie too, because she had seen him years later, when it was too late. He'd had a wife and child and now he had two, and she was a prisoner of the life she'd forged for herself one beautiful wonderful night, though she could never regret having Honour.

'I'm so sorry, Flo,' Honour said and hugged her. She wiped the tear from her cheek. 'Roy loves me, I know he does. He wants to get a ring and get married, but I told him Dad wouldn't allow it. If I'd permit him, Roy would visit Dad and tell him we want to marry, but I know he wouldn't let us. Roy says we could get engaged anyway...'

'You would still need permission,' Flo reminded gently. 'I know it sounds hard, Honour, but you hardly know this young man. Wait for a while – six months – and then I'll find a way for you to get what you want...'

Flo mentally crossed her fingers. She was Honour's mother, she'd insisted her name was on the birth certificate, even though the world thought of them as sisters, and she could sign the permission for her daughter to wed, but that would mean telling her the truth and there was a part of Flo that shrunk from doing that... Besides, marriage meant she would lose her and although it might be selfish Flo dreaded the thought of her life without her.

'Oh, you're wonderful!' Honour hugged her again. 'Roy doesn't expect us to marry before next summer. He will have done his time in the army by then and he wants to find us a house and a little shop not too far from you. His father and his uncle were both tailors by trade and Roy wants to follow in his father's footsteps, but he's going to tailor-make women's clothes...'

She showed Flo a magazine that she'd been looking at earlier, with women wearing smart lounging pyjamas and an article saying that capes were the fashion this winter because of the backless gowns everyone was wearing.

'Roy gave me this magazine. He says I've got good taste in clothes...'

'He sounds just right for you,' Flo said, because it was the truth. Honour loved smart clothes and had a flair for them. Sometimes, she sketched what she wanted and made up a pattern for herself. She could be a real asset to the man she'd chosen – but it was all too soon.

Flo's eyes watered but she blinked the selfish tears away.

'I'll be good,' Honour promised. 'Roy is going to buy me a ring for Christmas and we'll be engaged – and get married next summer. I thought in August, on your birthday, Flo. Then it will always be something we can celebrate together – the three of us…'

'Yes, that will be lovely,' Flo agreed. She heard the thumping from upstairs and sighed. 'I'd better go upstairs and see what Dad wants…'

She left her sister dreaming as she mixed another batch of truffles, carefully weighing the ground almonds and the icing sugar, cocoa and essence before starting to mix the delicious soft paste and rolling them into balls.

Flo's heart was heavy as she went into the bedroom that smelled of her father despite all the polishing she did to keep the room sweet. He refused to have the window opened even a little, which meant there was always a faint tang of sweat and urine.

He was sitting on the edge of the bed, about to put his feet to the floor. She watched as he straightened and hoped he would use the commode without her help, but he'd sensed she was there.

'What are you waiting for, girl? Do you want me to mess myself and make more washing?'

'No, Father,' she said and went to him, taking his arm to steady him as he pulled up his nightshirt and sat on the wooden commode seat. The smell as he opened his bowels was pungent and made Flo want to turn away, but compassion made her hide her feelings. It was hardly his fault that he'd had a stroke and needed so much help to perform the everyday functions of life, even if she suspected that he could do more than he let on.

Walking to the window, she looked out, waiting until he'd finished.

'Take that mess away and then bring me some water. I want a wash,' he grunted. 'And my shaving things…'

'Yes, Father,' Flo said dully, because she was past resenting the way he ordered her around. Once, she had rebelled inside and many times she had dreamed of escape, but this was her house, her business and it was Honour's inheritance. Flo was damned if she was going to let him drive her away, because then he would win and she'd have nothing to pass on to her beloved daughter one day. 'I shall be out this afternoon for a while. I'll clear up but please don't ring after I bring the water. I have work to do…'

She left without waiting for his reply. Anger was there inside her, because Honour was right. She had let that man waste her life. If she'd had the courage to make him leave, she could have brought Honour up on her own, perhaps employing a little help in the shop, but he'd always held that power over her – the threat of exposing her as a whore and a woman of no morals. He had no proof of it, because Honour's birth certificate was well hidden, but he'd hinted that he knew – and he had stolen all her mother's documents: the deeds to the property, the copy of the will and other things that Flo needed. He pretended that he'd never seen them, but Flo knew that everything was hers, because the lawyer had told her; it had been a provision of her maternal grandfather's will that the shop should pass to Mrs Hawkins' first-born and not her husband – and yet she'd never had the courage to throw her father out.

When he'd been fit and strong, she'd been afraid of him. He'd used his strength to bully her mother and he'd threatened Flo with a good hiding if she defied him – and yet he'd never done more than pinch her arm and say nasty things to her. She'd seen her mother's bruises and knew what he was capable of, and at first she'd been afraid of what he might do to her and Honour. If he'd destroyed the will and hidden the deeds, he might be able to take what was rightfully hers and her daughter's.

Over the years, Flo had grown stronger. She'd stood up to him more and then, one day, when he'd bullied Honour and made her run from the room crying, she'd finally told him that unless he mended his ways he could go.

'This is my house, my business,' she'd said angrily. 'Talk to Honour like that again and you can leave. I've let you stay here and I've given you a share of the profits because you're my father and I thought it was right you should have something – but I shan't tolerate you mistreating my sister.'

'Your sister?' he'd sneered and something in his eyes told Flo that he knew. Yet how could he know for certain? She and her mother had been to so much trouble to hide it from everyone. 'If I revealed your dirty little secret to the world how long do you think it would be before you had to shut up shop? All the customers who smile at you would cross the street to avoid a dirty little slut like you...'

His words had cut deep, but she'd lifted her head and looked at him proudly. 'You don't know what you're talkin' about,' she said. 'You're a liar and no one likes you – they wouldn't believe you. Especially when I tell them how you hit my mother and hastened her death...'

'Bitch! That's a lie. It wasn't my fault that she had a weak heart...'

'No, but you made her life wretched,' Flo answered bravely seeing the way his fists clenched as if he was itching to hit her. 'Who do you think people will believe – you or me?'

Her father had slammed out of the room in a temper. That night he'd had his first stroke. Only a slight one, and after a short stay in the infirmary he'd come home, seemingly back to normal. Yet he'd never been as strong again and one of his hands wasn't quite right, because things slipped through his fingers, which was why he'd lost his job at the docks.

He'd blamed her for his illness. Said she'd upset him and demanded she give him more of her profits, but Flo had refused.

'I shan't throw you out,' she'd told him. 'But just remember that I could if I wished...'

He'd glared at her, but Flo knew she'd won a small victory. Her father wasn't the man he'd been before the stroke. He understood that he would find it impossible to find permanent work; other, better men than he were standing on street corners now. Flo had given him enough money for himself and she'd paid all the household bills, but still he insisted he was due a share of her profits. She knew it rankled that her mother had left the shop to her rather than her husband. Flo supposed it had hurt his pride, but she gave him a few pounds and let it go.

What she wouldn't put up with was him hurting Honour. If he did that, she would ask the doctors to take him into the old people's infirmary. It was a horrible place and, despite his spite, his temper and the mess he made, she would be reluctant to do it – but he wasn't going to destroy Honour's life as he had hers.

Yet Flo knew that wasn't quite the truth. Her father had had a hand in making her life unhappy, but she'd shaped her own life when she lay with a charming young man who promised to love her and then ran away when she'd whispered to him a few weeks later that she thought she might be with child...

Tears ran down Flo's cheeks as she emptied the chamber pot, rinsing it before returning to the bedroom with water for her father to wash and shave. She brushed her tears away first, because he must never see just how vulnerable she was inside.

'Thank you,' he said when she settled him back in the bed comfortably after his wash. 'You're a better daughter than I deserve...'

Flo looked at him, hardly believing what she'd just heard. She shook her head at him and took the used water away to tip it down the sink. He'd never said such a thing to her before and she didn't believe he meant it – he was just trying a new tack but she wouldn't be fooled.

Downstairs, Honour had changed into her best skirt and twinset. Her coat was ready and she looked at Flo uncertainly as she entered.

'Are you off already? Don't you want anything to eat?'

'We'll have something out if we're hungry,' Honour replied. 'I've made a sandwich for you, Flo. I'll be back in time for you to go out...'

'All right.' Flo went to kiss her cheek. 'Have a lovely time, dearest.'

Honour glowed as she shrugged on her coat and went out of the side door that led through the little passage to the street. As it shut behind her with a small thud, Flo shuddered. The house suddenly felt empty and she knew that was how it would be when Honour married. She would have the business she'd worked so hard to keep going, but somehow that would mean nothing when Honour was no longer a part of it.

For a moment, despair swept over her, but Flo fought it. She would manage somehow and she had so much more than many others. She thought of Robbie's children and the way their little noses pressed up against her window as they looked at the cakes and sweets. And then there was Millie Waters lying sick in her bed, while her elderly husband tried to cope alone.

Rolling up her sleeves, Flo did what she always did when she was upset or lonely. She began to measure flour, sugar, butter and dried fruit; she would make a light fruit cake with a few cherries in it for the couple she was going to visit, despite her father's objections, the very minute her sister returned from her day out...

7

Robbie put the fish paste sandwiches on the table in front of his children and turned his back as they reached for them and started to eat. He made a cup of tea for himself, feeling wretched. Was this what he'd come to – the best he could do for his children's Sunday dinner was fish paste sandwiches?

He'd planned on buying them all some meat this weekend, but he'd lost that wretched card game and been left with ten pence by the time he'd bought them all a drink. Of course they'd all asked for a pint, but Robbie had refused; the stakes were a half-pint of bitter each and that's what he'd bought, despite the jeers and the moans that he was stingy. It was money his kids ought to have had and he felt bad about it.

He was a rotten father. Madge had told him what a useless father and husband he was several times in the weeks before she died. He'd still been on half-pay then, but she hadn't accepted that everyone had been put on to half what they normally earned. She'd blamed him for having a drink on his way home. Her nagging had driven Robbie to the pub more often, because he didn't want to go home to a sick wife who never stopped complaining and children who looked at him with sad eyes. After her death, he'd tried so hard to look after them – and sometimes he managed to put a proper meal on the table, but that happened less and less recently.

He wasn't a good father, but he did what he could and they'd never yet starved, even though sometimes they didn't get much.

'I'm goin' out in a few minutes,' he said and he put a mug of milky tea in front of each of them. 'I've got to see someone about a job – not on the docks but my real trade.'

Ben looked at him for a few moments, chewing in silence, then, 'You used to be a carpenter, didn't you?'

Robbie smiled at him. 'Still am, son. I just need someone to give me a decent job so we can have proper food on the table and buy you kids a bit of a treat for Christmas.'

'I want a sugar mouse,' Ruthie piped up and picked up her mug with both hands, slurping noisily. 'I saw them in the window of Miss Flo's shop – a pink one and a white one. I want a pink one…'

'We must see what we can do,' Robbie said and turned away lest his kids should see the pain in his eyes. He ought to be able to buy his beautiful daughter a sugar mouse for Christmas! 'What about you, Ben?'

'I don't care, Dad,' his son said. 'We're goin' round to Granda's this afternoon.'

'And who is Granda?' Robbie asked the corners of his mouth quirking.

'Bert Waters,' Ben told him and finished his sandwich. 'Granny Waters isn't well so I thought we'd go round and help…'

'Since when have you been callin' them Granda and Granny?' Robbie asked.

'Since this mornin'. We go there to sit in the warm until you get home some nights, Dad. It's cold here until the fire gets goin' and she always gives us a drink and a piece of cake…'

'You shouldn't intrude on people, Ben.'

'It isn't intrudin'.' Ben was defensive. 'They haven't got anyone else, Dad. Granda told me both his sons were killed in the war. They don't have a lot of money and I wouldn't take it if they offered, but I earn what they give us – cleaning winders and carryin' in the coal. I do jobs fer others too, but they give me tuppence or sixpence if I do all the downstairs winders… I buy food for Ruthie and me sometimes, but I put some in your pot for the gas, Dad.'

Robbie thought he'd fallen as low as he could get before this, but his son's words were like a blow to the stomach as he recalled the one shilling and tuppence he'd wasted on drinks for those card players on Friday night. What the hell had he been doing? His son was not yet ten years old and he did jobs for neighbours for pennies, which he spent on his sister and added whatever was left to his dad's fund for the gas. Robbie had seen pennies and a sixpence in the pot, in which he saved shillings for the gas meter – and, assuming he'd put the money there, he'd taken a few coppers out more than once to buy a half of bitter down the pub. The shame of it was like scalding water. He turned away fiercely, holding back the tears that sprung to his eyes. Anger swept the weakness away – he was a useless fool!

'Well, that's great, son.' He hid his emotion. 'I never knew what you get up to when I'm not here.' He faced his children, who were both looking at him with innocent open faces, and forced himself to laugh. 'I hope you won't have to buy your own food for a while, kids. If I get this job it should mean I'll have a little money for Christmas – and after that perhaps things will pick up.'

Robbie knew that it was very unlikely things would pick up anytime soon. The Depression was biting and more and more businesses were struggling to keep going, especially the kind that employed lots of men. Shipyards, factories, warehouses were all working short hours or closing their gates, and no one was taking on new men. This work John Hansen had promised him was like a gift from heaven and he hoped it was more than a couple of hours, which would hardly pay for the sugar mice his children wanted as their Christmas treat.

He wanted so much more for them – toys, clothes and lots of good food.

Robbie reached for his clean shirt, fastening the starched collar with a silver-plated pin he'd had as a young man. He didn't wear a tie but thought it best to make a bit of an effort when going for a job at the mission. His scuffed boots had been polished with spit and a soft brush, and his trousers had an army crease down the middle.

'You look posh, Dad,' Ruthie remarked. 'Are yer goin' ter church?'

'Dad's goin fer a job like he told us,' Ben answered her. 'Good luck, Dad.'

Robbie smiled and thanked him. 'Well, be good, both of you,' he said. 'I'll call for you and say hello to Mr Waters when I get back – if that's all right?'

'Yes, Dad, we'll be there for a while,' Ben said seriously. 'I think Granda needs a bit of help in the kitchen. Granny wouldn't like to see it the way it looks now so I'll be doin' a bit of cleanin'.'

Robbie nodded but didn't say anything more. He felt choked as he inwardly vowed to find the kind of work that would give him back his pride and put proper food on the table for his children.

Honour held Roy's hand as they walked slowly through St James's Park. It was very cold and hardly anyone lingered as they did; a few children ran laughing down the paths between the greens and past the lakes, one of them with a hoop that he hit with a little stick to keep it going, but no one sat on the wooden benches and only a few stood listening to the Salvation Army band playing hymns.

'I love it when they come round at Christmas singing carols,' Honour said, smiling at Roy. Her breath made little patterns on the cold air. 'Flo always gives them two shillings in their tin. She gives the children who come a cake rather than money, but the Sally Army is a good cause, don't you think?'

'Yes, I'm sure it is,' Roy agreed and smiled down at her. He looked so handsome in his uniform that Honour's heart jerked and fluttered in her breast. She was almost sure she loved him as much as he said he loved her, even though Flo thought she should be cautious.

'You won't mind that Flo says we have to wait until the summer to get married? She says she will make it right for us – though I don't know how she'll get Dad to sign his name...'

'Perhaps she has her own methods.' Roy grinned. 'She'll refuse to feed him if he says no...'

'Flo couldn't be so hard-hearted,' Honour asserted and then giggled. 'She's been the best sister to me, Roy. I was miserable when Mum died, but Flo took me in her bed and held me all night as I cried. She's looked after me better than most mothers. She never has much for herself, but she makes sure I have nice things to wear and there's always a lovely present for me at Christmas.'

'What sort of ring would you like me to buy you at Christmas – do you like rubies or sapphires or just diamonds on their own?'

'I don't know... Anything,' Honour said and blushed, because she was too shy to say that she loved the colour blue. She was wearing a dark blue coat with a little velvet collar and her cloche felt hat was pale blue with a satin band and a bow at the front. The coat was new, when she'd had it last winter, but it had been Flo's gift and came from a shop and not the market. She wasn't sure yet that she was ready to marry but she couldn't tell him that because he might take offence.

'We'll make it a surprise then.' Roy squeezed her hand. 'I know it seems a long time to wait until the summer... I want us to be together more, Honour. I want to kiss you and...' He stopped and shook his head. 'We have to be careful, though, because I'd hate you to get in trouble...' He sighed and Honour wondered what he meant.

Flo was never critical of the young women in their road who sometimes got married in a hurry. She just smiled and said as long as they were happy in the end it didn't matter. Honour had seen one of those young women pressed up against the wall, kissing her fellow and wrapping her arms and legs around him. It was soon after that she ordered a small wedding cake.

Honour thought that perhaps passionate kissing led to babies but wasn't quite sure how. Flo had told her to be careful when she went out with Roy and she knew that she meant something about not doing things that led to having babies but wasn't sure what that was. She ought to ask her sister, but until now it hadn't mattered and Flo was always so busy.

'I trust you, Roy.' Honour smiled up into his eyes lovingly. 'I know you'll always look after me.'

Roy made a little noise that sounded like swearing but he didn't say it out loud, just bent and kissed her softly on the lips – right there in the middle of the park. A smartly dressed woman wearing a fox fur round her neck was strolling past with her husband and a little boy, who was carrying an expensive sailing boat under his arm and walking just ahead of his parents. The woman raised her eyebrows as if she didn't think it was quite right for Honour to be kissing her boyfriend in public, making a sound with her tongue that indicated disapproval, and that made Honour blush. She squeezed Roy's arm and tried to ignore the woman's look but thought that she would ask Flo if there was anything very wrong with kissing in a public place.

'Will you meet me tomorrow evening?' Roy asked as they approached the bus stop. She'd told him they had to catch this one so that Flo could go out when they got back. 'I might be sent away for a while soon and I want to make the most of our time together, Honour darling.'

The passion in Roy's voice sent little shivers of delight down her spine. She looked up and promised that she would get out for a little while, even if she couldn't come for the whole evening.

'We bake at night if it's something that will still be fresh in the morning. Otherwise we have to be up at five to get ready – and one of us has to answer Dad's bell.'

'Don't you have a parlour downstairs?' Roy asked, frowning as Honour shook her head. 'He could have his bed there and save you having to run up and downstairs all the time.'

'Flo says we should never have a moment to ourselves if he could hear us in the kitchen. I think I would rather run up and down than have him listening to all we say.'

'Can't be much of a life for any of you.' Roy looked thoughtful. 'Wouldn't he be better off in one of those homes where they look after old folk? My mother is well looked after in hers.'

'Flo says the ones she's seen are awful. She told me it made her feel sick to see the old folk lying in the infirmary – and she said the smell was terrible. They were left to lie in their mess for hours. I wouldn't want him put in a place like that, Roy. Flo should get someone to help her with him...'

'She may have to when we get married,' Roy said. 'I'd like to live somewhere near your sister for your sake – but we might have to go further afield to get a decent workshop. If it meant a bus ride you couldn't be there so often – especially when we have a family...'

'I know...' Honour bit her bottom lip. It made her feel guilty to think of leaving her sister to cope with everything. She knew that Flo wouldn't manage it all on her own. 'I'll help her in the shop if I can...'

'I thought you might like to work in our place when it's set up,' Roy suggested. 'You can help me design the things we sell in our showroom – and you could model them for the customers too...'

Honour giggled at that, because she couldn't see herself parading up and down to show off clothes. Yet the idea of working with him, of learning how to cut out beautiful suits and dresses, as well as draw them, was attractive. Much as she liked making her fancy cakes and sweets, clothes were more exciting. The idea of marriage was becoming more real – besides, she didn't want to be stuck with her father forever.

'It might be fun,' she said and looked up at him, eyes wide and innocent. 'I'd never have thought you could make clothes for women...'

'Both Dad and my uncle were men's tailors, but I liked making smart things that women could wear; I made Mum a suit when I was fourteen and she told everyone it was the best she'd ever had. Uncle Ken wants me to work for him when I'm demobbed, but I've got plans. I don't want to settle for a small tailoring workshop in the East End. I'm heading up to the West End as soon as I can afford it. If you can come up with more ideas as good as that dress you wore on Saturday night, we shall soon be able to expand. One day I want a big store in Regent Street as well as several workshops in the East End...'

'You've got ambition. You're so clever, Roy. I never thought I'd do anything exciting with my life...'

'When we're rich we'll have a beautiful house and we'll travel – to Paris and Italy,' Roy said. 'You'd like that, wouldn't you?'

Honour agreed that she would, but felt as if a rushing wind had swept her off her feet. Roy seemed as if he were in a hurry. He wanted so much and he wanted it quickly. She found it exciting but also a little scary. A part of her needed to cling to Flo, to stay where she was warm and safe and knew what she was doing – and yet Roy's ambition was catching and she'd started to see how much more there was to life than working every day in a small cake shop in the East End.

The only thing wrong with the future that Roy was promising her was that there didn't seem any place in it for Flo... and that made Honour feel guilty and a little sad, because she did love Flo.

'Don't look sad, darling,' Roy whispered and squeezed her hand. 'We'll find someone to look after your father so that Flo has a life too...'

8

Robbie was whistling as he made his way home that evening. He could hardly believe that he'd been given what looked like a month or more's work at the mission hall. It was an old building and John had explained that he wanted a good job made of the repairs.

'That coving and the door frames are both Victorian,' he'd told Robbie. 'I need you to go to the scrapyard and find something that will blend sympathetically with what is here. If you buy new wood it will show and the Church Commissioners are very particular about having things right...'

'I understand,' Robbie said. 'You're looking to restore rather than rip out and use new wood and plaster coving.' He'd smiled then, because he knew just the place to buy what he needed. 'Too many old buildings are being torn down and replaced by modern. The slums do need replacing but they're tearing down the good with the bad.'

'This place is old and it suits us that way,' John explained. 'We couldn't afford to pull this down and build new – but some of that coving is about to fall and that wood is rotting. I have a small budget to repair what I can – but if you make a good job my bosses will be pleased.'

'It's just the kind of thing I like doin',' Robbie had told him and looked round at the various jobs. Some of it wasn't carpentry, but there was nothing here he couldn't manage, even a bit of brickwork. He'd turned his hand to all kinds these past years and this would be a pleasure. At least that was one good thing the Depression had brought, a temporary pause to the constant destruction of the heart of London.

Robbie looked at the street he was walking down. He knew it was on a plan somewhere for demolition but had been reprieved until money was less tight than it was now. The little terrace where his son and daughter were right now was one of those destined to disappear in the push for progress – and then what would happen to the elderly folk who lived there?

'Wot yer, Mr Graham!'

Robbie saw the lad who had greeted him and smiled a welcome. 'How are yer, Mick?'

'I'm all right, sir. Me dad's sleepin' it off at 'ome – but I cooked some sausages fer dinner so I ain't 'ungry.'

'You can have a cup of cocoa with us later if yer like...'

'Thanks...' Mick grinned at him and ran off but turned back to call out: 'Me dad sent me to see someone... he wants a bet on fer the first race tomorrow...'

Robbie watched him disappear round the corner. Mick's father was a fool betting the few shillings he earned with illegal bookies. Robbie had never fallen into that particular trap, because he knew it was always the bookies who won in the end. Often they had the police on their payroll, overlooking their activities. A lot of them were gangsters and Robbie stayed clear of them; even when he hadn't two pennies to rub together he refused to give way to the temptation to steal or work for those that did...

He arrived at the second from last house in the terrace and he stopped, and then knocked at number six. Ruthie opened the door to him.

'You're to come in and have tea and cake,' she announced importantly. 'Granda wants to say thank you for lettin' us help him.'

Robbie smiled and followed her into the kitchen, which was the main room of the house and had a black range at one end with an oven, a pine dresser – its shelves filled with crockery – at the other, and a big pine table in the middle. A hotchpotch of wooden chairs stood round the table, which had been set with plates, cups and saucers. A fruit cake and some bread and butter and a dish of jam were on the table – and making the tea was Flo Hawkins. Robbie could smell her perfume, which didn't come out of any bottle, but was a mixture of soap and her own freshness.

She turned as he approached the elderly man who had stood to welcome him. Robbie was conscious of her eyes on him as he shook hands with Bert Waters.

'How is your wife, sir?'

'Not well, Mr Graham, but Flo took her up a cup of tea and a piece of her cake and she did eat a little. We have to just wait and see... the doctor came a little while ago and said it is a nasty case of bronchitis...'

Robbie nodded, because there was nothing else they or anyone could do but see how she went on. Millie was in her seventies and like her husband she'd worked hard all her life, but the upside of that was that she was strong.

'Miss Hawkins,' he said as he turned to greet Flo, his heart racing wildly. 'What a pleasant surprise seeing you here. I came to fetch my two – and now I'm invited to tea.'

'We all are,' Flo told him and her cheeks were a little pink. He thought she was as much affected by their meeting as he was. 'Bert insisted and I shall enjoy having tea with your children, Mr Graham – they are a credit to you and Mrs Graham.'

'We lost Madge some months ago.'

'Yes, I know. You must miss her – and I'm sure the children do.' She turned away and smiled at Ruthie.

'Shall we all sit at the table? I'm hungry and that strawberry jam looks delicious…'

'The bread was fresh yesterday,' Bert Waters said as he took his usual chair. 'My Millie always made fresh every day, but we have it delivered now, because she can't manage to bake bread these days.'

'No, of course not, making bread is hard work,' Flo said. 'We make our own bread and my sister makes lots of lovely soft rolls. I will bring you some next time I come, sir.'

'Thank you but you must call me Bert – or Granda like the children…' Bert's watery grey eyes were kind as he looked at Robbie's children. 'They're good kids – good to me and Millie…'

'Yes, I know,' Flo agreed and for a moment her gaze met Robbie's. His heart felt as if it was being twisted, because by rights, they might have been her children…

Memories swept back as he thought about the night she'd slipped out of her father's house all those years ago and told him she feared she might be having a child. Robbie had panicked and instead of telling her he would marry her, he'd run off without answering her. Some months later, when he'd been ready to accept his responsibility and tell her they would get married her father had driven him away.

'My daughter isn't at home to you or your kind,' he'd growled and shown Robbie his fist. 'Come near her and

I'll thrash the life out of you – I'll kill you, you filthy little worm…'

Robbie had tried to argue, to explain that he'd been foolish and was sorry; he'd told Mr Hawkins that he truly loved Flo, but her father had knocked him down and then kicked him in the head and face. He'd run then, feeling ashamed and sorry for himself. It was that night he'd joined the army and been swept into a terrible war. Only after ten years had he come back to this town and then he was married and had a one-year-old son.

He'd caught sight of Flo in the market and in her shop more than once over the years, but he'd never been into the cake shop and shame had kept him from speaking to her until they'd met in the grocer's by chance – and now he felt the bitterness of regret rush through him as he looked into her clear eyes and saw there was no anger or accusation. He deserved that she should be angry, but she smiled and gave her head a little shake.

Robbie felt the food stick in his throat but managed to swallow it, though he felt as if it were being forced down. He spoke very little, but it hardly mattered, because the children chattered away happily, clearly enjoying not just the food but the company. They liked their Miss Flo and, as he watched and listened, Robbie realised how much he'd lost by his cowardice. This pleasant, smiling and gentle woman could have been his wife, if he'd only been braver at the start. He should have stood up to Flo's father and insisted that they be allowed to marry.

Robbie was awkward, on the back foot, wanting to apologise but not knowing how. Flo was taking it all in her stride, but then she had nothing to be ashamed of – it was he who had let her down, though she'd obviously been mistaken about being pregnant that night, because there had been no scandal and no rushed marriage to a respectable older man. She was so serene and confident that he knew she'd put the past out of her mind. He would be a fool if he thought he could ask a woman like her for a second chance. What could she want of him that she didn't already have – and what could he give her when all he had was a few weeks' work ahead of him? He'd missed his chance of happiness with Flo – and besides, he didn't deserve her.

After they'd all finished eating, and the table was cleared, the dishes washed, Robbie asked his host if there was anything he could do to help before he left the house and took his children home. He was told that, between them, his children and Miss Hawkins had done everything.

However, on the way home, Ben told him that the catch on the back scullery window was broken. 'Anyone could get in,' Ben said. 'You could fix it fer him, couldn't yer?'

'Yes, of course,' Robbie agreed and ruffled his hair. He would be working up until Christmas, still nearly three weeks away, but he'd find time for the repair. 'I'm starting work tomorrow – but I'll fix that window for yer friend, son.'

'Good.' Ben grinned at him. 'I'm glad yer stayed ter tea, Dad. Miss Flo makes a lovely cake – and that was 'er jam too. She made it in the summer and brought two pots round for Granny and Granda.'

'You know they're not really yer grandparents, don't yer?' Robbie asked gently and Ben nodded. 'Yer mother's parents died soon after yer were born, and my mother and father both died of diphtheria when I was twelve. I was sent to live with me grandmother and she was a scold. I left home at sixteen and made me own way in the world after that…'

'You were a soldier, weren't you?'

'Yeah, I joined up before I was eighteen. Spent eight years learning me trade as a carpenter with the army and started out married life in yer mum's home town – and when I came back here to London you were just a year old…'

'Miss Flo asked about you, what you did these days,' Ben chattered on. 'I told her you were a soldier once, but you worked wherever you could now. She said a lot of men had to do the same because so many factories and yards had closed down…' He looked up at Robbie. 'She's lovely, ain't she? Did you like her, Dad?'

'Yes, I liked her,' Robbie said. He felt the sting of shame over the way he'd ignored Flo all these years, knowing that he owed her an apology even though it wasn't all his fault. Her kindness to his kids made him awkward and uneasy. 'You mustn't go round to her shop, son. I know she gave you a cake, but you mustn't expect her to do it again – besides, I'll have more money in my pocket soon. I'll be able to buy some proper food for Christmas – and maybe a present for you and Ruthie…'

'I ain't bothered about a present,' Ben said solemnly. 'As long as yer all right, Dad…'

His father put a hand on his shoulder. 'I promise I won't drink all me wages away down the pub, son. It was just… with me havin' ter do all the dirty jobs and yer mother…'

'Yeah, I know,' Ben agreed and leaned into his father's side.

Ruthie saw Ben leaning into him and ran around the other side, reaching for his hand. She hadn't been listening to their conversation, but now she looked up at him with her big innocent eyes. 'Miss Flo promised me a sugar mouse,' she confided. 'Her sister – Miss Honour – makes them and she's goin' ter give me one at Christmas…'

'You're a lucky girl then,' Robbie said and hadn't the heart to tell his little girl that she mustn't go round to Flo's shop. 'But wait until Christmas – you mustn't keep askin' fer things, love.'

'I didn't,' Ruthie protested indignantly. 'She asked me what I liked in her winder so I told 'er...'

Robbie sighed. He was hurting inside and pride would keep him from calling into the shop – pride and the knowledge that he'd let Flo down. Yet he couldn't stop his kids visiting when Flo so clearly enjoyed their company...

Flo was singing softly to herself as she opened her kitchen door after visiting Millie and walked in. It was past seven in the evening and she hoped that Honour had taken some supper up to their father because if he had it too late he would be awake half the night and calling out to her to help him.

'Honour...' she called and then halted, staring in surprise as she saw who was sitting in the wooden rocking chair beside the kitchen fire. 'Father – what are you doing down here?'

'I suppose I can do as I like in my own house...'

Flo bit back an angry retort, because he was still her father and, in some ways, entitled to think of this as his house – or at least his home.

'Where is Honour?'

Honour had promised she would be there to look after him while Flo went out. The girl had returned at four as she'd promised, but Flo had only been gone a few hours – surely she hadn't gone round to her friend's?

'You tell me…' her father retorted. 'I rang the bell for half an hour and no one answered, so I came down and got myself a glass of water…'

Flo stared at him, because he'd been pretending he could hardly get to the commode without her half lifting him on, and now he was sitting down here and watching the clock.

'So where have you been, miss? Out with some man, I suppose?'

Flo looked at him but didn't answer. She'd already told him she was visiting Mrs Millie Waters, but he was obviously in a bad mood.

'I'm sorry no one brought you your cocoa, Father. I'll make it now, if you like?'

'You'll have to help me upstairs,' he grumbled. 'I came down on my backside but I can't get back on me feet now…'

Flo knew he was lying. If he'd had the strength to come down in the first place, he couldn't be too weak to stand up alone, but there wasn't much point in arguing. She bent to give him her arm, heaving him to his feet and moving slowly towards the door leading into the hall. He leaned on her heavily, making her take his weight deliberately.

'Flo – wait, I'll give you a hand,' Honour offered as she suddenly entered the kitchen door and saw them struggling. 'I'm sorry. I just went next door. Sarah Jones wanted to borrow some sugar and she asked me to show her how to make coconut ice...'

Honour's cheeks were pink and Flo knew she was lying but shook her head at her. 'We'll manage,' she said. 'You can make cocoa for us all please...'

Her father made it as difficult for her to help him up the stairs as he could, but in the end he tired of the struggle and they reached his bedroom. Flo balanced him on the edge of the bed and took his slippers off, raising his legs to settle him in the bed. She plumped up his pillows and straightened the bedspread.

'Do you want to read for a while?'

'I think I'll sleep once that wretched girl brings my cocoa,' he said and suddenly looked weary. Flo realised that he'd got himself downstairs out of sheer stubbornness, but it had taken more out of him than she'd thought.

'Here she comes,' Flo told him and took the little tray from Honour.

'Goodnight, Dad,' Honour said and turned away.

'If you bring shame on us, girl, I'll not have you in the house...' he called after her sharply.

Honour gave a little sob and rushed out of the room. Flo could hear her running downstairs.

'There was no need for that, Father. She's a good girl...'

'Like her mother, I suppose?' he asked and gave Flo such a look that she felt hot all over.

'Can I get anything else for you?' Flo asked.

'I'll ring if I need the toilet,' he said. 'Get downstairs and ask that girl what she's been up to – or she'll land herself in trouble...'

Flo walked away without answering.

Honour was by the stove and she picked up the little saucepan as Flo entered the kitchen, pouring the warmed milk into two mugs and stirring the thick cocoa. She didn't look at Flo until she sat down opposite her.

'You promised to stay here until I returned. You've been out all day.'

'I'm sorry,' Honour apologised. 'Roy came to the window and waved at me. He wanted to tell me something he'd forgotten. I just popped out for a few minutes.'

'It was more than a few minutes – and you'd had most of the day with Roy,' Flo scolded. 'Dad kept ringing because he was thirsty. It must have taken quite an effort for him to get downstairs.'

Honour looked ashamed. 'I'm sorry for lettin' you down, Flo. I don't care about Dad. For all I care he can ring until kingdom come and I wouldn't bother to answer – I only do it for you...'

'Oh, Honour...' Flo shook her head sadly. Honour didn't love the man she believed to be her father. In truth, he was her grandfather but it was sad that she felt nothing but anger against him. 'I know he's bad-tempered and sometimes cruel – but he is our family. He's ill and it can't be much fun lying up there all day alone.'

'He isn't on his own. We're up and down all day making sure he has what he needs.'

'It isn't like being able to go out – and he never gets any visitors.'

'Because he doesn't have any friends. He drove all his workmates away. One or two came to see him after he had the stroke and he swore at them – told them to clear off…'

'Yes, I know,' Flo sighed. 'I get fed up with his demands too, Honour – but what else can I do?'

'You could put him in the infirmary…'

'No! I would never do that to anyone,' Flo declared firmly. 'It used to be the workhouse and all the old people are afraid of it. Bert Waters told me Millie is terrified of being sent there. She is convinced she wouldn't come out alive and I think she might be right. It is an awful place.'

'Oh, I know, I didn't mean it,' Honour said and looked down. 'But I'm not goin' to spend all my life lookin' after him, Flo – and you can't manage him and the baking and the shop all by yourself when I get married. You'll have to get help with him – or send him somewhere…'

'The only place is the infirmary. The hospital wouldn't keep him once he was over the worst of the stroke and a nursing home is too expensive. I'll get help when I need it, but I've already told you, it's too soon for you to think about gettin' married, love. I know Roy is nice and he's good-lookin' – but you don't really know him yet.'

'I know I love him,' Honour said, suddenly stubborn. 'He kissed me and it was wonderful, but I understand I have to be careful not to do anythin' wrong… only, I'm not sure what that means…'

'That's my fault,' Flo admitted ruefully. If Honour got into trouble it would be her fault for not warning her. 'I should have told you about makin' love.' She hesitated uneasily. 'I don't know very much either – but I do know that kisses lead to touchin' each other and then… if you let a man go all the way it can mean you have to get married quick…' Flo's cheeks were hot as she tried to explain, but she hardly remembered much about that sweet, muddled fumbling in the park that had led to Honour's birth. However, she explained as best she could and Honour blushed scarlet.

'Is it just for havin' babies?' she asked. 'Only, when Roy kisses me, I feel as if I want him to touch me places and… that other thing… is that wrong?'

'Oh no, it is for pleasure too,' Flo explained. 'I haven't been married, but I think people in love do it all the time when they're married – perhaps not so much later in life. Sometimes babies come and sometimes they don't, but if you wait for all that until you have a husband you don't need to worry.'

'So kissing doesn't make a baby?' Honour looked relieved.

'No, dearest – as long as that is all it is... but sometimes it might be hard not to do other things when you kiss. Men do want more and sometimes they get carried away and you do too... but you have to be careful that doesn't happen before you're wed.'

'Thank you for tellin' me.' Honour kissed her cheek. 'I think I'll get an early night and read in bed for a while. We need to be up early for the baking.'

'Goodnight, my darling,' Flo said and took the used cocoa mugs to the sink to wash them. She wasn't in the least tired, but she knew they had to be up early. Her shop had a reputation for freshness and that meant most cakes had to be baked each day.

As she went up to her room, the thoughts were going round and round in Flo's head. Honour had been a woman for a while now, but Flo had wanted to keep her safe from the world. The time when she could protect her was over now though, Flo realised; Honour wanted to spread her wings and go out into the wider world. She had discovered love and Flo could only hope that things would turn out better for her...

Meeting Robbie that afternoon at the Waters' house had turned back the years, making Flo so aware of all that she had lost. Her mother had claimed she was protecting her from the censure of the world, but instead Flo had been a prisoner in her own home, denied a husband, children and a life that consisted of more than work. It was too late for her. She must forget her own hurt and loss and make sure that her daughter was safe and happy…

9

Robbie mended two broken window sashes first, and then started work stripping out some worm-eaten wood from skirting boards, and window frames, replacing them with weathered wood from the reclamation yard. He'd used it often in the past and enjoyed the feel of old wood in his fingers; he loved to see a good walnut or mahogany begin to shine after he'd stripped it back, rubbed it down and oiled it before bringing the wood to a soft smooth shine.

Here, it was just a case of stripping out wood that had wormholes or was splintered and damaged beyond repair. However, he liked to see things looking proper and there was a right way and a wrong way of doing restoration work.

'How are you getting on?' John asked, standing a mug of hot tea on a little table. 'I imagine there's a lot more needs doing than we spoke about on Sunday?'

'I believe there are a lot of small repairs needed,' Robbie agreed and ran his hand down one of the thick wooden beams, which had turned almost black with age. 'But these supports are basically sound. I think you've been very sensible having this damaged wood stripped out. It's poor-quality stuff and not original to the building. I imagine it was used for repairs some years ago and they didn't bother what they used... they probably imported the worm into the building at that time.'

'I'm afraid the woodworm has got into the roof structures and these beams,' John said, looking up at the structures that were a basic part of the centuries-old ceiling. 'If that is the case my bosses might decide to pull the place down. That's why I thought that if we got these repairs done for a fair price, they may let me have the roof done before it goes too far.'

'It would be a shame to lose this place,' Robbie murmured, looking round him appreciatively. 'It's the thing to sweep away the old and build new at the moment – or it would be if anyone had the money to undertake large projects.'

'Unfortunately, you're right,' John agreed, shaking his head. 'I should hate to see the whole of old London disappear...'

'At least we can try and save this place.'

'Call me if you run into a problem,' John said with a sigh. 'I have to get ready for the lunchtime crowd. We're giving out hot soup and bread as usual and we'll be busy for a couple of hours. You're welcome to some soup once we start serving if you're hungry.'

'I'm fine, thanks,' Robbie said. 'Cheers.' He picked up his mug of tea and drank a mouthful. It was hot, strong and sweet, just the way most working men liked it. Robbie drank it gratefully and went back to his task. He would be sorry when it was finished and he was back looking for work.

He grimaced, because after some weeks of doing the job he loved it would come hard standing in line again, shivering in the cold wind as he waited to be picked and was always left to the last. The dirtiest jobs were all he'd had offered for months and Robbie had considered going off to look for work elsewhere in the country – but he didn't know where to try and couldn't think how to provide for the children while he was gone. Buying a newspaper was something he considered an unnecessary luxury, but he saw the billboards and read the headlines as he passed the newsstands. It was every bit as bad up north and perhaps even worse down in Wales, where pits were closing.

If his wife had still been alive Robbie could have left the children in her care and gone searching for work. He would have done it before now, because it had been made abundantly clear to him that he was never going to get a decent job on the docks again. The gaffer had spread the word; he was branded as a troublemaker – just for standing up for a man who was in even more desperate need of a job than he'd been at the time.

Robbie couldn't desert his children, and he couldn't drag them all over the country while he looked for a job that suited his talents. He was caught tight in a noose and struggling only made it worse. He shook his head and looked at the door strut he was about to rip out. He had several weeks of work for fair pay and he must make the most of it. Robbie's kids would have a good Christmas and after that... well, perhaps he would have more luck if he went to the factories that were still working rather than the docks.

Feeling satisfied at the end of a good day's work, he left the mission and started to walk home, passing the pub on the corner without a glance. Seeing his son's friend hanging about near the end of the lane, Robbie beckoned to him and Mick came running. His face looked dirty and his hands were blue with cold.

'Come and have some supper with us,' he offered. 'We've got sausages, mash and onion gravy tonight. I bought plenty from the pie shop and you're welcome to share.'

Mick's thin face lit up. 'Thanks, Mr Graham. Dad ain't home 'cos he's got a job that took him up West – and I don't like goin' back there until he gets in; there's a bloke... He frightens me.'

Robbie looked at him in concern. Mick was too young to be on the streets all night. 'Will yer dad get home tonight?' Mick shook his head. 'Right – you can sleep on the couch in the kitchen. I'll give yer a blanket and a pillow – and yer can have a wash while yer here… and we might find yer somethin' clean to put on.'

Mick nodded, trotting happily down the road beside him.

The next day, Mick left the cottage feeling warmer because of the cocoa and the bread and dripping Ben's father had given him. He wished he didn't have to leave his friends, because it was the only place he felt safe these days. Even at school the teachers gave him odd looks and told him that if he couldn't come to class clean he should stay away. Mick didn't care about learning or the other kids, but he liked Ben and Ruthie was all right, even though he knew she thought he smelled. He'd washed his hands and face in Ben's sink, but his hair itched and he knew he had nits.

If his mother had still been alive she would have combed them out of his hair and scrubbed him in the sink with carbolic. They'd never had an inside toilet or a bathroom, but Mick's mother had been fussy about keeping their clothes clean and there was always food waiting on the table when he got home from school.

His dad had been different then, more like Ben's dad, ready to tell him off and give him a clip of the ear if he played up, but not unkind or drunk. These days Mick's dad was always drunk unless he had work, and sometimes he slapped Mick for no reason. He hadn't told him about the man who terrorised all the kids because he wouldn't have listened.

Yet Mick still felt safer when his dad was around. He just wished Taffy would find a proper job and a couple of rooms in a decent house for them rather than the cold, dark slum where they slept now. Ben's father had lost his wife too but he still had a place for his kids to sleep and he didn't collapse in a drunken stupor soon after he came home...

Mick's cheek was damp but he brushed the tears away angrily. He wasn't a cry baby and he would get by somehow. It wouldn't be so bad if he could find a job like Ben but as soon as they saw him, shop keepers and landlords turned up their noses and told him to clear off.

The only place that allowed him to sit in the warm was the mission and Mick went there some days, but the trouble was that Scrapper did too and Mick was afraid of him... yet some days the soup and bread were the only food he was given.

'There's over twenty pounds in the Christmas fund,' Nurse Mary told John later that morning, when she locked the cash box away in the drawer of the office desk. It was a sturdy roll-top, much scarred from its use at various locations before it finally came to John, almost on its last legs. 'What are you goin' to spend it on this year?'

'What do you suggest?' John asked. 'We could give the men cigarettes and the women chocolates, boiled sweets or lollipops for the kids…'

'I was thinking we should cook a proper Christmas dinner for them rather than waste money on cigarettes and sweets,' Nurse Mary said and pursed her lips. She was a thin woman with a straight nose and a small tight mouth, her light brown hair scraped back off her face, but although she came over as harsh, she had a kind heart. She worked for meagre wages as a nurse at the infirmary but gave her personal time to his mission for nothing.

'Yes, that is an option,' John agreed, brushing his short wiry hair back from his forehead with his fingers. 'We should need several willing helpers to cook the meal here – and our regulars do appreciate little gifts. I'd hoped to have more in the fund before this – are you sure it was just twenty pounds?'

'I counted it twice,' Nurse Mary confirmed. 'You give them money all the time, John. They come in with their sob stories and you give them five shillings to pay their rent, because otherwise they will be on the streets, or half a crown to buy medicine for their sick child… It all adds up.'

John sighed, because he knew that Nurse Mary was right. He could afford to provide a chicken dinner with all the trimmings for his regulars or he could give them small gifts of five cigarettes, a bar of chocolate and a twist of sweets for the kids; he couldn't manage to do both.

'I suppose you're right,' he agreed. 'A good dinner is a treat for them… I just wish I could do more. Some of those children have never had a proper Christmas present in their lives.'

'You can't take all the troubles of the world on your shoulders,' Nurse Mary said. She looked thoughtful as she heard Robbie hammering in the next room. 'It must be costing quite a bit for the repairs?'

'Robbie is working for his wages and we paid the cost of the materials – but that is a different fund, Mary. The Church authorities grant me money for repairs and I couldn't take that money for our Christmas party. I'm given enough funds to offer the destitute a place to sit in the warm for a few hours, mugs of tea, bread and a bowl of soup. I have asked for extra money for Christmas but there isn't much to spare these days and the commissioners turned me down.'

Mary made a little hissing noise. 'You keep this place running, John. If it weren't for the tombola evenings and the raffle tickets you sell, this place would close down…'

'I dare say they would keep it open for just three hours in the middle of the day, which is what was intended; it was just meant to be a soup kitchen, Mary. I fought hard to get them to let me open it at night and to fund it by whatever means I could... raising money by bring-and-buy sales and tombola evenings makes it possible to give our regulars more than a bowl of soup at least one night a week.'

'Yes, I know.' She stood up and came round the desk, touching his arm sympathetically. Mary's heart belonged to this slight, hard-working man, but he would never know. 'If there was anything I could do... but I don't know how we can make more money in time to do what you want.'

'No, of course you don't, Mary,' he agreed. 'You give so much of your time. I know you'll be one of my volunteers serving that dinner on Christmas Day. It's my problem and I think your idea is very sensible. A proper dinner is far more valuable than small gifts...'

John knew she was right, of course she was, even though he'd had his Christmas party all planned. A tree with candles, strings of tinsels and little parcels. He'd hoped to provide sausage rolls, mince pies and sandwiches with the help of a few generous ladies who gave to his mission whenever asked to provide food for the tombola. Yet how many of the poor folk who frequented the mission ever had a proper meal, let alone a Christmas dinner?

He went through to the antiquated kitchen, where two ladies wearing turbans and brightly coloured cotton aprons were stirring the vegetable soup they would soon be serving to the large queue that had already started to gather outside. It smelled delicious and he smiled at them.

'Good morning, Emily and Sal. Thank you for coming in today – that soup smells wonderful. Is it ready?'

'Yes, Reverend,' Sal said. 'It tastes as good as it smells, too. Fancy some?'

'Later perhaps,' he murmured. 'I'll go and open up – welcome our guests. I think we have the usual queue, perhaps more.'

'It grows every day,' Emily said. 'I sometimes think we're feeding the poor of London rather than just the dock area and part of Poplar.'

John laughed at that, because sometimes it felt like that to him too, but his smile faded, because the growing queues were a sign that the Depression was biting ever deeper. The men and women who came to his door now sometimes included workers, men who looked ashamed of being forced into a position where they had to accept charity. They were decent men who had never been out of work in their lives, proud men who hated it that they had nothing to do but stand about on street corners all day.

John felt sorry for all those who came to his mission seeking help. Some would always need his help. Nurse Mary tended sore feet and nasty boils on the neck and other small ailments that would otherwise go untended, because her patients could not afford to visit a doctor and were afraid of the infirmary, which was still thought of as the workhouse in these parts. Her tongue was often as stringent as her disinfectants, but folk respected her and they trusted her. Sometimes, she told them they must go to the infirmary because there was nothing she could do, but she knew they ignored her. She and John talked about it, but both understood that what they did here would never be enough. All they could do was to offer a warm secure place to be for a while, a little food and a soothing touch where it was needed; there was just too much poverty and sickness to make much difference.

'It should be free for everyone to see a doctor,' John had said to Nurse Mary on more than one occasion. 'Not just the infirmary, which they all hate – but a doctor of your choice. A stay in hospital should not mean that folk run up debts they can never pay.'

'The authorities talk about it,' Nurse Mary said. 'I hear the doctors at the hospital discussing it – some agree with you, others think it is a terrible idea to introduce free medicine and say they would refuse to treat patients if it was brought in.'

'They should come here and listen to the chests you listen to,' John had suggested wryly. 'You do your best, Mary, but you can't cure the chronically sick. They should be in hospital...'

'Most of them would rather be sleeping under the bridges or wherever they have a place to lie down,' she'd told him. 'I've tried sending some of them to hostels where they can have a bed for a night, but they say it's like being in prison to them. They come here because I don't question and nor do you...'

'We're here to help, not to inquisition,' John had said with an odd smile. 'I know why I do it, Mary – but why do you? You already work hard at the hospital. Why give up your free time to work with the destitute?'

'Because it's right,' Nurse Mary had told him. She hadn't met his eyes as she spoke and he had a feeling there was more to it, but he hadn't probed. Everyone was entitled to their privacy.

At his mission people came for food, warmth and a place to sit for a while. He asked no questions of them, nor did he demand that they use the showers provided, though they were there with soap and clean towels if needed. He also provided good, clean second-hand clothes for anyone that asked; the Sally Army gave him what they could and any donations were gratefully accepted. Many of the men who came to eat here wore garments that were threadbare, but only a few asked for clothes. There was a rail in the room just off the showers and toilets and John let people decide for themselves if they wanted anything from the rails, all they had to do was just ask to take them.

John looked at the crowd of people waiting outside his door. It was mostly men but some women too, and a few children. Many children were at school and often got a free meal there, but others lived on the streets and those children didn't go to school. John never asked why they were not at school; he knew that they would run away and forgo their meal rather than explain. He wasn't here to criticise or enforce the law, only to help where he could.

He opened the door and let the people enter, greeting many of them by name and smiling; he watched, as they went up to the counter and were given a bowl of fragrant soup and a chunk of fresh crusty bread. They helped themselves to mugs of tea at the other end of the table and then found a place to sit down. Soon all the tables were in use and every bench seat was taken. Now men sat on chairs lined up at the side of the room; some squatted on the ground to eat their meal, and still they kept coming. He wondered if they would have enough soup and bread to go round, but then, all of a sudden, everyone had been served.

John went through to the kitchens where two more women had arrived to take a turn at washing the pans and used soup bowls.

'Jane, Catherine,' John called to them. 'Thank you for coming. I thought we might run out of mugs and bowls today. I'm afraid you will have a lot of dishes to wash...'

'That's what we're here for,' Catherine replied easily. 'Yer know we don't mind what we do fer yer…'

John smiled at them. He couldn't manage the mission at all if it were not for his little band of volunteers. There were ten or twelve ladies of the parish who worked tirelessly at the mission, most of them war widows, performing whatever tasks he asked of them cheerfully and with no thought of reward, filling their lonely lives with good works.

'You're all angels,' he told them and looked at his cooks, who were about to leave after finishing their job. 'That was splendid, ladies.'

'Anythin' for you, Revd,' Sal quipped with a cheeky grin. She winked at the women who had come in to deal with the washing-up. 'Don't do anythin' I wouldn't!'

'That's given us plenty of scope,' Catherine responded and plunged her hands in soda and hot water as she started to clean the piles of soup bowls. 'We can manage 'ere, Revd,' she told John with a wink. 'You'd best keep yer eye open out there in case they pinch the silver…'

'I'd pinch it myself and sell it to buy Christmas treats if we had any…' John retorted and grinned back. These women were the salt of the earth in his opinion and made his day seem worthwhile.

He walked back through to the large hall where the men and women were drinking tea now and talking. He could smell cigarette smoke and wondered where the money came from for such luxuries, but probably it was butts picked up from ashtrays in cafes, pulled apart and rolled in cigarette papers. Not many of the men looked as if they could afford to buy even a packet of five cigarettes or an ounce of tobacco for roll-ups.

John frowned as he traced the man who was smoking. He was a large man with black hair and a thick dark beard sprayed with grey hairs, bushy eyebrows and filthy clothes. His eyes were a startling blue and looked rather wild, and he was a stranger. Hesitating for a moment, John walked over to him and offered his hand. 'I haven't seen you before, sir. Have you come to the area recently?'

'Yeah; I've bin walkin' lookin' fer work, but there ain't none wherever yer go...' His eyes narrowed menacingly. 'What's it to you?'

'Nothing at all,' John said mildly. 'This mission is just for a hot meal I'm afraid, sir – but if you're looking for a bed for the night I can give you an address.'

'Mind yer own business,' the man growled. 'When I want yer advice I'll ask fer it...' He turned and walked off, his shoulders hunched.

There was no point in going after him. John hadn't intended to offend, but the man wasn't of this parish and not really entitled to come here at all, though John never turned anyone in need away. His intention had been to offer help to a stranger in giving him an address where he might find further help – but the man had taken offence. John shrugged. He seldom offered advice, but something had prompted him to speak to the stranger; now he wished he'd followed his usual path and let the man come to him.

'Don't take no notice of 'im, Revd,' one of John's regulars muttered, jerking his head at the man's retreating back. 'That sort ain't no good to anyone, least of all their selves. He'll be from up north I reckon – and a bad 'un by the looks of 'im.'

'I think you might be right, Michael,' John agreed and smiled. 'How are you now – your chest any better?'

'That medicine your Nurse Mary give me done me a power of good,' Michael asserted. 'Brought me a big bottle of it she did, and I'm nearly through it – if she's 'ere I was goin' ter ask 'er fer another bottle if she's got any…'

'Go through to her room,' John suggested. 'I'm sure she's seeing people now. I know she will do what she can for you.'

Nurse Mary was handing out bottles of cough medicine now. She must have purchased it herself – unless she'd got it from the infirmary. He knew that she sometimes brought bandages and ointments that bore the name of the infirmary on the packaging. Strictly speaking, she was stealing from her employer, even though it was for an excellent cause. John hoped she knew what she was doing, because he didn't want her to lose her job over it – or worse.

10

Ben left his sister sitting in Granda's kitchen while he went down the road. The newsagent on the corner had a job for him sorting out his back room. He wanted a load of old cardboard boxes flattening and taking round the corner to the junkyard.

'I'll give yer a shillin' to clear 'em for me,' Mr Arnold offered. 'Yer a decent lad, Ben, and yer made a good job of me winders last Saturday, so I'll give yer this job. Sid Foster will give yer a tanner fer takin' me junk to him. He sells cardboard once he gets a big enough load and I reckon you'll need to make two trips with that little trolley of yours – are yer on?'

''Course I am, sir,' Ben said. 'I don't mind what I do and a shillin' will get me two sugar mice fer me sister fer Christmas...'

'Is that what she fancies, lad?'

'Yeah, she's got 'er 'eart set on a pink one, sir – out of Miss Flo's winder...'

'Well, that's a good brother she's got ter buy 'er two,' the newsagent said. 'Look, why don't yer call me Arnie like everyone else?' He winked at Ben. 'Mebbe, come Christmas I'll 'ave a little present fer the both of yer – 'specially if yer continue ter do little jobs fer me. I might ask yer to run down ter the bookie with a little bet fer me… if I can trust yer? I wouldn't ask most of the kids round 'ere 'cos they'd take me money and scarper…'

'You know you can trust me, Arnie,' Ben said and grinned. Arnie was generous if you did little jobs for him and Ben was up for anything that wasn't actually wrong. His dad might not like him going to the bookies much, because it wasn't strictly legal and if the coppers found out they'd cart him off to the station and give him a talking-to – but it wasn't like being a thief or a burglar, was it?

'That's what I thought, lad,' Arnie confirmed. 'I like a little bet – and some of me customers feel the same, but they don't like bein' seen going into them places. Think of them as dives – well, they ain't decent some of 'em, but the one I'll send yer to is honest. He gives good odds and pays out if yer win – not like some of the cheatin' buggers. Trouble is, all sorts hang around there; the women ain't what they ought ter be and rough types an' all – just go straight in and ask for Finney, give 'im the slip and the money and come straight orf – understand me?'

'Yeah, all right, when do yer want me to go?'

'Saturday mornin',' Arnie said. 'Tell yer dad yer cleanin' winders if he asks and I'll give yer half a crown after yer get back – now how's that?'

'Cor that's great, Arnie!' Ben grinned at him. 'I can buy Dad somethin fer Christmas as well as Ruthie.'

'Yer'll be rich if yer stick wiv me.' Arnie winked again. 'Now get that cardboard flattened and trundled round the corner to Sid Foster and you'll be well on yer way to making yer first fortune.'

Ben giggled to himself as he set to with a will, stamping on the old cardboard boxes to flatten them before loading them on to his little trolley. There were all kinds of boxes, from thin ones that had held chocolate bars to heavy-duty cardboard that was used for carting tins and other heavier goods. Arnie's stock room was filled up with all sorts. Ben saw that some of the wooden crates had bottles of what looked like whisky in them and wondered what they were doing here. This was a newspaper shop that sold cigarettes, tobacco, sweets, magazines and birthday cards, also a few tins of mints and some tinned fruit. The whisky looked out of place and it was pulled out of sight behind boxes of other stock, but Ben had revealed it when he'd started clearing out the old boxes.

Arnie came in just as Ben was about to leave with the first load. His eyes went to the boxes of whisky and he frowned.

'One thing, Ben… anythin' you see 'ere, you keep ter yerself, right?'

''Course, Arnie,' Ben said and left through the back door. Ben was innocent but not so innocent that he didn't know when he'd seen something he shouldn't. That whisky didn't belong in a shop that sold newspapers and sweets – you had to have a licence to sell spirits. Ben was sure that was right and it made him feel a bit uncomfortable knowing Arnie's secret. He liked Arnie and he wanted to earn money for Christmas. Ben couldn't tell anyone what he'd seen, but he was uneasy as he took the cardboard to the scrapyard.

Sid told him that if he brought another load just like it he would give him sixpence.

'Threepence for this one and the same for the next,' he offered. 'Is it a deal?'

'Yeah,' Ben said and grinned at him. 'What else are yer lookin' fer?'

'Scrap metal mostly,' Sid told him. 'Bring me a load of metal – and I'll give yer twice or three times as much, more if it's lead, but I don't want pinched stuff, young 'un. I'm an honest man, see. I don't get no trouble with the coppers and don't want any – understand?'

'Yeah, I don't want none either,' Ben agreed. Ben knew that life was hard for lads that got taken up by the law. His dad had told him that until earlier that year young boys were often birched for small misdemeanours. He walked back to Arnie's shop, his mind busy. He often saw bits of metal lying around in the gutters or under sheds or on waste ground. If he picked them up and saved them until he got a load, he could earn money for his sister and his dad. Ben missed his mum and knew that his sister was pining for her. His dad was busy trying to find enough work to keep them going for a while, so it was down to Ben to make this a good Christmas despite everything.

When he got back to Arnie's stock room, he discovered that the boxes of whisky had gone, just as if they had never been there. Ben felt relief sweep over him. If he didn't know where they were, he couldn't tell anyone and that was a good feeling. He didn't mind running errands for Arnie, but the idea of stolen goods had made him uncomfortable; now they'd gone and the shadow had lifted.

With what he'd earned that evening, he could already buy Ruthie two sugar mice for Christmas, and that made him smile – and he'd keep a lookout for old bits of metal to take to the scrapyard.

He could hear the Sally Army singing as he walked back to the Waters' house to collect his sister. They had started to sing carols, which meant Christmas was coming ever closer, just over two weeks to Christmas Eve. Some of the shop windows were already decorated with bits of holly and cotton wool to look like snow. A shop that sold books, puzzles and games had a display of Father Christmas and his sleigh pulled by reindeer.

Ben saw a large box of Meccano at the back of the window and sighed, because he knew there was no way he could ever afford to buy that for himself. He had a very small set that his father had bought him three years earlier and he'd made up the model that was displayed on the front of the box and then pulled it to pieces again; he'd done it many times, but try as he might he couldn't make anything much different with the set he had. If he had that large box of pieces, Ben could make all sorts of things – and it was what he liked doing for fun. Putting things together, working out how they went; he thought perhaps he would like to be a mechanic of some kind one day, though he didn't know anything about engines.

As he went into the big warm kitchen, Granda had the kettle on the range. 'Have a cup of cocoa, lad,' he offered. 'We saved yer a bit of cake – and Ruthie has been making paper chains fer us. We're goin' ter decorate Millie's room upstairs so she don't miss Christmas. We've always put up decorations and Millie likes a tree – she likes the smell of a real one. I thought you could go to the market on Saturday and buy one for me. You can help me carry it upstairs, lad – and then we'll all decorate it together…'

'Yeah, great,' Ben said. 'I've got a couple of errands ter run fer Arnie at the newspaper shop, but then I'll fetch the tree fer yer. Ruthie loves Christmas decorations.

We've got a box in the attic. I'll ask Dad to 'elp us put them up on Sunday...'

'Will Dad want us to decorate this year?' Ruthie asked doubtfully and a tear welled in her eye and ran down her cheek. 'It's the first wivout...'

'Wivout Mum, I know,' Ben said and put his arm about her shoulder. He sniffed hard to hide his own emotion. 'Mum would want us ter 'ave a good Christmas, Ruthie. You know she would...'

'Yes...' Ruthie smiled a little wobbly smile and wiped her cheek with the back of her hand. 'This is lovely cake – Miss Flo's sister brought it for Granny and Granda... but they shared it wiv us...'

Ben realised he was hungry. He'd earned his shilling treading all those boxes flat and trundling them round to the scrapyard, but it was worth it, because he knew Ruthie would squeal with delight when she got her sugar mice on Christmas morning.

'That looks good,' he said and then tasted the coffee icing on top of the slice of plain sponge cake, his taste buds bursting to life as he came to the butter icing in the middle. 'It's lovely. I've never had anythin' quite like that...'

'Miss Flo is a lovely cook,' Granda agreed and his eyes looked a little watery. 'People are so kind...I know my Millie is touched by what they've done for us and it has cheered her up no end...'

Ben nodded, because it was true. Folk like Miss Flo and her sister were kind, but he knew that not everyone was as nice. As he was leaving Arnie's shop to come here, he'd seen a big bloke with a thick beard hanging round the back of the shop. He'd nipped back in and whispered to Arnie what he saw, who just nodded and said it was all right... but Ben had a prickly feeling at the back of his neck. He didn't like the look of that stranger at all and he wondered if he had anything to do with the whisky that didn't belong in a newspaper shop...

'Are you sure you don't mind me going out again tonight?' Honour asked as they closed the shop and went through to the kitchen at the back. 'I know I've been out every night this week and it isn't fair on you...'

'I shall want to go out on Friday night as usual,' Flo said and hesitated. 'If you promise not to do anythin' silly, I'll let you invite Roy here that evenin'. Dad is often asleep after I give him his cocoa and he doesn't stir until I go in to see if he needs anythin' when I get back... but you must be quiet, because I don't want him tryin' to come downstairs again.'

Her father had been down a couple of times since the evening Honour had left him alone in the house. Flo had watched him inching his way stair by stair, but he'd refused her help, though he could never get back up alone. He'd sat in his chair by the range and watched her as she cleaned and then made some of the sweet treats ready for the morning.

'Don't yer ever stop?' he'd asked. He sounded humbled, concerned for her, something he hadn't shown her for years.

'I like to be busy,' she'd told him. 'The kitchen has to be spotless or they might stop me making cakes here. Besides, it's our living, you know that…'

'Don't rub it in that I'm a useless idiot…'

'I wasn't and you're not. You always worked while you could…'

'Too much! If I hadn't taken that job up north…' He shook his head. 'You were a fool, Flo – but your mother was a bigger one, and it was her fault. She ought to have told you or stopped yer goin' out with blokes. I hope yer told that girl of yours what's what?'

His words sent prickles down her spine, but Flo had concentrated on moulding the soft sugar paste into different shapes, not letting him see that he'd unsettled her. Besides the sugar mice, she was making other fancy bits and pieces to sell in the shop; she'd bought some more moulds that she could use to cut out marzipan and decorate in various ways. Marzipan was too expensive to sell all year round, but there were only a couple of weeks until Christmas now and so she was trying something new. She'd made a little family of rabbits, some stars and a Christmas tree shape, which she was decorating with tiny pieces of angelica, sugared fruits and nuts.

Flo had felt shivery, because this was the closest her father had ever come to speaking of their secret. 'If you mean have I told her to be careful, yes, I have.'

Flo could feel his eyes burning into her as he muttered, 'I'm not a fool, girl. I always knew she couldn't be mine. I thought at first yer mother had cheated on me and I made her pay for it – but then I realised that you mothered the brat too much and there was something in yer eyes when I spoke harshly to her. I knew then that yer mother had been protecting yer.'

Flo had turned to look at him. 'You can't prove anythin'...'

'I might if I wanted to but I don't...' he'd muttered. 'I'd have been angry if yer mother had told me. I might have slapped yer a few times, but then it would've been over. She made me hate her – and then I hated you for what yer put me through, the pair of yer. I loved yer mother once, Flo. I ain't a man fer showin' me feelings – and I've always had a mean streak and a temper. Yet I cared fer her and it cut me up when I knew she'd shut me out...'

Flo was stunned. She could see the pain working in his face and it had struck her like a hammer fist. Neither she nor her mother had considered his feelings when they had hatched their plans to protect Flo from scandal.

'I'm sorry. We thought you would never know – that you didn't need to know...'

'That was what made me so very angry. At times, I wanted to kill her – and I nearly threw you all out, but it was her shop and, in the end, she told me that she would prefer that I left her if I couldn't accept your child and keep my mouth shut...' He glared at her. 'All she cared about was the shame you might bring on us... I kept quiet, but I made her pay by giving me a share of her profits.'

So that was why Flo's mother had started giving him money every week!

'You won't tell Honour she's mine?' Flo had felt hot all over. 'She might not understand... One day, I'll tell her myself.'

'She should be grateful for all you gave up for her.'

'I didn't give up anything that mattered...' Flo had turned her face so that he couldn't see her pain.

'No? You might have been married, had a husband and a home of yer own if she hadn't been born – oh, I know yer own this place, but yer could have sold it. Yer might have had a nice little nest egg, but once yer soiled yerself with that no good begger yer had no choice. No man would want yer if he knew yer were a slut... had a kid when yer were seventeen.'

Flo hadn't answered him. She'd felt bad for him, for his loss – but he was just using it to taunt her again. He'd done it enough times in the past, but this time she'd let him in.

'I shan't tell the girl or anyone else,' her father went on. 'What good would it do me? If I'd been goin' ter expose yer I'd have done it years ago – but I won't be put in the infirmary, Flo. I heard that girl of yourn talkin' about it and I'm warnin' yer – make any move to send me orf and I'll tell her what a slut yer are...'

Flo had raised her head proudly. 'Luckily for you, I've got a sense of decency, which you clearly don't have. I never intended to send you there – but if you say one word to Honour, you can lie up there in your own dirt and I'll leave you to rot.'

She'd walked out of the kitchen door into the little yard at the back of the shop, the tears falling. Sometimes, she hated that man in her kitchen, sometimes she almost wished he would die – and yet she knew that when her storm of grief was over, she would go back inside and help him back to bed.

Ben saw the man selling Christmas trees from a barrow at the side of the market. He'd got a notice up saying they were five bob each, but most of them were too big for Ben to carry home, and he thought they would dwarf Millie's room. He sidled up, looking the trees over and saw a much smaller one at the back of the stall. It was a nice shape but a quarter of the size of the others.

'How much fer that?' he asked. 'It ain't worth a patch of them others...'

'It's a bit on the small size, but yer could 'ave it fer half a crown – if yer've got the money?'

Ben had, but he wasn't willing to part with it. 'I reckon there ain't much more than a tanner's worth there...'

'Cheeky monkey, get orf wiv yer!'

'I'll give yer a bob fer it,' Ben offered. 'Go on, mister, I can't afford no more and me granny ain't well...'

'It's worth two bob...'

'You'll never sell it,' Ben persisted. 'I'll help yer unload them ones at the back... if I can have it fer a bob...'

'Persistent little bugger, ain't yer?' the man said and sniffed. 'All right, help me get the rest of me trees off the van and yer can 'ave it fer a bob – though I'm losin' me profits.'

'I bet they chucked that one in fer nothin',' Ben said and grinned, and the man aimed a light blow at his ear, but he was chuckling and Ben knew he was right.

He helped unload all the trees, paid the shilling and set off with his prize under his arm as the carol singers started to gather. He'd only spent a shilling of Granda's money and that was a bargain.

Mick saw Ben carrying the tiny Christmas tree. He envied his friend being able to celebrate Christmas at home with all the trimmings. Mick had had a home once, just a small terraced house up north and his mother had made presents and decorations to make the festive season special too. Taffy had seemed to be different then, saving his drinking sprees to Friday night and bringing his wages home, but after Mick's mother died he'd starting drinking too much and lost his job.

He hated being on the road, sleeping rough and never having a proper home or decent food unless it was a packet of chips or a pie and mash from the shop. Mick's mum had made wonderful apple pie and he missed that most of all.

Tagging along behind Ben, he saw him go into the terrace house next to the end of the small block of houses. He hadn't gone home but to visit some old people who lived here. Mick's hopes of being invited in for tea at Ben's home faded. He turned towards the dilapidated tenements that were his home until they moved on; it would be cold and dark and he was frightened of Scrapper. It might be best if he found himself a shop doorway to sleep in tonight...

11

'It's gone... the cash box and every penny that was in it,' Nurse Mary said as John walked into the office that morning. 'Someone must have taken it...'

John walked over to the desk and saw that the top right-hand drawer had been broken open. The little black cash box that had held the money he'd saved so painstakingly for the Christmas treats had gone!

'No! I don't believe it – who would do such a thing to us?'

'Who knew the money was there?' Mary frowned in concentration. 'Unless... I put another five shillings in yesterday and he was in here... the man you've got doing our repairs...'

'Robbie wouldn't do this,' John said, shocked by the suggestion. 'He was so pleased to be given this work... No, I can't think it...'

Robbie could be heard cheerfully whistling in the background, hammering away at something he was repairing. He'd looked so happy to be here, taking care and pride in his work. Surely he wouldn't throw away his chance to get back into a proper job.

Twenty pounds and a few extra shillings could mean a lot to a man like Robbie, especially with Christmas so near – but if he took money meant to buy a Christmas dinner for people who had nothing… it was despicable.

'You have to speak to him,' Nurse Mary was saying. 'You and I were the only ones who knew about that box and the Christmas fund – and him, because he came in while I was putting it away…'

She clearly believed Robbie Graham had taken their money. John knew that he had to ask, even though he shrank from doing it.

John nodded at her and went through to the other room, where Robbie was hammering a replacement floorboard into place. He stood watching for a moment, his heart heavy, but he knew Mary was right. Lots of people came and went every day, but the office was kept locked when no one was using it – and Robbie was the only other person at liberty to go in there…

'Robbie…' he spoke hesitantly. Robbie stopped hammering and looked up at him inquiringly. 'I don't suppose you know anything about the drawer in my office?'

Robbie got to his feet, a look of wary bewilderment in his eyes and John knew instinctively that he'd made a mistake. 'What drawer?'

'It was locked. We kept the Christmas fund money in a little cash box and it has been broken open...'

Robbie went very still and the look of hurt and bewilderment in his eyes was awful to see. John wanted to take the words back, to unsay them, but it was too late. He knew that he'd been wrong to ask such a question of a proud man, but Mary's conviction that he'd taken their money had forced his hand.

'You think that I would take money from you – after you gave me the chance to work here?' Robbie sounded stunned. 'You really believe that I would steal from the man who helped me get money for my kids at Christmas?'

'No, of course not,' John said at once. 'It was just that it has gone and you were there when Mary locked it away yesterday and...'

'I know she thinks I'm not good enough to be here,' Robbie said a little sadly. 'I understand that she might think it was me – but I thought you were different...' He looked back at the floorboard he was fixing. 'I'll make sure this is safe and then I'll collect my things and go.'

'No...' John's words wouldn't come out right as he saw the scorn in Robbie's eyes. 'I didn't mean... I know I should've trusted you...'

'But you didn't and so I can't work here,' Robbie said. 'I hope you find your money and I'm sorry if it means you can't give the old folk their Christmas dinner – but you owe me two pounds and you can keep that towards it...' He turned his back on John and hammered away violently.

John stood watching him for a moment and then returned to the office. Mary looked up as he entered, her brows arched.

'He didn't take it – and he's leaving as soon as he's finished that floorboard...'

'You believe him?'

'Yes, I do,' John asserted. 'So, how did whoever it was get in here?' He examined the window but the latch was secure. 'Not through this anyway...'

'The office door was locked when I came in earlier,' Mary said. 'Did you leave it unlocked at any time yesterday?'

'No... I did leave my jacket hanging over a chair last evening when I was closing up and I left the room and the key was in the pocket. I may have forgotten to lock the door after you left, but I locked it before I went home...' He hesitated, then, 'I can't be certain when the box was taken, because I didn't come back in here before locking up... Someone could have sneaked in and taken it while I was checking the other doors and windows...'

'So someone might have come in here late yesterday afternoon when you were checking round, making sure everything was shut for the night?' Mary nodded her head.

'It is possible...' John looked at her in dismay. 'I should never have asked Robbie. I should have known he wouldn't take the money...'

Robbie was collecting his tools. John went quickly to the office door.

'Please stay,' he begged. 'I know I should've trusted you...'

'Thanks for the opportunity. It reminded me of what I am,' Robbie said. 'Keep the money you owe me. I hope you get yours back for the old folk's party...'

Robbie walked to the door and disappeared through the opening, closing it behind him.

John swore quietly. He'd intended to help Robbie and now all he'd done was hurt his pride and rob him of the last few days of work. He would have to take the money he owed him round to his house and put it through the door. It was unlikely Robbie would make that much up in time to buy his kids anything this Christmas.

'I'm sorry,' Nurse Mary apologised. 'I was so sure it was him – would it make any difference if I went after him and explained?'

'No, he's angry and his pride is hurt. I'd hoped to help him into permanent work but even if...' He shook his head. 'I've made a mess of things.'

'It was my fault,' Mary looked upset. 'If there is anything I can do?'

'I'll have to ask for donations for the Christmas fund... or fund it myself...' John had very little personal money. He was forever putting his hand in his pocket for hard-luck cases, but perhaps he could sell something – the silver cigarette box and beautiful table lighter that had once belonged to his grandfather. The items had sentimental value for him, but he might raise enough to go ahead with the Christmas lunch for his regulars… But that didn't solve the problem of what he'd done to Robbie Graham. John would feel terrible knowing that Ben and little Ruthie were likely to go without a proper dinner this year because of what he'd done…

Robbie's anger kept him walking for the first ten minutes or so and then it began to hit him. He had exactly six shillings in his pocket. He'd used his wages thus far to buy food and a couple of small things for the children for Christmas: a new pair of boots for Ben and a good second-hand dress off the market for Ruthie. He'd been going to buy the special food, sweets and other gifts he'd planned when he'd got the rest of his pay – but now he would find it difficult to pay for food on the table and a few bob for the gas meter…

Robbie smashed his fist against the wall and gasped as he felt the sting of raw pain. He wished he'd taken the chance to hit John Hansen while he had it. Robbie might have had to stand in line for work and sometimes his kids were lucky to get a bit of bread and scrape for their tea, but he'd never stolen anything in his life and it humiliated him to know that John Hansen and that stuck-up Nurse Mary thought he would sink so low as to take the money they'd put aside for the destitute at Christmas.

He was so angry that he felt sick with it, turning this way and that on the pavement as he fought the desire to go back there and wreck the place. When he thought of all the care and pride he'd taken in doing those repairs...

Robbie's gaze fell on the public house across the road. He needed a drink. He needed several drinks – and although the money he'd got in his pocket wasn't enough to get him drunk, it would help.

He crossed the road, shoving the door back aggressively and walking up to the bar. Robbie was about to order a pint when a hand slapped him on the back and he turned to see one of the men he'd stood in line with on the docks. He hadn't seen Josh since that day and would have been glad to see him had he not been so wretched.

'Well met,' Josh greeted him warmly. 'Have a drink on me, Robbie. I've 'ad a bit o' luck – won a fortune on the 'orses...' He grinned, clearly well ahead of Robbie and half-drunk already. 'Two double whiskies, mate – and keep 'em comin...' he told the bartender.

Robbie accepted the drink, tossing it straight down. He couldn't afford to buy the same but offered a pint. Josh pushed the offer aside and two more whiskies appeared on the bar. Robbie downed his and turned to leave, his head already beginning to feel a bit fuzzy.

'Yer bought me half a pint when I were down and brung me luck,' Josh told Robbie with a grin. 'I got a job the next day – just a bit of sweeping up at the cigarette factory like, but I put five bob on the horses at five hundred ter one – and the bleeder only come in first... a hundred and twenty-five quid... that's a bleedin' fortune.'

'I'm glad,' Robbie said and grinned at him. He'd never in his life managed to accumulate that much. 'But you want ter hang on to some of yer winnings, mate. Yer won't always be lucky. Save a bit fer when yer need it.' He got up to leave because two glasses of whisky were already affecting his balance.

'You can't leave me yet,' Josh insisted, pushing a third double at him. Robbie drank it and hesitated as a fourth was pushed his way, then he shook his head. The other man snorted with laughter and downed both of them and then sank to the floor in a stupor. Robbie tried to lift Josh but succeeded only in dragging him over to a bench and setting him up. His own head was spinning as he left the man there and walked out, forgetting his tool bag, which he'd dumped on the floor of the pub. He wasn't used to whisky and was already wishing he'd stuck to a pint or two of bitter.

It seemed a long way home and he attempted the stairs but found it impossible to climb them, so he went through to the kitchen and collapsed on the sagging sofa at the far side, his eyes closing. He wasn't sure what had happened to his tools; he'd had them when he went into the pub, but somehow he seemed to have lost them along the way... A thought came into his head that without his tools he wouldn't be able to find work as a carpenter. He would go back in the morning and ask...

Ben finished his jobs for Granda and then told Ruthie to stay there while he went to the newsagent to see if Arnie had anything for him. She pulled a face at him, because Ben was leaving her here too much recently and she wanted to go home.

Ben ignored her sulky look. He'd been to the bookie for Arnie several times over the past couple of days and been paid five shillings in all, which was safely put aside at home. He knew that his dad wouldn't like him running bets, particularly as there were some nasty types hanging around. He thought that after Christmas he would tell Arnie he wouldn't do it any more, but he wanted enough money to buy his dad a gift too and so he needed to earn more than the pennies he got from doing errands for his neighbours.

Arnie gave him a list to take and some money in an envelope. 'Stick it inside yer shirt, lad,' he told Ben. 'If there's any bugger watchin' yer and thinks he'll have it orf yer, run like 'ell. That money belongs to me punters and I'm responsible fer it getting' ter Finney...'

'Yeah, all right,' Ben agreed and set off at a smart pace. The sooner he placed the bets with Finney and got his money from Arnie, the better. He would much rather be with his sister eating the bag of chips he was going to buy for their tea than running errands on this cold and foggy night.

When he got to Finney's premises, he saw a man leaving and something made him hesitate for a moment. The man looked unkempt and had long hair with grey streaks and a thick beard. As he walked up the street, he dumped something in a dustbin outside the grocer's shop and glanced furtively over his shoulder.

Ben waited until the man had disappeared round the corner and then went to the bin and looked inside; there, on top, was a small black metal cash box. Ben picked it up and turned it over. He could see that the lock had been forced, mangled and broken so that it was no longer any use, but he could add it to his collection and Sid Foster would buy it from him as scrap metal. For a moment, he stood there uncertainly, because instinct told him that this box had been stolen. He had no idea where it came from or who it belonged to, but he knew it didn't belong to the man who had put it there.

Making a sudden decision, Ben tucked the box inside his jacket pocket. Maybe he shouldn't, but instinct had told him to do it. He turned back and went to Finney's door, knocking twice.

Finney opened the door himself and pulled him inside. 'What yer got fer me, lad?'

Ben handed over the envelope and the list and Finney's foxy face lit up with a grin. 'There's a good lad.' He counted the money and then put his hand in his pocket and gave Ben sixpence. 'If yer ever need a proper job, come to me, lad. I'll see yer earn good money…'

'Will yer tell me somethin'?' Ben asked. 'I saw a bloke leavin' here a minute ago – big bloke, bushy beard…'

'Don't ask me no questions about that one,' Finney warned. 'He ain't a regular. Don't know where he got my name, but I don't like him – took his money, ten quid he put on the bloody favourite to win in the Christmas Stakes at Cheltenham termorrow. I hope the bleedin' thing loses… I dare say he pinched the ten quid anyway.'

'I think he stole somethin',' Ben said and showed him the mangled money box. 'He put this in someone's bin… so that might be where he got the money for his bet…'

'Yeah, his sort nick everythin' they get a chance of,' Finney said. 'Don't mess wiv 'im, lad. He'd as soon slit yer throat as not…'

Ben put the box away inside his jacket. He didn't know what he was going to do about it, because the right thing to do would be to take it to the police, but he wasn't sure they would believe him. They might think he'd taken it…

'Get orf back to Arnie and tell 'im I said 'e's on fer termorrow…'

'Yeah, all right. Thanks, Finney.'

'Don't forget what I said about workin' fer me when yer ready,' Finney told him. 'I've got loads more punters besides Arnie. I could do wiv a lad like you runnin' fer me…'

Ben thanked him and pocketed his sixpence. Finney hadn't taken any notice of the cash box, just warned him against messing with the man who'd dumped it in the bin. Ben knew he was right to think there was more than just a bit of betting on the horses or the greyhounds going on. Was Finney a fence? Ben had heard the word used in connection with stolen goods and Finney's acceptance that the bet he'd taken was probably with stolen money made Ben realise that he was getting mixed up in bad things.

Ben decided that perhaps he'd got enough to buy his dad something good for Christmas, or he would have by the time Arnie paid him. He didn't want to be sent away for being involved with thieves and that was what might happen if he got caught. Ben had thought it harmless to take a few bets to the shop for Arnie, even though he knew it was not lawful for the newsagent to take bets. He'd seen that whisky in Arnie's storeroom and now he suspected that Finney was a fence as well as a bookie – and that was too much.

This was the last time he was going to take Arnie's bets. He would tell him after he got his sixpence and he would have to look elsewhere to earn a few bob in future. Perhaps it wouldn't matter so much now his dad had a proper job...

12

Honour looked at herself in the dressing table mirror and didn't like what she saw. Her hair was messed up and her face looked flushed, her mouth a little swollen from Roy's kisses. She looked like a woman who had been making love and that was just what she'd done with Roy in the back seat of the car he'd borrowed. He'd taken her for a ride to a secluded pub by the river; they'd had a couple of drinks and then returned to the car. When Roy suggested climbing in the back seat so they could kiss properly, Honour had been eager and willing, excited by the car and the alcohol as well as his sweet words. Of course she hadn't meant to let him do all the things he'd done, but his touch had inflamed her senses and she'd been swept along by her love and a new-found desire – and it had been lovely. She couldn't understand why people said it was wrong, because it had felt so right.

Honour didn't regret giving herself to the man she loved, but she knew that if her sister saw her now she would know what she'd done – and the last thing Honour wanted was to hurt or upset her. She was well aware that Flo had given up a lot for her, doing all the things her mother would have done if she'd lived – and even when their mother was alive, it was Flo who had kissed her when she fell and scrapped knees and hands, and Flo who told her stories to help her sleep.

Honour was torn between the lovely secret she hugged to herself and fear that Flo would despise her. No, she wouldn't do that – she didn't despise the girls who had to get married in a hurry – but she would be angry. She had made it clear that Honour had to wait until next summer to marry, and that was fair enough. If anything happened... But it wouldn't, of course it wouldn't the first time.

Roy had held her in his arms afterwards as she'd shed a few tears.

'It doesn't happen the first time; lots of women have to wait for years before they have a child.' He'd smiled and kissed her nose. 'You know I love you, Honour – if anything happened, I'd marry you straight away, I promise.' He looked rueful. 'I never meant this to happen, truly. It was just... you were so sweet and trusting and I got carried away.'

'It wasn't all your fault,' Honour had admitted, because she'd been swept away on a wave of love and desire. 'I should have refused – but I didn't want to. I love you, Roy, and I wanted it to happen – and I want to be married so that it can happen whenever we want. It isn't fair that we have to wait...'

'It's best if we do,' Roy had said. 'Once I've finished my term of service in the army, I'll find us a house with a shopfront that I can use to set up my business. I want something like your sister's shop only a bit bigger – and if I can find somewhere not too far away you'll be able to see her often...'

'You're so good to me,' Honour had cried and threw her arms about him, kissing him passionately. Her embrace had almost led to them making love again, and she'd been lost in the heat of desire, but Roy had called a halt that time.

'I need to look after you,' he'd murmured and touched her mouth with one finger. 'I didn't come after you just to get my wicked way, Honour – I want you for my wife...'

Her feeling of guilt subsided as she scrubbed her face with cold water from her jug on the washstand in the corner of the room. Flo said that when she could afford it she was going to have a proper bath installed in the box room, but Honour knew they were lucky to have an inside toilet upstairs. Most of the houses in the road still had a toilet outside and used chamber pots during the night. Flo had a sink with hot and cold taps in the kitchen; the water was heated by the kitchen range, but she hadn't been able to afford to put the plumbing in upstairs yet. They used a zinc bath in front of the kitchen fire, which afforded privacy, because they locked the door and took it in turns to bathe. Roy had told Honour he was going to make sure that the house he got for them had proper plumbing upstairs and down.

As she jumped into a cold bed, Honour pulled the sheets up to her chin. Flo had put a hot-water bottle in for her hours ago, but it had gone cold and she pulled it out, dropping it to the floor. She was hours later than she ought to have been and had wondered if she would find the back door locked or Flo sitting up waiting for an explanation. Neither had happened and that had made Honour feel even guiltier as she crept in and locked the door after her.

She knew Flo would expect an explanation in the morning and she had one ready, though she hated the thought of lying. The truth was neither of them had realised the time and when they did it was already long past the hour Honour was expected home. Flo had obviously given up and gone to bed... but she would know that her sister had been very late in.

Sighing, Honour turned over and closed her eyes. She didn't want to think about facing Flo; she wanted to relive the excitement and tenderness she'd felt in her lover's arms.

Flo heard Honour come in and creep up the stairs. She heard the little click of her door and was relieved that she was back safe. That evening, Roy had come for her in a small Ford motor car he'd borrowed from a friend and Flo had foolishly worried that they might have had an accident. Of course they hadn't! No doubt they'd sat cuddling and kissing in the back seat and time had flown. Flo could still remember the stolen moments with Robbie; time had flown then, but she'd never dared to be late back, even when she'd been courting, she'd only ever been a few minutes late and her mother had looked pointedly at the clock.

Things were different now; Flo knew that decent young women were allowed to go out with their young men without chaperones and had been for some years, but her parents had been strict. Had Flo come home two hours late, her father would have taken his belt to her. Even now, he looked annoyed if she was a little late coming back from the mission on a Friday night. However, Flo couldn't find it in her heart to blame her darling daughter. She was in love and it looked as if Roy really cared for her. Flo prayed he wouldn't let her down; she didn't think she could bear it if history repeated itself – but surely it wouldn't. She'd explained what making love was, which, was something her own mother would rather have died than done. Flo was sure Honour had more sense than to make the same mistake now that she knew... and she made up her mind not to make a big thing of Honour being late. After all, the girl had made it clear she wanted to marry and she was old enough. Perhaps Flo was being unfair to make her wait until next summer…

It would be very hard to let her go. Flo would miss working with her each day and it would make things much harder for her. She couldn't manage everything without help – and no one else would work for the small wage Honour accepted without question. Her father would have to give up at least some of his share of their profits. She couldn't imagine what he needed it for these days, but he never failed to ask if she neglected to put the money by his bed every week.

Tossing and turning sleeplessly, Flo thought about the tea she'd shared with Mr Waters, Robbie and his family. It had been such a happy time for her, even though Robbie hadn't said much. She'd hoped he might come into the shop to buy something for the children, but he hadn't and she'd stopped looking for him. For a moment as he'd met her eyes, Flo had thought he still cared, but she was mistaken. Robbie had never loved her; he'd only wanted the excitement of the forbidden and he'd run away rather than face the consequences.

Tears were trickling down her cheeks. Flo rubbed them away and sat up as she heard her father moving about. He'd got out of bed by himself, but unless she went to check on him, he might end up spending the rest of the night on the floor and it was much too cold to let him lie there.

She went softly into his room and saw him getting up from the commode. He saw her and shook his head, annoyed with her or himself, she wasn't sure which, but could see that he hadn't wanted her.

'I didn't ring fer yer,' he muttered crossly. 'Yer 'ave ter be up again in a couple of hours.'

'I know, but I didn't want you to fall and freeze to death. It's cold enough for snow, Dad.'

'I dare say,' he muttered. 'Something woke me. I'm not sure what. I can manage if you just give me yer arm. I'm gettin' stronger.'

'Good,' Flo said. 'It will be better for you if you don't need help all the time – and you will be happier if you can come down more.'

'I'd be pleased if I thought you meant it, Flo.'

'Well, I do,' she assured him. 'It's easier to pop into the kitchen to make you a cup of tea than run upstairs.' He pulled a face at that and she smiled. 'Of course I'm pleased if you're feelin' better. You're my father. I don't want you to die.'

He looked at her and cleared his throat but said nothing.

Flo saw him settled in bed and then went to the window and glanced out.

'It's white everywhere,' she observed. 'Jack Frost is at work, but there's no sign of snow yet.'

'It's savin' itself for the week before Christmas, makin' it difficult for folk to get their shoppin',' he quipped and grinned.

'Yes, very likely,' Flo agreed. 'Ring if you need me...'

She left him and went down the landing, pausing as she looked at Honour's door. She was tempted to go in and make sure she was all right, but Honour wasn't a little girl now. It was time to let her grow up, even if it meant losing her.

Flo's eyes felt wet, but she brushed the tears away and returned to her bed. If she didn't get some sleep she would be too tired to work in the morning.

Honour was down first. She'd started making the first batch of sponge cakes and was mixing some buttercream with a light whisk. For a moment she concentrated on her work, looking up only when Flo spoke to her.

'What flavour have you made today?'

'I made two coffee sponges, four vanilla and two almond,' Honour told her. 'I'm doing a vanilla icing for the almond sponges with an almond buttercream filling, coffee icing for the coffee sponge with walnuts, and a strawberry jam and buttercream filling for the plain sponges.'

'I'll make some fancies then.' Flo turned away to start gathering what she needed for her little iced fancy cakes. 'Did you have a nice evening, love?' She looked at her daughter thinking she seemed a little quiet.

'Yes, lovely,' Honour said. 'We went for a drink at a posh place near the river and then just drove round for a while. Roy wanted to take me to the Christmas dance at the church hall tomorrow, but I told him I'd been out a lot lately and I would have to ask you first...'

'You may go if you wish,' Flo agreed. 'Of course you can, Honour. You do your share of the work; you deserve to have some fun...'

'I thought I'd make some more sugar mice and rum truffles this evenin' – we've sold all but two bags of the truffles and there are only two pink mice left.'

'I've taken several orders for the truffles and the sugar mice,' Flo said. 'I wrote them in the book so you could see what is on order – and we have twenty orders for iced cakes. It means we shall be busy the last few days before Christmas. I think we ought to start the marzipan icing this evening and keep them well wrapped. If we leave everything until the last moment we'll never get it all done...'

'I'll tell Roy I can't go out as much when we start the icing...'

'You can ask him to come round and when you've done your cakes you can go out for a little walk...'

'You're so good to me,' Honour murmured and her cheeks were bright pink.

'I was young once and I thought I was in love,' Flo said and then wished she could take the words back as Honour stared at her.

'What happened?' she asked.

Flo began mixing the smooth thick sugar paste she needed to ice her little fancies. 'Oh, he went away and forgot me... I've never been sure why...' A little voice in her head told her that it was because Robbie had been scared of responsibility and yet a part of her didn't believe that – had never believed it. Robbie had sworn he loved her. He'd been shocked when she told him her news and left her abruptly. Flo had always believed that he would come back – she'd gone on believing it right up until the day her daughter was born and she'd known Robbie wouldn't return to her.

'I'm sorry, Flo,' Honour apologised. 'I didn't know you'd been let down...'

'It was a long time ago and I'm well over it,' Flo said, but in her heart she knew she would never forget her first and only love.

'I wish I'd known...'

Flo shook her head. 'I'm goin' to make a light fruit cake I can take round for Mr and Mrs Waters,' she said. 'I thought I might pop round there at teatime – if you can manage on your own for an hour or so?'

'What happens if Dad rings his bell?'

'Ignore him if you're serving customers, but then put the "closed" notice on the door, go up and help him and come back down. I shan't be too long. I'm only going to deliver the cake and have a little chat.'

'All right, that's fair,' Honour agreed, though Flo knew she hated being left alone with the man she believed was her father. He didn't like her helping him and would demand to know where Flo was – so perhaps she would tell him before she went. If he made himself comfortable first, he might not need to call Honour upstairs at all...

Bert Waters answered the door and smiled as he saw who his visitor was. He welcomed Flo in and insisted that she went up to say hello to his wife.

'Millie is feeling a bit better today,' he said. 'I'll bring her a cup of tea up and a piece of your cake. You're spoiling us, Flo. She loved the last one you brought us... and I'll bring a cup of tea for you, too.'

'Don't worry about me,' Flo told him. 'It must be a lot for you, Bert – up and down stairs all day and looking after Millie. Is there no one who could help you?'

'I dare say Effie next door would if I asked,' Bert admitted, 'but Millie wouldn't care for it much – and I don't like to be a trouble to anyone...'

'I'm sure you wouldn't be,' Flo reassured him. 'I shan't poke my nose in, but don't wear yourself out,

Bert. I could manage to help a bit with the housework on Sunday afternoon… but I've got my hands full with the shop…'

'You work hard enough and you've got your father to look after,' Bert said. 'You're a kind young woman, Flo. I appreciate you coming like this – but you can't take on any more…'

Flo didn't argue the point, because he was right. She would come when she could, but she was tied to her own house. A quick visit like this and perhaps on a Sunday afternoon, but that was as much as she could manage.

She spent half an hour chatting to Millie, who seemed brighter than the last time she'd popped in but was still too weak to get out and use the commode herself. Bert was still helping her to wash, brush her hair and bringing up all her drinks and meals. Flo could see that it was tiring him out, but he would never dream of asking for help. Besides, he knew as well as she did, that the doctors would advise putting Millie in the infirmary and that was something Bert would never agree to.

Flo didn't want to leave him alone, but just as she was saying she must go, the door opened and Ruthie and Ben entered, their faces red from the cold and their eyes glowing.

'I bought some chips for us all, Granda,' Ben said and grinned at her. 'Nice ter see yer, Miss Flo. I'll be into the shop at the weekend.' He winked at her behind Ruthie's back and mouthed, 'Two pink sugar mice.'

Flo smiled and put a finger to her lips. She would make sure that the mice were freshly made and ready for him – and she would make something special for both Robbie's children.

Ruthie was making herself useful, setting out the plates that had been warming above the range. The children were clearly at home in this kitchen and she felt relieved that the elderly couple were not completely alone.

Ben followed her out of the door as she went. 'I want a few more bits for Ruthie, Miss Flo. I've got two shillings to spend on her… Can you make up a little parcel like you do in the window please?'

'Yes, of course I will, Ben,' Flo said, and then because she was anxious: 'If you notice anything about Mr Waters – if he isn't well – you come for me, do you understand? We need to make sure he doesn't do too much…'

'Yeah, I know, he's a bit unsteady sometimes.' Ben nodded wisely. 'I was goin' ter ask if it was all right to come to you, Miss Flo – I'd ask me dad, but he's down in the dumps at the moment, right fed up about things.'

'What happened? I thought he'd got some work at the mission?'

'Yeah, but he walked out – said they didn't trust him but wouldn't tell me why,' Ben said and Flo saw the anxiety on his face. 'He's back standin' on the docks, and he's got a cough. Yesterday, he came home after a couple of hours. He says it's no good – they've blacked his name and he can't get any work…'

'I'm sorry to hear that,' Flo said dismayed. She didn't like to think of Robbie out of work again. 'I'll speak to Mr Hansen about it and ask what happened. I know your father was doin' a good job there…'

'Thanks,' Ben said and grinned at her. 'I'd better get back. We're havin' some of Granny's mustard pickle wiv our chips tonight… it's much better than they have in the shops.'

'You go back then,' Flo told him and smiled at his eagerness. 'Remember, if you need anything at all, come to me. It doesn't matter what time of the day or night…'

'Thanks. Yer all right.' Ben nodded and returned to the warmth of the cottage.

Flo walked briskly through streets that were rapidly getting colder, the pavements slippery under her feet. Smoke from the chimneys mingled with the cold air, making an icy fog that seemed to flow in from the river. She could hear the horns of boats and tugs out on the Thames and they made an eerie backdrop to almost empty streets. Nobody wanted to be about much in this weather, though the lights were on in the pub at the end of Fettle Street. Men who had nowhere else to go would make a half-pint last all night just to keep warm by the landlord's fire.

She was glad to get back to the warmth and light of her home. Even though she had no parlour, her kitchen was familiar and comfortable. Taking her coat off and hanging it on the stand in the hall, Flo donned her crisp white apron and went through to the shop.

Honour was tidying the shelves and wiping the spaces between pretty tins and parcels tied up with cellophane paper.

'Everything all right?'

'Yes, he hasn't rung once,' Honour said. 'I've sold the last sponge and all of your fancies went to one customer. He says he's just discovered us and he wants one of our Christmas cakes, a dozen truffles and a box of coconut ice, some marzipan fancies and six of the sugar mice. He's going to pick them up next week – on the Thursday.'

'A special customer by the sound of it,' Flo replied, pleased with the order. 'We're going to be busy making replacements for those truffles again. I've got an order too...' She smiled as Honour's brow rose. 'Two pink sugar mice and some coconut ice chips, also some of those strawberry creams I made...'

'I didn't think anyone knew about those yet.'

'They don't,' Flo said, 'but I was given an order that I want to make special.'

'You're talkin' about those kids that hang around outside...' Honour teased. 'I think you care more about them than any of your wealthy customers.'

'Yes, perhaps. Ben has two shillings to spend on his sister's Christmas present and I want to make it special for him.'

Honour hesitated, then, 'Roy popped in the shop while you were out,' she said and disappointment was in her eyes. 'He says he can't take me to that dance at the weekend – and he isn't sure when he'll be able to see me again. It's something to do with his job; they're sending him on a course, but he doesn't know where yet or for how long...'

'Oh... I'm sorry,' Flo said. 'That's a shame for you, love. I know you were lookin' forward to that dance...'

'It was a special one for Christmas,' Honour said and her face showed how she felt. 'There was going to be wine and a buffet and prizes... all sorts of stuff especially for Christmas.'

'Roy can't help it,' Flo said, because Honour was clearly upset. 'I'm sure he wouldn't let you down on purpose – not after all he's said to you about gettin' married next summer...'

'No...' Honour said and sighed. 'He promised that he would come round before Christmas and bring me a present...'

'Well, there you are then,' Flo said. 'I know it doesn't mean much, but I'll be glad of your help and your company...'

'You know I like bein' with you,' Honour said, 'but it was fun goin' out with Roy all the time... and I should have loved that dance...'

Flo hoped that Roy didn't intend to dump her daughter, but there was nothing she could do to help. In one way she was glad that Honour would be at home more to help her in the busy run up to Christmas, but in another she felt sorry that Honour had been let down. It must be important if Roy couldn't tell her when he would be back or free to take her out again...

A day or so later, Robbie left the pub where he'd lost his tools the day he'd been accused of theft. The landlord had denied all knowledge of them but promised to ask his customers if anyone had seen them.

'Times are 'ard, mate,' he'd said to Robbie and given him a half on the house. 'I'll put a notice up, but I doubt you'll see them again, they'll probably be down the pawnbroker's by now.'

Robbie agreed gloomily. How could he have been such a damned fool as to lose the very means by which he'd hoped to earn his living? Christmas was creeping closer and he had no money to give his children what they deserved; it was the first Christmas without their mother and he wanted to make it as happy as possible for them, though inevitably they would miss the mother who had loved them.

He sighed as he saw a man selling Christmas trees at the side of the road and wished he could buy one for Ben. He knew his son had promised to fetch a small tree for Millie so at least he and Ruthie would have the pleasure of seeing it dressed, but they ought to have their own.

Robbie set his jaw hard. Somehow he had to find work, even if it was sweeping the roads!

Walking with his head down lost in thoughts, Robbie nearly bumped into a woman. He glanced up swiftly to apologise and became tongue-tied as he saw Flo.

'Sorry, I was in a dream,' he said and saw she was carrying a heavy shopping basket. 'You've got quite a load there – can I carry it home for you?'

She hesitated and then smiled. 'Yes, if you have the time, Mr Graham... it is heavier than I realised and I've walked all the way from the market. I left Honour managing the shop because we needed some extra supplies...'

Robbie took the basket from her. It was heavy but easy enough for him. It felt good to be walking by her side and he asked her about her father and her sister.

'Father seems a little better, but he gets tired and irritable,' she said. 'Honour is lovely. A beautiful, loving girl and I'm blessed to have her.'

There was something in her eyes then that made Robbie feel she was trying to pass a message but he did not know what.

The walk to her home was all too short. As he lingered outside he hoped she might invite him in but she heard the church clock strike and it seemed to stir her.

'Oh, I must go. Honour will be thinkin' me lost and I've got lots to do... thank you for helping me, Mr Graham.'

'Won't you call me Robbie, please.' She nodded shyly and took the basket from him.

'Thank you again...'

Robbie watched as she went in and spoke to the lovely young woman behind the counter. He wondered how old Honour was – perhaps eighteen or nineteen... something tingled at the back of his neck but he ignored it and walked on.

He had to think about finding some work...

13

'The commissioners are coming to look at what's been done here this afternoon,' John said to Nurse Mary as they prepared for the usual influx of visitors that morning. The increasingly bitter weather had ensured that they had a long line waiting outside their door. 'I wish Robbie was still here... That window isn't safe and I'm worried that someone might get in and rob us again.'

'You're not leaving money here now?'

'No, I've opened a bank account. It seemed foolish to waste time putting such small amounts in – but the post office woman was very accommodating. She said if it's only five shillings it's better to be safe than sorry.'

'Why don't you go round and ask if Robbie will come back?' Nurse Mary asked.

'I put the money I owed him through the door in an envelope. He was there but he wouldn't come to the door... I suppose he is still too angry.'

'He didn't throw the money in your face or put it back through our door though...'

'I don't suppose he could afford to,' John said. 'He's unlikely to pick up any work on the docks. They've closed down a couple more bays because there's no work...'

'Just before Christmas?' She looked at him in dismay. 'No wonder that queue outside seems to grow every day. It's a pity we can't give them a Christmas dinner...'

'That's all in hand,' John said and smiled. 'I didn't tell you – but I've managed to raise just under twenty pounds. All I have to do now is ask my little band of helpers to have their own dinner early and arrange for the chickens to be cooked.'

'You've got the money?' Mary was puzzled. 'How did you manage that?'

'I sold some little pieces of silver that belonged to my grandfather. Apparently, a couple of them were quite rare and sought after... vesta cases in the shapes of animals: an elephant, mouse and armadillo – that one was so rare he gave me six pounds for it...' John smiled in satisfaction, because the silver would help make Christmas joyful for those who needed his help. 'That's why I opened the account at once. I couldn't risk losing so much...'

'I should think not. You ought not to have to sell things that belonged to your family, John.' She laid a hand on his arm and gave him a concerned look that revealed far more of her feelings than she intended. John patted her hand kindly but averted his gaze, for although he appreciated her work and her help, only one woman had ever made his heart quicken. He'd loved Flo Hawkins for years, looking forward to her weekly visits to the mission, and he knew that unless he could wed her he would wed no one. He would just go on dedicating his life to the poor and sick, as he always had.

'The church board can't give me any more, Mary. They were debating whether it was viable to keep this place going if the repairs were too expensive... Robbie did so much for just a few pounds. I spent fifteen pounds and two shillings including materials and I'd had an estimate of thirty-five to do half what he did... He was doing such a good job...'

'Then go and tell him so and ask him to come back – or do you want me to? I know I caused this...'

'I don't think he would answer the door to you,' John said. 'I will try though – as much for our sake as his...'

'You'd better get that door open,' Mary said. She watched him go through to open the double doors that let the hungry crowd swarm into the hall and then picked up her nursing cloak and put it on. She had caused this problem by urging John to speak to Robbie about the missing money. It was up to her to put it right – until she did, she had a feeling that the man she cared about most in the world was never going to forgive her.

Mary looked at the grimy street in which Robbie Graham had his home. At the far end some properties had fallen into disrepair, the roof gone on at least one of them, and the windows boarded up. Colourful posters, now fading, advertised the Los Angeles Olympics earlier that year and sat side by side with posters of the new Austin A10 car and union propaganda telling the jobless to unite and march to bring down the government. Filth lay unswept in the gutters and a mangy dog was hunting amongst the rubbish in the hope of a free meal. Some small children were playing with a ball, kicking it relentlessly against the wall of one of the houses and a thin boy dressed in a jacket far too large for him, ragged trousers and boots tied up with string was kicking at an abandoned ginger beer bottle. He stared at Mary as she approached Robbie's house but didn't speak.

Robbie's cottage was right at the end of a row of terraced houses, all of which looked as if they too might be ready for demolition. After the Great War, the clearance of the slums had begun with several ambitious schemes, mostly planned and run by well-meaning do-gooders, often churchmen, who knew little of what they were doing. Families had been turned from their homes, pulling apart whole communities and scattering the inhabitants far and wide. Some people had begun to realise this was not the right way to go about it and to discuss how they might keep neighbours living together but in modern, more habitable dwellings. They had to be affordable and back-to-back terraced houses seemed to be falling out of favour; the popular idea was for high-rise buildings with tier after tier of flats that could accommodate whole neighbourhoods if need be. Only the shortage of money had stopped the plans going ahead full steam.

Nurse Mary wondered what would happen to the sense of community if that happened. These people might live in poor housing and they might be deprived in some senses of the word, but they helped each other. Many of them went in and out of each other's houses without a by-your-leave and nobody cared, because your neighbour was your friend and often your family. Some of these people would prefer to keep their neighbours and sacrifice the gleaming white bathroom and efficient range found in the new flats; most of them would struggle to afford the rent even if one was allocated to them.

Standing outside Robbie's house, Mary realised that this was probably one of the few privately owned houses in the area. At some time an attempt to update it had been made, and the wood surrounding its windows looked newer and less rotten than most of its neighbours. It had a small garden, just enough to plant a few rose bushes along the front path, and a bright blue door. Someone had once cared about this place, because the door was only a few years old and the paint was still good.

Mary knocked and waited. She heard something inside and guessed that Robbie was in, but he didn't want to answer the door so she opened the letter box and called through it.

'Please answer me, Mr Graham – this is important...'

She heard another sound and then the door was reluctantly opened and Robbie stood there. His hair hadn't seen a brush for days, he needed a shave and his clothes looked as if he'd slept in them. He coughed and she heard the wheezing sound, realising that he was unwell.

'I've got some medicine for that,' she said. 'If I could come in, Mr Graham...'

'Why? Do yer think you'll find yer money here?' Robbie growled.

'No, I'm sure it isn't,' she said. 'I should apologise for that, Mr Graham. John Hansen said it couldn't be you – but I insisted he asked because you saw me put the tin away. I was wrong to doubt you and I'm very sorry.'

'You shouldn't jump to conclusions. Just because I'm out of work doesn't make me a thief...' Robbie said, but he was no longer angry. His anger had worn itself out standing in line on the docks and knowing that he had no hope of being picked even if a ship came in.

'I know that and I have regretted it – especially as we still need your services,' Mary said. 'The Church people are coming this afternoon to inspect the work – and there's a window that needs doin'. The latch is broken and anyone could get in...'

'I was goin' to finish it after I'd done that floorboard...'

'Could I ask you to do it as a favour to John? He'll be in trouble if they see it like that... and it wasn't him who thought you might have taken that money.'

Robbie hesitated, then, 'I would help yer – but I lost me tools on the way home that night...'

'Oh...' Mary was taken by surprise. 'What do you need?'

'At the least, a hammer, screwdriver, nails... that's probably all for that window.'

'Right, well, I think I can find those for you,' she said. 'I'll meet you at the mission in an hour. I have what you need at home... and I'll give you something for that cough when you arrive.'

'OK,' Robbie said. 'I was grateful for the money Mr Hansen put through the door. I haven't earned a penny since...'

'Well, I know he'll be grateful to have you back... and perhaps we can ask round, see if anyone found your tools.'

'I doubt if they've been handed in. Those tools were worth a few quid,' Robbie said regretfully. 'I bought the best when I had money in my pocket... I'll never be able to afford them again.' In these hard times, it was unlikely that anyone would hand them in.

'Well, we'll ask and see,' Mary said. 'Some folk have a conscience… and I want to thank you for showing your forgiveness, Mr Graham.'

'The name is Robbie.' Robbie ran his fingers through his hair, conscious of what he looked like. 'I was maybe a mite hasty… It hurt me pride…'

'You're an honest man, Robbie Graham, and to be accused of theft was an insult. I am the one who should apologise and I do…'

Robbie shook his head. 'You're a good woman. I know what yer do fer others, Nurse Mary. I'll shave and meet yer at the mission in an hour…'

Mary left him, a little smile on her lips. She had a hammer and a screwdriver at home, but she had just thought of someone else who might have much more and surely didn't need them any longer.

'It's just a loan for a while,' Flo said to her father. 'Mr Graham lost his tools and he needs them to continue his work. He will give them back to you once his own have been found…'

'Is that Robert Graham?' Her father looked at her for several minutes and then inclined his head. 'Nurse Mary waiting for yer answer, is she? You can tell her that I shan't need them again. He might as well keep them…'

'Are you sure?' Flo was astounded because she'd thought her father would turn the request down. 'That's really good of you... thank you so much.'

'Mebbe it was owed,' he said. 'You know where they are – go on, get them out and give them to her. It's fer a good cause after all...'

'Yes, it is,' Flo said and bent to kiss his cheek on impulse.

She almost ran down the stairs in her excitement. Nurse Mary was sitting in the kitchen, drinking a cup of tea and eating a fancy cake. She looked up as Flo carried the large, much-worn leather workbag into the kitchen and placed it on a chair.

'Dad says Mr Graham can keep the tools,' she said. 'He will never need them again. I suppose they are worth something, but he says it's owed – I don't know what he means, but tell Mr Graham my father says it's for a good cause, because he's working for the mission.'

'Yes, I shall,' Nurse Mary said and picked up the bag. 'This is very heavy. The tools in here must be worth quite a bit of money.'

'My father collected them over a lifetime of work,' Flo said. 'Thank you for comin' to me, Nurse Mary.'

'I should be the one to thank you – and I will certainly call in to see Mrs Waters, as you suggest. I can take a look at Mr Waters at the same time. I doubt he'll let me examine him, but I shall know if he's unwell and hiding it.'

'Thank you,' Flo said. 'Can you manage that bag on your own?'

'Yes, just about. I shall catch the bus from across the road,' Nurse Mary replied and lifted the bag. 'I usually walk, but this time I think the fare will be well worth a few pennies…'

Flo saw her to the door and then washed her hands and changed her apron for a clean one, because the tools had been dusty. She went through into the shop and saw that a small queue had formed. People were beginning to buy their Christmas treats and the home-made cakes and sweets were selling well despite the general shortage of money. It was hard for some of the locals to pay their rent and put food on the table every day, but most of them saved a few pennies in a Christmas club and now they were spending them on what their loved ones liked most…

Flo and Honour worked side by side until the shop was empty.

'I thought we would never get through the queue,' Honour said. 'What did Nurse Mary want? Did she come to see Dad?'

'In a manner of speaking,' Flo said. 'She wanted to borrow Dad's tools – he had a big bag filled with all kinds of hammers, chisels and other things. They were needed for the mission and Dad let her have them just like that...'

'How odd,' Honour said and laughed. 'Shall we close for lunch today or shall we take it in turns?'

'You go first,' Flo said as she saw one of their better-off clients heading towards the shop. 'I think we'll keep open just in case. We must make the most of the trade now because no one will have any money for weeks afterwards...'

In the weeks after Christmas the shop would see only a handful of customers and they would spend only pennies on a few buns or the delicious soft rolls Honour baked and sometimes filled with cheese or ham. She went through to the kitchen to make herself a sandwich just as the door opened and a gentleman in an overcoat with an astrakhan collar entered.

'Ah, Miss Hawkins,' he said. 'I wanted to buy some of your marzipan fancies, a box of six sugar mice and perhaps I could try a few of those peppermint creams for myself. They are fresh made, are they not?'

'Yes; it's a new venture for us. I'm only just beginning to make them and they're not quite all the same shape, but do try one first, Mr Rolf...' She offered a little dish and he took one, popping it into his mouth. His eyes rolled and his mouth curved with pleasure.

'Delicious. I've never tasted anything like that. My grandmother used to make her own sweets when I was a boy – strawberry, violet and peppermint creams – the mint ones were always my favourite. I will take a box of those please. After all, it is Christmas…'

'Yes, or it will be soon enough,' Flo said and smiled at him. He was softly-spoken, in his forties and a frequent visitor to her shop. 'Would you like some of the almond macaroons for your wife?'

'Yes, please. How well you know me,' he said and looked pleased. 'It is a privilege to shop here, Miss Hawkins. I don't know anywhere in the West End that I like half as well… and to think I might never have found you if I hadn't come here on business for my factory…'

Flo nodded, because he'd told her the same thing many times. He was one of her regulars, one of the few that would continue to buy in the weeks after Christmas when others could not afford it.

'Are you on business today, sir?'

'In a way, though not my own. I sit on the board for the Church Commissioners and I'm on my way to the mission in Oldfield Street – do you know it?'

'Yes, I do,' Flo said. 'I help out there sometimes in the evening.'

'Well, well, what a small world,' he said and took out a pound note, placing it on the counter.

Flo picked it up and took his change from the till.

'No, no, you keep it. Give it to the mission next time if you wish.'

'Yes, I shall – because they need money for the Christmas lunch,' Flo said. 'Unfortunately some money was stolen and they will need all the help they can get this year...'

'Indeed, well, we must see what we can do,' he said, tipped his smart beaver hat to her and walked from the shop.

14

Robbie swallowed a dose of the cough medicine and went straight to work on the broken window, fitting the new catch he'd bought when he began the work. It seemed to have been damaged further since he was here and he wondered if it had been used by someone intent on robbing the mission more than once. When he arrived, Nurse Mary had handed him a tool bag and smiled, saying she hoped it would help. Robbie hadn't been able to believe it when he saw the amount of tools inside and the quality of them; they were equally as good as those he'd lost, though most had clearly been used for many years. All were still useable and the worn handles felt smooth in his hands.

John was busy in the dining room, overlooking the distribution of food and serving the mugs of tea himself, when Robbie walked in. He noticed that Mick had just been given a bowl of soup and some bread and nodded to the young lad. At least he wouldn't starve today.

He'd been working for a few minutes when Mick came up to him, watching him work. Smiling, Robbie asked him how he was. The lad said he was all right, but Robbie saw a little bruise on his wrist as he picked up one of the tools.

'How did you do this, lad?'

'I knocked meself,' Mick said, but his gaze veered away.

'No, you didn't,' Robbie said sternly. 'Was it yer father?'

'Nah, not 'im – the other bugger...' Mick said and jerked his head towards the hall. 'He comes here some days... that's why I came through to you. He grabs me and I 'ate 'im... I daren't go home if he's there...'

'Sit over there and wait fer me,' Robbie said. 'Yer can come back wiv me when I've finished and wait fer yer dad to come home.'

Mick thanked him and sat on the floor watching as he got on with his work. Robbie soon had his small task in hand and was just finishing the last screw when John entered.

'Thank you for coming,' he said and looked relieved as he saw the window had been skilfully repaired. 'I hope we can be friends again?'

'Yes, I don't see why not,' Robbie said. 'I was angry when I left last week but I'd almost finished my work here anyway. Thank you for putting the money through my door. I couldn't afford to refuse it.'

'It was yours, well earned,' John said. 'We do have more work here, Robbie – but I need permission from the board, because it is a big job. I think most of the rafters in the roof are rotten…'

'That will be a huge job,' Robbie said. 'I think it would need two men and take them the best part of a month – it's liftin' the heavy beams see.'

'You could find someone to help, I'm sure.' John smiled at him. 'If I can get the money and permission…'

'There are plenty of skilled men lookin' for a job,' Robbie said. 'Why me? You don't owe me anything, Mr Hansen. Nurse Mary explained – and it was only natural you should ask. If someone stole from you, you needed to discover who and how. I shouldn't have been so ready to take offence.'

'We think we know how it happened. I left my jacket with the keys to the office hanging over a chair back. Someone could have sneaked in after both you and Nurse Mary left that afternoon, gone into the office and taken the cash box. I didn't check it was there before I locked the office door. It never occurred to me that anyone would touch the mission's money. Everyone who comes here is always so grateful for what we do…'

'When a man is desperate, he might do anythin',' Robbie said but frowned. 'Yet I think it's mostly those who don't care about anythin' or anyone who steal

– especially from a place like this. Anyone could have got in this window and I noticed that the catch had been worked looser than I remembered it bein'.'

'We've lost other things since you stopped comin',' John said. He looked at Mick, but the lad was fiddling with Robbie's tools and did not appear to be listening. 'I did think about the window and I wedged it shut, but in the morning it was open again – and we had some clothes taken. There was no money, because I decided to bank it every day after the cash box was stolen – but I'd been given a donation of good clothing. I left it in Nurse Mary's office, because she sorts it out and we try to sell some of it, because we need every penny.'

'Yes, I understand that, that's why it angered me when you thought I might have taken your money. I know what it's like to go without, Mr Hansen. I wouldn't take another man's bread…'

'Excuse me…' A voice from behind them made them both turn to look at the tall well-dressed gentleman who had entered. His eyes went from one to the other and he extended his hand to John. 'Reverend Hansen, I imagine. I've come to look at the work you've had done – and to discuss the possibility of having the roof repaired…'

John went forward with his hand extended. 'Mr Rolf? I'm John Hansen and this is Robert Graham. He is the gentleman who has been seeing to our repairs. He finished the last window this morning and I told him about the state of the rafters…'

'Ah yes, Mr Graham.' The newcomer shook hands with Robbie. 'Yes, I'm pleased to meet you – have you had a chance to look at the extent of the damage to the rafters?'

'Not personally, but it is a large roof. I told Mr Hansen that it would probably take two men the best part of a month to repair – and would need quite a bit of timber. However, my advice is that you should pay your workman for his labour and buy in the timber yourselves; that way you'll get a good job done cheaper.'

'Yes, I imagine so.' Mr Rolf looked thoughtful. He turned to John. 'Perhaps you would be good enough to show me what has already been repaired and tell me what you feel is the minimum that needs to be done to ensure that the mission is safe for a few years...'

'I'll go and leave you to it.' Robbie beckoned to Mick. 'Come along, lad. Thank you for the work, Mr Hansen...'

'Nice to meet you. I'll leave Mr Hansen to give you my conclusions on the project...' Mr Rolf said and nodded, his expression giving nothing away.

Robbie picked up his tools and went through to Nurse Mary's room, Mick one step behind him. She was putting away some rolls of bandages and he could smell the strong odour of disinfectant.

'I wanted to thank you for the loan of your tools,' he said. 'I don't know where they came from but they've been loved and looked after...'

'I don't want them back,' she said. 'I asked someone I knew if you could borrow them and he said that he would never use them again – and told me that you could keep them...'

'I couldn't possibly accept.' Robbie frowned. 'These are worth money. Quite a bit of money...'

'Miss Hawkins said her father was quite clear that you were to keep them – something about it was owed, but neither she nor I understood that. I dare say he just wanted them to go to a good home...'

'You mean Miss Flo Hawkins' father owned these tools?' Robbie hesitated. A part of him wanted to throw them back at the man who had so casually given away such a precious gift, but another part of him held back. His pride and temper had led him to make one mistake, and if he was to work as a carpenter he needed tools like these. Robbie's own had been lost the day he got drunk and no one would hand them in; they would be sold to buy someone drink or cigarettes or perhaps food for a family.

'You should think before you give them back to him,' Nurse Mary was saying. 'You're a skilled man, Robert Graham, but you can't work without tools.'

'Thank you for gettin' them for me,' Robbie said, surprised that a man who had always hated him should give him such a gift but feeling he should repay it. 'I must find a way to repay him...'

'Perhaps you might think of visiting the poor man,' Nurse Mary said. 'From what I hear, he hasn't had a visitor other than the doctor or his daughters for years…'

'Yes… I mean, I'm sorry to hear that.' Robbie picked up the bag of tools and left.

Mick walked quickly to keep up with him. Robbie had almost forgotten that he'd told the lad he would take him home, then noticed Mick was having trouble keeping up and slowed his steps.

'I've got somewhere to go first, lad, but you can keep me company.'

Mick grinned but didn't say much, then, 'I reckon you're a skilled man, Mr Graham. I should like to do what you do.'

'It takes a long time to learn. I learned my trade in the army…'

Mick nodded, drinking it all in. Robbie relaxed a little. He knew that he would need to find a way of repaying Flo's father for his gift. His pride told him to take them right back this minute and let that be the finish of it, but if he was offered the work at the mission he would need all these tools… and even if he wasn't given the job, he was never going back to standing in line on the docks. He was a skilled man and he'd proved that he'd lost none of the flair and artistry he brought to his work.

He walked past the labour exchange, seeing the queue

of men outside hoping for the chance of a job. Robbie could go and sign on, as he had many times in the past, or he could try round all the small businesses that abounded in the busy streets. Most of them were just about managing to eke a living in these troubled times and couldn't afford much in the way of modernising or refitting their old premises, but repairs could save a place from falling into dereliction. If he took his time, just carried his tools with him and asked if there were any small repairs that needed to be done, he might earn enough to get by. A lot of people put up with a window that didn't shut or a door that stuck but a man at the door ready to work for the price of his labour and do the job here and now might be lucky.

It was a risk, because he had only a few pennies in his pocket, but it would buy the kids some pie and mash for their supper. If everyone turned him down he would earn nothing... and yet if he didn't try he would always feel a failure. If he wanted to repay Flo's father for the tools he had to earn some money, and more than the odd couple of bob he got for doing a bit of cleaning or lifting on the docks.

He saw a baker's shop just in front of him and noticed that the sign above it was hanging off and in danger of slipping. It would take him perhaps half an hour to fix and he would charge two bob for his labour. Nothing ventured, nothing gained, he thought as he went round to the back of the bakery and saw the door was open at the back. It was a split door and he saw the top half hung drunkenly from its hinges. He could fix that for another couple of bob.

Lifting his head, he walked to the door and poked his head over it. A ruddy-cheeked man turned to look at him, his arms floured right up past his elbows.

'What can I do fer yer, mate?' he asked cheerfully.

'It's what I might be able to do fer you,' Robbie said and nodded at the door. 'I could fix this and the sign above yer window – two bob each. What do yer say?'

'What's that lad hanging around fer?'

'He runs my errands,' Robbie said and Mick grinned for all he was worth.

'Get on with it,' the baker said. 'I've been meanin' ter 'ave that bloody sign fixed fer months, but the builder charges an arm and a leg. If yer charge the same rates as yer've quoted, I've got a few more jobs inside an all… but any fancy bills and yer out the door; understand? I'll give yer what yer asked but no more.'

'I shan't ask more than I've told yer,' Robbie said. 'I'll take this door down and fix it and then I'll borrow yer ladder and do the sign…' He looked at Mick. 'Stand on the bottom rung, lad, and hold it steady for me.'

'Yeah, thanks, Mr Graham,' Mick said his grin even wider.

*

Robbie was whistling as he walked home that evening, Mick still tagging at his heels. He'd earned four half a crowns that afternoon, doing five separate small jobs for the baker, whose name was Ted Green. Robbie had been glad of the work, because it was more than half what he could get on the dole for a week and he'd earned it in a few hours. The baker had been delighted with the price and asked him if he wanted more work. Robbie assured him he did and Ted told him he would be in touch in the new year – and he'd given Mick a bread roll and winked at him.

'I know a few people round here with small jobs that need doin' fer a fair price. Most of the builders don't want ter know unless it's a big job – and if they come out fer small repairs they charge a day's work. Yer a fair man, Robbie, and I'm glad we've met. I'll spread the word.'

Robbie had thanked him, pocketed the money, which was more than he'd earned in a day for months, apart from the few pounds he'd earned at the mission. He'd charged John ten shillings a day for his work, but he'd given good value and he'd done all the work needed in less than two weeks. A builder would probably have been there for a month, if Ted Green were to be believed. Ted had been grateful. Robbie wasn't sure whether he could find enough work to keep him going by asking round at the doors, but it was worth a try – and he felt better about himself than he had in a long time.

Passing the cake shop, Robbie stopped to look in the window. He could afford to buy a couple of those sticky buns with the pink icing, and Mick had helped out, handing tools and standing on the ladder, and Robbie would buy him a bun and give him threepence for himself – and, while in the shop, he would take the opportunity to thank Flo Hawkins and her father for the tools.

He opened the shop door and entered. Flo was serving a lady with a box of her rum truffles. She tied the ribbon on a white box and took the money, giving change and smiling at the lady as she left before turning to Robbie. He saw the way her eyes changed, became uncertain and nervous, and his heart ached with regret. If only he hadn't been such a cowardly fool all those years ago...

'I wanted to thank your father for the tools,' Robbie spoke first because Flo seemed to be struggling to find the right words. 'I finished the work at the mission, but Nurse Mary said I could keep them – is that right?'

'Yes, my father said he no longer needed or wanted them...'

'I'm very grateful,' Robbie said. 'I earned some money doing repairs for a baker this afternoon. If I can pay for the tools a little at a time I should like to...'

'They were only going to rust away in the cupboard under the stairs,' Flo said and she was smiling. 'We don't want anythin', Robbie, truly. When I heard yours were lost, I asked Dad and he agreed…'

'Thank him for me. Tell him I'm very grateful.'

'You could go through to the kitchen and tell him yourself if you wish,' Flo said. 'I'll be closing soon and I'll come through when I've tidied up…'

'I wanted to buy those two sticky buns in the window first – and what would you like, Mick?' Robbie asked. Mick indicated a coconut pyramid. 'That one for Mick please.'

Flo was looking at Mick and handed him his coconut pyramid in a bag, then winked and slipped in a rock bun. Mick grinned but didn't speak. 'Those buns are popular with all the kids, and the sugar mice. We're sellin' so many of those, Honour can hardly keep up… but your Ben has bought two for his sister.'

'Ben earns a bit of pocket money runnin' errands,' Robbie said, hesitated, then: 'If you're sure yer father won't be upset I'll go through and thank him.'

Flo put the buns in a little bag for him and took the sixpence he offered, ringing it into the till. 'He will be pleased to have a visitor, I think…' She turned as Honour entered. 'Here is my sister come to help me clear up for the evening.' She turned the 'closed' sign on the shop door. 'I'll let you out of the side door when you've spoken to Dad…' She gave Mick a little look as he paused. 'You too, Mick…'

She lifted the flap in the counter and invited them through. Robbie noticed that it was a little awkward because the hinge was loose.

'I could fix that before I go,' he said. 'That hinge just needs a screw tightening. If you like, I'll do it after I've spoken to your father…'

'Oh, would you?' Honour said and smiled at him. 'It is the kind of thing my dad used to do all the time and it's not something you can call a builder out for, is it?'

'No, you need a handyman like me,' Robbie said and smiled at her.

Mr Hawkins was just trying to stand up as Robbie entered the kitchen and he saw him sway and almost fall, going quickly to support him until he was steady.

'Thanks…' he grunted. 'I'm a bit tippy on me feet these days. I wanted ter get upstairs without the girls havin' ter lug me up there…' His eyes narrowed. 'Do I know yer?'

'I'll give yer a hand if yer like,' Robbie said. 'I came in to thank yer for the tools you let me have. I can pay a few bob at a time once I get goin'. I'm startin' up as a carpenter-cum-handyman – fixing all the little jobs that never get done because people put off askin' a tradesman to come out.'

Flo's father gave another grunt. 'Yer don't have ter pay me fer the tools. I reckon I owe yer – and yer know why, so don't ask and don't tell her either…' He jerked his head towards the door that led into the shop. 'I'll make me peace with me daughter in me own way – but it can't come from you.'

'I don't know what yer mean,' Robbie said, but of course he did. He would never forget the day he'd been told that if he ever went near Flo again he would be beaten to a pulp.

'She don't want the likes of you,' Flo's father had told him. 'Come near her again and I'll beat yer head in... now go...'

Robbie had gone, shuffling his feet, his head down, beaten, bruised and defeated, because Flo didn't want to see him. He'd sent a note and asked her to meet him and her father had come in her place.

So Robbie had gone. He'd left London and joined the army, because the war was raging and it was the only place left for a young man with no family and a broken heart – and, worse than that, the shadow of failure. He'd let down the girl he'd loved with all his heart and he would never cease to regret it.

Looking into Mr Hawkins' eyes now, Robbie saw guilt and the anger rushed up inside him, but then he saw the hurt and pain. Whatever he might have done, whatever lies he'd told, Mr Hawkins had paid for them.

Holding the anger inside, Robbie took the weight of the fragile old man's body and carried him up the stairs, placing him on the edge of the bed as carefully as he would a child.

'Do yer need the commode?' he asked, because helping this man was helping Flo.

'I'm all right, thanks,' Mr Hawkins said and then clasped his wrist as he turned to leave. 'You won't tell her it was me that ruined her life?'

'What do yer mean?' Robbie asked, genuinely puzzled.

'Yer knew – yer must have known she was havin' a kid?'

'Yes, I knew – but I thought she must have lost it… or did she have to give it up? Did you make her give the baby away?' Robbie's gaze narrowed intently.

An odd smile twisted the old man's mouth. 'Yer've got another daughter, Robbie Graham. Most folk think she's Flo's sister – but I thought you would've twigged the truth afore now…'

It was like a lightning strike. Robbie felt as if he'd been punched in the stomach, the way he had more than seventeen years earlier when the fragile man sitting on the edge of his bed had been strong and had taken him by surprise, hitting him on the back of the neck and as he staggered, punching him to the ground and then standing over him to kick his head and face until he was barely able to see from one eye and his head was whirling.

'You mean… that lovely girl is my daughter?' Robbie was astounded, his thoughts in utter confusion. And yet he'd felt something that morning he'd carried Flo's basket and watched her talking to Honour. It had occurred to him that she must be about eighteen, which is what she would be if their loving had made a child. How could it be that all this time he had a daughter he'd known nothing about? Because no breath of scandal had ever touched Flo, he'd assumed that she'd been mistaken and there was no child. Now, he was being told that for all those years he'd been away in the army he'd had a daughter.

'Yer ain't stupid. Work it out. Flo and her mother tried to hide it from me and the world. I was fooled fer a bit, because I was away and the babe was born when I got back – but I soon cottoned on and then I found the letter you sent Flo through the door.'

Robbie stared at him, the gorge rising in his throat. He'd blamed himself all these years for running like a coward. He hadn't been much older than Flo and, at first, he'd been scared of the responsibility of a child and marriage, but when he'd got over his blue funk, he'd tried to see Flo again, but she wasn't in the shop and she never went anywhere. In the end he'd sent a letter – and this wretched man had intercepted it and waited for him, giving him a beating that had left him too bemused to think.

He'd gone then and when he'd finally returned to the area, married with a young son, he'd tried to discover if Flo ever had a child and all he'd found out was that she had a sister and he'd accepted it… What a fool he'd been all these years but Flo's father had been as much to blame and suddenly his anger boiled over.

'It would serve yer right if I went right down there and told her what you did…'

'What good would that do now?' Flo's father asked. 'She has put yer behind her, Robbie Graham. She lives for this shop and her daughter – and she'd do anything to stop Honour knowing the truth. She wouldn't thank you fer tellin' her, believe me.'

'So I'm supposed to just ignore it?' He felt a pain in his chest, making it difficult to think or breathe.

'That's what you've done for the past eighteen years. What's different now?'

It was the truth and Robbie couldn't deny it. He should have contacted Flo long ago and asked her what happened – and told her that he'd never forgotten her, but now… it was useless, just as her father said.

'So what then?'

'Just leave us be – at least until I'm dead. Don't throw those tools back in my face. It wouldn't hurt me, but it's yer only chance… and I do owe yer that much.'

Robbie stared at him in silence for several seconds. Giving them back would ease his pride, but the tools were his only chance of earning a decent living.

'You're right, I am owed,' he said. 'I'll take the

tools – and I shan't tell Flo what you did, but one day I want Honour to know the truth. When I have something to give her – something to be proud of…'

Robbie turned and walked from the bedroom. His emotions were churning because he wanted to tell Flo that her father had sent him away when he'd offered to marry her. He wanted Honour to know that he'd never known she was his… but he couldn't speak, not because that old man had given him the means to win his pride and a future of some kind, but because he was a fragile old man and Robbie couldn't destroy what little life he had left.

'You helped Dad upstairs,' Honour said, coming into the kitchen with a plate of cakes. Mick was sitting at the table drinking a glass of milk and eating a piece of sponge cake. 'Would you like to stay for a cup of tea and a couple of these rock buns? We can't sell them tomorrow, because they will not be perfectly fresh by mornin'.' She laughed; her cheeks pink. 'That sounds awful, but you offered to do the hinge and I wanted to thank you – I assure you they are perfectly fresh now.'

Robbie felt a glow of pride. She was a lovely girl and she was his! He longed to claim her but knew he must wait until he had the right. Instead, he just smiled warmly at her. She was his daughter and the thought filled him with pride and love, and he wanted to be able to embrace her and show her affection.

'I'm sure they are, Honour, and I'd love one, but I can't stop to eat it. I'll just fix that screw and then I must get home for my kids – Ben and Ruthie.'

'Look, I'll put these rock cakes in a bag for you and the children,' Honour said. 'It was so kind of you to put Dad to bed... it isn't easy for us to get him upstairs and he insists on coming down most days...'

'I expect it gets lonely up there on his own,' Robbie said. 'I'll fix that screw and then come back this way...'

He went swiftly through to the shop just as Flo was tidying the last few bits and pieces. Robbie searched through his bag and took out the right size screwdriver. It took seconds to mend the counter.

'Thank you for calling in and doing that,' Flo said. 'Shall you be at the mission for the Christmas bazaar on Friday evening? You should bring Ben and Ruthie. There will be games and prizes for the children... and you should come too, Mick.'

'I'm not sure... I might,' Robbie said and smiled at her, because the thought of seeing her there was tempting. Mick just grinned and patted his stomach. 'How long has your father been so ill, Miss Hawkins?'

'He had the second stroke nearly a year ago, and the doctor thought he might die, but he seems a little better in himself recently... though he's not good on his feet.'

'Very unsteady, I would say,' Robbie said. 'He ought not to come down on his own. Do you have a downstairs parlour?'

'No, it's just the shop, which was once a parlour, I suppose. We have the large kitchen, which we needed for our business – and our bedrooms upstairs. We don't have much time for sitting anyway.' She frowned. 'It isn't ideal for Dad, but it's the best I can do...'

'Yes, I expect so,' Robbie said. 'Well, I must go. My children will be expecting me to fetch them, and I've got to feed this lad and then see him safe home. Perhaps we'll all come to the mission on Friday... if I can manage it...'

Flo nodded, smiled and walked him to the back door. Honour reminded him to take all his cakes. He accepted them from her hand, smiled and left, his thoughts in turmoil.

He'd given his word that he would say nothing while the old man lived – but one day he wanted Honour to know that she had a father who would love her, if she would give him the chance. Yet before that he had to make himself worthy – of her and of Ben and Ruthie too...

Robbie knew that whatever he did he could never redeem himself in Flo's eyes and the thought of what she must have gone through, having the child in secret and always pretending to be her own daughter's sister... Robbie felt his heart bleed for her and everything she had lost because of him – because of a foolish young man's desire and his subsequent cowardice. He was the one who had ruined Flo's life, not her father!

No, there was no hope of Flo ever truly forgiving him, but perhaps Honour would one day...

15

Would Robbie bring his children to the mission that Friday? The thought made her heart flutter a little, because having him in her shop and her home had made her realise how much she'd missed by not having him there all these years. Walking back with him from the market the other morning had made her realise how pleasant it was to talk with him about little things and his smile made her feel happier.

Flo looked forward to her one evening a week at the mission. She hadn't missed going since the first time John Hansen had asked if she could help out, except for the few times she'd been ill or either her father or Honour had needed her.

Honour was a little quiet as Flo prepared to leave that evening. She'd been tying a silky headscarf over her hair to keep it from blowing all over the place and caught sight of her daughter's forlorn face in the mirror behind her.

'What's wrong, love?' she asked, turning to look at Honour. 'I said you could ask Roy round in the evening while I'm out...'

'He hasn't been into the shop for ages,' Honour said and sniffed. 'He said he would be away for a while and I haven't seen him since... but he promised to write and it's more than a week and I haven't had a letter...'

'Roy is a soldier,' Flo said. 'Maybe he's been put on extra duty – it isn't always his choice, Honour. You went out nearly every night for a week. Perhaps he needs to save his money for something...'

'We often just walked or had a drink. I didn't want him to spend lots of money on me...' Honour said and her eyes didn't meet Flo's. 'Do you think he has thrown me over?'

'Well, for a girl who was all set to get married next summer, you don't sound very sure of him.' Flo touched her arm. 'Roy seemed sincere to me, dearest, and he's been courtin' you for a while now. Give it a few more days before you start breakin' your heart. After all, if he doesn't come back he's not worth your tears...'

'You don't know what it's like to love someone so much you can't bear not to be near them,' Honour said sharply. 'This shop is your life...'

'Yes, it has had to be,' Flo said and turned away before her own tears welled up. Honour had no idea of how she was hurting her. 'Well, listen out for Dad please. I'll be back by a quarter to eleven...'

Picking up her coat, Flo hurried from the house before she said something she might regret. Honour was upset and hadn't meant to hurt Flo. Perhaps it wouldn't have hurt so much if Robbie hadn't come back into her life. Seeing him in her home, talking to him and being near enough to touch, had set off memories she'd buried deep inside her, and she'd spent half that night crying into her pillow. If only he hadn't gone off and deserted her when she was sixteen, giving her no choice but to do what her mother had told her was the only way.

She remembered the look of disappointment in her mother's eyes when she'd discovered Flo being sick in the toilet, the way she'd dictated how things would be in a cold, stern manner that made Flo freeze inside.

'I can't believe that my daughter would do such a thing,' she'd told Flo in her first shock. 'Behaving like a filthy little whore – and sneaking out to meet some beast of a man, who doesn't even have the decency to stand by you! I hope you're ashamed of yourself, Flo, because I am – but you won't shame me before the world. You'll stay in this house and out of sight until the child is born and I shall let everyone think I'm carrying my husband's child – and that's the way it will always be. Your father is away working up north. He'll believe it when I tell him we're havin' another child and so will everyone else. Once you've got over the birth I'll let you work in the shop sometimes, but you will go nowhere without me. I'll take you to church to beg for forgiveness, but you've shown you can't be trusted, so you will stay in this house and work. No respectable man would want you in his life to shame him with a bastard child. So I'll protect you from your father's anger and the scorn of the rest of the world, but you will never go dancing again. I was a fool to spoil you by giving you freedom and nice clothes.'

Flo had felt the shame of letting her mother down. It stung far more than her father's belt would have done, and sometimes, when she'd seen him looking at her oddly, she'd thought she would prefer his anger to her mother's cold disgust. Looking back on her life now, she wished she'd defied her mother and let the world know that she had a child, but it was too late now. She'd been a young and very frightened girl when Robbie left her to face her disgrace alone, and now that she was old enough to do as she pleased there was nothing left but the shop and caring for her father and Honour.

Walking into the warmth and noise of the mission, Flo's spirits lifted and she forgot the pain that had been so sharp earlier. She had so much to be thankful for when compared with the people she saw here – people dressed in patched and worn clothing, who often had nothing to eat and nowhere to sleep but the streets or, at best, a hostel. The food and pleasure this evening of entertainment gave them meant everything and Flo felt glad to be a part of it.

'Miss Hawkins,' John Hansen greeted her warmly as always. 'How good of you to come out on such a cold night!'

'I wouldn't have missed it for the world,' Flo said and smiled. He was such a kind man, to her and to all the people he helped. She had always liked him and working here was a pleasure. 'You're full to bursting tonight...'

'It's all the children,' John told her, his eyes sparkling with enthusiasm. 'Some weeks we just get the card players and the tombola enthusiasts but tonight everyone knows it's the Christmas party.'

Flo looked about her. Paper decorations had been looped about the dreary hall, brightening its dull greyness, and the little Christmas tree in the far corner was hung with tinsel and lit with tiny wax candles that flickered in the slight breeze from the door. A large sack of what looked suspiciously like presents was set by the tree and she knew that somehow John had raised the money for this evening as well as the Christmas dinner for the homeless.

'How did you do all this?' she asked, looking at the plates of sausage rolls, little cakes and sandwiches.

'People were kind – like you, Miss Hawkins. Your Christmas cake has pride of place, but other people helped – and I had a donation of twenty-five pounds, more than the sum we lost. It enabled me to buy the small gifts I had hoped to provide this evening and still keep to my plans for the Christmas dinner.'

'That was kind,' Flo said, because few people in this area had the money to give a donation of that size. A cake or a few sausage rolls or perhaps half a crown, but twenty-five pounds was a small fortune. No wonder John was looking so pleased with life. 'How extraordinary that you should receive such a gift...'

'Mr Rolf said that someone had told him of our loss and he wanted to help in a personal way. He is a businessman and sits on the board of the Church Commissioners, but I had never met him until the other day when he came to inspect the work we'd had done.'

'Mr Rolf...' Flo felt a little uncomfortable, because she recalled telling her customer of the mission's loss. 'Well, it was very generous – and I'm sure you are grateful to him.'

'Yes, I am and not just because of the money. He told me that he thought the mission was even more important now than it had ever been – and he promised that he will recommend the roof repairs be funded.'

'I didn't realise that you needed repairs to your roof...'

'Very few people do,' John told her ruefully. 'It isn't just a case of a few slates falling off. The rafters have rotted and it will mean a major overhaul. I hadn't dared to ask until recently, because I feared they might try to close us down – or move the mission to another building. Mr Rolf was very understanding and it seems he hates to see the old buildings torn down and so we have an ally in him...'

'Well, that is wonderful,' Flo said and looked about her again. 'I'd better go through to the kitchen and see what I can do to help.'

'You mustn't spend all your evening in there,' John told her. 'You should come and join in the carols later, Miss Hawkins. It will be after Father Christmas has given the presents to the children...'

'I shall come and watch that,' Flo said. Christmas was surely for the children and the children here this evening would not receive gifts from their parents; unless they came to the mission they might not even have a cooked dinner on Christmas Day. 'It looks as if most of the food has been donated by your helpers tonight so I'll just help with the washing up...'

She heard a shriek of laughter and turned to see some children playing a game of trying to stick the tail on the donkey blindfold. She caught sight of Mick, Ruthie and Ben chasing some balloons and felt pleased that Robbie had brought his children. Her eyes eventually discovered him beneath a red suit with a hood and a long white beard. Clearly, he'd been dragooned into playing Father Christmas for the children that evening. John Hansen was very good at getting people to do things for the mission, but Flo was a little surprised that Robbie had been drawn into his net.

Most of the children wore shabby clothes, some with holes in their boots. One or two had bare feet, lank greasy hair that was thick with nits and grimy faces. She felt tears sting her eyes. There was so much to cause concern these days: men standing on street corners because they had no work aroused her sympathy, but hungry kids made her want to cry. This poverty was all wrong! Most of these kids would hardly know it was Christ's birthday if it were not for the mission and John Hansen. Yet tonight they were shrieking with laughter, not a care in the world and that made a warm glow start inside her.

Feeling happier than she had when she left home, Flo went through to the kitchen to join the ladies who were supplying more sandwiches, endless cups of tea, fruit squash and cocoa for those who preferred its chocolatey taste.

Robbie saw Flo go through to the kitchen. He wondered if she'd seen him in this uncomfortable outfit and wished himself rid of it, but John Hansen had asked because his usual Father Christmas had let him down at the last moment. Robbie could hardly refuse after John had told him the news that the inspector from the Commissioners had approved his work and assured John that he would recommend the work needed on the roof to the board.

'Mr Rolf could not guarantee it,' John had told him earlier that evening when he'd brought the children to the Christmas party. 'But he is going to give it his approval – and he has told me he thinks your work is excellent...'

'I don't know what to say... but thank you,' Robbie had said emotionally. 'I've been offered some small jobs locally. They pay me enough to keep food on the table and I shall manage a proper dinner and a couple of little gifts for the kids...'

'I doubt they will expect more,' John had told him. 'You have good children, Robbie. I've heard they are kind and thoughtful to others and that is a credit to you.'

'I think it's more down to their mother,' Robbie had said with a twisted smile. 'Madge was a good woman and she looked after them – even if we didn't always get on.'

'I imagine life has been hard for a while...'

'For the majority of the working men in this country,' Robbie had said, refusing to accept sympathy. 'The hunger marches in October were an eye-opener for me. I went to watch as they marched into Trafalgar Square and I saw the police set on them with truncheons.'

'The papers reported that it was unruly youths who caused the fighting by smashing car windows and setting fire to things...'

'Yes, I saw some of that,' Robbie had agreed, 'and I know that elements of the crowd were communist led out to cause trouble – but the majority of those men had marched all the way from Lancashire to protest against the means test; they were just ordinary workin' men who were desperate.'

'Yes, I do understand. That is why we're always so busy here. The men on that march asked for bread, and that's what we give our people – bread and soup. An evening like this is made possible only by the generosity of those who often have little enough themselves, but also by those who can afford it and do what they can to help.'

'I'm not a radical,' Robbie had said and relaxed. 'I didn't throw stones that day or jeer at the police, but I felt sorry for the men who had marched so far and were blamed for riots that were none of their doin'.'

'We must hope that the government can find a way to improve the unemployment figures in the coming year,' John had said. 'Anyway, this evening we're doing what we can to make it happier for at least a handful of people.'

'You help more than a handful,' Robbie had told him. 'Without this place, a lot more people would be starvin'. I want you to know how grateful I am for what you've done for me.'

'I did very little and your work speaks for your worth, Robbie.'

'You made me remember that I had a skill. It was so long since anyone had offered me carpentry work that I'd forgotten I could...'

'You won't go back to the docks?'

'Not if I can find enough work,' Robbie had said. 'I've turned a corner, John, and I'll try my utmost to be a good father to my children.'

'I think you already are,' John had said.

John had left him to struggle into the heavy Father Christmas suit and gone off to greet the people who came to the mission on Friday nights. They were not the same people who queued for bread and soup every day, but the ordinary working people of the area, some who struggled on poor wages but still supported the mission with their tuppences for raffle tickets and their sixpence entrance fee, and others who ran the little shops and businesses that had managed to keep going during the Depression, and also the elderly who managed as best they could on what they'd saved. The women had contributed some of the food and the men put a couple of bob in the collection tin when they had it. None of them had much money to spare, but all of them pitied those of their community who had been driven to the breadline. Britain was struggling under its war debts, some of which had had to be repaid this year. Bonds were issued and those who could afford them bought them to help the government fund the debt, but the people here seldom bought a newspaper and only heard second-hand of the political and financial problems that had brought the Depression; they only knew that life was harder than it had ever been in living memory, and it wasn't just here in London, but all over the country.

Yet tonight in this hall, it was warm and there was light, laughter and good humour. Women gossiped with friends, children played games and the men drank a cup of tea and played cards with their mates or slipped away for a crafty half at the pub down the road, returning in time for Father Christmas and the giving of gifts. It was a tradition that had gone on for some years now, and it was accompanied by squeals of delight as boys ripped the paper from a *Little Jimmy*, *Mickey Mouse* or *Rupert* comic, or a little tin toy car, and girls had bead bracelets, colouring books or paper dolls to dress; little packets of boiled sweets were also given to every child.

Everyone waited for the carols. Nurse Mary played the piano and everybody gathered together to sing the old favourites: 'Away in a Manger', 'The Holly and the Ivy', and others that they all knew the words to and could sing lustily.

Afterwards, mothers collected children and started to leave in small groups to walk home. The party at the mission would be the highlight in many homes this year as it had been for several past. Food of some kind would be on the table for Christmas Day, but only a few thrifty mothers had managed to save enough to buy a small gift for their loved ones.

Robbie called Ruthie and Ben to him, and Mick tagged along behind; he lingered until Flo said her goodbyes and moved towards the door. Robbie smiled at her as he caught her up.

'We'll walk you home, Miss Hawkins.'

'You should call me Flo, as the children do,' she said and looked at Ruthie and Ben, as he walked and Ruthie skipped beside them. Mick hung back a little, giving her an uncertain look until she nodded and smiled at him. 'Did you all enjoy the party?'

'It was lovely,' Ruthie said, clutching her colouring book and pencils, her sweets already almost gone. 'Ben got a Rupert comic and some crayons... he's always wanted some...'

Ben grinned. 'They're great for drawin', but I'd like a Meccano set if I could afford it. I'd like to build a crane or a lorry or something...'

'Ben is going to be a mechanic when he leaves school, I think,' Robbie said. 'Did you have a good evening, Flo? I didn't see much of you. I was hiding in that suit most of the time and struggling out of it ready for the carols.'

'I was helping in the kitchen, but it was fun,' Flo said. 'Mrs Goodison brought in some cooking sherry and we all had a glass and a mince pie. I watched Father Christmas give presents to all the children.'

'That was Dad,' Ben said. 'I knew him all the time, but I didn't let on – some of the kids still believe in Father Christmas...'

'The real one comes on Christmas Eve, doesn't he, Dad?' Ruthie said. 'Mum told me he did. She said because everyone was hard-up last year Father Christmas was too – but he still brought me that set of covers for my dolly's cot and some sweets – and we got a silver threepenny bit in our Christmas puddin'!'

Ben looked at his sister but shook his head. Robbie smiled and ruffled his son's hair.

'I think Father Christmas might have a little something for us this year, don't you, son?'

'He might,' Ben agreed and winked at him. 'Are we goin' ter walk Miss Flo right home, Dad?'

They had reached the corner where their ways parted. Robbie hesitated, wishing he could take her home but uncertain what to do. His eyes met hers, but she settled it for him.

'Mr Waters still has his light on. I'm just goin' to pop in and see how he is – goodnight, Robbie, Ruthie – Ben, I'd like you to come into the shop one day before Christmas. I'll have a little something for you all... and you, Mick.'

'Thanks, Miss Flo,' Ben said and took Ruthie's hand. 'Tell Mr Waters I'll be round in the mornin' as usual – goodnight, Miss Flo...'

Robbie watched Flo as she walked the short distance to the Waters' front door and then followed in the footsteps of Mick and his children, whose happy voices echoed on the still frosty air. They were still caught by the excitement of the evening. It was the first Christmas party they'd attended at the mission. Madge wouldn't have let them go if she'd been alive, because she'd come from better things. Before she was married, she'd been an upper parlour maid to a titled family. She would have considered the folk at the party beneath her. Madge had gone back to her home town for the funerals of both her parents. Her mother had died a year before her father and she'd been left to pack up the house and dispose of the contents herself. She'd brought all her mother's silver and linens back with her and she'd made a point of setting the table with a cloth for the children's tea – but once Robbie lost his job and couldn't get another, the silver had started to disappear and so had his wife's smile.

Madge had blamed Robbie for bringing her down. She didn't belong in this shabby cottage close to the docks. Her father had lived in a pleasant house with a big garden within sight of the sea, and she'd played on the beach as a child. She'd been proud of the family she'd worked for and used to a good living. Robbie had met her on holiday when he was in the army and they'd fallen in love – at least it had seemed that way then.

Perhaps it was his fault. He hadn't been able to settle in her home town once he'd left the army and started work as a carpenter. All he had been able to afford was a couple of rooms in a shared house and the legacy of his grandfather's cottage had seemed a godsend, and, at first there had been more work for him in London.

At least the years in the army had given him a trade, one that he'd excelled at. It wasn't Robbie's fault that he'd had an accident at work and been flat on his back for weeks afterwards. He'd gone back to work as soon as he was fit enough, but then the recession started to bite and that meant that he was the first to be laid off. It had led to months of humiliation, but at least he had money to make a good Christmas for his kids this year.

Robbie quickened his stride and caught up with the children as they arrived at the door of their home, taking the key from his pocket. Mick waved as he walked off on his own, and Robbie hesitated. He felt he ought to offer the boy a place to sleep, but if he took Mick on it would be another mouth to feed, so he reluctantly let him walk away.

'Up those stairs and into bed,' he told his two and bent to kiss Ruthie. He looked at his son and smiled. 'Do you want some cocoa or have you both had enough for tonight?'

'I'm fulled right up,' Ruthie announced.

'It's filled up,' Ben said with all the knowledge of his superior years. 'I am too, Dad. It was fun. Did you have a good time?'

'I enjoyed myself,' Robbie said. 'Get some sleep both of you. I'm going to bank up the range and then I'll be up myself…'

He bent to pick up the coal chute, which was filled with coke and tipped most of it onto the range. It was good stuff and would hold in overnight.

He heard the kids scampering upstairs, laughing and giggling and looked round the kitchen that had seemed unbearably empty to him until recently.

'I'm sorry I wasn't a better husband, Madge,' he whispered. 'I never stopped loving her...' He'd tried, because the humiliation of his rejection and the beating Flo's father had given him had made him angry, but he'd always known deep down that it was his fault. He'd let Flo down and her father had the right to be furious.

Robbie dusted the coke from his hands and hung up his jacket. He had a job to do in the morning that would bring him in a couple of pounds. Life was looking better and he would be a fool to want or expect more... and yet Flo's smile as she left them that evening had made him want so much that he knew he could never have...

16

Nine days before Christmas Eve and trade in Flo's shop that Saturday was the best she'd known it for ages, as if people had decided that they were fed up with the Depression and lack of money and they were going to buy treats for themselves and their children no matter what. Honour could hardly keep up with the demand for their deliciously soft home-made rum truffles and the sugar mice.

'You just can't buy things like this anywhere else,' one lady wearing a warm wool coat with a fur collar and a matching fur hat told her as she bought box after box of the truffles. 'I want these for my party – and those marzipan fancies look wonderful. I always buy your lovely iced fruit cakes, Miss Hawkins, but this year I decided on the truffles as presents for my friends. The ones that come from a factory in a box are not as nice. Besides, your sister makes them look so elegant in all that cellophane and we've had to stick to a budget this year...'

As the customer handed over the two crisp white five-pound notes and received only a few coins in change, Flo smiled and nodded until the customer left the shop with her baskets filled to the brims with all kinds of treats, but inside she was fit to burst. She was grateful for the trade, which had nearly doubled her normal takings, but the woman's attitude made her smart with anger.

'Most people think buying one box of truffles is a luxury but she took fifteen – because she is cutting down on what she gives her friends this Christmas and they make a nice little gift...' she said to Honour when the shop was empty for a moment. 'I couldn't believe my ears... as if those truffles were just cheap trifles...'

Honour giggled. 'You looked so red in the face I thought you would pop,' she said. 'I don't mind if she does think she's economising – think how much profit we've made from her purchase...'

'I wish I could charge someone like her double,' Flo said vengefully and then laughed as she saw the teasing look in Honour's eyes. 'I know that is nonsense and I wouldn't do it if I could – but she was so...'

'Rich is the word,' Honour said. 'There are lots of people like her, sis. She may be feelin' the pinch a bit if she's had to cut down on how much she spends this year, but it just shows how bad things are…' She sighed. 'Roy told me his parents had it hard when he was young. His father had an accident on an icy road one winter and died after being bedridden for a year – and his mum was left almost penniless.'

Sadness had come to Honour's eyes now and Flo knew she was thinking about the man she'd fallen in love with, from whom she'd had no word. 'That was sad for Roy and his family, darling, but he's a man now and I expect his mother managed somehow.'

Honour looked at her oddly. 'We've been lucky, haven't we? I know I grumble about Dad – but we've never gone short of anything and I think that's because of how hard you've always worked…'

'I do a job I love and I'm happy here,' Flo assured her. She wanted to say more, but the brief respite was over and two women entered with their children, a boy and girl home from boarding school. They were smartly dressed and had clearly come to spend money.

Flo served them and Honour went through to the pantry to bring in replacements for the truffles they'd sold that morning. They'd made them fresh the previous evening but would run out before the day was over if everyone wanted the same thing.

However, these ladies had come for previously ordered iced cakes, some marzipan fancies and the children had two sugar mice each. The boy bit the head off one of his immediately and continued eating it while his mother settled the bill.

Flo thought about the way Ben had saved all his hard-earned money to buy his sister two of the sweet treats for Christmas – and of all the children at the mission party who wouldn't even get an orange in their stocking this Christmas: the difference between those who had and those who had not made her suddenly angry. As Honour had remarked, they were luckier than most. Flo had her own business and they lived comfortably, though she would never be rich, but she never had to worry about a shilling for the gas; she didn't have to wonder whether she could afford to buy a meal for her family.

There was so much poverty that no one person could ever change it, but perhaps Flo might do something small to help a few children. It was the children that tugged at her heartstrings. She thought that perhaps she might make a large batch of the sugar mice and take them to the mission. John would know where the children lived – probably some of them would be at the mission on Christmas Day.

Flo would have liked to help with the lunch that day, but she had Honour and her father to think of. She'd ordered a cockerel for their Christmas dinner, because her father preferred the taste to goose or chicken and she would spend the day here with him and her daughter – but there was nothing to stop her making cakes and other things to take to the mission. John could distribute them as he saw fit...

Flo smiled as she thought of all the money she'd taken that day. She and Honour had worked hard for it and her daughter would have her share of the profits this year, but Flo didn't need anything personally; she'd made up her mind, she was going to make sure that this year Christmas came to some of the houses it would otherwise have missed...

'I'm really pleased with your work, Mr Graham,' the butcher said as Robbie finished the new cutting block for him. 'My old block was falling apart; it belonged to my father and I knew it was wrong to keep it, because it was no longer hygienic, but I couldn't get around to buying a new one. When I saw your work and you offered to make me another, I knew it was the right time to get rid of the old one – and this looks as if it will last at least fifty years.'

Robbie looked at the solid cutting block he'd made with pride. 'The problem with your old block was that the water you scrubbed it with soaked in and rotted it inside,' Robbie told him. 'This is just as solid as yours was once, Mr Jones, but when you scrub it, the water will drain off through those runnels and stop it rotting for longer.'

'I'll be able to scrub it thoroughly and have it ready to use again by morning,' the butcher said. 'When you repaired those window sashes for me and I complained about the old block, I never thought you could make me something better.'

'It only needs a bit of thought and time,' Robbie said. 'I was happy I could find the right wood and create something you needed.'

'What do I owe you?' Bill Jones asked.

'The wood was expensive,' Robbie said and added it up with a pencil on a scrap of paper. 'I paid four pounds for it – and the work I've done here is another five pounds and fifteen shillings altogether, so that's nine pounds fifteen shillings.'

'I looked at prices in a catalogue I sent for,' Bill Jones said. 'The cheapest I could get was ten pounds and it wasn't anywhere near as good as the one you've made for me, and you've done all those other jobs as well.' He took ten pounds from his pocket and thrust it at Robbie. 'I don't want any change. I'm very satisfied and I'll be recommending you to my friends…'

Robbie hesitated and then nodded and thanked him. He'd earned the money but he'd charged as little as possible, because he wanted this man to recommend him. Bill Jones was a member of the Chamber of Commerce locally. He met the other members regularly and a word from him should bring any work that was going Robbie's way.

So far the jobs had not exactly been flowing in. He'd done a couple of days' work here and there since finishing at the mission, but this was the most he'd earned. For the moment he was able to pay for food, gas, and buy a few things for Christmas, but what happened when the work dried up?

The thought of having to join the jobless queues again would haunt him, Robbie knew. He was determined not to go back to the docks, but he might have to be prepared to do other work.

The ten pound notes were burning a hole in his pocket. He wanted to get Ben something nice, because he knew his son had been helping him out for months, putting a few pence in the jar on the mantle when he earned them from his errands, and Robbie hadn't noticed. He'd taken the money for a half of bitter more than once without wondering how it came to be there and now he wanted to make up for it – but what did Ben want?

Stopping in front of the toy shop, Robbie looked at the display in the window. There was a pretty doll that Ruthie would like; it cost thirty-five shillings and he felt a warm glow inside as he realised that he could buy it for her. The extra money Bill Jones had paid would more than cover it... But what about Ben?

What was it his son had said about his ambition to build things... mechanical things? Robbie's eye lighted on a large Meccano set at the back of the window. It was three pounds, sixteen shillings and eleven pence... very nearly four pounds. More than he could afford to pay at the moment, Robbie decided. He would go inside and ask the man to reserve the doll. He might as well pay for that, though he wouldn't take it home until the last minute – but he couldn't afford that big set of Meccano. It would leave him with not much more than four pounds to pay for everything else, because at the moment he had no more work lined up.

He paid for the doll and asked the man behind the counter if there were any smaller sets of Meccano in stock.

'We had a few,' the man said sadly, 'but I didn't stock too many this year. I wasn't sure how many I could sell with things the way they are. All the thirty shilling and two-pound sets have gone, but that bigger one is still here, because most people can't afford it.'

'I can't either,' Robbie said and sighed. 'I could pay thirty-five shillings and come in after Christmas to pay a bit more...'

'I'll knock it down to three pounds and ten shillings,' the man offered. 'I'd let you take it and pay over time, but I can't afford to lose the money if you find you can't manage it.'

'No, I shan't do that,' Robbie said. 'Look, I'll give you thirty-five shillings if you'll put it by until I can pay you the rest.'

'All right, I'll do that – and you can have it for three pounds and ten bob, like I said.' He smiled now. 'I'll wrap the doll for you so it's ready when you come in. What is your name, sir?'

'Robbie Graham. I'm a carpenter lookin' for work if you hear anythin'.'

'I'll pass it on,' the man said and took Robbie's money. He gave him a receipt and wrote the purchases down in his book. 'I'll see you on Christmas Eve then…'

'Yes, thanks. My little girl is going to love that doll…'

Leaving the shop, Robbie walked home. He'd spent more money than he ought but he was pleased with himself. If another job came along before Christmas, he could get Ben that Meccano set and if it didn't… well, he'd have to make do with the boots and a packet of sweets. Ben wouldn't complain. He wouldn't expect anything, but Robbie really wanted to buy that set for his son this Christmas – but if not, he'd just have to try and get it for his birthday in January.

He began to think of what he had that he might sell. All the small trinkets that he'd had when in full time work had been pawned or sold when he was out of work all those months. After his wife died, he'd sold the rest of her parents' silver to keep food on the table. Madge's clothes were still in the wardrobe upstairs. Robbie hadn't felt able to touch any of his wife's personal things. He'd always managed somehow, though sometimes they'd only had bread and jam for their tea, but the memory of that Meccano set was like a stone in his shoe and it wouldn't leave him. He just needed to earn a few more pounds and he could get Ben a present he would love...

Robbie shook his head. It would feel wrong to buy Ben's present by selling anything of his wife's. First thing in the morning, he would make a round of the shops and factories he hadn't tried yet, though with only a few days until Christmas it was unlikely he would find anything before then...

Bert Waters rubbed at his chest. The pain was more persistent now and getting worse. He'd put it down to indigestion at first, but now his instinct told him that it was something more. It worried him that he might be ill, but he knew he couldn't be ill, not while his Millie was sick. All the traipsing upstairs with trays wasn't helping him, Bert knew, but he didn't have much alternative. He would break Millie's heart if he told her she had to go into the infirmary. He wasn't going to let that happen, but he was so tired.

Sitting down, Bert closed his eyes and immediately fell asleep. When he woke, it was to find that it was almost teatime. He got up to put the kettle on and felt the pain in his chest again. Rubbing it with his hand, he turned the tap on and let the kettle fill. He set the kettle on the fire and started to take plates from the dresser.

Damn this pain, it made everything twice as hard. Bert wasn't getting any younger, but he'd always been strong. At least he had a little pension from his work at the jam factory, which made his life and Millie's just about bearable. They could pay their rent and the gas and put decent food on the table, and Bert thanked God for it. When he saw the reports of men fighting with the police because their families were starving, he wondered what the world was coming to.

Bert had worked all his life, most of the time in the same place – except for the years he'd spent in the ammunitions factory during the Great War. Bert had risen through the ranks to become foreman and he'd taken his turn on fire watch; he'd helped to put fires out when the doodlebugs came over with their death and destruction, and he had done all he could because he had sons fighting out there on the Somme. Bert had never stopped thinking about his sons risking their lives. He knew that lots of men had sons fighting but many of them had come back after the war: Bert's sons hadn't.

At first it seemed they bore a charmed life. Terry and Jamie wrote regular letters home. They'd told their parents all about what it was really like out there and about how they longed to come home.

Bert recalled the first Christmas of the war. They'd called it the war to end all wars and the men who had made it back carried such terrible memories that they'd sworn it must never happen again. Because of Terry's letters, sometimes, Bert thought he could smell the stench of the trenches; the awful odour of death and rotting flesh trodden into the mud by countless feet. Even worse was the rats feeding on bloated bodies that lay in no man's land and couldn't be buried until there was a ceasefire. Bert had seen it all through his son's eyes and he'd wished he could change places with him, but Bert was considered too old, even then, for the trenches.

Yet that first Christmas, the soldiers had come together regardless of orders and faceless generals that dictated what went on from somewhere far in the rear. It had started with someone singing carols. Terry was sure it had begun on the German side, though other people said it was theirs – what mattered was that it did start. Then one of the German soldiers came out of the trench and the British men emerged from theirs and suddenly in the spirit of Christmas they were giving each other toffees and cigarettes, exchanging little things and someone – Terry had never said who – had brought out a ball and they'd started kicking it about...

Bert's eyes were damp as he thought about that respite in a bitter war. Jamie had been killed earlier and then Terry, his boy that he loved more than life, had died just a few weeks before it all ended – finishing the destruction of Millie's heart and nearly killing his father, but Bert was strong. He'd hung on for Millie's sake and she'd become his reason to live. He wasn't sure what he would do if she left him alone...

Bert had made the tea when he heard the little tap at his door and then Ben and Ruthie entered, their small faces red with the cold and eager at the thought of somewhere warm to sit with their friend. They were like a little ray of sunshine, the grandchildren he would never have. Feeling an easing of his loneliness, he poured tea for them and his wife; his own could wait in the pot until he came down.

'There's a new loaf Effie from next door fetched for me this mornin',' he told the children. 'And we've always got jam. They send me some from the factory once a month because I worked there all those years...'

He picked up the tray and took his wife's tea and a custard cream biscuit in the saucer. Millie might have a bit of bread and jam later if she fancied it, but often she only wanted her tea and a biscuit...

The pain in his chest had gone off a little as he climbed the stairs, taking it slowly, careful not to spill the tea for his Millie. She was still as precious to him as she had been the day he met her. He recalled it now and smiled as he thought of the years that had been so good for them – except for losing their boys.

Bert's eyes misted. He supposed the war wasn't truly God's fault. Men made wars. And those children of Robbie Graham's – well, sometimes, he thought they were a gift from God.

Millie was sitting up against the pillows. She looked a little better and he smiled as she looked at him.

'Are you ready for your tea, love?'

'Yes, thank you. I think tomorrow I might start to come down... save you coming up and down those stairs so much...'

'Well, we'll see,' Bert said and took her tea to her. He bent and kissed her cheek. 'Don't get up too soon, love. I can manage a bit longer...'

She nodded. 'I know. I heard Ruthie's voice. I think I might fancy a slice of bread and jam, Bert. Send the girl up to me with it. I do like to see them. It makes me think...' Her voice died away on a sigh.

'Yes, I know,' Bert said. 'I was just thinking what a blessing they are to us. We've got a little bit saved in the housekeepin' pot. Would you mind if I gave them two shillings each for Christmas?'

'Give them half a crown each,' Millie said. 'We've got everythin' we need, Bert. Yes, give them a nice present. We've been blessed since they started coming.'

'I'll give it to them on Christmas Eve,' he said, pleased. 'The poor little mites haven't had much luck since their mother died...'

'No, they haven't and no one but us and their father to care for them. Go down and have your tea with them,' Millie said, 'and then ask Ruthie to come up to me...'

17

Ruthie spread her jam thick on the fresh crusty bread. It was strawberry, her favourite, and she loved it. She loved Granda for letting her have it as thick as she liked. He was lucky because the jam factory gave him two big tins a month.

At home, they didn't always have the jam Ruthie liked so much. Ben told her that Dad couldn't always find the work he needed and that was why he sometimes had a little bit too much to drink; she sort of understood it because of the sadness in his eyes. He tried to give them what they needed, but Ruthie longed for a new doll and a pretty dress. Her mum had made her dresses, but Mum was dead and Ruthie's dress was too tight. Ruthie missed her mum so much! Her teacher said she needed new dresses for school, because hers had split under the arms and the other girls had taunted her. Dad had mended Ruthie's dress twice, but it kept splitting because it was too small.

She ate all her slice of bread. When Granny was well, she made a lovely seed cake or sometimes a jam sponge, but Granda couldn't make cakes. Still, it didn't matter, Ruthie had filled up with the lovely sweet jam. She smiled at Granda as he spread jam thinly on Granny Millie's bread and cut the crusts off for her. He always cut the slice into four little bits, to tempt Granny's appetite, he said.

'Can you take this upstairs for me, Ruthie?' he asked. 'Granny Millie wants to see you.'

'Yes, of course I can,' Ruthie said and beamed at him. She loved the elderly lady and missed her now that she wasn't well enough to come down. 'I'll sit with her if she wants, Ben.'

Ben nodded. He was well into his second slice of bread and jam but spread half as thickly as Ruthie liked hers. He grinned at Granda when he asked if he wanted another cup of tea.

'Yeah, love one,' he said. 'How is Granny Millie?'

'A little better,' Granda was saying as Ruthie closed the kitchen door and went carefully up the stairs. Granny called out to her to come in and she took the small china plate to her friend, who was sitting up and looked a little brighter.

'What a good girl you are, Ruthie. Both you and Ben are good to us – and your dad was kind to mend our window. I don't know what we'd do without you all...'

'I like to help,' Ruthie said. 'Ben is goin' ter clean yer windows in the mornin'. I heard him tell Granda. I'll come round too and help if I can...'

'Yes, you do that,' Granny Millie said and smiled. 'I've got something you might like. If you look in the top drawer of that chest...' She pointed across the room at a big mahogany chest.

Ruthie hesitated and then went over to open the drawer. It was heavy and she found it hard to shift, but in the end she managed it. Lying on the top was a picture book. She knew at once it must be what Granny Millie was talking about and lifted it out, bringing it back to the bed.

'Is this what yer mean?' she asked uncertainly.

'Open it and look inside.' Granny's eyes were bright. 'It's about fairies. Years ago, when I was about your age, this book was given to me. I thought you might like to have it...'

Ruthie opened the book and stared at the lovely pictures. She could read some of the words but not others, though the pictures told everything themselves.

'It's beautiful,' she said shyly, 'but you're always giving us things. My mum said not to take charity and my dad might not like me to take it. Unless I earn it...'

'Well, you can look at it with me,' Granny Millie said, 'and perhaps we'll think of a way for you to earn it.'

Ruthie climbed on to the bed beside her and Granny put an arm about her shoulders, turning the pages so that the jewel-like colours dazzled her eyes. She thought that she had never seen anything as lovely in her life and stroked the pictures with her fingertips.

'Did your granny give this to you?' Ruthie asked, looking at the pages reverently.

'No, my mother's employer gave it to her. It wasn't new when I had it, but the child it belonged to had grown up – so it came to me and now I want you to have it. We'll have to ask your dad first…'

It was then that they heard the cry from below and a moment later Ben came to the stairs and called for Ruthie.

'You'd better see what your brother wants,' Granny Millie said. 'The book will be here next time you come.'

Ruthie nodded, smiled and went out, running down the stairs. When she got to the kitchen, she stopped and stared in unease. Granda had fallen on the floor and his eyes were shut. Ben was on his knees beside him.

'What happened to him?' she asked in a hushed voice.

'He was talking about what we were goin' ter do tomorrow,' Ben said, 'and then he groaned, clutched at his chest and fell to the floor.' He rose to his feet. 'I have to get help. I'm goin' to Miss Flo 'cos I don't know if Dad is home yet. Ruthie, you've got to stay here in case Granda wakes up. Make him lie still and put that rug off the couch over him. I'll be back as quick as I can…'

Ruthie watched as her brother shot out of the kitchen door. She did as he'd told her and put the rug round Granda. He gave a little moan but didn't stir and she felt frightened. Supposing he died... Ruthie didn't know what happened, but she knew people did die because her mum had, and she didn't know what to do. She wanted to run upstairs to Granny and tell her, but Ben had told her to sit there and so she did, her heart beating fast and tears running down her cheeks.

Granda mustn't die, because they would take Granny away to the old people's home and then she wouldn't see her every day – and she wouldn't be able to look at the pretty book... Ruthie knew she loved both the old lady upstairs and the man lying on the ground, and she closed her eyes, praying as hard as she knew how.

Ben was out of breath by the time he reached Miss Flo's shop. He rushed inside and saw that there was only one customer, though both Miss Flo and Miss Honour were there. Flo immediately lifted the counter flap and came out to him.

'What's wrong, Ben?'

'It's Granda,' he gasped. 'He sort of moaned and fell on the floor. I think he's alive, but I left Ruthie with him and ran all the way here.'

'I'll come at once,' Flo said and looked at her sister. 'I may be a while, so if you need to see to Dad, put the "closed" sign on the door...' She rushed into the kitchen, grabbed her coat and returned to Ben. 'We'll go back there first,' she told him. 'I'll see how he is and then I'll phone for the doctor. He may need to be taken into hospital...'

'What about Granny Millie?' Ben asked when he could get his breath back.

'We'll talk about that when we get there,' Flo said. 'I think it would help if you could fetch your dad – if he's at home. If not I'll phone Mr Hansen at the mission...'

Ben was half running to keep up with her. When they reached the Waters' terraced house, he apprehensively followed her into the kitchen. Ruthie jumped up and ran to him, looking scared.

Flo knelt beside the elderly man and felt for a pulse. 'He's still alive,' she said as Bert gave a little moan and his eyelids flickered. 'Ben, please go home and see if your father is there and ask him to come. Ruthie, just sit here quietly for a minute while I make a phone call. Mr Waters needs a doctor...'

'Hello...' a voice said from the kitchen door. Flo looked and saw the plump, pleasant-faced woman who stood there. 'I'm Effie from next door. Is there anything I can do?'

'Oh, Effie, I'm so glad you're here,' Flo said relieved. 'I'm going to call a doctor for Mr Waters, but perhaps you could stay here with Ruthie until I get back?'

'Of course, what about Millie – does she know?'

Flo looked at Ruthie, who shook her head and looked miserable.

'Right, I'll tell her when you get back,' Effie said. 'I'll make sure she's all right, but she mustn't get upset… Bert is so proud. I've been beggin' him to let me help more, but would he?' She shook her head.

'I shan't be long,' Flo said. 'Just wait with Ruthie until I get back…'

Ben had gone running to see if his father was home. If the doctor said Bert had to go to the hospital they would need an ambulance, but if he thought it better for him to stay at home, Robbie could help her get their patient upstairs into his own bed.

Flo had her purse in her coat pocket. She put some pennies in the box and made a telephone call to the doctor from the kiosk on the corner of the street. She was told he was in surgery but would come out as soon as he could. Her second call was to the mission and Nurse Mary answered. When she heard Flo's story, Nurse Mary said she would come immediately. Thanking her and feeling reassured, Flo returned to the kitchen and discovered that Bert was stirring. His eyes were more or less open, but he was clearly confused.

'He spoke Millie's name,' Effie said. 'Now you're 'ere, I'll pop upstairs and tell Millie. She would never forgive me if anythin' happens and she didn't know…'

Flo was bending over Bert and stroking his cheek. He opened his eyes and looked at her in confusion.

'What happened?' he asked his voice a little slurred but his words clear.

'You had a little do,' Flo said, 'and you passed out. The doctor is comin' and we're goin' to see what he says – whether you need to go to the hospital...'

Bert struggled into a sitting position. 'I'm not leavin' Millie on her own,' he said firmly. 'I'll be all right when I get my breath back...'

'Is this the first time it has happened, Bert?'

He looked at her in silence for a moment. 'I've had a couple of breathless moments when I felt a bit shaky, but I haven't blacked out before. It starts with a pain in me chest... I thought it was indigestion.'

'I think it might be something a little more serious,' Flo said gently. 'Do you think you can get to a chair if I help you?'

'Of course I can,' Bert said stoutly, but when he tried, he flopped back against her. 'I need to rest a bit and then I'll be all right...'

The kitchen door opened and Ben entered, followed by his father. Robbie took one look at Bert and crossed the room. Effortlessly, he bent and picked him straight up, lifting him under the arms and hoisting him, to take his weight evenly against his shoulder, and then deposited him in the comfortable old armchair Bert favoured.

'Had a bit of a do then, Bert,' he said and smiled. 'Makes you feel rotten for a while I reckon. Ben told me the doctor is on the way and once he's been I'll get you upstairs and into bed.'

'You won't let them send me to the infirmary, Robbie lad?' Bert said apprehensively.

'Nobody wants you to go there,' Robbie said. 'No need for it when you've got friends, is there?'

'We'll be the judge of that,' Nurse Mary had entered the kitchen unnoticed. She walked forward, a figure of authority in her uniform and stood over Bert. 'I'll check your heart and your pulse, Mr Waters, and then we'll see what the doctor thinks...'

Bert gave Robbie a look of appeal; he winked at him behind the nurse's back and Bert acquiesced without further protest as she checked his pulse and used her stethoscope. She made a reproving noise in her throat as she stood back and looked at him.

'It looks as if you've been lucky, Mr Waters – but you've been overdoing things and next time you might not get away with it. I don't think the doctor will send you to hospital, but he's probably going to give you some pills to take – and if he does, you must take them. This was a warning and it's a good thing you had friends to help you... you'll be needing a bit of help now with Millie still laid up.'

Bert looked at her. 'Millie's not well enough to get up yet...'

'I think we can sort things,' Nurse Mary offered. 'I'll put you on my list for two visits a day. I'll come in the morning and help Millie to wash – and you too if you need me. And I'll come at night to see everything is all right – but you'll need help from others.'

'I'll pop round in my lunch hour,' Flo said at once.

'I can come in a few times a day,' Effie said, coming back into the kitchen. 'Millie is all right, Bert, so don't worry – she wanted to come down, but I persuaded her not to. I've told you I'll get her meals and take them up to her – yours too, if you need to stay in bed.'

'Bert is going to be all right,' Nurse Mary said. 'But he won't if he continues to charge up and down those steep stairs a dozen times a day. I'll make sure he has regular visits…'

Bert protested he didn't need to be looked after and the doctor arrived in the middle of a babble of voices all assuring Bert that he needed help and they all wanted to give it.

A hushed silence descended, because doctor's word was law and next to God, and they went through to the parlour while he talked to Nurse Mary and examined his patient. When Flo and Effie were allowed back in, Dr Miles told them that he agreed with his nurse. Bert had been lucky. He needed bed rest for a few days and then he would be better, but he had to slow down, because next time it might be fatal.

'I can hear a murmur on your heart, sir, and I'll be arranging for you to visit the hospital for a few tests after Christmas – no, we shan't make you stay in, Bert.

Goodness knows, we never have enough beds. In the meantime, I'm going to start you on some pills I think may help.'

'Are they expensive?' Bert asked suspiciously.

'You've always paid into my panel,' Dr Miles said. 'Which means you get the first month's supply free – and after that we'll see…?' He smiled kindly at his patient and left.

'I'm goin' ter carry you upstairs now and help you into bed,' Robbie told him. 'Are you using the same room as Millie?'

'No, I'm in the spare room while she's ill. I didn't want to disturb her, because I'm sometimes up in the night a few times.'

'I'm like that when I can't sleep,' Robbie said. 'Put your arms about my neck and I'll lift you…'

Bert managed a chuckle, his good humour restored now that he knew he didn't have to go into hospital. 'Where did you learn to lift like a fireman?'

'I've done all sorts when I was younger,' Robbie told him. 'But I learned this in the army. It's the best way to lift another man – saves the strain on yer back…'

Robbie carried Bert up the stairs, joking and encouraging him as he helped him undress and into bed.

'I'll be all right now, lad,' he said. 'You'd best get those kids of yours home.'

'They will be round first thing in the mornin',' Robbie told him. 'I'll be here too and I'll be comin' every day until we've got yer on yer feet again.'

'Thanks,' Bert's eyes were watery. 'I don't know what we'd do without you and your youngsters, Robbie. We look forward to their visits every day...'

'I'm proud of them both,' Robbie said. 'I just want to deserve them. I haven't always given them the life they should have since their mother died...'

'Poor lass! You're not the only one who's had to watch their kids go hungry on occasion,' Bert said. 'A lot of folk round here are in the same fix...'

'Yes, I know, but it doesn't make it any easier,' Robbie said. 'I've been lucky enough to earn a few pounds... enough for Christmas.'

'You deserve some luck,' Bert said and grabbed his hand as he turned away. 'Thank you fer every thin'...'

'You're welcome, Bert. I'll pop my head in next door and let Millie know you're all right...'

Bert nodded and lay back against the pillows, his eyes closing. 'You do that, son, you do that...'

Robbie tapped on Millie's door and looked round it as she invited him to enter. 'I've settled Bert for the night,' he said. 'The doc says he needs a few days in bed – and that means we'll all be about, lookin' after the pair of yer.'

'Oh, Mr Graham, I'm so grateful. I wanted to come down, but Effie threatened me with everything under the sun if I did. She says Nurse Mary is going to stay here tonight just in case she's needed...' Millie flicked away a tear. 'People are so kind, but I hate to be a trouble...'

'That's the last thing you are,' Robbie said. 'Miss Flo is goin' to pop in as much as she can and we'll make sure someone is visitin' all through the day until you're able to cope again.'

'I am feeling a little better...'

'That doesn't mean you can get up and look after Bert,' Robbie said. 'Besides, you won't need to. We'll organise somethin' between us...' He smiled at her. 'Bert is right next door and I think he's sleepin'. Before you know it, he'll be up and about again...'

'He's been worryin' over me, up and down those stairs far more than necessary. I was thinkin' – maybe we could get my bed downstairs and then if I'm not well enough to get up he wouldn't have to do so much.'

'I think that is a good idea,' Robbie said. 'I'll get a fire goin' in there in the mornin' to warm it up and then I'll move the furniture and I can get a mate of mine to help me bring your bed down. It would be easier for you to get up for a cup of tea and much nicer when Bert is on his feet again.'

'Thank you...' Millie sighed her relief, her soft face looking younger as the worry sloughed off her. 'I should've asked before. Those stairs were too much for me a long time back, but I knew we couldn't move the bed and there was no one to ask... you know we lost both our boys in the war...'

'I know,' Robbie said. 'I was too young to be there right at the start, but I saw some of the worst of it and I know how bad it was. I feel lucky that I survived when so many didn't, Mrs Waters – and anytime you need help, you just send for me. I'll be round as soon as I can...'

'You're very kind. We think of your children as if they were our grandchildren,' Millie said. 'You don't mind if I give Ruthie little things, do you? I've no one else to pass my bits and pieces on to – and Bert would like to do the same for your boy...'

'Think of them as your grandchildren,' Robbie said. 'My wife's parents have gone. I never knew my father and my mother passed away when I was a kid. I ended up with my grandparents until they died – and I'd like some family for my children...'

'That's grand.' Millie nodded. 'You get my bed moved, Robbie. It will be half the battle to gettin' us on our feet again...'

Robbie nodded, smiled and left her to settle back in bed. He went down the stairs, feeling thoughtful. Madge had always hated charity, but life was all about give and take. So many people were lonely, especially folk like Millie and Bert who had lost their sons to the

Great War. It didn't take much to give folk a helping hand and it gave him some of his pride back to think he could be of use to others.

Nurse Mary was settling down with a cup of tea in the kitchen. Effie and Flo had gone and he felt disappointed as he'd hoped to speak to Flo again.

'You'd best get these two home,' Nurse Mary said, nodding at Ben and Ruthie. 'That girl is half asleep. I'll stay here tonight in case Bert has a relapse, though I don't think it likely. Effie is coming in to get their breakfast in the morning, and Flo is goin' to shop and bring food in the lunch hour. I'll line up a couple more helpers – but the children can visit and keep Millie's spirits up...'

'I'm goin' to bring her bed downstairs,' Robbie said. 'A mate of mine will help. We'll see about putting Bert's bed in the parlour too – his is just a single. They might be better together and neither of them needs those stairs.'

'A bungalow or a ground-floor flat would be better for them – if the council could arrange it...'

'I think using the parlour as a bedroom is as far as either of them would be prepared to go,' Robbie said. 'Move them away from what they know and their friends and I think that would be the finish of them...'

Nurse Mary stared at him hard and then nodded. 'I dare say you're right, Mr Graham.'

'I thought you were goin' ter call me Robbie?'

'Yes, so I was...' She gave a short laugh. 'I was so wrong about you, wasn't I? I think they are very lucky to have you, Robbie.'

'Maybe it works both ways,' Robbie said. 'They've been good to my two.' He ruffled Ben's hair. 'Time to go home... you can stop looking so worried, son. Your granda is goin' ter be all right...'

18

'How is Mr Waters?' Honour asked when Flo walked into the kitchen that Saturday night. 'I've given Dad his tea. He asked where you were, but when I told him, he just grunted and said it was what he would expect you to do. I thought he would be annoyed, but he gave me thirty bob and told me to buy a Christmas present for myself.'

'I'll go up and see him,' Flo said. A few weeks earlier Honour's announcement would have surprised her, but her father had been changing gradually for a while. He was less spiteful, more accommodating when she helped him. She thought he was trying to make up for the way he'd behaved in the past. 'I've had a cup of tea and I'll grab a sandwich when I come down – we need to make some more sugar mice and truffles this evening.'

'You look pale,' Honour said. 'You're not ill are you?'

'Just a bit tired, I suppose,' Flo said. 'We've been busy recently and seeing poor Mr Waters lying on the floor was upsetting. The doctor says he will recover. It was a warning because he'd been overdoing things – but it made me think about Dad. He could have another stroke and that might be the end…'

'And that would upset you, wouldn't it?' Honour looked slightly ashamed. 'I'd be sorry too, Flo. I get fed up with his constant need for attention, but he is my father too…'

'Yes.' Flo smiled and reached towards her, kissing her cheek. 'Dad needs us, Honour. I will never let him be put into that place… Poor Mr Waters was terrified of being sent there.'

'No, well, we'll manage Dad between us,' Honour said. 'I don't suppose I'll be getting married anyway…'

'If Roy doesn't come back to you, someone else will in time…' Flo said, seeing Honour's hurt and disappointment.

'I don't think I'll ever trust anyone again,' Honour replied in a muffled voice and turned away. 'I think I'll get on with making the sugar mice…'

Flo nodded and moved towards the hall door. She sympathised with Honour's hurt, but she knew there might be an explanation why Roy hadn't been round. A soldier had to go where he was sent – and if he'd been taken ill or had an accident who would know to contact Honour? She wasn't his wife or even his fiancée. Flo hoped that her beloved daughter wouldn't end up with a broken heart, but at the moment there were other more pressing matters on her mind.

Her father was sitting in his armchair beside the bed when she went upstairs. He had a large wooden box on his lap and was looking inside it. As she entered the room, he closed the box and locked it.

'You're back then...' he said. 'How is Bert?'

'The doctor said he'd been lucky – but Nurse Mary is staying over tonight, just in case either of them needs her.'

'They've got no one of their own left now.' Her father looked serious. Flo realised he must have known Bert Waters well when they were younger. 'I was luckier. I had a daughter who stayed at home and took care of her mother – and me...'

'Most daughters look after their parents,' Flo said and turned away to gather up his used plate and cup. 'I've got some work to do for the shop – is there anything you need before I start, Dad?'

'No, thanks, Flo. I shan't ring unless I have to. I know how busy you are. I've heard that shop bell ring a hundred times these past days...'

'We've been busier than I expected,' Flo said and smiled. 'One lady told me she was giving her friends our truffles because she was cuttin' down on what she spent this Christmas...'

'More money than sense,' he grunted and frowned. 'It's good fer you, Flo. You deserve to do well because you work hard.'

'Yes, I do and so does Honour,' she said. 'But thank you for sayin' it...'

'I haven't said a half of what I should,' he muttered. 'One day you'll realise...' He shook his head. 'Put this box back in the top of the wardrobe for me please – and then go and get on with your work...'

Flo did as he asked, wondering what was inside. She'd never seen it before, because she never pried into his secrets. He would have been angry if she had.

She went back down to the kitchen, wondering at the change in her father recently. For years he hadn't had a kind word for any of them, but now he was polite, almost considerate – and he'd given Honour the money to buy herself something nice for Christmas. She could buy a pretty dress or a fully fashioned wool twinset for thirty shillings.

Honour had filled all her moulds with the sugar paste, alternating them with equal amounts of pink and white. She had pricked the eyes and inserted tiny sweets in the holes, and they all had tails of thin liquorice strips or barley sugar twists, which was one of the things that made her sugar mice so different to those the other shops sold. Her smile was bright as she looked up.

'I was just goin' to start on the truffles... unless you want to do them?'

'I'll make some marzipan fancies and ice that last unsold fruit cake. I'm goin' to give it to John Hansen for the mission on Christmas Day,' Flo said. 'I'm goin' to make another batch of sugar mice as soon as those are set and some coconut ice – but not for the shop. I shan't get it all done this evening, but I want to finish them before Christmas Eve, because John needs to distribute them to the families he chooses...'

'What do you mean?' Honour was puzzled.

'It's somethin' I want to do. There must be so many kids in this area that won't get a present this Christmas, Honour – not even an orange in their stockings. They won't even hang them up, because they know Father Christmas doesn't come to their house.'

'You're going to give the sweets away?' Honour stared at her in amazement. 'Can we afford that?'

'We've earned more than I expected this year – and I don't need anything for myself, Honour. I'm goin' to do this because I can't bear to think of those kids who have nothin'... and Christmas should be for children. We celebrate a special baby's birth – and I can't bear to think of all those children who have nothin'.'

'Then I'll spend what Dad gave me on the sugar paste,' Honour said. 'I don't need a new blouse or a jumper, Flo. You spoil me whenever you have a few bob to spare. We'll make as many as we can manage to turn out and ask Mr Hansen to distribute them...'

'Some of the kids may be at the mission on Christmas

Day and he'll give the sweets to them then, but others will have to be taken round to their houses on Christmas Eve...'

'John Hansen has an army of willing ladies able and ready to do whatever he asks,' Honour said and laughed, suddenly enthusiastic about Flo's idea. 'He'll be only too happy to oblige – besides, he would do anything for you. I've seen the way he looks at you...'

'Don't be daft,' Flo said and blushed. 'He likes me because I help him at the mission but that's all it is... and I haven't got time to waste. We have a lot of extra work to do if we're going to make enough sugar mice...'

Honour was dead on her feet when she finally tumbled into bed that night. She hadn't slept properly for several nights, because she couldn't get Roy out of her head. He'd pestered her to go out with him, visiting the shop for weeks on end before she'd agreed, and she'd been happy seeing him once or twice a week for ages, but then, after she'd got into the back of the car and let his kisses carry her away too far, he'd stopped coming. Did he think she was easy? Cheap? Nice girls didn't do things like that, Honour knew. She'd worried that she might fall for a baby, but her period had come and Honour wouldn't have to suffer that shame. Yet she felt shamed, abandoned and hurt.

Roy couldn't have loved her or he wouldn't have stopped coming round just like that. They didn't have a phone at the shop, even though Flo would like one, because a lot of the better off clients said it would be nice to phone their order in and then just collect it, but Dad always said it was a waste of money. However, Roy could have written to her or sent someone to tell her if he'd been posted somewhere new. He'd promised to write but hadn't bothered and that meant he didn't truly love her – he'd just wanted the conquest, because she'd turned him down for months. She knew where he lodged, but she was too proud to run after him. If he didn't want her, she wouldn't beg, even though her heart felt like it was breaking.

She'd fallen in love with Roy's smile and the way he teased her, and the way he'd seemed to care so much for her, making her feel special. She'd believed he loved her. It was her own fault. Honour knew that nice girls didn't cheapen themselves by giving everything before they were wed. Flo had told her the truth and she'd known what Roy wanted – what she wanted, too – because she wouldn't lie to herself. She'd been desperate to kiss and to touch and that had led to something she knew was wrong. Honour might not have fallen for a baby, but she knew she was wicked and perhaps that was why she was being punished.

Honour's tears stained her cheeks as she fell asleep, exhausted. She and Flo had worked tirelessly to replenish the stock and to make up little parcels of sugar mice and coconut ice for the children who would otherwise have nothing. Her heart was breaking, but she'd worked side by side with her sister, because it was what Flo wanted and she loved her: Flo would never let her down.

Flo left Honour to take their father a cup of tea and a ham sandwich up for his lunch while she did a quick shop on her way to Millie and Bert Waters. She'd noticed that their pantry was almost empty the previous night and knew it was because they hadn't been able to shop for themselves. A packet of tea, butter, bread, cheese, some nice slices of ham in greaseproof paper and a few rashers of bacon together with six eggs would see them right for a few days. She'd brought a freshly made jam sponge as well and felt pleased with herself as Effie let her in and she filled up their shelves.

'I was goin' ter nip down the market and do a shop, but you've saved me a journey,' Effie said. 'I took a piece of bread and jam up to Millie – and Bert had a bit of toast, but I'll get them an egg fer their tea.'

'I wish I could do more to help,' Flo said. 'I can only pop in for a few moments, but I'll come back this evening. Is there anything else they need?'

'I brought a tin of cocoa round this mornin' and the milkman left a couple of pints as usual, so we're all right, Flo. It's knowin' you'll come that matters – pop up and say hello if you've time...'

Outside, Flo could hear the sound of carols being sung and she thought it must be the Sally Army. They made a tour of the streets the last week before Christmas and it made her remember how close they were to the festive weekend.

Flo spent five minutes with Millie and exchanged a greeting with Bert before running back home. She had time for a cup of tea and a slice of her own sponge cake before she was back in the shop serving customers. With only a few more days to go before Christmas, people were buying cakes and a few last-minute Christmas presents. The buying spree for expensive gifts seemed to have peaked and now people wanted just a few treats for themselves or the ever-popular sugar fancies for their children.

In the middle of the afternoon, Flo took advantage of a lull to go upstairs to her father. He was sitting out again and smiled at her.

'Bert all right?' he asked.

'Yes. I only saw him for a moment – I did a bit of shoppin' for them.'

'You've got a good heart, Flo,' he said. 'I haven't told you this before – but I love yer, girl. I know I've not been a good father to yer – but when I've gone you'll be all right...'

'Don't talk like that, Dad,' Flo said, alarmed. 'You're

not goin' to die for years. You're much better than you were.'

'I feel better,' he agreed. 'That's due to my daughter and granddaughter...'

'Dad, please... you know she doesn't know the truth...'

'You should tell her,' he said. 'I'm not threatenin' yer, girl. One day she'll get married and she will want her birth certificate – and she will know the truth. You should tell her before it's too late...'

'Yes, perhaps...' Flo bit her lip. 'I will – when I think she's ready...'

'She's not a child any more...' he said. 'Take notice of me, Flo – being lied to makes folk angry. Tell her the truth before she finds out for herself...'

'Yes, I shall,' Flo promised.

She left him and went back down to the shop. She and Honour had agreed that one of them would be in the shop while the other made more and more little gifts for the children of the district.

'I've thought of something Mum used to do when I was little and had a holiday from school – do you remember her special burnt toffee?' Honour said when Flo finished work and went through for her evening meal.

'I called it stick-jaw toffee,' Flo said with a smile, remembering when she'd been small and her mother had made the treat on birthdays or special days. 'Do you remember how she did it?'

'Yes – do you?'

'It's just melted sugar, a little butter and vinegar right at the end,' Honour said. 'You made it for me after Mum died, because I wouldn't stop cryin'…'

'Yes, you add just that little drop of vinegar right at the end to make it set – and if you use an enamel dish to set it, remember to use buttered greaseproof on the bottom or it will fetch the enamel off.' Flo was laughing. 'I remember once when Mum forgot the greaseproof and we kept hammering the toffee, but it had set to the enamel and it brought great lumps of it off…'

Laughter brought back happy memories to both of them and they hugged each other. 'Do you mind if I try making some toffee for the kids as an extra treat in their stocking?' Honour asked. 'I'll buy the sugar myself…'

'We'll use some of the profits from the shop,' Flo said, but in the event it didn't happen quite that way.

Flo's father got himself downstairs for supper that evening. When he saw the rows and rows of sugar mice and baskets of coconut ice, he looked at them and raised his eyebrows.

'You'll never sell that lot before Christmas…'

'These aren't for sale,' Flo told him. 'I've asked John Hansen for a list of the children whose families come to the mission, the ones who won't get a Christmas present or even a tangerine in their stockings. So we're goin' to make up little boxes of sweets and I've ordered a crate of tangerines – we're aiming to make up a hundred and twenty gifts – and John and his volunteers will distribute them, some at the lunch on Christmas Day and some to the door…' Flo held her breath expecting an outburst of indignation.

'What are you giving them?' her father asked, looking interested.

'Two sugar mice, some coconut ice, a couple of penny lollies from stock, two tangerines – and Honour is going to make some of Mum's toffee…'

'You can save me a bit of that,' her father said and grinned. 'It sticks to your teeth and if you don't get it right it goes soft and sugary – but your mother got the knack of it in time…'

'I didn't know you liked it?'

'I used to pinch a piece when you were in bed,' her father said and looked at her oddly. He turned to Honour. 'Run upstairs, girl, and look in my wardrobe. You'll find a big sweet jar filled with silver sixpences. If you give them a wash in soap and water they'll look bright and new. I think you'll find there's more than enough to give each of your urchins a sixpence as well as the sweets.'

Honour looked stunned but did as he bid her and came back down in a few minutes with one of the sweet jars they used in the shop. It was filled to the brim with silver sixpences and very heavy.

'How on earth did you collect all these?' Flo asked

and laughed as Honour poured them into the washing-up bowl and started to scrub them with soap and water.

'I started years ago when you were a little girl. I used to give you sixpence on Saturdays but you've forgotten...'

'No, I remember now,' Flo said, smiling because she was remembering happier times. As a child her father had often given her treats but that was before it all went sour. He and his wife had drifted apart, quarrelling frequently, and the love had gone from the house. Flo's mother had blamed him and she had too, but now she wondered how much of the bitterness had been caused by her mother; when a marriage went wrong there was usually more than one to blame. 'So you just went on collecting them.'

'Yes. I thought they might come in handy one day and now they have...'

'It's good of you to let us have them, Father,' Flo said. 'Sweets are lovely, but they're gone very quickly – a sixpence of their own is something the children can keep or spend on whatever they like.'

'You saved yours to buy a fairy doll for the Christmas tree one year,' her father said, his eyes watering. 'Right, I'll have a cup of tea and sit here by the fire. You'd best get on with yer work – you've a shop to run as well as these waifs and strays you're set on spoiling. I shan't get in yer way...'

Honour had got all the sixpences in a towel and was rubbing them dry. Flo poured her father a cup of tea and cut him a slice of sponge cake and then started to make another batch of coconut ice and some fudge. She was finding that a lot of her customers were coming back for the home-made sweets as much as the cakes and every time she added something new it sold out quickly.

Once Honour had finished drying the silver sixpences, she put them back into the jar. 'I think we should give these to the children after they've had their Christmas dinner with their sweets,' she said. 'At least, Mr Hansen can do it...'

'You and Flo will go round after we've had our meal,' her father said. 'I'm not a child and I intend to come down for Christmas lunch. I shall sit here on my own for a couple of hours while you play Father Christmas at the mission...'

Honour raised her eyes at her sister, but neither of them said anything.

They worked solidly, making the treats they intended for the children and more of the ever-popular chocolate truffles for the shop.

Flo took her father upstairs when she'd finished. He was yawning but seemed happy enough in himself and when they got into the bedroom, he took something from the little chest by the side of his bed.

'Here,' he said, pushing two five-pound notes at her.

'That's my contribution to your Christmas for all the waifs and strays of the East End...'

'I wouldn't say we're goin' that far, Dad,' Flo said, but she took his money and thanked him.

Flo didn't know what had changed her father's mood of late, but she was glad of it and she kissed his cheek once she had him settled in bed.

'It was all for your own good,' he said cryptically as she reached the door.

She turned and looked back at him, but his eyes were closed and she didn't ask what he meant. For years Flo had blamed her father for her mother's unhappiness – and her own. Yet she knew that her mother had played a large part in it. Mrs Hawkins had been the one who had planned it all, forcing her daughter to lie all these years and warning her of her father's anger if he'd ever found out – but he'd known all along. He'd told her that he might have belted her, but then it would have been all over and she could have brought Honour up as her own. She might even have found a life for herself rather than hiding in shame all these years.

Flo went back down to the kitchen. Honour had scrubbed all the pans and moulds, putting them away for next time. She had one hundred and twenty little boxes with their sugar mice already inside; they would add the coconut ice tomorrow and then put in the lollipops and the tangerines last thing – and if Honour's toffee turned out well there would be a little bag of that too. Honour was going to wrap the open boxes in cellophane and tie them with a little ribbon and a cut-out paper Christmas tree.

'You've worked so hard, love,' Flo said, looking at the neat kitchen. 'Get to bed because you'll be tired in the morning. It's a pity you don't have anywhere to go on Christmas Eve... Couldn't you go out with Kitty?'

'She's going to her boyfriend's house for a while, but we might get together later. I thought we might all go to the carol service – if Dad doesn't mind...'

'I think he'll be all right on his own; he can listen to the wireless.'

'Yes, I'm glad he's feelin' better.'

'Me too... Up you go, love.'

Flo took a last look in the shop, made sure everywhere was secure for the night and went up herself. She realised that a lot of the anxiety that had been hanging over her for a while had lifted.

Her father's gift of the silver sixpences and his tacit approval of what she was doing had given her a warm glow inside. She would have still gone ahead whatever he said, but that evening there had been laughter and a real family feeling in the kitchen that she had missed for too long...

As Flo undressed for the night, she thought about Robbie and his children. She knew things had been hard for them and wondered if they would be at the mission on Christmas Day. It would be nice to talk to him again and she had a special gift for Ruthie and for Ben...

19

Robbie finished repairing the shed door and stood back to look at his handiwork. When he'd started that morning, the roof had had great holes in it and the door was off its hinges. He had made it look almost new again and was proud of his work. The lady of the house came out to him with a mug of tea.

'That does look good, Mr Graham. My husband has been talking about gettin' a new shed for months but couldn't afford it. When I heard about you, I thought it would be the best present I could give him – two pounds five shillings I think you said?'

'Yes, that includes the materials for the roof,' Robbie told her. 'It should last another ten years now or more. Most of it was still good...'

'Here is your money,' she said and handed over two pound notes and two half crowns. 'I've got a few more jobs in the house – but I'd rather leave those until after Christmas.'

'Just let me know when you want me,' Robbie said. 'I'm glad to have been of help.'

He packed up his tools and walked out of the back yard, whistling. The money in his pocket meant he could buy that Meccano set for Ben; from the colourful picture on the box it looked as if it might have the pieces to make a train engine, and his son would be both surprised and delighted as he didn't expect anything.

It was three in the afternoon. He would call in on John Hansen at the mission and then he'd go round to Bert Waters' house and see if there was anything he could do to help.

John was about to lock up when he got there. He greeted Robbie with a smile of welcome.

'Just the man I wanted to see,' he said. 'I had a letter this morning, Robbie, and it's good news. They've accepted that the roof needs urgent repair – and they want you to do it. Mr Rolf really appreciated your work and your honesty – he told me he is ready to pay up front for all the materials and pay you a retainer. You can put your account in when you've done the work – that's if you're prepared to do it for us.'

'Yes, I'd be happy to do it,' Robbie said eagerly. 'I liked your Mr Rolf too and it's good steady work that will keep me goin' for several weeks. I've begun to get private work, John, but it's still slow. This job will set me on my feet for a while and then…' He shrugged. 'I'm determined to make a go of it…'

'I wondered if you would bring the children to the Christmas Day dinner,' John said

'I think the kids would enjoy it,' Robbie said. 'But I want to contribute in some way – what can I do to help?'

'Do you have a few extra chairs you could bring round? Kitchen or dining chairs – we've got a hundred and twenty sitting down on Christmas Day. Some of the other chairs that have been offered will need fetching too.'

'I've got four kitchen chairs I can bring,' Robbie said, 'but I'll give a hand with fetching whatever is needed – and even the washing-up afterwards. I know you have lots of willing helpers – but I need to earn my lunch.'

'We never say no to help,' John said and stamped his feet on the frosty pavement. 'It's too cold to stand about. I have a few visits to make…'

'Yes, and I'm goin' to pop into Bert and Millie Waters – see if there is anythin' I can do, fetch in the coal and make up the range. If that goes out, they'll freeze.'

'You brought Millie's bed downstairs, I understand?'

'I brought Bert's downstairs too. It was something they'd resisted for years, but it will be much better for them. Even when they're up and about again – those steep stairs were just too much for Bert. The doctor says he needs to rest more…'

'Well, I think his neighbour is popping in as much as she can, as is Flo Hawkins…'

'Yes – and Nurse Mary. My kids are round there every day, in and out all the time now they're off school. Ruthie sits with Millie and Ben just does what he can and pops in for a chat with Bert. I know Ben works at a lot of little jobs for various folk. I'm not truly sure what he does but I know he's been saving up for Christmas…'

John nodded and smiled. 'I've given Ben the occasional job myself. I'll see you on Christmas Eve to move the chairs… and on the day to help me carve up the chickens. I'm having the poultry cooked in Wright's Bakery ovens… because no one else would be able to cook them all.'

Robbie smiled. 'Even your devoted band of helpers might have found that too much on Christmas Day. I'll be there about three on Christmas Eve to help with the chairs, after your regulars have gone?'

'Yes, see you then…'

Robbie gave him a wave as they parted. A smile touched his mouth as he walked towards the row of terraced houses where Millie and Bert lived. These houses had once been marked for clearance but the Depression had put paid to schemes like that for a while and perhaps it was just as well, because where would the tenants go? He couldn't imagine most of them settling in the new flats the council had talked of building.

Robbie knocked at the door and then went in. It

felt a bit chilly and he checked the range; that needed making up, but first he had to let Millie and Bert know he'd arrived. He knocked softly at the parlour door and Bert said he should enter. Here the fire was still burning well. Millie looked as if she was asleep and Bert put a finger to his lips.

'I'm going to bring in the coke and coal and make up the range again,' Robbie said. 'Can I make you a cup of tea or a sandwich?'

'Effie popped in two hours ago and brought us some hot food,' Bert said with a smile. 'Your pair will be here any minute and Ben will make us all tea. Millie will wake up then. She likes to have Ruthie on her bed; they're looking at a picture book together...'

'As long as they're not a nuisance?'

'They could never be that,' Bert said. 'It makes my Millie's day to hear their voices and see their little faces. She's a lot better now – I reckon we'll both be on our feet for Christmas...'

'What about your dinner?' Robbie asked. 'John Hansen asked us to the Christmas lunch at the mission – I suppose you two would qualify...'

'I don't think Millie is up to it – besides, Effie would be put out. She's already said she's goin' ter bring us our dinner when they sit down to theirs. Her Keith will probably bring it round while she dishes up. We've never been so well looked after... Flo offered to bring us dinner too, but it's nearer for Effie.'

'You deserve it,' Robbie said. 'I'll make up that fire in the kitchen and put the kettle on ready for tea...'

Robbie finished work the next morning and went straight home. He thought he ought to catch up on some of the jobs he'd been neglecting, take the sheets round to the laundry and put the children's clothes in the bath tub to soak before he mangled them and hung them over the range in the kitchen.

The clean sheets from the laundry were wrapped in a parcel of brown paper and string, and starched so they crackled when he took them from the wrappings. He stripped his bed and Ruthie's and then pulled the sheets from Ben's. As he pulled the pillows from the bed, he saw a box hidden underneath and frowned. What was Ben doing with a cash box – and one that looked as if it had been pried open at some time. It was in his hand as Ben entered the bedroom carrying a small parcel, which he hid behind his back when he saw his father.

'Where did you get this box, Ben?' Robbie rattled it and opened it to see that there were several shillings, sixpences, threepenny bits and some pennies. 'That's a lot of money, son...'

'I earned the money doin' jobs for folk,' Ben said, 'and I found the box. I saw someone put it in a dustbin and I took it out after they'd gone...'

'What made you do that?' Robbie was puzzled, but

he didn't want to accuse his son of wrongdoing, because he knew how that felt.

'I went round to the bookies for Arnie at the newsagent and I saw this bloke coming out of Finney's…' Ben said, looking nervously at him. 'I know I shouldn't have taken the bets, Dad, and I've stopped, told Arnie I won't do it – but when I saw this odd bloke bring something out from under his coat and put it in the bin I was curious. I thought he might 'ave stole it, so I took it and showed Finney. It wasn't his and he told me not to mess with blokes like that… said he'd put ten pounds on a special Christmas race. That's a lot of money to bet, isn't it?'

'Yes – if it was honestly earned.' Robbie frowned. 'Why did you keep the cash box?'

'I wanted somewhere to keep things… and I've been collecting old bits of metal to sell round the junkyard, things I pick up in the street. I sold most of it but the box was more useful…' Ben said and Robbie nodded, because his son was nothing if not enterprising. But there was a line between enterprise and breaking the law and Ben needed to learn.

'I wouldn't be pleased if I knew you were doing something dishonest, son. I know it's hard going without things, but once you step over that line you could ruin your life.'

'I know,' Ben said. 'I've told Arnie I won't do

anything wrong again – and the cash box had been thrown away.'

'I'm asking you about this, Ben, because a little while ago I was accused of stealing a cash box very like this one from the mission; I didn't take it and John Hansen apologised, but this might be it. I want you to empty your things out, Ben. We're going to take this to the mission and you're goin' to tell John exactly what you told me – is that all right with you?'

'Yes, Dad,' Ben looked at him uncertainly. 'Are yer mad at me fer running bets for Arnie a few times?'

'No, not if you've realised it was wrong and stopped.' Robbie frowned, because if Ben had been less honest or less wary he might have got into trouble – and that was Robbie's fault, because he'd neglected to ask what his son got up to after school.

Ben took the box from him. He opened the drawer of his little bedside chest, put the parcel he'd been hiding behind his back into it and emptied the money in to the drawer.

'We'll find you something better to keep your wages in,' Robbie said. 'If you can describe the man you saw that evening to John it may help to prevent anything more being taken from the mission.'

'I'm ready, Dad.'

Robbie nodded and smiled at him. He put a hand on his shoulder. 'If it belongs to the mission we must give the box back, but otherwise you might as well keep it – it's broken and it doesn't lock.'

'I don't need to lock it,' Ben said. 'I just wanted somewhere to save my money.'

'Perhaps you could have a little savings book,' Robbie said and smiled at him. 'I'm proud of what you've done, Ben – and I do trust you, but I had to ask about the box.' He smiled at his son as they left the cottage and walked to the mission.

John was in his office when they arrived. Soup and bread was still being served in the large canteen, but John was making a telephone call. They saw him through the glass partition and waited until he'd finished.

'Hello, Ben,' John said. 'To what do I owe this pleasure?'

'Ben has something to show you,' Robbie said. 'He found it and I wondered if it might be the one you lost... Tell Mr Hansen just how you found it, son.'

Ben described seeing a man leaving Finney's and thinking he looked furtive as he dumped the box in someone's dustbin.

'I thought he might have pinched it, so I took it to Mr Finney and he said it wasn't his... so I brought it home,' Ben finished. 'I didn't mean to steal it. I thought no one wanted it.'

John took the mangled box and turned it over, looking at a mark on the bottom. 'Yes, I do believe it is ours – the one that was stolen. Could you describe the man who put it in that dustbin, Ben?'

Ben obliged, recalling how the man was bulky, dressed in filthy clothes with long untidy hair and a bushy beard. 'He was mutterin' to himself,' Ben finished on a decisive note. 'That's what made me notice him – I thought he looked a bit mad… Finney told me he put ten bob on a special Christmas race.'

John frowned and then nodded as if Ben's words struck a chord. 'You're very observant, Ben, and that is slightly worrying – because I've seen the man you've just described hanging about outside the mission as recently as yesterday. I know he's been here for soup more than once – but if he stole our money…'

'You don't want that sort here,' Robbie growled. 'I don't grudge him a meal any more than you would – but his kind cause trouble.'

'Yes, he has caused bother on more than one occasion, pushing in before his turn.'

'Men who are forced to stand in line for what is probably the only food they get all day are bound to be tetchy,' Robbie said. 'Yet there are always some who seek to take advantage. You need to make sure this thief does not get another chance to rob you.'

'He will not be admitted if I can prevent it,' John said. 'I'm as charitable as the next man but you cannot help some people and one rogue may spoil it for others...'

'Let's hope we don't get any gatecrashers spoiling the fun for the kids,' Robbie said and lowered his voice to a whisper. 'Bert was telling me that Flo and Honour Hawkins are giving the children surprise presents after dinner...'

'Yes, they've been marvellous,' John said and his honest face lit up with pleasure. 'Flo wanted all the children of the area to benefit and she asked me for our list of the families who are likely to have nothing this Christmas – the fathers are out of work and some of them won't have a stocking at all, perhaps not much food either...'

'I've known how that feels,' Robbie said and frowned. 'Thanks to you, John, I made a fresh start and my kids won't go without this year – but I think Flo and Honour are wonderful to give up so much of their time...' He felt a little glow of pride in the girl he now knew to be his daughter, even though he couldn't claim her.

'Well, I've been sworn to secrecy,' John said a twinkle in his eye. 'I've already been given seventy gifts to distribute to families who won't come to the mission on Christmas Day for one reason or another. I think we have another fifty children who will be given a gift at the mission.'

'You must have nearly a hundred and ten or twenty

meals to provide... That's an awful lot of work for your helpers.'

'They've all decided to cook their own Christmas meal early so that they can serve a two o'clock luncheon for our regulars. As I said, the poultry is being cooked for us, but my helpers have mountains of cabbage, carrots and parsnips to prepare, as well as mashed potatoes and gravy – followed by tinned fruit and custard.'

'You're providing a slap bang up do for them,' Robbie said approvingly. 'I'm afraid it's a long time since we had anything like that; I wouldn't know where to start, but what you're doing is wonderful... and your helpers are marvellous, giving up their time on Christmas Day.'

'Indeed they are...' John smiled. 'I am blessed in my friends.'

'We'll leave your cash box here,' Robbie said. 'It's time we went home. Ruthie is sitting with Millie and Bert – and she'll be hungry. I've got a bit of ham today and we're having a few chips with it...'

'Cor, Dad, that's my favourite!' Ben said and licked his lips. 'I'm starvin'...' He looked at John. 'I'm sorry I kept your box, Mr Hansen. I didn't know it was yours.'

'I expect I shall just put it in the dustbin,' John admitted. 'You can keep it if you have a use for it.'

'I don't think I will,' Ben said. 'Pinched stuff ain't worth havin'...'

'Good lad,' John said and smiled. 'I'm glad you told me about the man who dumped my box – I shall keep an eye out for him in future...'

Robbie nodded his satisfaction. 'We'll all see you on Christmas Day...'

'I shan't stop you doin' any of the little jobs you're offered,' Robbie told his son as they left the mission. 'Arnie is a bit shady and if you're sensible you'll be careful of him, Ben. A paper round is all right – but if you suspect you're being asked to do something wrong walk away.'

'He knows I won't have anythin' to do wiv the shady side of his business,' Ben said. 'But if you say I can't work there I won't.'

'I'll let you decide but be careful...'

Ben promised faithfully he would and Robbie nodded. His son was growing up even though he wasn't ten until after Christmas. He knew wrong from right and he'd have a word with Arnie, make sure he knew that he would answer to Robbie if he got the boy involved in something shady.

Robbie walked with his hand on Ben's shoulder. He was proud of his son and his pride made him want to make a better life for them all. The work on the mission roof would be a good start, but he was not going to give up the small jobs he'd taken on for folk locally. If things went well he would be his own master. He would have time to be there when his children needed him and look after the house more than he had when he'd been forced to spend hours just standing in line waiting for a menial job. Now he was doing something that made him feel worthy again and life was suddenly so much brighter. There was a social evening at the church hall on Christmas Eve, perhaps he could ask Flo to come as his guest and take the kids, make it a family outing – though Honour would sadly have to stay home to watch over Mr Hawkins...

20

'Your father says you can take the things I give you,' Millie Waters said to the little girl who sat on the side of her bed and looked at the beautiful pictures in her book. 'You can take your book home with you if you like.'

Millie's bed was now in the parlour and Robbie had brought down the little Christmas tree that Ben had fetched from the market. Ruthie had hung some paper chains over pictures and the mirror so that it looked very festive.

'I'd rather look at it with you, Granny Millie,' Ruthie said shyly. 'I like being here with you. Ben is always busy doin' jobs, but I like to sit quiet in here and look at the pictures.'

'You're a little love,' Millie said and smiled at her. 'I've got somethin' else for you – but that is a surprise for Christmas. I'm goin' ter give it to yer dad and he'll put it in yer stockin'…'

'I don't know if I'll have a stockin' this year,' Ruthie said, looking wistful. 'Last year Mum was ill and she just gave us a tangerine and sixpence for sweets, though Father Christmas brought me somethin' – but I know girls who didn't get anythin', not even a tangerine…'

'Times are hard just now,' Millie said. 'When I was a girl, I always got a few nuts, an orange if Ma could get one, a sixpence and a packet of sweets in my stockin'. Sometimes we'd get a new pair of boots or a dress if we were lucky. My dad worked on the railways and he never lost a day's work until he took ill of a fever and died sudden at the age of fifty-four. I was fourteen then and I worked in the glove factory for one shillin' and sixpence a week. My mother took a shillin' from my pay each week – but while my dad lived we never went short. My Bert was the same; he worked in the jam factory most of his life, except for his war work, and my Terry was goin' ter be a motor mechanic. Me youngest would've been a railway man if he'd 'ad a chance. I've never been rich but I've never been poor, neither…'

'Ben's friend from school sometimes has nothin' to eat all day,' Ruthie said and frowned. 'He smells and his hair is full of nits. Sometimes we get them at school and the nurse scrubs our head with stuff that stings and smells bad.'

Millie laughed. 'All the kids had 'em when I was your age, love. We was used to 'em and didn't take much notice – 'cept when we got our heads put under the pump in the yard and scrubbed with coal tar soap. The water was freezin' and I usually ended up wiv the sniffles…'

Ruthie loved hearing about when Millie was young, about the dresses with hoops in and how Millie used to hide in the outside toilet and take them out before she went off to work. Millie's mother was strict and made her wear long bloomers and corsets that pulled her in so tight she felt like fainting. She used to take her corsets off sometimes, too, and if her mother found out, she got the cane on her legs.

'I remember when I first set eyes on my Bert,' Millie said. 'I was sixteen then and earning two shillings and sixpence, and I didn't tell my mother I'd had a raise. I spent the extra on some shiny black patent button boots so I'd look smart and get Bert to notice me. He was all dressed up and off to church and he smiled at me as I lifted my skirt just enough to show me ankle. That was a flirty thing to do in them days. Bert told me later, when we was courtin', that I had neat ankles and that's what he liked – that and me cheeky smile…'

Ruthie laughed and then leaned in and kissed Millie's soft, papery thin skin on her cheek. She smelled of talcum powder and violets and Ruthie wanted to put her arms about her and stay there forever.

They heard the kitchen door go and Ben's voice calling to her. He popped his head round the parlour door.

'Me and Dad went to the chip shop and we've brought yer a bit of fish between yer and some chips. Dad's puttin' 'em on plates now and he'll put yer a bit of salt and vinegar on – and bring you both a cup of tea, and then we're off for our dinner. Is there anythin' else yer want, Bert – Millie?'

'You shouldn't 'ave gone to all that trouble,' Bert said. 'A bit of bread and jam would've done – not that fish and chips won't be a real treat. We used to 'ave that every Friday night once, didn't we, gel?'

'I can smell it and it has made me feel hungry,' Millie said. 'You're a good boy, Ben – and Bert has got a present for you…'

'I don't need nothin',' Ben said. 'Yer pay me when I do a big job – the chips are Dad's treat…'

'I meant a Christmas present. I'll give the presents to yer dad fer yer to open when you wake up.'

'No need, we'll be round ter see yer early afore we go to the mission,' Ben told her. 'I might 'ave somethin' fer you an' all…'

Millie shook her head at him. 'Silly boy. You do too much fer us now…'

'I like comin' 'ere and so does Ruthie,' Ben said and grinned. 'We need to do somethin' fer all that bread and jam yer keep givin' us...'

His father arrived then with two trays of fish and chips set neatly on plates and sprinkled with salt and vinegar. Their cups of tea were placed on the little chests beside their beds. Robbie settled the trays on their laps and looked round the room.

'Is there anythin' else yer need, Millie? I want to get off, because it was snowing a bit as we came in, not sure it will settle, but if it gets worse I want this pair home in the warm.'

'No, thank you, Robbie. We're all right now, aren't we, Bert?'

'More than,' Bert said and forked a mouthful of the crisp batter and tender fish. 'Just the job, lad. I fancied somethin' different...'

'Effie will come in later and see to your fire – and then I'll come last thing,' Robbie said.

'I think Flo is goin' to come round when she's closed her shop,' Millie said. 'She and Honour have been workin' so hard on their gifts for the kids that she hasn't been in as much as she'd hoped, but we've had lots of folk poppin' in to see we're all right...'

'Come on, Ruthie,' Robbie said and held out his hand to her. 'We're goin' home for our dinner now. Say thank you to Millie for havin' yer.'

'Thank you, Granny Millie...' Ruthie said.

'It was a blessin',' the elderly lady said. 'I'll see yer in the mornin' then...'

'It's Christmas Eve tomorrow,' Ruthie said and her eyes lit with excitement. 'We've got paper chains and a tiny Christmas tree at home... Ben got it fer a shillin' off the market.'

'I bet that looks nice,' Millie said and popped a piece of fish in her mouth. She smiled across at her husband as she swallowed. 'This takes me back a bit...'

Robbie shepherded his children from the house and told Ben to keep hold of his sister's hand as they crossed the road. They could hear the sound of carols on the frosty air. The snow was very light and would probably be gone by morning, hardly enough to make a snowball. He was whistling and felt happier than he had for a long time. It had felt good to buy a small treat for the elderly folk and it had put a spring in his step, because he was suddenly feeling like the confident man he'd been before his luck turned bad...

'Now, you'll be all right, Dad?' Flo asked that evening after they'd all eaten sardines on buttery toast and a slice of hot jam roly-poly suet pudding with custard. 'I'm goin' round to Millie and Bert's house. I've got a few treats for them and I haven't been for a couple of days, because we've been too busy, but we've got all the children's gifts ready. Honour has counted them three times to make sure there's enough – and we've got lots more sixpences than we need.'

'Well, keep them for another time,' her father said. He looked at Honour. 'What about you, girl? Don't you want to go out? What happened to that boyfriend?'

'He's been too busy to come round,' Honour said and looked away quickly from eyes that saw too much. She'd never told him about Roy and it made her feel hot because it seemed he'd known all along.

'Why don't yer pop round and see that girl Kitty yer friendly wiv for a while. I'll be all right here by the fire for an hour or so...'

'I could take her Christmas present,' Honour said. 'I made her some fudge and I bought her a pair of silk stockings...'

'Wastin' money on fripperies,' Mr Hawkins shook his head, but there was no malice in his words. 'Off with the both of yer then. I'll listen to the wireless and doze here by the fire.'

'I've heard the King is going to broadcast to the nation on Christmas Day.'

'Aye, I'll be listenin' to that,' her father said and nodded, pleased. 'It's the first time an English monarch has done it and that's history, my girl.'

'I'll get Kitty's present,' Honour said and dashed upstairs.

Flo packed her basket with the small treats she'd made for Bert and Millie: mince pies, ten rum truffles, a little bag of fudge and a small tin of mint humbugs, also a tin of pink salmon and a jam sponge.

'Off yer go then, love,' her father said. 'Don't linger on the streets and catch cold.'

'I shan't,' she promised and then bent to kiss his cheek.

It was about six minutes' walk through dimly lit streets which were a little icy underfoot and might be treacherous later, but Flo was wearing sensible flat shoes and she trod safely. She knocked at the door of the terraced house and then entered, calling out as she did so.

Millie's voice invited her to go through; it was the first time she'd visited since they'd had their beds downstairs and she looked about her with interest. The stained wooden boards of the parlour were covered with a faded carpet in a blue and red pattern Flo thought might be called Persian. Obviously old, it had probably been bought second-hand in one of the many shops selling such things in the East End, but it looked nice and good quality. The old-fashioned settee and chairs had been piled up in the corners and the beds were placed fairly close together so that the couple could talk to each other and the commode was in easy reach of both. The room had been decorated for Christmas and the couple had several festive cards on the sideboard, some of which looked as if children had made them.

Someone had done some polishing that day, giving the room a pleasant smell of lavender, and Flo thought that must have been Effie. She saw that the window was opened just a little and there was a tiny vase of Christmas roses on a table.

'How lovely they are,' Flo said, admiring the flowers. 'Where did they come from?'

'Bert grows them in a cold frame in the back garden and Effie picked some for us,' Millie said. 'It's not much more than a yard really, but it's big enough. In the summer we grow a few tomatoes and we managed a couple of cucumbers one year.'

'You must have green fingers, Bert,' Flo said. 'Dad never got anything to grow in our back yard, though Mum once had a window box with pansies in it – but they died and she never bothered again.'

'I like a bit of green,' Bert said. 'I couldn't live in the country – but I like me cold frame...'

'I brought a few small things for you, because I know you can't get out, Millie. If you need anythin' you just ask and either I or Honour will get it for you.' Flo thought they both looked rested and happy and it lifted her spirits.

'Only if you let me pay for what you bring,' Millie said. 'We can't keep takin' for nothin'…'

'I've only brought a few Christmas things and I don't want payin' for them,' Flo said, 'but if you need groceries, of course I'll take your money.'

'Then I'll give yer a list,' Millie said. 'I was goin' ter ask Effie, but she's already doin' so much…'

'I will be happy to help. We've been workin' flat out but we've finished all the extra sweets we made for the children now and I'll have more time.'

'I heard what you and that sister of yours are doin' fer the kids,' Millie said. 'I thought it was a lovely thing, Flo – Christmas is fer the kids after all, ain't it?'

'Yes, that's how I felt,' Flo confided. 'We've been busy in the shop. A lot of my customers are not as hard hit by the Depression as folk around here and they bought our home-made sweets to save money – told me they were cuttin' down on what they spent on their friends and families. It made me think of how little some people have. Those truffles would be a luxury for most people – but one lady thought she was lowerin' her sights to give them to her posh friends. I suppose I got angry and thought about the children who will have nothing at the bottom of their beds on Christmas mornin'.'

'There's so many of them in the same boat.' Millie nodded and dabbed at the corner of her eyes with a hanky. 'Last year Ruthie and Ben didn't get much, but this year we're giving them somethin' – and so is their dad. It won't make up for not havin' a mum, but it helps a little...'

'They will get one of our Christmas boxes at the mission,' Flo said and smiled. 'I've also got both of them a little present. They're lovely children, aren't they?'

'That girl is a little angel,' Millie said sentimentally. 'I look forward to her visits every day. Ben helps Bert – he started long before either of us were ill and we don't forget that, but Ruthie makes my heart melt with love...'

'Yes, I know just what you mean,' Flo said and tears stung her eyes. 'Speaking of angels...'

They heard the kitchen door open and then the sound of children's excited voices, and then Ben and Ruthie entered, their father just behind.

'Don't jump on the bed, Ruthie,' her father said. 'Ben bring the coal scuttle through and I'll fill them all up while I'm about it. I'm goin' ter make the range right for the night, Bert. Effie saw us come in and said she'll be round first thing.'

'I'll be up in the mornin',' Bert said. 'I'm glad yer brought the beds down, Robbie lad. It will make all the difference if Millie wants a rest in the afternoon, but we're both feelin' better and we'll be able to get up a bit fer Christmas...'

'That's wonderful,' Robbie said and grinned at him. 'I'll bank that fire up and make a cup of tea – or cocoa if you would rather?'

'We need some cocoa – that's on my list,' Millie told Flo. 'My purse and the list is on the table there, love. If you can bring the shoppin' round tomorrow...'

'I'll come over when I've got a free moment,' Flo agreed. 'I'll be on my way now that you have more visitors. I'm so glad you're feelin' better...' She followed Robbie back into the kitchen. 'I've got something for the children at home,' she told him. 'They'll get one of our boxes at the mission – but I bought a little gift for both of them, if you could nip in and fetch it tomorrow?'

'I've got a lot on – it may not be until later in the evening...'

'That doesn't matter,' Flo said and smiled at him. 'John visited my father this afternoon. He told me that you'd been offered the job of repairing the mission roof. That's good isn't it?'

'It's the answer to my prayers,' Robbie said and looked at her in such a way that her heart raced. 'I owe it to you and your father, Flo – if he hadn't given me his tools I couldn't have done it.'

'You never heard anything about those you lost?'

He shook his head ruefully. 'They were worth good money. In these hard times folk keep what they find too often... but it was my own fault. I shouldn't have had that whisky Josh bought me. I can handle a couple of pints but the whisky made me stupid.'

'Well, it seems to have turned out all right,' Flo said. 'I'll expect you tomorrow evening, Robbie.' He picked up her coat and held it for her, his hand just brushing her cheek. She smiled up at him, her heart jumping. 'Thank you.'

'I don't suppose you'll have time to pop down the church social with me tomorrow evening? I thought we could take the kids for an hour or so...'

Flo shook her head but looked regretful. 'I'll be busy, but thank you – perhaps another time?'

'Yes, why not?' He sounded disappointed and Flo wished she might have gone with him, but there was a lot to do on Christmas Eve, preparing the stuffing and food for the next day. A roast cockerel was a delicious meal with a deeper flavour, but it took more preparation than a chicken and needed to be cooked slowly to make it tender. Besides, she'd promised Honour she could visit her friends if she wished.

'You'll call for the children's gifts?'

'Yes, thank you – my children are being spoiled this year, but they've had enough grief recently and they deserve a few treats.'

Flo nodded. 'Tomorrow then...' she said and went out into the cold night air.

Was she being silly to think there was anything in the way Robbie had smiled at her? For a moment she'd felt that the years had melted away as if they'd never been... But of course that was foolish. Nothing could come of her secret yearnings. Flo was just imagining the look that seemed to say that he still loved her...

21

Robbie spent most of Christmas Eve volunteering at the mission. John needed extra chairs, plates and cutlery and some of them were borrowed from the Sally Army canteen, which always had plenty of spares. The mission in Oldfield Street was a local charity set up to help the poor by the church and a few good people, but the Salvation Army was countrywide and had many thousands of helpers and members; they thought of themselves as God's army and their mission was to spread His word. Captain Arnott smiled at Robbie when he arrived with one of the other volunteers and a borrowed van.

'Mr Hansen is making a bold move,' the man said. 'I don't think we could manage a Christmas dinner for over a hundred people. We shall have the soup kitchen open as usual and we've planned some mince pies as a treat for our regulars – but that dinner is a huge undertaking.'

Robbie smiled and agreed. 'I think Mr Hansen has probably realised it by now but he has an army of volunteers. All his ladies are cooking their own meal early so that they can be at the mission to serve up the Christmas lunch at two o'clock.'

'Well, good luck to you, that's all I can say,' the captain saluted and laughed. Robbie noticed that their side door was half off its hinges and Captain Arnott nodded when he mentioned it. 'Someone broke in the other night. I think they were looking for money, but all they got was an almost empty collecting tin; it only had a few coppers in.'

'Still, they were given to help your work,' Robbie said. 'I hate thieves, Captain Arnott, and just because you're broke it doesn't mean you should take from others. After all, most of us are in the same boat.'

'I don't think it's a local man,' Captain Arnott said thoughtfully. 'I've noticed a few rough types hanging about – they may have come from somewhere up north. At least I think it was a northern accent, but it might have been foreign. I turned one of them away from the soup kitchen the other day. He tried to get a second portion and we do serve whoever comes, but we don't tolerate that kind of behaviour.'

Robbie nodded and took the last of the chairs out to the van. 'I'll pop back after I finish at the mission and fix that door for you if you like.'

'Thank you. I've been meaning to get it done, but no one seems to bother about small jobs.'

'I do,' Robbie said and grinned. 'I'll come back about four – OK?'

'Yes, I'll still be here.'

'You're a glutton for work,' Reg, the other volunteer, said as he drove the van away from the Salvation Army Hall. 'My missus volunteered me for this job and once we've unloaded I'm off for a drink with me mates.'

Robbie laughed. Once he might have felt the same, but now he wanted to make a name for himself. He had no intention of charging the Sally Army for the small repair to their door, but he hoped they would remember his name and pass it on. Although he had work for the next month or so, Robbie wanted to make sure that he had work every day in future.

He'd looked into Flo's sweet face the previous evening and something inside him had ached to take her in his arms and kiss her. He wanted to tell her how much he loved her, had always loved her – but he couldn't ask Flo to forget the past and give him another chance unless he was certain he could provide for his family – all his family.

Flo had her own business, but Robbie wasn't going to live off another's earnings. He had too much pride for that and so he couldn't ask her to wed him until he'd begun to make a proper living instead of earning a few bob for the day, which was enough to subsist on but not enough to build a new life.

His mind twisted this way and that, because there was so much he wanted to say to Flo – and to Honour, though he knew he could say nothing until Flo gave him permission. He'd given up all rights when he'd run away and left her to face her predicament alone. Somehow he had to find a way of making up for what he'd done, even though it wasn't all his fault. Robbie knew now that Flo's father had lied; Flo had never seen his letter. She must believe that he'd just kept on running.

Robbie spent the next hour and a half helping to clean the canteen after the soup kitchen closed, getting it pristine and decorated with paper chains and decorations for the next day. John's ladies had brought in various bits and pieces from their homes and by the time the tables were laid the room looked very festive.

When John locked up, Robbie set out for the Salvation Army Hall, his tool bag over his shoulder. It was in Spitalfields and a fair walk so he caught a bus. Captain Arnott looked a little surprised when he turned up, as if he hadn't truly believed Robbie would come back.

The Salvation Army captain made him a mug of strong hot tea as he worked, fitting the door with a metal bar they could put across when they locked up at night.

'That should stop any more break-ins,' Robbie said and smiled. He finished his tea. 'I'll be off now – Happy Christmas…'

'How much do we owe you?'

'Nothing for this,' Robbie replied, 'but spread the word for me if you can. I'm looking for work and my rates are very reasonable…'

'We've got a lot of repairs we need done in one of our premises in Stepney,' Captain Arnott said. 'It's a row of almshouses we let to our retired members and they are all in need of repair. Would you consider giving me a price for renovating the whole lot?'

'Do you really mean it?' Robbie was stunned. 'I've got a roof restoration for the mission, but I'll be free to start sometime in February next year.'

'It would take that long to get it approved,' Captain Arnott said and smiled. 'Yours won't be the only tender, but my approval goes a long way – if your rates are truly reasonable I would throw my weight behind your bid.'

'When can I look at them?' Robbie asked.

'I'm free on Boxing Day…'

'Give me the address and I'll meet you there…'

Captain Arnott extended his hand. 'Thank you for doing this for us, Mr Graham – and I look forward to showing you the almshouses…'

Robbie nodded and left. He felt as if he was walking on air as he hopped on a bus and paid his tuppenny fare.

The future was looking brighter and if he got that job for the Sally Army... But he would be a fool to put too much on the word of one man. He had to see what needed to be done first, work out a sensible price and then hope for the best, but it made him feel that perhaps life was going to change for the better for him and his family – and perhaps that might include Flo and Honour one day.

Flo was busy for the whole of the morning, but by mid-afternoon the trade had almost dried up. She'd sold all the fancy bits and pieces and all that was left were a few buns and mince pies and when Honour told her that she would take over, Flo decided she would do Millie's shopping and pop it round for her. She packed some of the mince pies into a little white box and put that in her basket. Her father was sitting by the fire reading a newspaper Honour had fetched for him and nodded as she told him where she was going.

It took Flo only a few minutes to buy the goods Millie had asked for and to walk to their house. She was surprised to see that Bert was dressed and in the kitchen. He was just making a cup of tea and invited her to stop for one.

Flo thanked him and unloaded her basket, setting out the mince pies on a plate and putting the other bits and pieces in the pantry.

'Don't do too much, Bert,' she said, looking at him in concern. 'Now, have you got all you need?'

'We don't need a lot,' Bert said. 'Will you take Millie's tea in for her, lass – and one of your mince pies? I know she likes to see you…'

Millie was still in bed but looked brighter than she had done for days and Flo thought she was genuinely better. She placed the mince pie on its plate beside the bed and handed Millie her tea.

'Thank you, lass – that looks lovely,' Millie said. 'Our neighbours have been wonderful. We've had a sponge cake and a casserole brought in this mornin' – and Effie is cooking us a dinner on Christmas Day. Folks are so kind…' She wiped a tear from the corner of her eye. 'I don't think I could ever bear to move away if they do want to pull our houses down.'

'You've made friends over the years,' Flo said. 'I know there have been times when you've helped others…' Millie nodded as she sipped her tea. 'Now folk are helping you a little and glad to do it…'

'Robbie has been as good as a son to us these past few days,' Millie said. 'He's done everythin' – emptied the commode and all…' She gave a little cackle of laughter. 'These old places bring down all the barriers, lass. We've only the lavvy in the back yard and so we're used to carryin' a night pail out in the mornings – but Robbie didn't bat an eyelid.'

Flo laughed. 'It doesn't worry me – but not many men care for the job.'

'My Bert never made no trouble of it, but lookin' after me nearly killed him,' Millie said, looking anxious. 'I'm glad we let Robbie bring the beds down. We can't expect folks to keep runnin' after us forever and those stairs are too much for my Bert.'

'I don't intend to stop comin' when I can,' Flo told her with a smile, 'and I'm sure Effie won't – I can't do as much as I'd like, but I shall make sure you're all right...'

'You've been an angel,' Millie said and the emotion in her voice showed that she meant it. 'Robbie has his work to do, but the children are here most days and that means we don't feel cut off... we know someone will always be about and that takes away the fear of lying ill and no one caring if yer die...'

'A lot of folk care about you and Bert.'

'Aye, they've shown that...'

Flo smiled and chatted for several minutes and then wished Millie a Happy Christmas. She said goodbye to Bert, who thanked her for coming and told her he was going back to bed for a little rest.

'I'm doin' what the doc told me,' he said and winked naughtily as she took her leave. 'I don't want to get carted off to hospital and leave my Millie on her own...'

*

Flo closed the shop at half-past four on Christmas Eve. They had very little stock left and what they did have they could eat themselves. Flo would make some fresh mince pies in the morning before she cooked their dinner, but other than that she intended to have a rest from baking.

They ate lamb chops, mashed potatoes and buttered carrots and cabbage for tea and then washed up. Honour said she was going next door to see her friend Kitty.

'We're going to cut out a new dress for Kitty's little sister,' she told Flo. 'I'll be back later if you want to go to church for the midnight service...'

'I'm not sure,' Flo said. 'I think I'll just sit and listen to Dad's wireless – if it works...' Her father's wireless was a Bakelite model and a nice-looking set but a bit temperamental, but Flo didn't mind if she just sat quiet for a while. It would make a nice change to read her library book, something she seldom had time for. She was hoping that Robbie would keep his promise to call that evening.

He came at eight fifteen and brought a big terracotta pot of hyacinths for her as a Christmas gift. The flowers were still green and tightly shut, but it was a lovely surprise and made Flo feel a little fluttery inside. She hadn't expected a gift and hardly knew what to think or say...

'I grew these bulbs myself,' Robbie said. 'I think they should be pink when they open, but I'm not sure.' He looked at Flo's father, who was sitting by the fire and looking at his newspaper. 'Happy Christmas, Mr Hawkins. I hope you have a good day tomorrow – all of you.'

'Thank you, Robbie,' Flo said. 'I'm glad you found time to pop round. I've got a little parcel for each of your two – but I didn't get you a gift. I'm sorry.'

'I didn't expect it, you've done enough for the children,' Robbie said and accepted her gifts. He hesitated, glancing at Flo's father. She knew he'd hoped they would get a moment alone. 'I suppose I'd better get back. I left the kids with Bert, but he won't want to be up late...'

'Oh, before you go, I wanted to show you something in the shop... a little job...' Flo said and led the way through the hall, closing the door after Robbie. 'There isn't anything wrong... I just wanted a moment alone. It's awkward with Dad there...' she confessed, slightly breathless because her heart was racing. She hadn't been alone with him for years and felt a little shy, her cheeks pink.

'I wanted to be alone with you,' Robbie said and smiled. He reached out and took her hand. She didn't draw it away. She couldn't, because she could hardly breathe. 'We've never had time to talk, Flo – and I know I don't deserve that you should listen but...' He hesitated, then: 'What I did all those years ago was wrong and cowardly...'

'We were both so young,' Flo said at once. 'I was as much to blame as you... and neither of us really knew what we were doin'...'

'I did,' Robbie said. 'I never thought you would fall for a baby just because we made love once... I was shocked when you told me and I ran, Flo, but I did come back... Only it was too late...'

'You came back?' She looked up at him in shock. 'I never knew...'

'I wrote and then I came but I was told you wouldn't see me... and given a black eye as well as a broken rib...' Flo gasped in shock and he shook his head. 'Don't be upset, Flo. It was such a long time ago, but I do want to make it up to you if I can...'

'Was it Dad?'

He nodded and she clenched her hands as the anger flared.

'He had no right...'

'Perhaps he did,' Robbie said. 'You were his daughter and too young to have a child – too young to marry a callow youth with no prospects...'

'That should have been my choice...' Flo's eyes stung with tears. She had never known that Robbie had returned for her and been sent away! It shocked and distressed her, because she'd thought he had not truly loved her. 'Oh, Robbie, I'm sorry for what he did to you...'

'I'm the one who should apologise. I took advantage and I let you down,' he asserted and reached out to touch her cheek. 'I don't blame your dad any more and neither should you, Flo. He was taking care of you – and, as it happens, he was right. I wasn't much of a provider for my wife or my kids. It was fine for a while, but then I had a fall at work and was in bed for months with a damaged spine and a broken ankle. I mended, but it took ages to get back to work and then the work started to dry up...'

'None of that was your fault,' Flo said. She gazed up at him, feeling the love she'd suppressed for years flow out of her. 'You worked hard when you could – and you're a good man, Robbie. Please, don't put yourself down.'

'I'm tryin' hard now to get on my feet,' Robbie said. 'I've got work for a month or so after Christmas – and there might be a lot more comin' my way, but I don't know for sure... I just wanted to tell you that I still care, Flo.' He met her gaze. 'Is it possible that one day...?'

Flo felt her eyes moisten and she offered a wobbly smile as he faltered. 'I still care for you, Robbie. I never stopped. I can't promise anythin', because I've got Dad to consider and Honour...' She hesitated, then, 'You do know she's your daughter?'

'I thought she might be,' Robbie said and caught his breath. Tears stung his eyes to hear her say it, even though he'd known. 'She's beautiful, Flo – just like you.

I'd like us to be together as a family one day – if that's all right with you?'

'One day perhaps,' Flo said and pressed her face into his shoulder, inhaling the lovely masculine scent of him and willing the tears not to flow. It was all too new, too painful to take in. 'It's what I would like, Robbie – but Honour doesn't know… and I couldn't leave Dad – despite what he did.'

'I wouldn't ask you to, love,' he said. 'Let's face it; I couldn't support a family yet. I'm managing now, but it will take me months before I have money in the bank and could offer you anything…'

'We'll have to think about what we do next, Robbie – but I want to be with you in time…' She gave him a loving smile, because she knew that now there was something to look forward to. Her grief over the years had not been his fault. He'd come back to marry her but her father had sent him away.

'I love you, Flo. I always loved you and Madge knew it… She didn't know it was you, but she sensed there was someone.' He held her close. 'I didn't mean to say all this yet, because it is too soon – but I couldn't help myself…'

'I'm glad you did,' Flo said. 'We both need time, Robbie – you have to get on your feet again, and I have to think of Honour and Dad. Maybe in time we'll be able to do what we want, but for the moment… But I want you to know I'm not bitter or angry.'

'I know.' Robbie kissed her softly on the lips. 'I know we have to be patient, but you've given me something to look forward to, Flo – far more than I deserve. And you will come out with me after Christmas?'

'Yes, I will...' Flo said and gave him a little push. 'Get those kids home and in bed – they will be beside themselves with excitement thinking about Father Christmas comin'...'

22

Ben tore the wrappings off the large box and yelled with excitement. It was the big Meccano kit he'd set his heart on. He'd got a new pair of boots too from his father and they were nice, but it was the Meccano that had him jumping up and down on his bed with glee.

'Thanks Dad…' he yelled and then his father entered the room just in time to see Ruthie tear the paper from her pretty new dress. 'That's lovely, Ruthie – does it fit?' Ben asked.

Ruthie held it up against her. It might be a little on the long side, but she didn't care; at least she wouldn't have splits under her arms at school now.

'It's lovely, Dad,' she said. 'Thank you…' She stroked the pretty pastel pink material with her hands, her face alight with pleasure before turning to her other parcels.

Ruthie and Ben both had one of their dad's long socks stuffed with little things. A few nuts in the bottom, a tangerine wrapped in silver paper, a long tin whistle, some humbugs and a comic in Ben's, and a hair slide, ribbon, a red lollipop and a pretty mirror with flowers painted on the wooden back for Ruthie. She had her doll from Father Christmas, because although Ben no longer believed in him, his sister did, and there were still more parcels to explore.

Flo had given Ben a set of drawing tools in a beautiful wooden box so that he could design the things he wanted to build, and she'd bought Ruthie a little papier-mâché jewellery box with a bead necklace inside. Bert had given Ben a train set in a box; it was clockwork, missing a little paintwork here and there, and had belonged to his sons when they were young, and Millie had given Ruthie a musical box with a fairy on top that rotated to the music when you wound it up; it looked new, but Robbie knew it belonged to a bygone age. The gifts were far beyond anything they'd ever expected and they were both thrilled.

Ben had given Ruthie two sugar mice and some sweets and he proudly handed his father a packet of five tiny cigars which made Robbie smile and pop one under his nose to inhale the delicious aroma. He couldn't remember the last time he'd smoked one and it was a real treat.

'Just like yer mum used to buy me,' he said. 'Thanks, son. Happy Christmas, both of you.'

'It's the best Christmas ever, Dad,' Ben said. 'I've wanted this Meccano set for ages – and Miss Flo's present is great too, because I'm goin' ter build things when I leave school.'

'You like Miss Flo, don't yer?' Robbie asked.

'She's great,' Ben said. 'When we were hungry sometimes, we used to look in her window and if she saw us, she gave us a bun or something... There ain't many do that... and that makes her special.'

'Yes, I think so too,' his father said. 'Well, you'd best get dressed and come down and have yer breakfast – and then you must go round to Millie and Bert and thank them for their presents.'

'Bert gave us half a crown each yesterday as well,' Ben said. 'I didn't want ter take it, Dad, because it wasn't earned – but he said it was fer Christmas...'

'Well, the train set he gave you belonged to his sons,' Robbie said. 'He wanted you to have it, but you mustn't get into the habit of takin' stuff too often even if Bert wants to give it to you.'

'I know, Mum wouldn't have liked it,' Ben agreed. 'She would've said we don't need charity – but I think they give us things because they haven't got anyone else and it makes them happy.'

'You see a lot more than most,' Robbie said and ruffled his son's hair. 'I told Millie she could give Ruthie things and no doubt Bert will give you stuff sometimes, but just be careful you don't let them give you too much, especially money. They don't have much money, even if they have things stored away.'

'I won't and I'll do their jobs for nothin',' Ben said. 'I've got a few folk I do jobs fer now, Dad: cleanin' winders mostly. I told Arnie I wouldn't take his money to the bookie again and I thought he'd tell me to clear orf – but he says I'm an honest lad and he's goin' ter give me a newspaper round next month when I'm ten. I help him sort the papers now and he gives me a shillin' fer doin' his winders, sweeping outside the shop and clearin' up what folk drop on the floor.'

'You're quite the entrepreneur,' Robbie said and laughed. 'I reckon you will build things one day if you want to – and I'm very proud of you.'

'I'm glad you bought Ruthie a new dress,' Ben told his father seriously as he helped set the kitchen table for their breakfast. 'She got into trouble at school because she was always splittin' it under the arms; she needs some more let out a bit...'

'I'm glad you told me, Ben,' Robbie looked thoughtful. 'I could take yer mum's old clothes and sell them to buy her some things – or I could get someone to cut a couple of the dresses up to make new ones for Ruthie, but I didn't want to touch yer mum's things without yer permission, son.'

'I think Mum would want you to sell most of her things, but if you could make some of them into skirts or dresses for Ruthie that would please her too.' Ben looked serious. 'Mum's gone and we have ter look after Ruthie, Dad.'

'That's what I'll do then,' Robbie said and felt his throat close, because his son was such a thoughtful lad. 'Do you need any clothes for school, Ben?'

'A couple of weeks ago, Bert offered me two pairs of good trousers that belonged to his son,' Ben told him. 'They were all right and fitted me so I wore them – Mum always said it wasn't worth gettin' me new because I grow out of them so fast and I don't bother much what I wear. I was thinkin' I'd give one of me old pairs to Mick; they'd fit him...'

'I think that's a good idea, son.'

'Mick has it a lot worse than us, Dad. We never went without food all day, even if it was just bread and drippin'.'

'I haven't been much of a dad since yer mum died, have I?'

'Yer the best dad ever,' Ben said and gave him a quick hug round his waist.

At breakfast, Flo opened the parcel from Honour and smiled as she saw the pretty blue velvet slippers and the handkerchiefs with embroidery in the corners. She looked across the table at her and smiled.

'Thank you – they are just what I wanted.'

'You always say that,' Honour said. 'Thank you for the lovely bracelet, my new cardigan and the silk scarf and everything...' She seemed a little subdued and Flo guessed it was because she hadn't even had a card from Roy. He'd promised so much and now it looked as if he'd let her down. She leaned over to kiss her cheek and give her a little hug.

'You're welcome,' Flo said. 'Don't look so disappointed, love. Roy may turn up yet, but if he doesn't – you'll find someone else. You're too pretty to cry over someone who let you down.'

'I know – but it's Christmas and he promised...'

'We have so much to be thankful for, Honour. Perhaps Roy just couldn't get in touch...' Honour nodded and Flo knew she was making an effort to cheer up. 'I'm looking forward to giving the kids their gifts later...'

'Dad gave me another five pounds,' Honour said. 'I went in to wish him Happy Christmas and he just sort of thrust it at me and told me to buy myself a new dress or put it towards somethin' I need...'

'Well, that was generous of him, especially after he gave us those sixpences for the children,' Flo smiled at her. 'I dare say he's making up for the past...'

Honour went up to fetch down his tray and Flo started on their dinner. She peeled potatoes and stuffed the cockerel with a sage and onion mixture, putting it into the oven after she'd baked some fresh mince pies for their own use. She had the vegetables prepared and the rich fruit pudding steaming in a saucepan by the time Honour came down again.

'You should have left some of it for me to do,' Honour said. 'Dad wanted to talk – he said he was sorry for not being kinder to me and asked me what I wanted to do with my life…'

'What did you say?'

'I said I wanted to get married one day but not yet…'

Flo looked at her and her heart ached as she saw the dark shadows beneath her daughter's eyes. 'Are you upset over Roy?'

'I loved him, Flo,' Honour said. 'Just because he has let me down that doesn't go away. I can't stop thinking about him even if I try…'

'You'll meet someone else in time…' Flo said but knew that if her daughter was anything like her it would not happen. She felt angry with Roy; because surely he could have told her face to face that he was finished with her?

'Perhaps,' Honour agreed. 'Maybe I'll just stay here and grow old in the shop…'

'Don't say that! It's nonsense and I won't have it,' Flo said sharply. 'I may not be here forever either, so you can just put that nonsense out of your mind…'

'I'm sorry – but you asked,' Honour said and left the room.

Flo sighed as she looked around her large spotless kitchen. She'd thought they were happy here, but it had become obvious to her that Honour thought of the shop as a prison. After Christmas, Flo would have to make inquiries about taking on some help, because she didn't want to keep Honour here against her will. If she would be happier elsewhere then she should be free to try...

'That was a good dinner, Flo. I do like a nice cockerel, so much more flavour,' her father said as he pushed back his empty plate. 'You should put the dishes to soak in the scullery and get ready. You have other things to do than washing up today.'

'I'll get some of it done before I get changed,' Flo said. 'But the pans can soak until later.' She hesitated, then, 'Are you sure you'll be all right alone, Dad? Honour can take the gifts round and I could stay here...'

'She'll never carry that lot on her own, you daft girl,' her father said. 'You don't get out much, Flo. Do as I say and leave that lot in the scullery. You've got tomorrow off, so it don't matter if you don't get finished today...'

'We should go if we want enough time to carry it all,' Honour said. 'Let's get changed, Flo – and then we can get goin'. I don't want to miss all the fun...'

'All right,' Flo said. 'That sweet jar of coins weighs a ton...'

They ran upstairs to their separate rooms and changed quickly into their best skirts and jumpers before meeting on the landing. Honour looked really beautiful and Flo's heart turned over; she was so proud of her daughter for thinking of others instead of sulking because of her own disappointment.

'I can't wait to see those children's faces,' Honour said. 'Ben and Ruthie weren't the only ones to press their noses against the window when we put the sugar mice out this year. They won't be able to believe they've actually got two each...'

'We've got enough for all the kids, haven't we? I'd hate to leave any of them out.'

'John gave us a list,' Honour said. 'We planned it down to the last sugar mouse...'

'Yes, I know – I'm just nervous I suppose...'

Honour laughed. 'I'm not. I'm excited. We worked so hard – but seeing those children's faces light up will make it all worthwhile...'

'Where are yer goin'?' Mick asked, kicking a brown beer bottle in the gutter. Ben had stopped to speak to him as his father and Ruthie carried on walking.

'We're goin' to the mission hall for a proper Christmas dinner,' Ben told him and saw the way his friend's eyes widened. Mick looked thin and dirtier than ever and Ben felt pity for him. 'You should come too. I reckon there's sure to be enough for one more – and if there ain't I'll share mine wiv yer... unless yer dad is gettin' dinner at 'ome?'

Mick gave a harsh laugh, but his eyes were miserable. 'He's bleedin' drunk as usual. There ain't nothin' to eat in the 'ouse – he spent every penny he had on drink… but I've hid half a bottle so he sobers up later.'

'Come on, Ben. We don't want to be late,' Robbie called.

'I've got ter go,' Ben said. 'Follow on behind us, Mick – they're sure to let yer in and it's better than goin' hungry on Christmas Day…'

Mick nodded but hung his head, kicking at the bottle in the gutter. Ben ran on to catch up with his father and sister. He felt vaguely guilty because he didn't have the right to invite the young half-Irish boy to lunch at the mission and yet Mick needed it as much as anyone.

When they entered the busy mission hall the smell of roast chicken dinner was mouth-watering and people were already finding places at the tables and being served with plates filled with delicious food. Ben caught sight of Mick as he dodged in and ran straight to the tables, finding a place right at the end. He grinned, because first come first served and they would have to find a place for whoever else turned up.

When Ben looked for a seat, he saw one next to Mick and took it, grinning at him as the lady brought them both a plate of chicken, mashed potatoes, veg and Yorkshire pudding with gravy and stuffing.

'This is a bit of all right,' Ben said, but Mick was too busy filling his mouth to answer.

'Did yer know Mick was comin'?' Ben's father asked softly, and sat next to him when he'd finished helping John cut the chickens.

'Yeah,' Ben lowered his voice. 'His dad's drunk and there's no food in his house.'

'He needs a wash,' Robbie murmured. 'Bring him home afterwards, lad, and we'll sort him out...'

As Flo and Honour carried their heavy baskets into the mission hall, every child's head turned towards them, and Flo guessed that somehow word had got out. Perhaps from the children who had already had their gift that morning or perhaps from some of John's band of devoted helpers, but there was a buzz of excitement as John Hansen greeted the two women with a smile and a wave. They took their places behind the serving counter, which had now been cleared of the luncheon dishes. In the mission kitchens the volunteers would be busy washing up.

John held up a hand for silence, then, 'Now, children, this is what you have all been waiting for – Miss Flo and Miss Honour have brought a present for all of you. Will you please form a line at the counter and you will each receive your gift.'

Ben nudged Mick in the ribs. 'Come on,' he said. 'Miss Flo has got something for all of us.'

John Hansen was speaking again. 'As well as a Christmas box, there is a silver sixpence for each child.' He gestured towards the sweet jar filled with sixpences.

'Don't wanna go,' Mick said, holding back. 'I ain't supposed to be here.'

'That don't matter...' Ben said and pulled at his arm.

Mick rose reluctantly to his feet and was so slow that by the time they got to the counter they were the last in the line, Ben just in front of Mick.

They patiently waited their turn and then something happened. It was so quick that most people didn't realise what was going on. A large, rough-looking man had thrust his way through the children to reach the counter and snatched the jar of sixpences. He barged back through the crowd of bewildered and frightened children and was on his way to the door when Ben realised what he'd done and yelled.

'He's pinchin' our money!'

At almost the same moment, Robbie sprang to his feet and sprinted towards the door, reaching it seconds before the thief. He opened his arms wide and stared at the unkempt figure in front of him.

'No you don't,' he said in a loud voice that caught the attention of all. 'That money belongs to Miss Flo and she intends it for the children. Just give it back and I'll let you go...'

'Get out of my way or it will be the worse fer yer...' the man muttered fiercely.

'You don't leave here with money intended for our children,' Robbie said, standing firm as the man tried to barge his way past him. He grabbed the sweet jar and the two men tussled over it, but Robbie wrenched it clear. The other man threw a punch at him, but he ducked and it swung his attacker off balance. John Hansen had realised what was happening and arrived with two other men. As the thief tried to snatch the jar back, they grabbed hold of his arms and hustled him through the door.

He struggled violently and then spat in John's face. 'I'll bleedin get the lot of yer...'

'This is Christmas Day, so I shan't call the police,' John told him calmly. 'But if I ever see you hanging round here again I will – and you are not welcome at the mission. You will never be served here again.'

The thief lifted his hand as if he would strike John, but Robbie moved forward. His hands were free of the heavy jar now and he put them up in a challenging manner.

'If you want ter fight pick on someone yer own size,' he growled.

The thief rushed at him, but Robbie was ready and punched him in the face. He staggered back, his mouth cut and bleeding, shaking his head from the blow. For a moment he looked as if he might try to come back at Robbie, but several of the men had clustered at his back and the thief turned away, spitting on the ground.

'I'll remember yer...' he muttered and slouched off.

'Well done, Robbie mate,' some of the men clapped him on the back. 'Yer saved the day...'

Robbie shook his head and looked at John. 'I reckon we know that thief and this isn't the first time he's robbed the mission...'

'Well, thanks to you, he didn't get away with it this time.'

Someone had restored the jar to its rightful place on the counter. A few of the children had run to their parents in fright, but now the line formed again. Ben and then Mick were still at the end.

Robbie glanced at Flo and she gave him a smile that seemed to speak of love and pride, making him feel that he was his own man again. He grinned at her and went back to his place.

Miss Flo handed out a box of sweets to each child and Miss Honour gave them all a bright shiny silver sixpence. Small faces lit up with delight. For some of them this was the only pocket money they had ever received. Cries of excitement and pleasure filled the hall. When it was Ben's turn, he saw that there was just one box left on the counter. Miss Flo offered it to him, but he shook his head.

'If that's the last one, Miss Flo – give it to Mick…'

'Oh…' Flo looked upset. 'We were sure we had enough for everyone…'

'I've had plenty of gifts this Christmas,' Ben said. 'Mick, this is yours.' He took it and handed it to his friend. Honour gave them both a sixpence.

'I'll have some sweets for you if you come to the house tomorrow,' Flo whispered. 'That was well done of you, Ben.'

Ben shook his head, his cheeks pink as he pocketed the sixpence and walked back to where his dad was sitting. Ruthie had her box open and was sucking a red lollipop.

'Ain't yer got one, Ben?'

'Nah, but it don't matter,' Ben said. 'You eat yours, Ruthie.'

'Yer can have one of me lollipops,' his sister offered, but Ben shook his head. 'I ain't hungry. You keep it fer later.'

'I saw what you did,' Robbie said in a low voice. 'That was a good thing to do, son. I'm proud of yer.'

'That man – the one who tried to steal Miss Flo's money…' Ben frowned. 'I'm sure he's the man who threw that cash box in the dustbin near Finney's.'

'Yes, I thought it might be.' Ben's father nodded his agreement. 'He has been hanging round here and at the Sally Army offices – and they think he broke in and stole a collecting tin left on their counter. They don't leave money in the office, but there were a few pennies in the tin.'

'It's still pinchin', ain't it?'

'Yes, it is, Ben. John Hansen wouldn't call the police because it's Christmas Day, but he'll telephone tomorrow and ask them to keep a watch over this place.'

'Are we goin' now, Dad?'

'After I've had a word with Miss Flo and Miss Honour.' His father looked at him and then ruffled his hair affectionately. 'If Mick wants to come to our house for a bit of cake and some clean clothes – you can ask him if you like.'

'Thanks, Dad,' Ben said and turned to look for Mick who had disappeared while he was talking to his father. He searched the hall for him, but by the time his father came back for them, he knew that Mick had gone.

'Your friend didn't want to come?' he asked.

'He left while me back was turned,' Ben said. 'He's like that, Dad. Sometimes he'll speak ter me, others he won't... he has a terrible time at home. When Mick comes to school, he has bruises all over him, but a lot of the time he just stays away. The teacher tried to talk to Mick's father about it once, but he was drunk and threatened him and no one has dared to say a word since... but a lot of days no one sees Mick at all.'

'Someone should be told,' Ben's father said. 'It's

wrong that this kind of thing can go on and no one dares to stop it... maybe we should tell the police.'

'Mick would never speak to me again if we did that,' Ben said. 'Please don't, Dad. Not the police...'

'Well, I'll have to tell someone. I'll speak to John Hansen after Christmas...'

Ben nodded and followed his father from the mission hall. When Mick showed up again, he would invite him round to the house, but who knew when that would be.

23

Flo deposited her basket on the kitchen table and sighed with contentment. Her father looked at her and nodded.

'Went all right then, did it?' he asked.

'Yes – thanks to Mr Graham,' Honour said, depositing the still half-full jar of sixpences. 'A rough-lookin' man tried to steal your sixpences, Dad. Mr Graham went after him and stopped him. Some of the men put the thief out...'

'They should've called the police,' her father growled.

'John Hansen said he wouldn't because it was Christmas Day.'

'Sentimental fool. If the bugger was low enough to try to steal from the kids, he will do it again elsewhere.'

'Robbie's knuckles were red where he'd hit the man. I should think they will be sore,' Flo said and went to put the kettle on the hob, but she was filled with pride and glad that Honour had been there to see Robbie's bravery. 'I'll make us a cup of tea.'

'So was it worth all your hard work?' her father asked.

'It was lovely,' Honour answered first. 'The children lined up properly like Mr Hansen told them and there was hardly any pushing – but we were one box short and so Ben didn't get one. Luckily we had plenty of sixpences so I gave him one of those – but he missed out on the box of sweets.'

'I thought you double-checked your list?'

'We did,' Flo said. 'There was a young lad there on his own – he looked dirty and uncared for. I think he just turned up out of the blue. One of the other women told me they had to fetch a stool from the kitchen and use an enamel plate for one dinner. They had plenty of food and several people had seconds – but they had checked the numbers too and they're sure an extra child turned up.'

'By the sound of it he needed that meal more than most,' Flo's father said.

'Yes, I think he did, poor lad. Ben was before him in the queue, but he gave the gift to the other boy – Mick… he's a good-looking lad with black hair and blue eyes, but as thin as a rake and filthy.'

'Sounds as if he might be Irish,' her father observed. 'It's a pity Ben didn't get his box of treats – but you can give him something next time you see him.'

'I told him to come tomorrow, but I don't think he will.'

'Shame, because I know the Graham children were a big part of the reason you did it.'

'Yes, at the start,' Flo agreed, 'but Robbie is gettin' on his feet again now, Dad. He can provide for his children – and there were so many little faces there. Most of them hadn't had anythin' for Christmas. The way their eyes lit up was wonderful to see. I felt like cryin'...'

'No need for tears. They will remember this Christmas as special all their lives – and that's down to you two,' Mr Hawkins told them. 'You've worked so hard, the pair of you – and I'm proud of my girls. Rich people give money to charity, but you were prepared to work for what you did – and that makes it special.'

Flo's cheeks were warm and her father's praise made her glow. He'd seldom given her a kind word over the years and, though he'd softened of late, this was high praise.

'I'm goin' to...' Honour said and broke off as there was a knock at the door. 'Who can that be?'

Flo was the closest. She went to open it and stared as she saw who stood there. For a moment she was silent and then she opened the door wider.

'You'd better come in,' she said. 'You have a lot of explaining to do...'

As she led the way into the kitchen, Honour gave a little squeak of surprise, staring at the man in uniform as though she couldn't believe her eyes.

'Roy! What are you doin' here?' she asked, looking shocked.

'I came to see you,' he said. He looked from her to Flo. 'From what you said, I think you didn't get my letter, Honour...'

'No, I didn't get a letter...'

'Why don't you take Roy through to the shop – or go for a walk?' Flo suggested. Roy's unexplained absence had cast a shadow over Christmas for Honour but already she looked happier.

'Will you come for a walk?' Roy's eyes held a look of appeal.

'Yes, all right...' Honour reached for the coat she'd taken off earlier. 'I shan't be long, Flo...'

'If you hurt that girl of mine you'll be sorry...' Mr Hawkins said, suddenly fierce and clenching his fist. 'I may be old, but I'm not too weak to give you a backhander...'

Roy looked at him. 'I never meant to hurt her, sir,' he replied. 'I just want to explain – if she will let me...'

'I'm ready,' Honour said. 'I'll see you later, Flo...'

Flo nodded but didn't speak as they left.

She made the tea and brought a tray to the table.

'I don't know whether he's lyin', but I haven't seen a letter for Honour...'

'No need to look at me, girl. I didn't take it this time...'

'You mean you took Robbie's letter. The one askin' me to forgive him and to meet him...'

'Told yer about it has he?' Her father's eyes dropped. 'Yer mother opened it and gave it to me – demanded I do somethin' about it, so I did... I told him to clear off and I gave him a good hidin'...'

So many years of not knowing, of believing that Robbie hadn't wanted to wed her, hadn't loved her... Between them, her parents had ruined her life. For a moment bitter tears threatened, but then Flo realised it didn't matter. Robbie loved her and one day they would be together.

'I was never good enough fer yer mother's family,' her father said suddenly. 'Her father didn't like me and he put that bit in his will to make sure the shop came to you when she died and not me. I was angry over that – and I hated your mother lying to me; that's why I made her share her profits with me. Robbie Graham was too young to have a child and so were you – but if you'd told me you loved him it might have been different...'

Flo looked at him and believed him. Her mother had threatened her with what her father would do and she'd let herself be dominated, but he'd been hurt and he'd had a right to be angry.

'Do you swear to me that you didn't take Honour's letter?'

'I swear on me life.'

Flo nodded. 'I hope she will believe you. I do, but she may not. She was very hurt because Roy just stopped comin'. He'd asked her to marry him and she thought he'd been lyin' to her.'

'You never told me anythin' about this...' He glared at her and then his gaze dropped. 'I suppose I can't blame yer after the way I've been. You'll hate me now if yer didn't before...'

'No, Father, I don't hate you,' Flo said. 'My life hasn't been all bad. I like my shop and I enjoy my work. It might have been better if I'd had Robbie too – but that is the past.'

'There's nothin' ter stop yer now,' he said. 'That man thinks the world of yer – I saw it in his eyes. You could have him now if yer want...'

'Perhaps...' Flo hesitated. 'Robbie has to get on his feet again. He's too proud to live on what I earn from the shop. If he is successful, we might marry – but Honour is more important for now. I told her she couldn't marry until next summer, but I'm not goin' to stand in her way. If she wants to get married sooner, she has my blessin'. It means I'll need help in the shop though – and I might need some help in the house too...'

'I shan't be a trouble to yer for much longer...'

'Don't talk like that!' Flo said sharply. 'Sometimes I've been angry with you because you hurt me – but I don't want you to die. You're my dad and, despite everythin', I love you... and I'll always look after you.'

Her father didn't answer. He just sat and looked at her and the tears trickled down his lined cheeks. His tea sat on the table in front of him turning cold, but neither he nor Flo touched their cups.

'It's time I went up,' he said a few minutes later. 'Honour will want to talk to yer alone when she gets back...'

'I'll get you to bed,' Flo said and ignored his angry shake of the head. 'Don't be daft, Dad. You can't manage alone...'

Robbie took the children to see Bert and Millie that evening. The elderly couple were sitting in front of their kitchen table and they wanted to know all about the Christmas lunch at the mission. Ruthie was bubbling over, telling them how good the roast chicken had tasted and the tinned fruit with custard, and showing them what was left of her box of treats.

'What about you, Ben?' Bert asked. 'Did you get one, lad?'

'Ben gave his up because there was one short,' Robbie answered for him. 'A young lad came on his own to the lunch. He wasn't on the list, but they fed him and Ben insisted he have the last box.'

'I got lots of presents,' Ben said. 'I didn't need it – and Mick didn't get anythin' else. His dad was drunk and there was no food in the house. I told him to come to the mission. I knew they'd have lots of food – and if they hadn't, I'd have shared my dinner with him.'

'Yes, you would.' Bert nodded his approval. 'Yer a good lad, Ben. Where does this Mick live?'

'I think it's one of them derelict places what the council boarded up. I've seen him headin' in that direction, but he never says anythin' – he only told me he hadn't had anythin' to eat 'cos I said we were goin' to the mission for our dinner…'

'I'm goin' to have a word with Nurse Mary tomorrow,' Robbie said. 'She will know the proper people to tell. Everyone at that lunch today was hard up, Bert – but most had scrubbed their kids' hair and spruced them up best they could. Mick was filthy and probably had nits…'

'It's not his fault,' Ben defended his friend swiftly. 'There ain't no water in them derelict houses…'

'No, there wouldn't be,' Robbie agreed. 'They were not fit for use when the council boarded them up. If it hadn't been for lack of money, they would've been pulled down now. They must be damp and rat-infested – and dangerous…'

'Mick hates it, but there's nowhere else…'

Robbie frowned. 'I'm worried about that lad. I think

I'll go round to John Hansen's house, Bert. Is it all right if I leave Ben and Ruthie here with you until I get back? I'll be as quick as I can.'

'Of course it is. You know we love havin' them,' Millie said. 'You do what you can to help that lad, Robbie. We look after our own round here…'

'Does Mick go to your school, Ben?'

'He did for a while, but we often don't see him for days.' Ben shook his head. 'He hangs around outside and I've seen him sneak into the school kitchen.'

'Surely the school should send the inspectors round after 'im?' Millie said, looking anxious.

'He's slipped through the system,' Robbie said. 'Right, I'm goin' to tell John about this. He'll know the right people to deal with it…'

'Not the police, Dad…' Ben pleaded.

'Not the police – but the lad needs help,' Robbie insisted. 'We can't just stand by and do nothin'.'

Robbie walked swiftly. He tried the mission first but it was locked and there were no lights inside, so he went round the corner and into Lonely Lane, where John lived in an old three-storied house that had been divided into three flats. John had the ground-floor flat and answered his door as soon as Robbie knocked.

'I saw you coming,' he said. 'Is this about that incident today?'

'No, it's about a young lad who turned up at the mission uninvited – well, Ben told him he could come, but he wasn't on your list…'

'Yes, my ladies told me we had an extra child for lunch – but there was enough food to go round and more.'

'The point is that lad was filthy, neglected and near starvin' – and the father is often drunk. Ben says he thinks the lad and his father are livin' in one of those derelict houses the council boarded up near the docks.'

'Ah, I see what you mean,' John said. 'I'll get in touch with the children's department at the council. They will send someone round – but in the end it may be a job for the police. If the father doesn't want to be helped, he'll scarper…'

'Yes, I realise it is a difficult situation, but after what I saw today I had to do something. He looked thinner than ever and pale. Nurse Mary visits a lot of homes where the men are out of work; I wondered if she might know of the family.'

'If she does, she hasn't told me. You don't know the father's name?'

'The boy is called Mick but Ben didn't know his father…'

'Well, we must see if we can do something for the lad,' John said, 'but the father may be beyond help…'

'Everyone needs a chance,' Robbie said. 'I've been lucky and if I get all the work I've been told about, I shan't ever look back – but perhaps Mick's father needs a chance too. It's hard for all of us right now.'

'I'll certainly make inquiries, Robbie,' John said. 'Get home to your kids – and thank you for your prompt action at the mission today.'

'Goodnight then,' Robbie said. 'Sorry to disturb you. I'll see you after Christmas…'

Robbie left John to close his door and walked away. He didn't see the shadow walking up behind him and when the heavy object hit the back of his head he went down without a sound. The dark figure bent over him, searching through his pockets and taking the few coins that were in his jacket. Robbie was unaware when the man spat in his face and then kicked him in the side before walking away. Blood was seeping from the wound to the back of his head as the cold night settled around him…

24

'Roy was sent off on a special trainin' course. They only told him where he was goin' that mornin'. He wasn't allowed to leave camp, so he couldn't come to the shop and tell me. He scribbled a note to me and asked one of his mates to bring it round, but Roy thinks he must have forgot... and he says he did send me a card but only on Christmas Eve, because he wasn't given leave until then, so it might get here after Christmas...' Honour looked at Flo a little accusingly. 'If we'd had a phone he could have rung me...'

'Do you think he was tellin' the truth?' Flo looked into Honour's eyes and saw the sparkle was back. Her cheeks had a healthy colour and she looked beautiful. 'Are you sure he won't just disappear again, love? I just don't want you hurt...'

'Look what he gave me...' Honour held out the little blue velvet box. Flo took it and opened it, gasping as she saw the beautiful sapphire and diamond three stone ring inside. 'Roy wants us to get engaged now and married next spring or summer. He's still lookin' for a nice little shop with living accommodation over it... and when he finds it we can move in and settle down.'

'Then, you have my permission to get engaged and married when you're ready,' Flo said and smiled as she saw Honour's eyes light up.

'Roy was goin' to ask Dad tomorrow...' Honour looked apprehensive. 'Dad was angry – but he will give Roy a chance, won't he?'

'It's me you have to ask,' Flo said and met Honour's questioning look. She was trembling inside because she knew she had to tell her daughter the truth but wasn't sure whether Honour would accept it. Taking Honour's hand, she said gently, 'Let's sit by the fire and talk. There's something I need to tell you... something you need to know.'

Honour looked uneasy. 'What?'

Flo took a deep breath, 'You're my daughter, Honour – not my sister, and I've always loved you. I got into trouble when I was sixteen. Dad scared him off and Mum made me hide what she called "my shame" from the world. She pretended she was pregnant and two months before the birth she closed the shop and took me away to a small seaside village, where I gave birth to you. When we returned, she let everyone believe you were her daughter... and her middle name was the same as mine so she just put Florence Hawkins on the birth certificate and no one guessed.'

Flo stared at her daughter, waiting for the outburst of indignation or disbelief, but it didn't come.

Honour was crying, staring at her with the silent tears running down her face.

'So it is true...' she said and wiped her cheeks. 'Dad hinted at it a couple of times, but I thought he was just bein' horrible... because you never said and I thought you would tell me the truth...' The expression in her eyes was a mixture of regret and accusation, but there was no anger. 'Why didn't you, Flo?'

'I wanted to... so many times I wanted to,' Flo said. 'Can you ever forgive me for lyin' to you all these years? I love you so much, Honour. I didn't want to hurt you... I always wanted you to know I was your mum, but I was afraid to tell you in case you hated me.'

'Don't you know?' Honour asked a little sob on her lips. 'You've always been my real mum – you were there when I was ill and when I fell over. You were the one who spoiled me and made me pretty clothes for my dolls. I always knew you were special. You were the one I loved...'

'Oh, Honour...' Flo burst into noisy sobs as they sought each other's arms and hugged, crying and laughing at the same time. 'My own darling girl. I'm so sorry. All these years I've had to pretend you were my sister when I longed to tell you how much I loved you and how proud I was to be your mother. I want you to be happy and if Roy makes you happy that's fine with me...'

'He does love me, Mum,' Honour said and smiled at her. Flo felt the tears because it was the first time Honour had called her mum. 'He's the only one for me – just as Robbie is the only one for you. He's my father, isn't he? I've seen you lookin' at him and I've seen him lookin' at you...'

'Yes, Robbie was the only one I ever loved.'

'Surely you will get married?'

'Perhaps, if things go well for him,' Flo said and gave her a quick hug. 'For the moment you're more important. Now, put that pretty ring on your finger – in the morning you can show Dad and your friends. And if Roy has time, you will ask him to stay for lunch...'

'Oh, Mum,' Honour said and hugged her. 'You're the best. No one is like you and I hope you'll be as happy one day as I am...'

'Seeing your eyes shine makes me happy,' Flo said. 'It hurt me to think that Roy had let you down – but at least you weren't pregnant like me...'

Honour's cheeks flushed and Flo guessed that perhaps she'd done more than kiss Roy on one of their dates, but thankfully she hadn't been punished for it the way Flo had – and even if Honour had come to her to confess she was pregnant, Flo would not have made her feel ashamed. Honour would never have felt the sting of shame or been made to feel unworthy just because she'd had a child out of wedlock.

'Why didn't they let you marry Robbie?' Honour asked, looking distressed.

'It's a long story. Dad played his part, and some of it was Robbie's fault, but, I think now, mostly my mother's.' She kissed Honour's cheek. 'Robbie wants to get to know you, but he didn't want to upset your grandfather or me...'

'My grandfather?' Honour nodded. 'It's so strange... Ben and Ruthie – they're my brother and sister?'

'Yes, your half-brother and half-sister,' Flo said. 'Do you mind?'

'No...' Honour smiled and hugged her. 'I'm glad. It means we could all be a family...'

'Yes, perhaps – and now it's time we got to bed,' Flo said and smiled. 'It has been a long and exciting day, my love, and we're both tired...'

'I'm tired,' Ruthie announced and rubbed her eyes. 'Where's my dad? I want ter go 'ome...'

Bert looked at the mantle clock. It was half past ten and Robbie had been gone hours. 'Yer dad has been gone a long time. I'm not sure why...'

'You should go to bed, sir,' Ben said, because he could see that Granda was weary. Granny Millie had said goodnight after Ben had made them all some cocoa at nine o'clock. Granda Bert had sat up with them, but he kept yawning behind his hand. 'We'll be all right here by the range. It's warm and neither of us is hungry. We can sleep on the sofa until Dad gets here...'

Bert hesitated, clearly uncertain. 'I wish we knew where yer dad has got to,' he said. 'It's a bitter night, Ben. I never expected he would be this long just speaking to Mr Hansen...'

'He must have gone somewhere else,' Ben said and tried not to show how worried he was. His thoughts kept goin' round and round in his head and he was afraid his dad was in some trouble but didn't know what to do about it. Ben wasn't sure where Mr Hansen lived. He could find his way to the mission, but it was late and he knew the mission would be locked up for the night. 'If you don't mind us stayin' here in the kitchen, we'll just wait for him...'

'I wouldn't dream of sending you home alone,' Bert said. 'You're a sensible lad, Ben. You'll be all right here if I go to bed?'

'Yes, Granda,' Ben said and watched as the old man struggled to heave himself out of the sagging chair. 'Can yer manage on yer own?'

'Yes, thank you, I'll be all right – look after Ruthie. I'm just in the next room if yer need me.'

Ben saw that Ruthie was already curled up on the sofa. He tucked Granny Millie's blanket over her and sat down on the peg rug in front of the range. It was warm there and Ben wasn't ready to sleep yet. The ticking of the old marble mantle clock reminded him of the lateness of the hour and his unease grew as the minutes passed and still his dad didn't come to fetch them. Ben didn't even consider that his dad might have gone home and forgotten they were here. Ben's father had got drunk a few times after their mum died, but things had been bad in those first months. Ben knew instinctively that his dad was in a better place in his life now. If he didn't come back for them, it was because he couldn't and that meant something had happened.

If Dad still wasn't back by the morning, he could find people and ask for help, but until then he had to wait even though it was the hardest thing he'd ever done in his young life...

Flo woke with a start and looked at the little alarm clock by her bed. It was half past six and she was usually up by now. She'd slept well and a smile touched her mouth as she remembered Honour's happiness the previous evening when she came back from her walk with Roy, to show her her lovely ring.

Pushing back the bedclothes, Flo put her feet to the floor. It was freezing and she hurriedly pushed her feet into fluffy slippers and pulled on her dressing gown. She hadn't heard her father ring the little bell he used to alert them when he needed to get up and use the commode. He must be bursting to go now, because she was – but she could hold on until she got him settled.

Walking softly along the hall, she opened his door and went in. Her father was lying back against the pillows, his eyes shut. It was unusual for him to sleep this late, because he'd always been up early and out to work until his illness struck him down.

'Dad...' Flo said softly, not wanting to disturb him if he was resting. 'Dad...?'

She could see that his mouth was open slightly and his face was white – he wasn't breathing. Flo's heart stopped for a moment and then raced on as the dread gripped her and she felt a rush of panic and grief and she touched his cheek with her fingertips. He was very cold. She knew then that he must have passed during the night.

'Oh, Dad, no...' Flo said and the tears started to trickle down her cheeks because it was so sad: all the years they had spent estranged, hardly speaking to each other at times, separated by a secret that need never have been. 'Please, not now...'

For a moment she sat beside him on the bed, mourning him, regretting that she hadn't found a way to reach him long ago. They might have discovered how to love each other again.

Sighing, Flo got to her feet and walked down the hall to Honour's room. She knocked and entered. Her daughter was sitting up in bed, admiring the ring on her finger.

'Are you all right, Mum?'

Flo went to sit on the edge of her bed and hold her hand. There was only one way to say it, 'Honour, I'm so sorry, dearest – but Dad is dead... He passed away in the night.'

Honour's face drained of colour. She stared at Flo and then the tears started flowing. 'No! I wanted to tell him about Roy, to let Roy tell him about... We had such a lovely day...' Flo embraced her, comforting her as she wept. 'I know I grumbled about him a lot, but I didn't want him to die... Oh, Mum – what are we goin' to do?'

'I'm goin' to slip my clothes on and then I'll ring for the doctor and tell him. Once he's been we'll have to contact...' She shook her head. 'Go down and put the kettle on, Honour.'

Honour nodded and looked at her mother with agonised eyes. 'Roy is comin' round later... I'm not sure how to contact him...'

'Let him come. You can go out with him for a while, get away from the house until things are settled...'

'I'm not leavin' you to cope with everythin' on your own,' Honour said. 'I'll pop in and say goodbye to Dad and then I'll put the kettle on...'

Flo didn't argue. Her daughter was old enough to fall in love and marry; she was old enough to face the reality of death.

Flo dressed hurriedly in the clothes she'd worn the previous day – such a lovely day giving presents to the children and Honour's engagement and finally telling her that she was her mother – and now this. It was with a heavy heart that she went downstairs, out of the kitchen door and through the little passage to the main street where the red phone box was situated. She knew the doctor's telephone number by heart and dialled it, putting in her pennies when she was told and pushing the button when directed.

'Dr Forrest here...'

'It's Flo Hawkins, Dr Forrest,' Flo said. 'I think my father is dead; I found him first thing this morning...'

'I'll be round as quickly as I can, my dear.'

Flo replaced the receiver and left the phone box, retracing her steps almost reluctantly. She wasn't looking forward to what followed and wished it hadn't happ-ened so soon after Christmas Day.

Honour looked at her as she entered the kitchen. Her eyes were red and she couldn't stop her tears.

'The doctor is coming to confirm...' she said.

Honour made the tea and poured it. 'Do you want a piece of toast?'

'No, just tea. I couldn't eat. The food would stick in my throat...'

Honour nodded. 'I feel the same. Why now – why did it happen now, when things were gettin' better between us?'

'Maybe he sensed he didn't have much time left,' Flo said and sipped her tea. 'I wouldn't have wanted it to happen at any time, Honour – but now...' She sighed and toyed with her spoon. 'It was awful when Mum died, but Dad took charge then...'

'Will the doctor tell us what to do?'

Flo understood her fears and gently explained what would happen after the doctor's visit.

'I'll use the same people that looked after Mum,' she said. 'They took her to a chapel of rest – and then the hearse brought her back to the street on the day of the funeral so we could follow to the church.'

It seemed ages before Dr Forrest arrived. He looked sombre and was very sympathetic. The death was expected and he patted their hands in a paternal way and told them what good girls they'd been to look after their father as they had. After he'd gone, the men came to take Mr Hawkins away and told Flo that they could visit once he was prepared for them.

The house seemed empty and horrible when they'd finally gone and neither of them knew what to do with themselves.

'I've made my bed. Is there anything you need me to do downstairs?' Honour asked.

'We'll have visitors when folk hear,' Flo said. 'We need to make sure the kitchen is spotless – and we're closing the shop until after the funeral...'

'Yes, I think Dad would expect that,' Honour said and looked at Flo oddly. 'I know he was my grandfather, but I can't stop calling him Dad...'

'Why should you? He stood as a father to you for years – and he felt shut out, Honour. Mum lied to him until she needed him to know the truth and so did I and that wasn't fair...'

'I think you're the one who was unfairly treated,' Honour said. 'Neither of them was fair to you.'

'No, perhaps not – but it's over now...'

Honour looked at her but didn't say much as they started to clean and tidy the large kitchen that served as their workplace and their resting place. It was where they received friends and where Dad had sat in his rocking chair by the range.

'Go up and wash your face and powder your nose. Roy will be here soon and you don't want to be red-eyed for him,' Flo said and smiled. 'Cryin' won't change anythin', love. Dad has gone and we can't change that...'

Someone knocked at the kitchen door. It was too early for Roy's visit, so Flo went to answer it and saw Ben standing there, looking as if he too had been crying.

'Is somethin' wrong, Ben?' Flo asked. 'What has happened?'

Ben followed her into the kitchen. 'Dad went to see Mr Hansen about Mick last night – and he didn't come back. He left us with Bert and Millie and we've been there all night...'

'Oh no!' Honour cried her face pale. Her eyes met Flo's and there was panic in them, as she realised that something might have happened to the man she'd only just discovered was her father. Flo was close to panic too, but she couldn't give way to it, because Ben was already frightened and worried.

Flo's spine felt icy and the back of her neck tingled. 'That's not like your father. He's never left you all night before – has he?'

Ben shook his head. 'After Mum died he had a bit too much to drink a few times and came home a bit daft... laughin' and then cryin', but he never stayed out all night – not once. I'm worried, Miss Flo. I don't know what to do...'

'I'll telephone Mr Hansen,' Flo said and grabbed her coat. 'Honour, find Ben some milk to drink and a piece of cake while I'm telephoning...'

Ben shook his head as Honour offered him a cake. 'I ain't hungry, miss. I just want ter help me dad...'

'I know how you feel,' Honour said and the tears started again. 'Flo's dad died in his sleep last night, Ben. He was a lot older than your dad – but I didn't want him to die...' She put an arm round him protectively. He was her brother, even though he didn't know it.

'I'm sorry, miss... I shouldn't have bothered yer, but I didn't know who else to ask.'

'Ben you can always come to us,' Honour said, hugging him. 'We care about you and Ruthie – and your dad. We're your friends and we'll always help you if we can...'

'Thanks...' Ben ground his fists in his eyes to stop the tears, but she heard the muffled sob and knew that he was worried out of his mind for his father. 'Yer very kind, miss...'

'Why don't you call me, Honour?' she said. 'We're friends, aren't we, Ben?'

'Yeah, I reckon,' Ben said. 'It was a good thing yer done yesterday, miss... Honour. All the kids were excited and Ruthie loved everythin' she got...'

'I remember you didn't get any sweets,' Honour said. 'You let your friend have the last one.'

'Dad bought me a Meccano set. I didn't need nothin' else,' Ben said. 'Mick's father never gives him anythin'. Most days he don't get enough to eat. I told him to ask Arnie fer work, but he said no one would give him a job…'

'Perhaps if he had a wash and some clean clothes,' Honour said. 'I remember he was a bit dirty.'

'Mick is always filthy and he smells,' Ben said, 'but he's all right and I feel sorry fer him.'

Flo returned then and told them that she'd spoken to John Hansen. 'John says your father spoke to him last night and then left. He is goin' to make inquiries and speak to the police and ring round some of the hospitals… just in case he had an accident or was attacked.'

Ben rubbed at his eyes fiercely. 'Why would anyone hurt me dad?'

'Well, you remember the man who tried to steal the sixpences?' Ben nodded and Flo put her arm round him. 'He threatened everyone, particularly John and your father. It is possible that he might have been hanging around last night…'

Ben nodded, his hands curling into tight balls at his sides. 'He was a rotten devil and they ought to have called the police…'

'Yes, I agree with you,' Flo said, 'but it was Christmas Day – and, besides, we don't know for sure that anything has happened to your father...' but even to herself she sounded unconvincing.

'Where is he then?' Ben demanded. 'He wouldn't have left us if he could help it – somethin' bad must have happened and I don't know what to do, Miss Flo. We can't stay with Millie and Bert all the time. They've said we can, but they can't afford to keep us and it's too much work...'

'No, you're right...' Flo looked at Honour.

'Why don't we go round to your house and fetch some clothes for you and Ruthie?' Honour said. 'You and your sister can stay here. You can sleep in my bed and I'll sleep with Flo for now. We'll get your things and collect Ruthie on the way back...' She glanced at the clock. 'If Roy comes before we get back, tell him I shan't be long, Mum...' She put her arm about Ben's shoulders again, because he was so upset he didn't seem to quite know what she was saying.

'Yes, all right, love.' Flo smiled at her gratefully. It was exactly what she would have suggested herself, but she hadn't known what Honour would think – especially with Dad just dead. Yet there was nothing more they could do for him and these children needed help. 'I'll change the sheets on the beds and make room in your chest of drawers for their clothes...' She needed to keep busy, because her mind was racing with all the possibilities. Robbie must be hurt; he couldn't have disappeared into thin air!

'Come on, Ben,' Honour said, slipping her coat on and offering her hand. 'We'll go to your house and bring a bag full of things and then call at Bert and Millie's to tell them you and Ruthie will be staying with us – you can still go there each day and help them, just as you have been doin'…'

'All right,' Ben said and looked at Flo. 'It's good of yer, Miss Flo – me dad said yer were all right, so I thought you'd know what to do…'

'We'll find him, Ben,' Flo said and smiled. 'I can't promise he isn't hurt but don't say anythin' to Ruthie. You'll be company for us – cheer us up in this sad time and your dad will probably be home before you know it…'

After Honour had gone with Ben, Flo received a visit from Mavis next door. Her daughter Kitty was Honour's best friend and Mavis had been friends with Flo's mother.

'I couldn't help noticin' a lot of comin' and goin',' she said to Flo as she answered the door. 'Is everythin' all right, love?'

'Dad died in his sleep last night,' Flo said, tears on her cheeks because it was all too much. She'd lost her father and now Robbie was missing! 'They've taken Dad to a chapel of rest… the doctor thought it best…'

'That's a terrible blow fer yer,' Mavis said. 'Losin'

yer poor father. I thought I saw them take a coffin out and I said ter Kitty as it was yer dad. I'm sorry fer yer, Flo...'

'Yes, it was a shock to find him,' Flo said. 'I'd believed he was gettin' better, but he'd been ill for a long time.'

'If yer need anythin' – anythin' at all, let me know,' Mavis said. 'Yer will be closin' the shop for a while no doubt.'

'We're never busy after Christmas,' Flo said. 'I shan't open again until after the funeral – and I'm not sure when...' She shook her head.

'Did I see a little lad leaving with Honour just now?'

Flo hesitated for a moment, then, 'Yes, you did, Mavis. We've promised to look after two children for a friend and she's gone to fetch their things...' There was no need to tell her neighbour that Robbie was missing.

'Well, I never! At a time like this... I should've thought you would tell your friend it wasn't convenient. With yer dad just gone... God bless his soul...' She crossed herself fervently. 'May he rest in peace...'

'Well, they will make it feel less empty, cheer us both up a bit...' Flo said.

'Well...' Mavis was clearly shocked. She took her leave soon after that, leaving Flo hardly knowing whether to laugh or cry. Her neighbour would think she was showing her father no respect and probably spread the word that she was heartless, but Flo had more to worry her than her neighbour's gossip.

Looking after Robbie's children would be more a pleasure than a bother but she couldn't help the nagging feeling at the back of her mind that something terrible had happened to him.

'Robbie, where are you?' she whispered. 'I've just lost Dad. I can't bear to lose you too. Please, come back to us… wherever you are…'

25

Flo pulled the sheets from all three beds and bundled them up for the laundry. She would put them out in the scullery cupboard until the man came round again the next week. She polished the furniture in the bedrooms and enjoyed the smell of lavender when she closed the doors on them and went downstairs. She had just put the kettle on when someone knocked on the door and she opened it to Honour's fiancé.

Inviting Roy into the kitchen, she explained about her father's death, Ben's arrival and his father's disappearance.

'Honour went to fetch the children's things,' she said. 'They can't stop with their friends indefinitely, because Millie couldn't cope, even though she loves them. Honour suggested we have them here and I believe it is the best solution. Hopefully, their father will be found soon.'

'What will you do if he isn't?'

'I'm not certain,' Flo said. 'I think Robbie would want me to care for them – if I'm allowed to. I have the business to look after here, but I can afford to employ some help in the house – and to be honest, the children will not be more trouble than an invalid father.'

'Growing children are expensive,' Roy said and looked thoughtful. 'I've known what it's like to be hard up. I couldn't do much for a start – until I have my own business up and running, but I would like to help if you need me later on...'

'I couldn't take your money,' Flo said and smiled at him, because at least he had shown willing. 'You and Honour will need that – for yourselves and your own family once you have children.' She gave him an old-fashioned look. 'You are planning to marry Honour I hope?'

'Of course.' He had the grace to look ashamed. 'I was thrown into a tough training course, and to be honest, I was too exhausted every night to think straight – but I should have found a way to let Honour know.'

'I shall forgive you, providing you never let her down again.'

'I promise I won't – but this other business. How will you manage with two young children and a shop if their father doesn't turn up?'

'I'll find a way,' Flo said and lifted her head proudly. 'I haven't given up hope yet, Roy. I'm hoping perhaps we shall find him in a hospital and all will be well once he recovers…'

'Of course, that is the best solution and I pray he's safe somewhere…' Roy frowned. The door opened and Honour came in. She was carrying a large but very old leather suitcase and held tightly to the little girl with her other hand. Ben followed behind, carrying a bag filled with various bits and pieces.

'We brought a few clothes and some toys,' Honour said and smiled at Roy before looking down at the very nervous little girl who still clung to her hand.

'Hello, darling,' Flo said, bending down to be on Ruthie's level. 'Would you like some milk and a piece of cake?'

'Yes, please…' Ruthie said in a small voice.

She followed Flo to the old sofa and sat down. Ben gave her the doll she'd had for Christmas and she hugged it to her, looking anxious as her gaze moved about the big kitchen.

'Why don't you take Roy into the shop for a while?' Flo said to her daughter who had gone to her fiancé's side and was whispering to him. 'Its cold out for walking – I'll get Ruthie and Ben settled.'

Ben sat beside his sister, clutching his Meccano set. He looked uncomfortable, because it was all so strange.

'Granny Millie said we could stay, but she looked

tired and Granda said it was best we came here until Dad gets back…'

'Mr Hansen will find him,' Flo told Ben.

'Yeah, I know,' Ben said and put his Meccano set down. 'What can I do – fetch in some coal or wash the window…'

'You can fetch the coke in for the range,' Flo said, understanding that he needed to make himself useful. She too needed to be busy. 'I'm going to take your case up and show you where you and Ruthie will sleep – and we're very lucky, we have a toilet upstairs and one in the back yard. When you've had something to eat, you can play with your Meccano or go out to meet friends – this is your home for the time being, Ben. You can do what you like…'

'I filled Granda's coal buckets this mornin',' Ben said. 'I'll go round this afternoon and see what they need – but the shops are still closed fer Christmas, 'cos it's Boxing Day. They won't have no jobs until the mornin'.'

'Then play with your Meccano set,' Flo said. 'You can set it up in the kitchen or in the bedroom if you like…'

She carried the case into Honour's bedroom and unpacked their clothes, Ruthie watching with her thumb in her mouth. Apart from Ruthie's new dress, her clothes were very shabby. Ben had two decent pairs of trousers, but the rest of his things were patched and his jumpers were worn thin. Flo knew that several of Honour's dresses she'd kept from her childhood would fit Ruthie. She could get them out, wash and iron them and see if the little girl liked them, but there wasn't much she could do for Ben – the only way was to buy something decent off the market and cut them to fit him. Second-hand clothes were all right, providing you bought only the best and were good with the needle.

Ben looked round the spacious bedroom and grinned. 'Can I set up the Meccano here and leave the models half built?'

'I'm sure you can,' Flo said. 'Come and have a drink of something and a piece of cake and then you can play...'

After they'd eaten, Ben went back upstairs to set out the pieces of his Meccano set, but Ruthie sat on the sofa and watched as Flo started to prepare their lunch. She sliced some potatoes and put them in the oven to roast, prepared some sliced carrots and cabbage and then cut meat from the large cockerel they'd roasted the previous day. Flo then started to make a strawberry jelly, which she intended to offer with some tinned fruit and cream for their tea. The smell of the jelly melting in hot water brought Ruthie to the table.

'My mum used to make strawberry jelly,' she confided shyly to Flo.

'Do you like it?' Flo asked and the child nodded and smiled for the first time since her arrival. 'I like it too – especially with tinned peaches and cream.'

'Ohh that's lovely...' Ruthie said, her face lighting up. 'I haven't had that since I was five on my birthday...'

'That's a long time ago,' Flo said. 'I'm going to put this outside in the scullery so that it sets quickly. Do you want to help me set the table for lunch?'

Ruthie nodded and looked at the large oak dresser that took up most of one wall and was set with lots of blue and white crockery. 'Do I get the plates from there?'

'Yes, please. The middle-size ones, I think. I'll get the knives and forks – and the place mats.'

Between them they set the table and Ruthie started to chatter. She talked about Granny Millie and school – and how her friends had laughed at her because her dress split.

'Mum used to mend my things,' she explained, 'but Dad doesn't know how to. Granny Millie put patches under the arms of one, but the other girls called me names because of the patches... they were a different colour...'

'Well, I might be able to sort something better out

before you go back to school,' Flo said. 'I've got some pretty dresses we could look at after lunch – and if you find something you like, I'll alter them to fit you.'

Ruthie nodded happily. She was used to second-hand clothes. As long as they fitted her, she didn't mind. Her school friends had second-hand things too; they'd taunted her because hers had big splits and odd patches under the arms. Yet none of them were much better dressed, but for some reason they'd decided to pick on her, perhaps because she cried easily after her mum died.

Flo called Ben down for lunch when Honour came through to the kitchen. Roy was on duty that afternoon, but he was coming back the next day and would stay to lunch then.

The meal was easier than Flo had thought. Both children ate their food with evident enjoyment, and Honour managed a little too. She seemed to have stopped crying now and Flo was too busy to dwell on her father's death. It was something that she would always regret, because she'd just begun to know him, but at least they had broken down some of the fences before he died. She just wished she'd been with him at the end so that she could have said goodbye... but that was most people's lament and Flo had to think about Robbie's children. At the back of her mind the shadow of Robbie's disappearance haunted her, but she tried not to let it weaken her resolve.

It was mid-afternoon when John Hansen came to the door. Ben had taken Ruthie round to see if Granny and Granda were all right, and Flo was just thinking about what she ought to do next when he knocked on the door. She smiled and invited him into her kitchen, which was not quite as tidy as usual, but John knew she didn't have a parlour and was relaxed as he sat on one of the kitchen chairs.

'I was so sorry to hear about your father, Miss Hawkins,' he said. 'I know he has been ill for some time, but he did seem a little better in himself when I last called.'

'Yes, that's why it upset us so much…'

'Your father was a stubborn man. You've been very patient and kind, looking after him so devotedly, Miss Hawkins…'

'Please, call me Flo,' she said. 'We know each other too well for you to be so formal, John.'

'Yes…' He smiled and looked pleased. 'Am I right in thinking you're looking after Robbie's children while he's… missing?'

'Yes.' Flo looked at him anxiously. 'You haven't heard anythin'? He isn't at the hospital or the infirmary…'

'Neither of our local medical facilities had taken in a man of his description,' John said and looked anxious. 'I thought he might have slipped on the ice but…'

'He can't just have disappeared, unless…' Flo couldn't say the words. If he'd been murdered, his body might have been hidden or thrown in the river, but she daren't think about that eventuality.

'He may have been hurt and wandered off in a daze,' John said. 'I'm so sorry, Flo. I wanted to bring you better news, especially at a time like this…'

'It isn't your fault,' Flo said. 'We just have to pray that Robbie will be found and that whatever happened to him, he will be all right soon…'

'Yes – and now we had best discuss the details of your father's funeral. Once the authorities give you permission to bury your father you will wish to have it all in place.'

Flo agreed and they talked about her father's favourite hymns. Talking with John eased the tension inside her and made it possible for her to grieve for her father without regret.

'You will continue your visits to the mission?' he asked as he was leaving.

'If I can,' she said. 'The children are my first priority now – and Honour is courting, so she must have time to go out. I just hope Robbie is safe and comes home soon.'

John looked at her a little oddly, hesitated as if he would say something, then smiled and left. Flo wondered if she'd shown her feelings for Robbie too plainly, but she couldn't hide how she felt. She needed Robbie to come back.

The children came home for their tea and everyone enjoyed the strawberry jelly, tinned peaches and bread and butter. Even Honour ate all hers and Flo knew that she'd begun to get over the shock of losing her grandfather and the suddenness of his death. As for how she felt about her real father, Flo could only guess that her thoughts were in turmoil, because she had not yet come to terms with her feelings.

Flo sent the children to bed at half-past seven but told them that they could play for a while. Normally, they would be preparing to open the shop the next day and to start baking, but the shop would remain closed until after their father was laid to rest.

'Have you and Roy talked about the future?' Flo asked as they sat over a cup of tea.

'Yes...' Honour sighed. 'He can't find premises large enough for a shop with a workshop behind and living accommodation over the top. He found a good workshop which would be just right, but there were no rooms over the top. It would take all the money he has saved, which means we should have to rent some rooms for ourselves.'

Flo nodded thoughtfully. 'You could live here for a while – if you wanted?'

'I'm not sure that would work,' Honour said. 'I love

you, but this is your home, your shop – and I'd like my own home.'

'Yes, of course,' Flo agreed, though she was a little disappointed that Honour should feel that way. 'Well, I'm sure something will turn up.'

'I wish we had news about Robbie,' Honour said suddenly. 'I feel mean talking about my plans when he's still missing...' She gave a little sob. 'Oh, Mum, I don't want him to die... I've never even spoken to him properly...'

'We're all worried,' Flo said, 'but I don't think Robbie is dead. I'm sure I would feel it inside if he were. He must be hurt or he would have come home before now – but I can't – I won't believe he's dead...'

'I pray you're right,' Honour said. 'He's my father and I want him to give me away when I get married – and I want to see you happily settled too...'

Flo smiled and got up to kiss her cheek. 'I love you, Honour, and your happiness is my chief concern – but I do hope that one day I shall be Robbie's wife and those children upstairs will be mine to love and care for until they're ready to leave us...'

'They should always have been yours,' Honour said and put an arm about her waist as they prepared to go up. 'It wasn't right what Mum did to you. If I have my way, Robbie will marry you and give you the happiness you're entitled to...'

Flo made sure the kitchen door was locked and followed Honour upstairs. As she looked in at the sleeping children, her thoughts were with Robbie, wherever he was, and she prayed that if he had been hurt his injuries had been attended to, unable to bear the thought of his lying injured somewhere. John Hansen had told her that he wasn't in the local hospitals... so where could he be?

26

He opened his eyes with a groan as the pain struck, closing them again quickly because of the light shining into his eyes, and put an arm across his face to shut it out.

'So you've come back to us then,' a gruff voice said. 'You'd have been a gonner if my Mick hadn't spotted yer and come runnin' ter fetch me. 'Tis lucky for yer I couldn't afford a drink or I'd never have got yer back 'ere.'

Robbie became aware of the pain in his head. He put up a hand to touch the source of the pain and discovered a roughly tied bandage. He tried to sit up but fell back on what was possibly a pile of sacks or rags. The lantern being held over him was bright, but the rest of his surroundings were dark. He was aware of the odour of damp and neglect and suspected the rustling sound he could hear was rats.

'Where am I?'

'It's where we kip fer the moment,' the gruff voice said. 'Me and the lad – we came down lookin' fer work, but there ain't none fer the likes of me. Me name is Taffy and me home's in Ireland, so 'tis – but I've been working up north for the past ten years. I married a northern girl and she gave me my lad – but she died these two years past and I've been on the road since, so I have.'

Robbie struggled to sit. His head was swimming, but he made it this time and looked into the face of the man who had brought him here and tended to his injury. 'Do yer know what happened to me?' he asked.

'Mick says you were struck on the back of the head. He was too far away to warn you, but he saw what happened; you were bleeding and the night was bitter. If we'd left yer there yer might have died – so I carried yer here and tended the cut on yer head. It's not that deep, but yer were out for a whole day and I was thinkin' mebbe I should have got a doctor to yer, though I tipped the last of me whisky what Mick hid on yer wound…' He looked a bit regretful that he'd wasted good whisky.

'Thank you for what yer did,' Robbie said. He'd managed to sit up but knew he couldn't stand. 'Where is Mick?'

'He comes and goes,' Taffy said. 'He knows who hit yer, so he does, but whether he'll tell yer…' Taffy shrugged. 'I've no food in the place, but Mick fetched me a drop of the hard stuff…' He offered a half-bottle of what smelled like whisky and Robbie remembered what he'd been doing the night he was attacked. He shook his head. 'If I've been out for more than a day my kids will be frantic…'

'Mick went to yer house ter tell them, but it was empty. He thinks he knows where yer kids go after school. I told him he'd better go round and tell them where yer are…'

Robbie's sight was clearing. He realised he was in a derelict house and the windows were boarded over, which was the reason it was so dark. 'Is this place the old tenements – they were going to pull these houses down, but the charity decided they couldn't afford it…'

'We're not the only ones kipping here,' Taffy said. 'There are a few rough types – and that's one of the reasons I've decided to move on. I'm going to take the lad back to Ireland. We've relatives there and they'll take us in fer a bit…'

'What's yer job, mate?' Robbie asked. 'I might be in a position to offer yer some work soon.' That was if he hadn't lost the chance of restoring those buildings for the Sally Army.

'That's the first decent offer I've had since I came south,' Taffy said and grinned at him. 'I'd have taken yer up on it – but I've made up me mind. I can't take care of the boy on me own. Back home he'll be made ter wash and have regular food in his belly…'

Robbie looked at him, nodding because he understood; it was hard for a man alone to keep his children safe, especially one who had no home and no work. 'Give me a hand to stand, will yer?'

'Yeah…' Taffy took his arm and pulled until he was standing. Robbie was forced to hold on to him until his head stopped whirling and then he let go. 'Are yer all right?'

'I will be in a moment,' Robbie said. He heard rather than saw Mick arrive and then the young lad was standing by his father's side.

'I went ter the 'ouse where the old folk are and told 'em yer were alive,' Mick said, lookin' at Robbie. 'Yer kids are stayin' wiv Miss Flo – so the neighbour said. She asked if we wanted 'er husband to come and fetch yer back, but I told 'er no…'

'Good lad…' Taffy said. 'I'll find yer something to eat today, so I will…'

'If yer could give me a hand home, I'll give yer both somethin' ter eat,' Robbie offered. 'You and Mick are welcome to wash at mine and I've some clothes that might fit you – and Ben may have a pair of trousers and a shirt Mick could use…'

'I'll help yer home,' Taffy said, 'and if Mick wants ter wash I'll not stop him – but the food would be welcome.'

'I owe you for fetchin' yer father to me, Mick,' Robbie said. 'The food is the least I can do...'

'Yer me mate's dad,' Mick said, 'and yer stopped that rotter takin' our money at the mission. I reckon that's why he hit yer...'

'You know it was him?' Robbie asked and Mick nodded.

'He hangs round 'ere some of the time and he clouts me when he feels like it. He's a bad 'un. We're all scared of 'im. I know they call him Scrapper, but it probably ain't his name – just what they know him by. No one likes him. He steals other folks stuff and if they argue he beats 'em up...'

'If I catch him touching you I'll give him a hidin',' Taffy said and glared at his son. 'You didn't tell me...'

'Yer were drunk; you'd probably 'ave 'it me,' Mick said and Robbie saw the other man flinch, but he didn't strike back at the boy.

'Mick, let me put a hand on your shoulder,' Robbie said. 'I reckon I can manage now – and the sooner you get me home, the better...'

Flo opened the door and stared at Effie in surprise. Her first thought was that either Millie or Bert had been taken bad and her heart jerked as she invited the woman inside her warm kitchen. It never rained but it poured!

'It's lovely and warm in 'ere,' Effie said. 'I had ter come round, love, as soon as I heard – Robbie's all right. Leastwise, he's had a nasty bang on the head and he's been unconscious fer a few hours, but the lad said ter tell his kids he would be all right...'

'Oh, thank goodness,' Flo said and sat down on the nearest chair as her legs felt as if they would give way under her. 'It's such a relief. Where is he?'

'I don't know – the boy wouldn't tell me. He said he was Ben's friend and that he and his father were lookin' after Robbie... a bit of a scruffy lad...'

'I wonder if that's the boy Ben brought to the mission...' Flo said and shook her head when Effie looked curious. 'It doesn't matter. It was good of you to come round, Effie – will you stay for a piece of my Christmas cake and a cup of tea?'

'I don't mind if I do,' Effie said, clearly relishing the prospect of a good gossip. 'You ain't openin' the shop fer a while then – but yer wouldn't wiv yer poor father gone. I was sorry ter 'ear that, love...'

'Dad had been ill for some time,' Flo answered. Her throat caught but she didn't cry. 'It's always a shock, but it wasn't unexpected.'

She brushed over it as lightly as she could, hoping that Effie would talk about something else. The woman liked to gossip and soon started talking about other things, including some good news she'd heard.

'They say there's a new factory openin' in the spring,' she said. 'Well, an old one openin' up again – cannin' food, so they say. I reckon there will be queues ready to sign on once they open the gates…'

Relieved the subject had been changed, Flo joined her in speculation as to whether the worst of the Depression was over or whether the factory was just batting against the tide. Either way, it would bring some relief to the local people.

As soon as Effie left, Flo ran upstairs to the children. Ben was building something with his Meccano set; she thought it might be a crane but wasn't certain. Ruthie was nursing her doll and looking pensive. They both stopped and stared at her as she entered the room.

'Your friend went round to Bert's and told them that your dad is all right,' she said and they both jumped to their feet, running at her. She caught their hands as they clutched at her arm in sudden excitement. 'Effie came to tell me. The boy – Effie said a scruffy lad – said your dad had a nasty bang on his head and he was unconscious for a while, but he says he will be all right…'

'Where is he?' Ben asked.

'I want my dad…' Ruthie said and two tears slid down her cheeks.

'I'm not sure where he is,' Flo said. 'Your friend wouldn't tell Effie, but it's good news. Your dad will come here lookin' for you as soon as he can…'

'I want my dad…' Ruthie whined louder now. 'Where is he?'

'I bet he's round Mick's…' Ben said and darted past Flo.

'Where are you goin'?' Flo whirled round and caught him. He struggled, but she held on to him. 'No, Ben – if it's those condemned houses, it is dangerous for you to go there alone.'

'I've been there before with Mick,' Ben lied and tried to get away. 'Please let me go, Miss Flo…'

'He might not still be there,' Flo reasoned. 'I think if your dad woke up, he'd want to get home, don't you?'

Ben looked up at her mutinously for a moment and then nodded. 'I'll go home first…'

'We'll all go,' Flo said. 'All of us together. I can't let you go alone, Ben. Robbie would never forgive me if anythin' happened to you – and I've seen some rough sorts hanging round the tenements.'

'Mick says there are some nasty blokes,' Ben admitted. 'He hates it, but his dad never stops anywhere long enough for them to have a proper home…'

'Let's all put our coats on and we'll go to your home first and then we'll think about what we do next. We need a man to go with us if we're going to the old tenement block…'

'All right,' Ben agreed. 'Mick is scared of them blokes, so we'd be best together…'

Honour came into the kitchen as they fastened their coats. She wanted to know where they were going and when they told her, insisted on going with them.

'The more of us, the better,' she said and picked up her coat. 'Come on, Ruthie. Hold my hand. We don't want anyone gettin' lost, do we?'

'I know my way 'ome...' Ruthie said indignantly.

'Yes, but I don't know the way and I might get lost,' Honour said and Ruthie went into a peal of laughter and took Honour's hand. 'That's it; you take care of me...' Honour smiled down at her. She glanced at Flo. 'Do you really think Robbie will be home now?'

'If he is conscious, his first thought will be for the children...'

Mick cleared the bacon, sausage and chips, from the chip shop, from his plate, wiping a piece of slightly stale bread round the edge to soak up the grease. Robbie had showed Taffy where the food was and let him get on with it, because his head felt as if it were splitting.

'Here, get that down yer, mate,' Taffy said and slid a mug of strong tea in front of Robbie. 'Sure yer don't want a drop of the good stuff in it?' He poured a generous measure of whisky in his own and smacked his lips.

Robbie smiled weakly and sipped his tea. It had

several lumps of sugar in it and he felt it doing him good, giving him strength. He was feeling better now that he was in his own home, sitting in his chair by the range, which Taffy had made up for him.

He hadn't been able to face much food himself, but he did manage a few bites of a sausage Mick put on a plate for him. It made him feel a bit queasy, but he held it down, because he needed all his strength if he was going to fetch his children. He couldn't face the walk just yet, but he'd get them before nightfall somehow.

'We'll be going now, mate,' Taffy said and Robbie realised that he'd been sitting with his eyes shut.

'Don't you want to wash and change?' Robbie asked. 'I haven't really thanked yer for what yer did for me... I've got some money here somewhere...' He looked around, trying to remember where he'd hidden a couple of pounds.

'Nah, thanks just the same,' Taffy said. 'I'm owed a few quid, so I am. I'll pick it up tomorrow when they open the office – and we'll be off, back to the old country. 'Tis where we belong – and the lad can go to school there...'

'Don't want ter go ter school...' Mick muttered rebelliously.

'You'll do as yer told,' his father said and glared at him. Mick submitted but didn't look happy. 'We'll be off then...'

'Let yourselves out…' Robbie didn't try to get up. He wasn't sure he could.

He closed his eyes again, drifting off as he heard the door close behind his guests. Somewhere in his thoughts there was one that said he ought to have tried harder to keep them here – because Mick needed someone to look out for him, but Robbie's head was throbbing and he couldn't keep two thoughts together.

'Oh thank God!' a voice said and someone else said, 'Is he all right…'

'Dad, Dad, speak to me…' a small hand was shaking his arm and a tiny form was climbing on his lap and it was that that brought Robbie back.

'Be careful, Ruthie, your dad isn't very well,' a voice from his dreams said and then he felt a gentle hand on his face. 'Robbie, love, I think we need to change the bandage and take a look at the injury to your head. We might need the doctor…'

'No, it's all right… I was just sleepin',' Robbie said and opened his eyes, looking into Flo's sweet face. The anxiety in her voice made him smile and he felt life flow back into his limbs. His head was still sore, but the fuzziness that had caused him to drift off had begun to clear. 'I felt terrible when Mick and Taffy got me here, and I just sat here and went to sleep after they left…' He held out his hands to Ruthie and Ben, who rushed to kneel beside his chair. 'I'm all right – don't cry, Ruthie.'

'Did they make you a meal?' Flo asked, looking at the mess.

'I told them to cook bacon and sausages for themselves. They were hungry and I can get more for us… when I can make my feet work again…' He gave her a lopsided grin. 'I don't know what that rogue hit me with but it scrambled my brains for a while.'

'I'm goin' to have a look,' Flo said and took off the makeshift bandage, which was a rather suspect red scarf that could have done with a wash. She gently inspected the wound to the back of Robbie's head and nodded. 'You've got a nasty cut there, but it hasn't gone deep and it seems to be clean despite that bandage…'

'I think Taffy said he'd put some whisky on it,' Robbie said with a grimace. 'That may be why it is so damned sore, but it probably stopped any infection taking hold.'

'Yes, it certainly looks clean, but I expect you have a headache. I've got an Aspro in my pocket, if you'd like one?' She took out a pink strip of the painkilling tablets she used if anyone had a bad cold or a headache.

'It might help,' Robbie said and accepted the small strip. 'Thank you for taking care of the children, Flo – Honour.' He looked at Honour and smiled and saw that she was crying but trying to comfort Ruthie. Something told him that she knew the truth about their relationship.

Ben had started to clear up the mess, hiding his own emotion.

'We loved havin' them,' Flo said. 'What can we do for you?'

'I'm goin' to clear up the mess Mick and his father left,' Honour said and flicked a hand across her eyes before eyeing the greasy dishes in the sink. 'I'll put the kettle on, Flo. Make us all a cup of tea.'

Flo brought Robbie a glass of water and he swallowed the tablet. He took another and swallowed some more water, smiling at her. 'That will help I'm sure – thank you.'

'We were very worried about you,' Flo said and sat on a chair looking at him, unable to take her eyes from his face.

'I'm sorry. I knew nothing until a couple of hours ago when I finally came round.'

'It's not your fault...' She smiled but couldn't bring herself to stop staring at him. 'I'm so glad you're all right...'

'So am I,' Robbie said and then frowned. 'I missed an important appointment, but I was unconscious and only started to come round earlier... I need to get a message to someone.'

'I can deliver it – or ask John Hansen to,' Flo offered. 'And if you were unconscious all that time we should have the doctor. I'm going to ring for him, Robbie. I don't care what you say…'

'Perhaps John could telephone the captain at the Sally Army and explain why I didn't meet him…' Robbie looked anxious. 'It was a big job and it's a shame if I missed it because of that rogue… Mick saw him and that's how I came to be at their place. Taffy carried me back there and looked after me as best he could. Feeding them was the least I could do…'

'Give me your message and I'll pass it on, but I'm also ringing for a doctor,' Flo said. 'Will you be all right here tonight? Shall I stop here with you?'

'What about your father?'

'Dad died in the night…' Flo caught back a sob. 'He looked peaceful when I found him…'

'Yet you still took the kids in?' He stared at her as if he couldn't believe she was really there.

'They took Dad away to a chapel of rest. The doctor thought it best, because of the shop selling food. To be honest I was glad to have your two in the house; they helped through the first hours…'

'I'm so sorry, love,' Robbie said and took her hand, holding it gently. 'I wish I'd been there for yer…'

'So do I,' she whispered, tears catching her throat. 'You could come to ours – or I could stay here. You shouldn't be alone tonight…'

'I can look after Dad,' Ben said stoutly. He'd watched in silence but now spoke out. 'I can manage, Dad.'

'Yes, I'm sure you can, lad,' Robbie said. 'I don't think we need to trouble the doctor, Flo. I'm feelin' a bit better now – but if you want ter stay, there's a spare bed upstairs. You could both stay if yer want...'

'Roy is comin' round later,' Honour said. 'I'll be there to meet him – but I'll be all right on my own, Flo – if you want to stay here...'

'We'll see how Robbie is by teatime...' Flo said and took the cup of tea Honour had made for her. The milk was out of a tin, because Robbie hadn't any fresh in the house. 'I'll fetch some milk for us before then... we've got plenty of food at home... and I think the shop on the corner is open for a couple of hours. He won't mind serving me anyway, even if he's closed; I'm his favourite customer.'

'Let me go,' Honour said. 'I'll bring fresh bread – is there anythin' else you need?'

'Some ham for the kids or cheese. Which sort of sandwich do you want?' Robbie looked at them. Ruthie wanted ham and Ben wanted cheese, so Robbie smiled at Honour. 'There's some money in the dresser drawer, get some of each please if he'll serve you.'

'He'll serve us,' Honour said and smiled at him. 'If not, I can get a tin of pink salmon or something from home...'

Honour took four half crowns from the purse in

the drawer, told them she would be back soon and let herself out of the front door. Ben told Ruthie to come upstairs with him, leaving Flo and Robbie together.

'Oh, Robbie, when they told me you were missing I was so frightened,' Flo said. 'I couldn't bear to lose you now...'

'And I ain't goin' anywhere,' he said and smiled at her. 'I love you, Flo. I let yer down once, but it ain't goin' ter happen again. I've been thinkin' – either we can move in with you and sell this place – or you can move in here, but we'll get married as soon as we can arrange it... You will marry me, won't you?'

'Yes, I shall and we'll live as a family,' Flo agreed and knelt at his side, looking up at him with love in her eyes. 'I've told Honour she's yours and I want to be with you for the rest of my life, Robbie – and I don't want to waste another moment...' She shivered. 'When I thought I'd lost you for a second time, I didn't know how to bear it...'

He bent to kiss her softly and then gave a wry smile as his head reeled. 'I can't bend my head without goin' dizzy yet, love, but I will soon – and then I'll show you just how much I love you. We'll be together for the rest of our lives.'

'Yes...' Flo smiled and kissed him softly. 'I do love you so much.'

'I want to be with you and the kids...' Robbie

sighed, 'but I'm not promising it will be easy. The kids like you, but they still miss their mother and I'm going to have to wait for the right moment to tell them they have a big sister.'

'Let Honour make friends with them,' Flo said gently. 'We'll speak of us as a family and of her as their sister – and when they're ready, you can explain to Ben and he'll make it right with Ruthie.'

Robbie looked at her and nodded. 'You know my son nearly as well as I do, Flo…'

'He's quite like his father,' Flo said and smiled. 'We all need to adjust slowly, but it will be better when we're married and living together.'

'Your money is yours to do with as you like,' Robbie said. 'If I had lots of it I'd probably want you to give up – but that would be selfish and I shall leave that decision to you.'

'I don't want to give up the shop just yet,' Flo said. 'Once you're on your feet I probably could, but for now it will make things easier for us all – but I wonder if you'd consider letting Honour and Roy have the cottage. He was looking for a workshop with accommodation over the top but couldn't find anythin' with rooms over – but he can't afford to buy a separate workshop and a home…'

'They can rent the cottage cheaply for a while and then perhaps I'll give it to Honour one day,' Robbie said after a moment's consideration. 'I have to think of Ruthie and Ben too – but if I succeed with what I'm hopin' to do, I'll be able to provide an inheritance for them as well…'

'That's for the future,' Flo said, 'but if Roy feels he'd like to move in here, renting would suit them for a start…'

Robbie smiled at her. 'If it makes her happy, they can have it for whatever they can afford,' he said. 'She's my daughter and I've never done anythin' for her. It's the least I can do…'

'Thank you,' Flo said. 'We must wait to marry until after Dad's funeral, of course – but I don't want to wait any longer…'

Robbie smiled and risked another kiss, even though it sent his head reeling. 'Nor do I, my love… nor do I…'

27

Flo stayed at the cottage overnight because she was worried about Robbie, who was dizzy for most of the evening and needed to sit quietly in his chair. She fed the children, made tea for Robbie and sent Honour home to be there for Roy when he arrived. In the morning, when Honour came to visit, bringing bacon, eggs, milk and bread from the shop, Flo didn't question her about what time her fiancé had gone home the previous evening. Her daughter's eyes were shining and she was happy and that was all that mattered to Flo.

Robbie was much better by the morning, but Flo persuaded him to go to the doctor's surgery. He seemed more cheerful when he came back and told her that on his way from the doctor's he'd called into the Sally Army headquarters and explained why he hadn't been there for his appointment to view the properties in need of renovation.

'We've made another appointment for the morning,' he told Flo. 'If I get that job too, I'll be earning a decent wage and when word gets round I should start to get more work comin' in...'

'Don't overdo things just yet,' Flo said, but knew she was wasting her breath because Robbie was feeling much better and full of enthusiasm for their future.

Roy was invited to dinner at Flo's later that week so that he could meet Robbie and it was decided that Roy would rent the cottage from his future father-in-law until he was in a position to either move into somewhere else or to buy it himself. He and Honour wanted a spring wedding and would move into their new home a few months before Roy was demobbed from the army and began his business venture.

Flo's father was buried in early January and both Robbie and Roy helped to bear his coffin into church. Flo was surprised at how many local folk turned out to say goodbye to him. They'd decided to have the reception at Robbie's cottage, because Flo had no parlour. The room was filled with guests who came to say farewell to her father – including Millie and Bert Waters, who were both much better and able to get about again with a little help from their friends and neighbours.

The pace of life had slowed a little for Flo now. It felt strange not to have to run after her father all the time, but instead she had Ben and Ruthie in for cake and tea and she'd begun to care for their clothes and do the things that a mother usually does, knowing that soon they would all be living together.

With Robbie's permission, Ben kept on with his odd jobs for Arnie, but his father had made it clear there was to be no running to the bookies or anything illegal. He also helped Fred Giles at the fish and chip shop, and Ruthie spent as much time as she could with her granny, reading about the fairies and looking much happier than she had since her mummy died. Although the Depression was still hard, everyone seemed to feel that it must soon get better, and as the weeks passed, Flo discovered that a lot of new customers were coming in to buy her home-made sweets. Both kids seemed to have accepted that Flo and Honour would now be a part of their lives and seemed happy enough to call her Flo, as their father did. She hoped that one day they might call her Mum but she would never ask: it would have to come from them.

In America things were changing. Roosevelt had defeated President Herbert Hoover in the Presidential election in the previous November of 1932 and would become the 32nd President later that year. He'd promised the Americans he would boost spending on railways, roads, electric power and farms to get their economy back on track; he would in the meantime introduce unemployment benefit for all to alleviate their suffering. The news made English people hopeful that perhaps their government might do the same.

In Germany, a man called Hitler was also voted in on a landslide to become the Chancellor of Germany; he'd promised an end to the poverty and despair for his people too and it was hoped that these things would mean the beginning of a new future for all.

In mid-January Robbie received a visit from John Hansen one evening at the cottage. He came to tell him some vaguely disturbing news.

'I spoke to the police concerning Mick – the lad you told me about. They seemed to know that some people had been using those abandoned houses down by Dock Road and yesterday they went round to investigate... There was no sign of either Mick or his father,' John said. 'However, the police found a body – no attempt had been made to hide it. They said the man had been stabbed in the neck and face several times and must have bled to death...'

'Good grief!' Robbie was shocked. 'Do they know who it was?'

'They believe it to be a man who came to the area only in the past six months or so... Some people called him Scrapper... and from the description I was given, I believe it might be the man who stole from the mission. You stopped him taking the children's money on Christmas Day. He had been dead for some time when the police found him…'

Robbie shook his head but said nothing. He remembered Taffy saying that if Scrapper laid a hand on Mick again he would kill him, but he didn't know what had gone on after Mick and his father had left his cottage that day. They had saved his life by carrying him into their shelter from the icy streets, and he wouldn't be giving the police any clues to the murder of a man who had been both a bully and a thief.

'I dare say there are quite a few rough types using those derelict buildings; anyone could have done it…' he offered.

'Yes, I imagine so,' John agreed. 'The police constable said as much to me. I think they put it down to thieves falling out… They found a great many empty whisky bottles and some stolen goods in the buildings…'

Robbie nodded. 'Hopefully, it will mean an end to break-ins at the mission and the Sally Army…'

'Yes, that may be the one bright thing to come out of this…' John was thoughtful. 'I thought I would tell you. I'm not sure whether to tell Miss Hawkins or not… I do not wish to upset her. She's had enough troubles with her father dying and then you were attacked…'

'I'll tell Flo,' Robbie said. 'Thank you for lettin' me know, John. I've stripped out the rotten wood, so I'll be startin' work on your roof rebuild tomorrow mornin' when the struts are delivered and then we're nearly done.'

'I shall be glad to see it done and get rid of the tarpaulins and the safety props.' John replied, then hesitated. 'Ah, there's the other thing that made me call; I believe congratulations are in order. Miss Hawkins is a lovely person. I know you will be very happy.'

'I love Flo and we ought to have married years ago,' Robbie said. 'Her father sent me packin', but in the end he regretted what he'd done... and now we're goin' to marry...'

John nodded, his face half turned away. Robbie didn't notice the little nerve flicking at the corner of his eye, but then, John Hansen knew how to hide his feelings. Only Nurse Mary would notice the grief it had caused him to hear of Flo Hawkins' coming wedding. She would offer him comfort in the only way she knew as his friend, working side by side with him to help the poor. She was a decent woman and John knew that if he wished to marry, Nurse Mary would always be by his side. For the moment his heart must heal, because he had truly loved Flo Hawkins, but he knew now that she would never be his. As for his constant friend and helper, their future lives remained to be seen. The signs that the worst of the recession might be beginning to ease a little, at least in some parts of the country, were hopeful, but it would be a long time before places like his mission were no longer needed. John thought that if the poverty here became less extreme he might consider taking a mission abroad – and perhaps Nurse Mary would also find that a good life, but that was for the future...

Flo had meant what she said about not waiting any longer than necessary and they arranged the wedding for the final week of January.

'I don't mind using Dad's things,' she'd told Robbie when they discussed what to do for the best. 'He would hate to think I'd just thrown everythin' out and I don't see the need for it.'

However, she'd had to clear her father's clothes from his large wardrobe. She packed them all into an old tin trunk and Robbie wheeled it round to the Sally Army in his barrow. In times like these a lot of men would be glad of the good things and the older stuff would go for pennies to the rag-and-bone man and be used for a good cause.

'I'm sure Dad would say it was the best thing to do,' she told Honour as they sorted through his possessions. 'He didn't like waste and it would be a waste to put his clothes up in the attic and let the moths have them – that coat and his best suit were hardly worn...'

In a locked box on the top shelf of the wardrobe, Flo found the deeds to the shop, which her mother had left to her in accordance with her grandfather's will, also a gold watch and chain, some one hundred gold coins, and five hundred pounds in notes: the money she'd given him each month from her takings for years. She doubted he'd spent a penny, just putting it all away in his box each month. There was also a letter addressed to Flo:

Everything is for you, Flo. I'm sorry I wasn't always the father I meant to be, but you and your mother hurt me, shutting me out and treating me as if I was a fool. I hope you'll find happiness in the future and the money I've saved will come in useful.

He'd signed it but there were no expressions of love and she thought perhaps it had been written before he'd forgiven her and started to make amends. She stared at the letter for several minutes, before putting it back in the box. The gold watch and chain she would give to Robbie, and she would share the gold sovereigns with Honour; the money would stay in the box at the top of the wardrobe until it was needed.

*

It was the morning of Flo's wedding. She rose to a dull and dreary view from her window, but nothing could dim the golden shine of her happiness as she remembered that this was the day all the dreams of a young girl were about to come true. She'd waited so long, but as Honour brought her breakfast in bed and told her that some gorgeous flowers had arrived, she jumped out and embraced her daughter.

'I'm so happy, my darling. I hope you will be just as happy on your wedding day...'

'I'm happy now,' Honour said and kissed her. 'Sometimes, Roy might seem a little careless, even thoughtless – but I know he loves me and he's the one I love.'

'Then I know you would never marry anyone else...' Flo said and kissed her. 'There was only ever one man for me and I've had to wait for a long time, but at last it has all come right.'

Honour nodded, looking thoughtful. 'I've decided to work in the shop with you until Roy has his business up and running, even when we're married – and by then you'll have found someone else to help you.'

'Thank you, darling; that is very thoughtful of you.'

'You've done so much for me, Mum, it's the least I can do...' She said and kissed her. 'I do love you very much...'

The sun managed to break through for a few minutes as Flo walked into church, looking young and pretty in her best pale blue frock and hat. Honour and a giggling Ruthie walked behind with their own little posies of flowers and Ben stood proudly with his dad. He'd been given the ring to keep safe and kept patting his jacket pocket to make sure it was there. Flo's friends had gathered to see her wed and she was aware of the smiles and happy faces all around her as she and Robbie left the church together as man and wife, standing for a few moments in the cool wind for some photographs taken by John Hansen, who was there with Nurse Mary looking happy and very smart in a blue tailored costume and hat.

Afterwards, they had a simple reception at the cottage, all the food having been prepared by the bride and her daughter. Flo noticed one or two odd looks when Honour called her Mum but ignored them; she felt no need to explain and neither did her daughter.

Honour stayed on after the others had gone, clearing the used plates and washing up, with Ben and Ruthie helping her. Ruthie already followed Honour everywhere and Flo felt warm contentment as she watched her family laughing and chatting together. Ben wanted Honour to show him how to make the sweets she produced for the shop, though Ruthie was just happy to eat them.

After all the guests had gone and the clearing up was

done, the children went back to the rooms over the shop, quite willing to stay with Honour for the night, leaving Flo and Robbie alone in the cottage. They had accepted her as a big sister without complicated explanations, perhaps because Honour had decided to call Robbie Pa. Ben thought it was funny, but it brought them all closer and he'd called Flo Ma a couple of times. Ruthie hadn't yet, but she would come round to it in time because she always followed Ben's lead. Flo had always loved them and was content just to see their smiling faces.

When they were alone, Robbie told Flo that Honour had asked him to give her away on her wedding day, which was set for May. 'Of course I said yes – but it should've been you...'

'No, you're her father and I'm glad she asked you.' Flo smiled lovingly at him. 'I wasn't sure she would accept it, but she has – and I know the children love her.'

'Yes, they do. It surprised me how easily Ruthie took to her...'

'Well they are sisters...' Flo said and then put her arms about him. 'It was a lovely wedding... thank you for my beautiful flowers...'

'I should have taken you to a hotel...' he said, looking at her regretfully. 'One day I'll give you all the things I can't now, Flo...'

'I have all I could possibly want or need...' Flo drew her breath as he held her closer and bent his head to kiss her. 'I love you so much, Robbie, and I've waited all these years for you. How could I want anythin' more?'

'I love you,' he said and there was a tremor in his voice. 'You don't know how often I regretted leaving you all those years ago. I was a coward and because of it you suffered so much...'

'I cried for you and I cried because I couldn't claim Honour as my own,' Flo said, 'but I always had her to love and I thought of her as being your gift to me... and I always hoped that one day...'

Robbie kissed her and then swept her up in his arms, taking her up the stairs to their bedroom. Flo surrendered to the passion of his loving with all the joy and love that was in her and knew that for the rest of their lives he would never leave her or stop loving her. She was filled with happiness because she'd never expected that she would be loved so much. It had been a long wait, but they were lovers at last, joined as husband and wife and so very much in love. Now they were older and their lovemaking was more thoughtful than when they were little more than children, but just as sweet as it had been on that long-ago night.

They had three children, all of whom were precious

to Flo, but she held a secret hope in her heart that she was not too old to perhaps have another baby and she knew that the years ahead would be filled with love and laughter. Even if she were not blessed with another child, she could always help other children who had nothing, especially at Christmas, because after all that was what it was all about...

About Rosie Clarke

ROSIE CLARKE is happily married and lives in a quiet village in East Anglia. Writing books is a passion for Rosie, she also likes to read, watch good films and enjoys holidays in the sunshine. She loves shoes and adores animals, especially squirrels and dogs.

Hello from Aria

We hope you enjoyed this book! If you did let us know, we'd love to hear from you.

We are Aria, a dynamic digital-first fiction imprint from award-winning independent publishers Head of Zeus. At heart, we're committed to publishing fantastic commercial fiction – from romance and sagas to crime, thrillers and historical fiction. Visit us online and discover a community of like-minded fiction fans!

We're also on the look out for tomorrow's superstar authors. So, if you're a budding writer looking for a publisher, we'd love to hear from you. You can submit your book online at ariafiction.com/we-want-read-your-book

You can find us at:
Email: aria@headofzeus.com
Website: www.ariafiction.com
Submissions: www.ariafiction.com/
we-want-read-your-book

f @ariafiction
𝕏 @Aria_Fiction
⊙ @ariafiction